Leslie Deane

HERO

HERO

Leslie Deane

ARROW BOOKS

Arrow Books Limited
3 Fitzroy Square, London WIP 6JD

An imprint of the Hutchinson Publishing Group

London Melbourne Sydney Auckland
Wellington Johannesburg and agencies
throughout the world

First published in Great Britain by Arrow 1981
© Leslie Deane 1980

Made and printed in Great Britain
by The Anchor Press Ltd
Tiptree, Essex

ISBN 0 09 924980 4

chapter 1

The yacht *Chanteuse* entered the harbor at Portofino late in the afternoon of a hot August day. The bay was crowded with pleasure boats of all types and sizes, power and sail. They were tied up three and four abreast at the quays, and many more rode at anchor, their flags hanging limp in the still air, their brightwork glinting in the sunlight. None of them was as big as the *Chanteuse*, or as elegant. She was a hundred and thirty-five feet overall, diesel powered, with a gleaming white hull and a blue-and-white superstructure. When she slid through the channel, heads turned to look at her, as if a spectacularly beautiful woman had walked into a ballroom.

On the flying bridge the mate stood beside the helmsman and issued commands quietly, his hands resting lightly on the throttle handles, his eyes flickering back and forth from the big yacht's bow to her stern as he took her carefully through the busy harbor. He was a tall man, young, an American named Hendricks. He wore a white shirt and trousers, the shirt open at the neck, and a pair of worn canvas boat shoes. His skin had been burned to the color of tarnished copper, and his blond hair had bleached streaks in it under the cap he wore pushed back at a careless angle. His eyes were a deep blue, and his teeth were startlingly white against his dark face.

The south end of the harbor offered a little more space among the glut of boats. "Come right," the mate ordered. He spoke in English, although the *Chanteuse* was registered in Cannes and most of her crew was French. At any time several languages could be heard aboard her.

The helmsman swung the wheel. "Right, sir."

"Now steady up."

"Steady up, sir."

The mate eased the throttles back until the gauges showed 1,200 rpm, just enough power to keep the yacht under way. The *Chanteuse* crept forward until she was at a point where she'd have room to swing at anchor without danger of hitting

1

another vessel, a location directly opposite the Splendido Hotel, perhaps a hundred meters offshore. Hendricks checked the fathometer and glanced over at the starboard wing of the bridge where the captain stood talking with the owner. The mate did not bother to ask if the anchor site was suitable. He reversed the engines and pulled the levers that released the anchors. There was a splash forward, followed by the sound of chain rattling through the hawsepipes.

The *Chanteuse* trembled slightly as she stopped and began to make stern way. When Hendricks felt the anchors take hold, he checked the fathometer again and shut down the engines. He engaged the auxiliary generators, then picked up the telephone and sent an order over the yacht's loudspeaker for the crew to put her in anchor trim and to rig the landing stage over the side. He put the phone down and said to the helmsman, "Tell the bosun I'll be down there in a minute. We'll use the big tender."

When the man had gone, Hendricks leaned on the polished teakwood rail and studied the shoreline of Portofino. It did not look much different from the other resort towns along the Italian Riviera, although it was the most famous of them. The old buildings on the waterfront were five and six stories high, jammed together, the walls made of Ligurian plaster in soft hues of yellow and pink and orange. Behind them the hills sloped sharply upward, their sides dotted with villas among the thick green foliage.

Hendricks looked over again to where the yacht's captain and her owner stood talking. Dubec, the captain, was as formal in his dress as Hendricks was casual. The visor of his cap was emblazoned with gilt, and he wore shoulder boards with four wide gold stripes. His whites were starched and sharply creased, and his tie was carefully knotted. Even the moustache under his fleshy nose appeared impeccably groomed. Pompous asshole, Hendricks thought. He looks like he's commanding the *France*. Hendricks turned his attention to the other man.

Claude Lemont, owner of the *Chanteuse*, was about sixty, Hendricks judged. Lemont was potbellied and soft under his tan. He gestured as he spoke, long slim fingers waving in the air. Hendricks's knowledge of French was limited, but he gathered that Lemont was talking about restaurants in Portofino. He heard the names Piccolo and Santini's. That was, the mate reflected, all Lemont had to think about. Where to enjoy his next extravagant meal, where next in the world to wander aboard the *Chanteuse*. The son of the man who had founded one of France's largest chemical companies, Lemont had not worked from the day his father died. He had immediately sold his inherited shares and that, together with the balance of the estate, had kept him in yachts, villas, jets, wives, and mistresses ever since.

Which brought Estelle to Hendricks's mind. He turned and looked aft. A group of people lolled in deck chairs on the fantail. They wore swimsuits, and several of the women were topless. One of these was Estelle Lemont. On board the *Chanteuse* the crew was expected not to notice, to look the other way when female passengers took the sun, but Hendricks stared directly at the owner's wife.

Estelle was a brunette in her middle thirties, as carefully trim as when she had been a major star in the French cinema. Her breasts were large and lush, with broad, dusky nipples. She had covered her body with coconut oil, and her skin glistened, its color a golden brown. She wore only the bottom of a black string bikini and a pair of oversized sunglasses. When she saw that Hendricks was looking down at her from the flying bridge, she smiled and raised her hand in a little wave.

The mate did not respond. Instead he held Lemont's wife in his gaze for a few more seconds, his expression blank, and then he deliberately looked away from her to the other women in the group, slowly inspecting each in turn. It would, he knew, annoy her.

One of the others was outstanding, even in this company. She was the girl friend of Benuzzi, the tennis player, and had come aboard with him in San Remo. She was young, probably no more than twenty, and quite pretty, in a fresh, natural way. Her body was slim and athletic, her breasts small but high and well formed. Hendricks decided that she would be very good in the sack. After another moment he turned his back on the group and resumed looking at the buildings along Portofino's waterfront.

What the hell was the matter with him anyway? He'd lucked into the best job he'd ever had, and instead of being happy about it, he felt morose and resentful. He had been second officer aboard the tanker *White Star*. When the ship put into Marseilles with engine trouble just five days out of Abadan in the Persian Gulf, loaded with five hundred thousand barrels of Iranian crude, Hendricks went ashore, got drunk, and shacked up. When he returned to the shipyard after a few

3

days, he was too late—the *White Star* had already sailed. A bartender told him that the mate of a yacht had suffered an attack of appendicitis and that her captain was anxious to replace the man and resume cruising, and Hendricks talked his way into the job. Life on board the *Chanteuse* could not be easier. Yet now, only a month later, he was bored and disgruntled.

"Hendricks."

He turned to face the captain. Lemont, he saw, had gone below. "Yes?"

The captain spoke in heavily accented English. "Mr. Lemont will have guests come aboard here in Portofino. You are to pick them up at seven and bring them out for drinks. Later on everyone may go ashore for dinner. Mr. Lemont has not yet decided."

"Okay." Hendricks saw the look of disapproval on the captain's face. He knew that the yacht's commander preferred strict adherence to yes-sir, no-sir responses among his crew, including his mate, but so far the captain had not made an issue of it.

To hell with him. Hendricks went down the ladder of the boat deck and oversaw the swinging out of the davits that held the larger of the yacht's two tenders. When the boat was in the water and secured to the *Chanteuse*'s landing stage, he walked forward to the crew's mess.

Benoit, the chief steward, was sitting at the table drinking coffee. Hendricks drew a mug and sat down opposite him.

"Welcome to Portofino, hah?" Benoit was cheerful. "One of the most beautiful ports on the whole Mediterranean. Where you have to beat off the girls with a club."

Hendricks grunted.

"Unless of course you have duty that keeps you on board," the steward needled.

"I'm in charge of the tender," Hendricks said.

"Ah. What a pity. But then tomorrow morning you can take me ashore. I need supplies."

"The bosun will take you tomorrow. I only make the important runs, with Lemont's guests."

Benoit smiled. "It gets on your nerves, I think, eh? A big deepwater ship's officer playing taxi driver. But then, it's not so bad. Worth it, for such a soft job."

"Maybe. And maybe not."

"But what more could you ask—unless, of course, it would be a yacht of your own?" The steward's smile widened to a grin.

4

Hendricks looked at him. "Could be that's exactly what I want. And when I get it, I'll hire you to keep the bilges clean."

Benoit guffawed. "Better you hire me to keep your harem stocked. Except first there is one small problem. You need to make some money. Say, a few million, eh?"

"More than a few, I think. Who's coming aboard tonight, do you know?"

"I have heard Vicente Morello. You don't know who he is? A movie producer. Very famous. A most distinguished man. No doubt he will bring a woman along, and you can bet she will be something special. He has a villa in Portofino. When we were here last summer, he came out for dinner."

Hendricks finished his coffee and left the messroom. When he stepped into his cabin, Estelle Lemont was standing in the middle of the room. She had put on a thin white robe over the bikini. "Hey," he said. "What are you—"

She placed a finger over his mouth. "I had to see you," she whispered.

He lowered his voice. "Where's your husband?"

"He's asleep." She pressed close to him. "Do you know I haven't been with you for two whole days?"

Hendricks grinned. "That's a long time, isn't it?"

"Too long."

He put his arms around her, and she moved her hips and opened her mouth to his kiss.

"We musn't let that happen again, do you understand?"

"Yeah, I understand."

"I saw you staring at that child's body this afternoon. You made me jealous."

"Did I?"

"Of course you did."

She continued to grind her hips against him, and Hendricks felt himself growing hard.

"You don't look at anybody else," Estelle said. She reached down and gripped him. "You belong to me and to me only."

He made no response.

She pulled away and slipped out of her robe. "Now hurry. We don't have much time." She hooked her thumbs into the bikini bottom and stepped out of it.

Hendricks eyes traveled down her body. The smooth skin was brown and still faintly slick with coconut oil. There was a white patch where the bikini had screened her from the sun.

Estelle's breathing quickened with excitement, and the full

5

breasts rose and fell. She lay down on his bunk and watched as he pulled his clothes off.

Without them Hendricks's body seemed even more massive. His shoulders were broad and heavily muscled, his chest deep, the pectorals clearly defined. Below his ridged belly his hips were as narrow as a boy's. Fully erect, his penis throbbed.

"Come on," Estelle whispered. "Come on."

Hendricks lowered himself to her, and she opened her legs and wrapped her arms around his neck. Her tongue flickered against his ear and her hips began to move again rhythmically.

"Put it in," Estelle commanded. "Now." Her fingers found him and guided him into her, and she let out a little cry.

"Sure," Hendricks said. "Anything you say."

The sarcasm was lost on her.

chapter 2

Vicente Morello swung the bright red Ferrari Boxer down the winding hillside road into the town. He turned left at the church tower and drove past the Nazionale Hotel. Even in Portofino the big sports car drew attention, and that pleased him. He was an extremely successful man, and he liked the world to know about it. Consequently he chose his personal possessions with great care—his cars, his clothes, his homes, his women. He reached over and patted the leg of the girl who sat beside him. Her name was Cecily, and in her way she was as distinctive as the Ferrari, and as high spirited. She had long auburn hair and a remarkable body, clad only in pyjamas of thin pale green silk.

The narrow streets were thronged with people. It was dusk, and the cafés and the restaurants were already crowded, as they would be until three or four o'clock the following morning. As always in the summer months, an air of festivity and good humor prevailed in the ancient seaport. Morello eased the Ferrari through the crowd, the V-12 snarling as he revved it. He enjoyed the admiring stares of the pedestrians, especially the girls.

Morello was in his middle fifties, but he looked much

younger. A vain man, he kept himself in excellent shape with tennis and swimming, and women thought him quite handsome, in a vital, athletic way. He was nearly bald, but his gray sideburns were thick and luxuriant, and this added to the impression he gave of virility.

When he reached the Pensione Lina, Morello parked the Ferrari in front of the place and stuffed a handful of lira notes into a porter's hand, telling the man that his job for the remainder of the night was to watch the car. He took Cecily's arm and guided her down to the waterfront.

Lights were coming on now on the boats, in the cabins and at the mastheads. Morello pointed out to where the *Chanteuse* rode at anchor. "There. She's easy to spot, hm?"

Cecily followed his hand. "Beautiful. And so big. Much bigger than any other boat in the harbor."

Morello smiled. A woman was a woman. He enjoyed Cecily, finding her not merely decorative but brighter than many of the young women he knew, and as a result easier to tolerate over a longer period of time. As an actress she was competent, if not inspired, and in bed she was outstanding. Nevertheless he had no illusions about her. Cecily was ruthlessly ambitious, and as eager to use Morello as he was willing to use her. She would star in the picture he planned to put into production in a few weeks.

They strolled along the quay, taking in the sights and sounds of the seaport. On many of the yachts parties were under way, mostly of the informal kind common to places where boats clustered. People sat in the cockpits or on the decks laughing and talking, some of them wandering from boat to boat, glasses in hand. Music from the cafés carried out across the bay.

At the end of a stone wharf the *Chanteuse*'s tender waited for them. A huge blond man in whites, a yachting cap pushed back on his head, lounged on the pier. Two sailors stood in the launch. As they approached, the blond man studied them. "Mr. Morello?"

Morello nodded.

"I'm Hendricks. Mate on the *Chanteuse*." He gestured toward the tender. "If you'll come aboard, we'll go right on out."

Morello watched as the blond man clambered into the boat and then reached up to take Cecily's hands. The mate swung her down onto the deck as lightly as if she had been weightless. Morello jumped into the tender and took a seat beside Cecily.

7

The mate gave an order, and the sailors cast off the lines and headed the tender out into the harbor.

In his long years in the motion picture business Morello had carefully developed his powers of observation, especially where the interaction of people was concerned. His ability to understand and to convey what went on between them was acute. What he had just witnessed was very interesting to him. First, this young man in charge of the tender was astonishingly good looking. There was about him a palpable sense of strength and masculinity. Second, Morello had seen Cecily react to him as if an electric current had passed between them.

* * *

Estelle Lemont kissed Morello and then Cecily as they came up the stage onto the *Chanteuse*'s main deck. Although she had fulfilled a lifelong ambition by marrying one of France's richest men, Estelle nevertheless missed the excitement of the film industry and welcomed any opportunity to see old friends and catch up on gossip. She did not know Cecily very well, but she and Morello went back to her days as a juvenile in repertory theater in the south of France, before Jacques Burstein had spotted her and given her a small part in a suspense picture that had not only been a hit in Europe but had even done business in the States. The picture had won her favorable mention from the critics, and far more important, it had given her wide exposure to the public, who found her dark good looks sexy and appealing. Morello was an assistant director in those days, and later they worked on two pictures together, one of them the first in which Estelle had a featured role.

"Darling," Estelle said to her husband. "You remember Vicente? And Cecily. Isn't she exquisite?"

Lemont offered a limp hand and a vague greeting, and Estelle introduced the couple to her other guests. Besides the tennis star and his friend, there was a stockbroker from Paris, a Swiss ballet dancer, Lemont's lawyer and his mistress, the owner of a chateau in the Domaine de la Romanée-Conti and his wife, and a pop singer from Monaco and her fiancé.

After a steward served Morello a drink, Estelle sat beside him. "You look good, Vicente."

"Better every year."

"Yes, you are like fine wine, or some such shit."

"Precisely. And how are you?"

8

"All right. A little bored, sometimes. I miss the business."

"Why? When you were in it, you bitched about it constantly."

"That is a woman's prerogative. At least there was variety. And excitement." She gestured. "With this life, everything is so much the same. Perhaps I retired too soon."

"Nonsense. You did exactly the right thing, to give it up at the pinnacle of your career. The biggest star in French films, undefeated, and always the champion."

"Balls."

"So come back, if you wish. I would always have a part for you." It was a little game they played when they saw each other, and both of them knew it.

"I'll think about it. How is business?"

"Superb."

"I hear your last two pictures were disasters."

"I do not produce disasters. It is only that some of my pictures may not be as successful as others."

"I hear the people ran out of the theaters holding their noses."

"The pictures could have been better."

"What's next?"

"I have a very powerful concept."

"Meaning you have no story?"

"I have a marvelous story."

"What is it?"

"A western."

"A what?"

"A western. You know—the American West."

"Vicente, are you out of your mind?"

He sighed. "Like most women, you can't wait to jump to a conclusion."

"But cowboys? Indians?"

"No, no. Nothing like that. What I plan to do is a kind of allegory. Its setting is a western, because that provides a natural reason for the violence."

"What is the title?"

"*The Hired Gun.*"

"Mm. Tell me the premise."

"The people in a Western town see that their village is being destroyed by outlaws, and so they hire a professional killer to rid them of this scourge."

"So he kills the outlaws?"

"Every one of them."

"And then?"

"And then they find themselves dealing with a new scourge—the killer. Because when he kills the outlaws, he becomes the power in the village. And, as we say, power corrupts."

"And absolute power corrupts absolutely."

"That is exactly right."

"It sounds boring."

"I believe it will be a tremendous hit."

She sniffed. "Perhaps. Is there sex?"

"Of course. Cecily will costar."

"And in your story that is how the town finally rids itself of the killer."

"How is that?"

"Cecily will fuck him to death."

Morello laughed. "You should be a screenwriter."

"Why not? My ideas are no worse than the *merde* most of them turn out."

The *Chanteuse*'s guests drank champagne and smoked marijuana in neatly rolled joints offered on silver trays by the stewards. Natalie, Benuzzi's girl friend, went below with a headache, and the tennis player immediately directed his attention to the ballet dancer. Lemont and his lawyer continued their discussion of the advisability of establishing residence in Switzerland for tax purposes, and the stockbroker and the pop singer compared notes on discotheques in Rome.

The lawyer's mistress asked the chateau owner if the grape crop would be a good one. Her name was Bette and she was a small, red-haired girl from Lyon who now lived in a handsome apartment in the Eighth Arrondissement in Paris.

"Fair," he replied. "A bit too much rain in July. But the crop will be acceptable. Not as good as last year, but not bad."

Bette inhaled deeply. "Maybe you should put part of your land in grass."

"Grass?"

Bette held up her joint.

He laughed. "The quality would not be high enough. You need a much hotter climate for really top-grade marijuana. That is why the best stuff comes from Africa."

"And Mexico?"

"And Mexico. South America is very good also."

"It's the coming thing, no? Someday huge plantations, and international judgings and vintage years."

"Of course. It is inevitable."

At around ten o'clock Estelle Lemont led her guests into the main dining salon for a dinner of asparagus hollandaise, striped sea bass caught that same afternoon, and cold mussels in mustard sauce. For dessert they had wild strawberries in heavy cream. The wines were an outstanding Chevalier-Montrachet, and in deference to the chateau owner, a Romanée-Conti. Afterward, back on deck under a dazzling blanket of stars, Lemont suggested they go ashore for a round of the clubs.

* * *

In his cabin Hendricks poured more champagne into Natalie's glass. The chief steward had slipped him two cold bottles and a handful of joints, and he was a little high now from the combination of wine and marijuana. "Where will you go from here?"

Natalie brushed her hair back from her eyes. She was naked, and the only light in the small room came from a candle Hendricks had stuck in an ashtray on his desk. They sat facing each other, spraddle-legged, on his bunk. "Spain. He plays exhibitions in Barcelona and Toledo, and then there is a tournament in Malaga."

"It sounds like fun. You go to a beautiful place, he plays a little tennis, and then you're on to another beautiful place."

"It's all right. The trouble is, after awhile all the beautiful places seem the same. There is no difference among them."

Hendricks blew out a stream of smoke. "It's always like that, isn't it? No matter what we've got, we're never really happy with it. We want more, or less, but anyhow always something different from what we've got."

"And you? Do you feel that way too?"

"Yeah, I do."

"But why? This is a good life for you, isn't it?"

"I thought so, at first. Until I realized I'm nothing but a fucking seagoing bellboy."

"So why don't you quit and go back to real ships, if that is what you want to do?"

He shifted his body. "Trouble is, I don't know what the hell I want. I thought I did, once. But now I'm not so sure."

Natalie sipped champagne, studying him over the rim of her glass. "Has this work made you see things differently from how you once did?"

He thought about it. "Yeah, I guess it has. I was never around money before, you know?"

11

She smiled. "And so now that you've seen it, you want it."

"Something like that."

"But not quite?"

He shook his head. "Just to have it wouldn't mean a damn thing to me."

"But what it could buy?"

"Some things. But others, no." He waved a hand. "Owning this tub, for instance. No interest at all. But on the other hand—"

"Yes?"

"*Getting* money could mean everything."

"Ah. It's the power, then, that you want."

"Maybe."

She dragged deeply on a joint. "You are a very unusual man, Hendricks."

He laughed. "Because I want money? That makes me just exactly like every other asshole in the world who hasn't got any."

"No, I didn't mean that."

"What, then?"

She leaned forward until her lips almost touched his. "I meant that there is something about you that is unlike anybody else. It is the way you send out these—signals, somehow. This afternoon, when we came into the harbor, you looked down at me and I felt it. As if your eyes were hands, and they were touching me. It was very exciting."

Hendricks brushed his lips against her mouth. "I think we have time—"

The intercom on the bulkhead emitted a raucous buzz, and the captain's voice snarled metallically. "Hendricks! Come topside at once."

The mate gritted his teeth. "Shit. You see what I mean? That fat fuck wants something, he just rings for the boy."

Natalie giggled. "It's a system I should have. Whenever I want you, I only have to yell into that thing, and you come running at once."

Hendricks grinned in spite of himself. "With you it wouldn't be so bad. I might even yell into it myself once in a while."

"I hope so."

He kissed her, gently at first, and then hungrily, crushing his mouth on hers, feeling her breasts against his chest.

The captain's voice grated again. "Hendricks! Get up here."

"Jesus Christ." He pulled on his trousers and reached for his shirt.

12

The Lemonts and their guests were gathered on deck at the head of the landing stage, Lemont gesturing impatiently to the captain, when Hendricks stumbled into view. The mate was still high. He was barefoot and bareheaded, and his shirt hung open, its tails flapping.

The *Chanteuse*'s captain looked at him and turned dark red with anger. "Hendricks—what are you doing?"

The mate returned his stare. "Doing? What the hell do you think I'm doing? I'm going to run your fucking dink to the dock."

A wave of laughter swept over the group. For a moment the captain was unable to move or speak. If there was one thing the man absolutely could not tolerate, it was to be laughed at. When he did act, it was as if his anger had caused him to explode. Teeth bared, he reached over and grabbed Hendricks's shirtfront with both hands.

The mate's reaction was instinctive and immediate. He put his own right hand into the middle of the other man's face and shoved hard. The captain stumbled backward out onto the top level of the landing stage, hit the rail, and somersaulted over it. His heavy body hit the water horizontally, creating an enormous splash. When he bobbed to the surface sputtering a second later, the people on the *Chanteuse*'s deck were all yelling at once, and the yacht's sailors scurried to throw a life ring to the man in the water.

In the midst of the confusion Hendricks ambled down the steps of the stage and climbed into the tender. He started the engine, cast off the bow line, and headed for the lights of Portofino.

chapter 3

At two o'clock in the morning the Ristorante Il Pitosforo was bustling. The kitchen would stay open for at least another two hours, and people continued to push into the place, hoping for a table. In one corner a group sang "Amore Libero," the new hit in the discos of Italy. Waiters in red shirts negotiated the crowd by holding their heavily laden trays with arms extended straight up over their heads.

Hendricks sat at the bar, drinking grappa, the cheap, fiery brandy made from wine dregs. He was on his eighth or ninth, and he was very drunk. He fumbled in his pocket for a cigarette, and when he got it out and into his mouth, the bartender lit it for him.

A hand touched his shoulder. Hendricks turned slowly. A man stood at his side, smiling. He looked vaguely familiar.

"Vicente Morello," the man said. "You took us out to the *Chanteuse* earlier."

"Oh, yeah. You had that great-looking chick."

"Correct. Mind if I join you?"

"I don't give a shit."

Morello elbowed in next to him and ordered a cognac. "I've been looking for you for hours."

"What for?"

"I wanted to tell you I was sorry you had that, ah, little difficulty earlier, with the captain."

Hendricks shrugged. "Sooner or later I was bound to have a run-in with that prick."

Morello's cognac appeared. He raised his glass. "Salut."

"Yeah." Hendricks swallowed some grappa.

"I was wondering what your plans might be."

"Now that I'm out of a job, you mean?"

"Yes."

"What the hell do you care?"

"I thought I might be able to help you."

"Why?"

"Why?"

"Yeah, why? What's in it for you?"

Morello smiled. "You are a very direct man, Mr. Hendricks."

"Fucking right."

"And so am I."

"Uh-huh."

"Do you know what business I am in?"

"I heard movies."

"That is correct. Tell me, have you ever thought about the possibility of working in that business?"

Hendricks shook his head. "Hell, no. I'm all through with being a flunky. Kissing ass on board that yacht was the end of it. No more."

"You misunderstand. I was not speaking of a job as a flunky. I meant the possibility of working as an actor."

Hendricks looked at him. "Are you a fag?"

"No, no. I assure you I am not. What I am talking about is a very serious proposal. I think you may have a distinct talent for pictures. As an actor."

Hendricks snorted. "Listen, buddy. I don't know what your hustle is, but don't try to con me. I don't know the first thing about acting, or pictures. Hell, I haven't even seen one in years."

Morello drank some of his cognac. "It is a very different business from what you might think. Especially today. Acting ability is not so important as personality. It is personality the audience reacts to. Some of the most successful actors can hardly act at all, and yet their personalities have great impact."

Hendricks put another cigarette into his lips. This time Morello lit it.

"What is more, acting can be taught," the producer went on. "To anybody. But the other thing, this personality thing, that is something no one can teach. It is something you must be born with."

"So?"

"So I think I see some of that natural talent in you."

"And I think you're full of shit."

Morello took a deep breath and exhaled slowly. "You know, there are probably several thousand young men here in Portofino right now who would give anything to have me say these things to them. Yet you do not even do me the courtesy of listening."

Hendricks drained his glass and signaled for a refill. "So talk. I'm all ears."

"Tonight I saw some things that interested me. I saw that

15

you have a lot of what we call presence. I saw how women seem to react to you. And as I am sure you are happily aware, they react."

"Mm."

"I also saw you in a situation in which there was a little stress. When you were under a bit of pressure. It was fascinating."

"Uh-huh. But that doesn't make me an actor."

"Perhaps. But if I am right, it could be something very good to discover. For both of us. So what I am suggesting is that we find out. To do that, we make a little test. We take some footage of you, and we look at it."

"Where do we do that?"

"In a studio in Rome."

Hendricks's eyes narrowed.

Morello gestured impatiently. "You will go there entirely at my expense. You will live well and eat well—a first-class hotel. When we see the results of the test, if I am wrong, what have you lost? Nothing. You have had a nice vacation in a beautiful city. But if I am right—"

"Yeah?"

"Hendricks, do you realize that there are actors who are paid a million dollars a picture?"

"For one picture? A million bucks?"

"That is correct."

"Sure, but—"

"Will you make anything like that, at first? Of course not. I am only trying to get you to understand what the possibilities are. And the truth is, they are unlimited."

Hendricks took a mouthful of grappa and turned it over on his tongue before swallowing it. The liquor no longer seemed to have any bite or any effect on him. It was like drinking water. "I guess I'd have to be a damn fool to turn that down, wouldn't I? At least the chance to see what happens?"

Morello drained his glass. "Yes. You would."

"Okay. So when do we go?"

"You go," the producer said. "I will provide you with some money to get you to Rome." He reached into a hip pocket and withdrew a black crocodile billfold. He counted out eight hundred and fifty thousand lire in crisp notes and laid the money in a stack on the bar. "I will join you there in a few days." He reached into the billfold again and took out a card which he placed on top of the money. "As soon as you arrive, contact my assistant at this address. His name is Antonio. I will have spoken to him, and he will take care of everything."

Hendricks picked up the card and squinted at it. Then he scooped up the bank notes and stuffed them along with the card into his pants pocket.

Morello smiled and extended his hand. "Arrivederci."

When the producer was gone, Hendricks finished his drink. The bartender looked at him and Hendricks put his hand over the glass.

"No more?"

"No more grappa," Hendricks said. "Give me a Scotch."

chapter 4

The Stazione Metropolitana was in the central part of Rome. It was much larger than the terminal in Santa Margherita, where Hendricks had caught the train, and was even more crowded. The tourists here were also more of an international mixture. Hendricks was pretty sure that he could identify the Germans and the French and the Scandinavians, as different as they were from the southern Europeans. The Americans were the easiest to spot, with their polyester shirts and the masses of photographic equipment dangling from their necks, the women invariably overweight, buttocks threatening to burst the seams of their garishly colored slacks. They were the most vocal as well, shouting to each other in accents of Pittsburgh and Houston and Atlanta. There were also many Japanese, well mannered and appearing affluent in their Western-style clothing. As lways, only the youth were impossible to sort out by nationality. They all looked alike, brown skinned and carefree, attired in the inevitable uniform of T-shirts and jeans.

Hendricks carried a plastic shopping bag. Getting cleaned up in the public toilets here, he thought, would be just as difficult as it would have been in Santa Margherita. So the hell with it. If Morello's assistant didn't like the way he looked, it was too bad. Sooner or later he'd find a place to bathe and change clothes.

There were rows of telephones against the walls. To reach

one, Hendricks had to stand in line. When his turn finally came, he pulled out the card the producer had given him. Vicente Morello Produzioni was printed on it, and under that, Antonio Crescia. There were two telephone numbers, one business, the other private.

He tried the business number first. No answer. The private number was answered on the second ring.

"Prego?"

"Antonio Crescia?"

"Si?"

Hendricks thought the man would probably speak English, but he wasn't sure. "My name is Hendricks."

"Oh, of course. Mr. Morello called me about you this morning." There was an accent, but the words were strong and clear. About what you heard in an Italian restaurant in New York, Hendricks thought.

"Yeah?"

"Where are you?"

"In Rome. At the railroad station. I just got here."

"Okay, fine. You have a place to stay?"

"No, not yet."

"All right, I tell you what. You get a taxi up to my place, and we'll get you lined up with a hotel. Mr. Morello gave you some expense money, right?"

"Yes."

Antonio quoted an address. "That's in central Rome, off the Via Condotti. The driver will know."

The address Antonio had given him was on a tree-lined street in what appeared to Hendricks to be a good neighborhood. It was an apartment house, modern and well kept, constructed of sand-colored brick. Like most of the other buildings he had been able to see in the city, it was not very tall. Rome had a relatively low skyline, he realized. Nothing like New York, and even London had more high-rise structures.

Antonio's apartment was on the third floor. Hendricks rang the bell, and a man about his own age opened the door.

"Hendricks, right?" The young man was slim and dark, his hair a thick black cap that curled over his ears. He wore a tight-fitting shirt of gray silk, open to the waist. He held out his hand. "I'm Antonio."

Hendricks shook his hand. From within the apartment he could hear the sounds of music and a girl's laughter. He was suddenly aware again of how grubby he must look.

"Come on in," Antonio said. "You didn't have any trouble finding it, huh?"

Hendricks followed him inside. "No. No trouble at all."

The apartment was sparsely furnished. It contained a stereo, a few tables and wicker chairs, and a zebra-skin rug. Several abstract oil paintings, unframed, hung on the stark white walls.

A man and a girl sat together, talking and drinking what appeared to be whiskey. The girl was a brunette, with large almond-shaped eyes so dark they seemed black, and a sensuous, full-lipped mouth. She looked at Hendricks with interest. The man paid no attention to him. He was broad and muscular and wore a short, spade-shaped beard. Antonio introduced them as Tina Rinaldi and Matt Weaver. They had just dropped in, he said.

Antonio waved toward a chair. "Have a seat."

"I was wondering," Hendricks said, "if I could change." He gestured with the plastic shopping bag. "I bought some clean clothes." He was aware that the girl was looking at his dirty whites, and it made him uncomfortable.

"Sure, sure," Antonio replied. "Come on, right in here." He led Hendricks to a bathroom. "You can shower if you want. Plenty of clean towels on the racks there. Take your time."

Hendricks thanked him and shut the door. He stripped off his clothes and stepped into the shower stall. The stream of water was strong and hot and seemed a great luxury. Hendricks stood under it for a long time, soaping and resoaping his body, feeling that heat soak into the muscles of his chest and shoulders and back. When he finally got out, much of his fatigue had left him. He found a razor and shaved carefully, but still nicked himself. Then he pulled on the new clothes he had bought, a blue shirt and a pair of light gray slacks.

Antonio smiled when Hendricks reentered the living room. "Hey, a new man, huh?"

"Yeah, I feel a lot better," Hendricks said.

Antonio indicated the man with the beard. "Matt here is a cameraman. He'll probably shoot your test."

Weaver glanced at Hendricks. "You ever done any acting?"

"No, never."

"How about a drink?" Antonio indicated a table on which stood bottles, glasses, and an ice bucket. "You probably could use one after that trip, eh?"

Hendricks smiled. "Scotch and some ice would be fine."

"Sure." Antonio made the drink and handed it to him.

"Luck," Hendricks said. The liquor instantly relaxed him, spreading its soothing warmth down through his chest and into his stomach. It also reminded him of his hunger. He had eaten nothing since the sandwich he had bought on the train, and the thought of food now made him wish he'd stopped for something before coming here.

As if he had read Hendricks's thoughts, Antonio said, "I will take us out to dinner in a little while. There's a good restaurant not far from here. This is your first time in Rome?"

"Yes," Hendricks replied. He turned to Weaver. "You sound like an American."

"Yeah."

"Where from?"

The cameraman sat back in his chair. He looked bored. "New Mexico originally. Lived in L.A. the last few years I was in the States."

"But now he is a Roman," the girl said. "They say that once you live in Rome, you are a Roman forever, and it is true." She smiled at Hendricks. "So you will become a Roman too."

"If I'm here that long."

"What do you want to be an actor for?" Weaver asked.

Hendricks drank some of his Scotch. "I'm not sure that I do."

"Then why go through all this crap?"

"I just thought I'd give it a try," Hendricks said, "as long as I had the chance."

Weaver rubbed his nose. "Not that it's all that difficult. Especially with Morello. What he requires as a range of emotion is that you can be glad, or mad, or dead."

Antonio laughed. "Don't be cynical, Matt. The thing is, the maestro understands his audience."

"What the maestro understands," Weaver replied, "is how to produce cheapo pictures that make a buck." He glanced at Hendricks. "And how to recruit low-cost talent."

Hendricks wondered why the cameraman was edgy, almost hostile. It could be because of the girl, he decided. He turned to her. "What do you do, Tina?"

She smiled. "I'm an actress. More low-cost talent recruited by the maestro."

"I've never seen any of his pictures," Hendricks said. "What kind of things does he do?"

"I just told you," Weaver said. "His major themes are killing and fucking."

"Mostly adventure stories," Antonio said. "Or crime pictures. Right now we're about to go into production on a western."

Hendricks was surprised. "A western?"

Weaver laughed. "Can you believe it? An Italian western. That's like doing a Polish minstrel."

Antonio refilled their glasses. "Personally I think it is a brilliant idea. American westerns usually do a good business in Europe, and particularly in Italy. So why not produce our own? Especially when the maestro can give his unique style to the film."

"Which brings us back to the classic Morello themes," Weaver said. "Murder and humping."

"But his pictures always make money, don't they?" Tina asked.

Antonio smiled. "Let us say, they often do."

"It's only when he tries to do something worthwhile that they bomb," Weaver said. "So he's very careful to avoid making that mistake."

Tina sat up in her chair. "That's not fair. One of his most successful pictures was *The Prince*, and the critics were very favorable toward it."

Hendricks studied her body as he swallowed more of his Scotch. Her breasts were firm and full, and her waist tapered narrowly before flaring to well-rounded hips. Good legs, too. If being possessive about her was what made Weaver touchy, it was understandable. He speculated as to just what their relationship was. Whatever it might be, he hoped he'd find a chance to make a run on her.

"It was a good picture," Antonio agreed. "But he doesn't really care what the critics say in any case. He has his own ideas about what the people want, and he always tries to give it to them."

"Sure," Weaver said. "Whether they agree with him or not."

"I don't know why you criticize him so much," Tina said. "You've done very well working for him, haven't you?"

"Yeah, it's been okay," the cameraman said. "But there's always plenty of work around Rome. And if there wasn't, I'd go to Paris or London." He looked at Antonio. "That's one of the advantages of having a reputation."

The Italian smiled. "He's reminding me that he is always in demand," he said to Hendricks.

"Correct," Weaver said. "It comes from my uncanny ability

21

to make any kind of shit look good. Shit material or shit directors."

I'll remember that, Hendricks thought. This guy is going to shoot my test, and if it's true that he has the power to make me come off okay, then he's going to be a friend of mine. Maybe I won't screw his girl friend, at that. Or at least, he decided, glancing at her, I'll postpone it awhile.

Tina returned his gaze, the hint of a smile turning one corner of her mouth.

Antonio put his glass down. "Let's go get some food. Everybody must be starved. I know I am."

They stood up, and Hendricks saw that the girl's body was even better than he had thought. He also noted that she seemed to like his observation of her. He decided that the problem of her relationship with the cameraman was something he'd just have to work out.

chapter 5

The restaurant was informal and crowded with people enjoying themselves. It was lighted by brass lanterns, and clusters of straw-encased wine bottles hung from pegs on the walls. It was called Nino's, after its proprietor. He was a big man, grossly fat, with a round, red, cheerful face. He greeted Antonio effusively and led the group to a table in one corner of the busy room. As soon as they were seated, two waiters hurried over and covered the table with platters of antipasto and trays of hot fresh bread.

"That's one of the great things about restaurants in Italy," Weaver said. "None of this waiting for half an hour until somebody feels like giving you a menu. Here you sit down and bang, you get something to eat right away." He shoveled food onto his plate.

Hendricks had learned enough from watching guests aboard the *Chanteuse* to restrain himself. Nevertheless it was with difficulty that he passed the dishes to Tina before he helped himself. There were slices of salami and sausage and pepperoni and olives and celery and cheeses and marinated mushrooms and pickled eggs and peppers and sardines and calimari and several kinds of salad. The way he felt, he could have cleaned off the table all by himself. As it was, he took a little of everything, which still gave him a hefty plateful. He forced himself to eat slowly, relishing the cold food.

Antonio spoke rapidly in Italian, and a waiter brought glasses and a two-liter bottle of Chianti to the table. He uncorked the bottle with a flourish and filled the glasses.

"To the start of a new career." Antonio smiled at Hendricks and held up his glass.

The wine was rough and hearty and tasted wonderful. Hendricks gulped down half his glass and saw that Weaver was watching him, a cynical expression on his bearded face.

"I still don't know why you want to do this," the cameraman said. "Unless it's because you want to be rich as well as beautiful."

Hendricks saw Antonio stiffen, but he had resolved that whatever was bothering Weaver, he wouldn't let it get to him. "I'll tell you what's going to happen. We make the test, I fall on my face, and then I go back to my old job. Meantime I've had a good time and a chance to see Rome."

The others smiled, but Weaver's expression did not change. "You're a sailor or something, aren't you?"

"That's right."

"I hear most of those guys are faggots," the cameraman said. "They like being on boats because they can all sleep together and cornhole each other. That true?"

Antonio opened his mouth, but before he could speak, Tina said angrily, "What is the matter with you, Matthew? Why do you want to start fights?"

Hendricks raised a hand. "Hey, it's okay." He leaned toward Weaver. "It's absolutely true. But don't knock it. You haven't lived till you've had a piece of a messboy's ass."

It broke the tension, and this time even Weaver smiled a little.

Antonio poured more wine. "With your permission I will order for us." He signaled to a waiter, and when the man approached, he spoke to him at length, giving him what Hendricks assumed were detailed instructions.

"Anyway," Antonio said when the waiter had left, "what is wrong with homosexuals in films? Or new about it, for that matter. Not that our friend is homosexual, but the industry's always been full of them, on both sides of the camera."

"That so?" Hendricks was being polite. He didn't much

23

give a damn about anybody's sexual preferences, in or out of the motion picture business.

"Absolutely," Antonio said. "You take Fellini. One of the best directors in the world. He even makes pictures that argue in favor of homosexuality as a way of life."

Hendricks stuffed marinated mushrooms into his mouth. "Really?"

"Absolutely. Did you see his *Satyricon*?"

"No."

"A fantastic success," Antonio said. "Big business everywhere it played. One of the sequences depicts the mythological story of the minotaur, in which a man is in a maze that will lead him to be killed by the bull-god, a creature that is half man, half bull. Fellini has the victim save himself by falling in love with the bull."

Hendricks ate some pepperoni. "No shit?"

Antonio nodded vigorously. "But it has always been so. Look at Noel Coward. A brilliant actor, a great playwright, a fine director."

"And a screaming queer," Weaver said.

Tina shook her head impatiently. "What difference does it make?"

"It makes a difference to me," Weaver answered. "I don't like working with them. Actors, okay. I couldn't care less. But taking orders from a fag director? Forget it. The only thing worse is working for a woman, which is maybe the same thing."

"When did you ever do that?" Tina asked.

"Never," Weaver said. "The closest I ever came was with Lina Wertmuller. She wanted me to work on a picture with her four years ago. It was before she made *Seven Beauties*. We had one meeting together, and I told her to stuff it."

Tina was contemptuous. "So you had a meeting with one of the most gifted directors alive, and you refused to work with her."

"Goddamn right," Weaver said. "She came on like Otto Preminger in drag. I said who needs this? There are enough good directors around so I don't have to put up with catching shit from a broad."

"Sometimes," Tina said, "I think you behave like an ass."

Weaver laughed. "What do you mean 'sometimes'?"

Their food arrived, and Hendricks ate ravenously. They began with linguine, delicious in a sauce faintly redolent of garlic, followed by veal rollatini, the meat tender and succulent,

24

the stuffing lightly spiced and fluffy in texture. As they consumed the meal, the conversation continued on the subject of motion pictures, ranging from what was presently in production to what films were being shown in the theaters to what grosses *Variety* was reporting. Antonio and Tina and Weaver compared current films to old ones and discussed actors and directors and writers. Hendricks began to understand that among people in the business, movies were virtually all they ever talked about when they were together.

"De Laurentiis is planning an enormous spectacle based upon the life of Christ," Antonio said at one point. "It is to be the greatest thing of this kind ever done. Much bigger than *The Robe* or anything that ever touched the subject before."

"I've heard that," Weaver said around a mouthful of veal. "He wants to because he's still stung by the *King Kong* flop. He can't understand why it went down the chute."

"I can," Antonio said. "It's because he turned the story into a kind of sentimental slop. The audience went to the theaters because they wanted to be terrified by a gigantic ape—a monster. Instead what he gave them was an oversized teddy bear."

"When a picture is a failure," Tina said to Hendricks, "everybody can tell you exactly when went wrong. And when one succeeds, everybody can tell you exactly what went right. The trouble is, nobody can tell you these things ahead of time."

"Even the erotic aspects did not work," Antonio went on. "In the original when Kong pulled Fay Wray's clothes off, the crowds were squirming with excitement. It still happens whenever the film is rereleased—I saw it myself. But in the new one nobody believed the relationship between the ape and the girl. It cost De Laurentiis a couple of million dollars to build that big monkey, but it gave you no real sense that it was alive. And most of all, it was threatening to nobody."

The food and the wine had made Hendricks feel very good. He decided to venture an opinion. "Maybe it's just monsters. Maybe people aren't scared of those things anymore."

"Bullshit they aren't," Weaver said. "Biggest moneymaker of all time was *Jaws*. And what the hell kind of a plot would you call that? Giant shark off Long Island chewing up everybody who goes into the water."

"The thing is," Antonio said, "that successful films cannot be formularized. Everybody always thinks they can, but they cannot. *Godfather* is a hit, so there is a flood of Mafia pictures, and all of them do nothing. Even the one with Anthony Quinn, *The Don*, I think it was called, was a failure."

"But then Coppola comes right back with *Godfather II* and makes another pile," Weaver said.

This was interesting to Hendricks. "Was everything else the same?"

"Pretty much," Antonio replied. "No Brando, but it had Al Pacino, and Mario Puzo worked on the screenplay."

"The author," Hendricks said. "I read the book."

Weaver glanced at him.

Hendricks grinned. "Don't be so surprised, Matt. I can read. It's something you have a lot of time for at sea."

A commotion sounded nearby. They looked around to see that the proprietor was arguing with two young men. They had shoulder-length hair and were dressed in rags. Nino waved his hands and shouted, and the young men responded with loud outbursts and gestures of their own.

"Communists," Antonio explained. "They are all over Rome."

"I saw the slogans on the way from the station," Hendricks said.

"Officially they are not in power," Antonio remarked. "But the truth is that they control the city. Nothing works because of them. The mail, the telephones, nothing. They have turned Italy into a bureaucratic swamp. If you tried to get something done, you could sink into it and never be heard from again."

The altercation between Nino and the young men grew louder.

"What are they yelling about?" Hendricks asked.

Antonio shrugged. "They are complaining that Nino does not hire enough help, and that the people he does hire are all his relatives."

Hendricks smiled. "What's wrong with that? I thought that's how most restaurants worked."

"It is," Tina said. "Mama and the girls are in the kitchen and the boys are the waiters and the cousins are the bus-boys."

"Mama is a hell of a cook," Hendricks said.

Antonio poured from a fresh bottle of Chianti. "Yes, and if Nino had to hire a staff of outsiders, it would ruin his business. He would have to pay them too much, and it would drive his prices a lot higher."

"And the food would be lousy," Weaver added.

"And there would go his customers," Tina said. "Right?"

"Right," Antonio replied.

Hendricks was puzzled. "So who benefits from that?"

"These jackals, or friends of theirs," Antonio said, indicating the young men who continued to argue with Nino. "When the business is ruined, they move in and buy it for a handful of beans."

"Ah," Hendricks said, understanding.

"Communists are really no different from anybody else," Antonio said. "They are people. Only their methods differ, a little."

"They're the reason there's no American merchant marine any more," Hendricks said. "They forced sailors' wages up until nobody could afford to pay U.S. shipping rates. Last three tankers I was on, two were Liberian and the other was registered in Panama."

"*Va via,*" Nino shouted. "*Va via da qui subito!*"

The two young men shuffled toward the door, their faces sullen. When they passed the table at which the Americans were sitting, one of them stopped and pointed, first at Hendricks, then at Weaver. "*Sudici capitalisti americani,*" he snarled. He was broad shouldered and hulking. Below his flat nose he wore a thick drooping moustache. "*Ladri.*"

Weaver looked at him. "Fuck you, buddy."

Before the man could react, Nino shoved his huge belly into him, shouting and gesticulating. There was another exchange of curses, and Nino pushed him out the door after his companion.

"Pigs," Tina said.

The conversation reverted, inevitably, to the subject of movies. Tina and Antonio exchanged gossip about a director who was keeping a ménage à trois with twin sisters who had appeared in one of his films, and Weaver told them about a stunt man he knew who had broken both legs on the Matterhorn earlier that summer while shooting a picture based on mountain climbing. The stunt man was still in the hospital and was having trouble getting the film's producer, a hand-to-mouth operator, to pay his medical bills.

"Guy's a real cheap-shot prick," Weaver said. "He makes Morello look like Santa Claus."

They finished the meal with cognac and espresso, and Hendricks felt marvelous. Antonio paid the bill, and Nino made a great fuss over them as they left.

"Say, you know," Hendricks said, "I have to do something about a hotel. Are rooms hard to get?"

"A little," Antonio replied. "But don't worry about it. We

27

give the Excelsior a lot of business. They'll find something for you."

Outside the air was cool and pleasant. As they turned to walk along the dimly lit sidewalk, Weaver and Tina in front, there was a sudden clatter of footsteps. Hendricks looked up as several dark shapes charged into their group. One of them, Hendricks saw, was the man with the moustache who had harangued them in the restaurant. The man's arm flashed in the light of a streetlamp, and there was a sharp crack as he laid a short club across Weaver's face. The cameraman staggered against the wall of a building and slid down it to a sitting position, blood spouting from a gash on his jaw. An instant later three others were swinging at Hendricks and Antonio.

As always when confronted with sudden violence, Hendricks moved instinctively, with great quickness for his size. Shoving aside the man who had assailed him, he stepped to the first club wielder, who now crouched over Weaver, his arm raised to strike again. Hendricks brought his left hand around in a short, vicious chop, catching the moustached man just below his ear. The man dropped as if he had been shot, and Hendricks snatched the club from him.

Whirling, Hendricks ducked as another of them flailed at him. He jammed the end of the club into his attacker's belly as hard as he could. The man fell to his knees, clutching his gut in agony.

Antonio let out a cry, and Hendricks was suddenly also aware that Tina was screaming. Out of the corner of his eye, he saw that she did not appear to be hurt but was standing with her hands clasping her face as her mouth emitted a piercing shriek. Antonio, on the other hand, was in trouble. He was bent backward over the hood of a parked car and one of the assailants was thrashing him with a length of chain. Hendricks brought the club down with great force across the small of the man's back. This one dropped the chain and tottered onto the sidewalk, howling in pain, and Hendricks put him out with a blow to the throat.

Weaver had pulled himself up and was leaning against the wall now, steadying himself with one hand while with the other he held his split face. The front of his shirt was spattered crimson. The moustached man was on all fours, struggling to get to his feet. Hendricks stepped toward him, but before he got there, Weaver swung his leg in a heavy kick, the point of his shoe driving into the man's mouth and snapping his head

28

back. The attacker collapsed, his lower face a welter of torn tissue, blood, and splintered teeth.

All of this had happened in less than a minute. Hendricks heard shouts and the sound of running feet approaching in the distant darkness. He grabbed Tina and the four of them ran to the corner when they flagged a taxi. Antonio yelled to the driver as they jumped in, and the machine roared away. Hendricks looked back through the rear window. He could see nothing but shadows in the street behind them.

chapter 6

They were in a bar on the Via Lazio. Tina had mopped Weaver's face with a towel soaked in cold water and the bleeding had nearly stopped, but the ragged lips of the cut gaped open.

"We ought to get you to a doctor," Antonio said. "That should be sewn up." His own face bore contusions where the chain had struck him, but the wounds were not serious.

"The hell with it," Weaver said. "If I can get some tape someplace, I'll put a butterfly on it, and that'll hold it together." He looked at Hendricks. "Jesus, that was some job you did on those bastards."

Hendricks grinned. "You got in a pretty good shot yourself. Kicked your pal's moustache right down his throat."

Weaver laughed happily. "Goddamn, that was beautiful. I haven't had so much fun in a month. Shit, in a year."

They were drinking Scotch, a bottle of Haig standing open on the table. Weaver poured a water glass full, no ice, and drank most of it. His face was flushed, and his beard glistened with water drops. The place was small and hot, and he had pulled his blood soaked shirt open.

Hendricks noticed scar tissue on Weaver's sweaty chest. The marks were irregular patches of shiny tissue, lighter in color than the skin surrounding them. "I think maybe you've been in a few ruckuses in your time."

Weaver finished his Scotch with another gulp. "Yeah, some."

29

"Where'd you get the souvenirs?" Hendricks nodded toward the cameraman's chest.

"Vietnam. That's where I learned cinematography."

Hendricks's eyebrows lifted.

"Marine Corps," Weaver explained. "I was a combat photographer."

It fell into place, then. Hendricks suddenly felt that he understood, that he had discovered much of the reason for Weaver's earlier truculence. "I got into Saigon myself once."

"Is that right?"

"Ran in a load of avgas. If I'd known the ship was going in there, I never would have signed on the son of a bitch."

Weaver was delighted. "I'll be damned. Should have known it. Say, you ever get to Pauline's?"

"Madame Pauline, the colonel's wife? That's where I spent all the time we were in port."

"Best joint in the whole damn Nam. You could get anything there, including buboes."

Tina had been trying to follow their exchange, looking slightly mystified. "What are buboes?"

Weaver grinned at her. "Honey, I hope you never find out."

"It is a terrible venereal disease," Antonio said. "Causes a huge swelling in the groin."

Tina made a face. "Ugh. How horrible."

"I have heard," Antonio said to Weaver, "that those sicknesses put more men out of action than the Vietcong."

"Absolute truth," the cameraman replied. "We had hospitals over there filled up with nothing but pussy casualties. Everything from a virulent clap that penicillin couldn't touch to Chinese crotch rot." He turned back to Hendricks. "So you were in Saigon. Wasn't that the asshole of the world?"

"One of them. I could think of a couple of other candidates for the number-one spot."

Weaver poured more whiskey. He was drinking at a much faster rate than the others, who had done little more than sip from their glasses. "So could I, now that you mention it. But that one'd be right up there."

"You say you actually learned cinematography in Vietnam?"

The cameraman shook his head. "The marines sent me to school to learn cameras, lenses, processing, all that. But where I really learned my business was in the field. You'd be amazed at how fast you can set up and then get your action in one take when some gook is trying to blow your ass off."

Hendricks smiled. "I'll bet."

They exchanged reminiscences for a time, most of the talk coming from Weaver. He told them stories about his Vietnam days, and also about a few of the experiences he'd had with various film companies, shooting on location in some of the more remote corners of the earth. All traces of his hostility had disappeared, and he got quite drunk on the Haig, having already established a fine base with the drinking he had done before and during dinner. In a departure from his earlier surliness he became friendly, almost sentimental, toward Hendricks. Antonio tried several times to get him out of the bar for some medical attention, but he brushed off these attempts, scoffing at the ragged gash in his face.

Hendricks was careful not to pay too much overt attention to Tina, but nevertheless he felt a strong rapport growing between them. Several times he glanced over to find her gazing steadily at him, a suggestion of a smile at the corners of her mouth. He knew from experience what that unspoken message meant, and receiving it produced a small tightening sensation in his chest as he contemplated what it could lead to.

When the bottle of Scotch was more than half empty, Weaver leaned across the table and squinted at Hendricks. "Hey, when are we supposed to make that test on you?"

"I don't know."

"Perhaps the day after tomorrow," Antonio said. "The maestro is driving down from Portofino in a few days, and he will want to see the footage. Of course, I cannot promise when he will look at it. He is a very busy man."

"Of course," Hendricks said.

Weaver drank more of his whiskey. "He'll look at it, all right. We'll shoot him the damndest test he ever saw. We'll make Hendricks look like Redford with muscles."

Hendricks laughed. "You'd really have to be a genius to bring that off."

"I am, man, I am." Weaver's speech had become slurred. "You'll see. And I won't just make you look good, either. There's a lot of stuff I can show you about handling yourself in front of a camera."

They talked and drank for almost an hour longer, until it appeared that Weaver might pass out at the table. Antonio finally half dragged him out of the place, getting him to agree that he would at least return to the apartment and get the cut on his face cleaned out and taped up.

31

Outside, as Antonio hailed a cab, Tina announced that she was going home.

"I've got to get a room," Hendricks said. "What did you say the name of that hotel was?"

"The Excelsior," Antonio replied. "It's on the Via Veneto. Tell them I sent you, and that you work for Mr. Morello. If there's any question, have them telephone me. You have my number."

Hendricks turned to Tina. "Can I drop you off?"

"You're closer. I'll drop you."

Weaver had started to sing a tuneless rendition of "The Yellow Rose of Texas." Hendricks helped get him into the taxi and thanked Antonio for dinner and his help.

"Check in with me tomorrow," Antonio said. He climbed in behind Weaver.

The cab pulled away, and a minute later Hendricks stopped another one. They did not go to the Excelsior at all, but instead had the taxi drive them directly to Tina's apartment. She lived on a side street a few blocks south of the Piazza Bologna. The area was run-down and dingy, nothing like the more fashionable neighborhood in which Antonio lived. Although it was late at night, a group of ragged children played in the narrow street.

The building was old and airless and smelled heavily of cooking. Tina's apartment was on the second floor in the rear. It consisted of one small room with a kitchen alcove, a closet, and a bath. The furniture was a table and chairs and a narrow bed which doubled as a couch. A single lamp on the table illuminated the room.

When she had closed and locked the door, Tina turned to Hendricks. "Would you like—"

He pulled her to him, a faint smile on his face. "I sure would."

Her eyes were wide with excitement, and he could feel her tremble slightly as their bodies pressed together. He loved this, the first time with a desirable, highly sexed girl, all of it new, full of discovery. He kissed her slowly, feeling himself grow hard, dipping his tongue into her open mouth. He wanted to savor the experience, to get every bit of enjoyment out of it he could, and he forced himself to go slowly, to be aware of each step of it.

He unbuttoned her blouse first, moving at that careful, unhurried pace, and when he pulled it from her body, he was rewarded by the sight of the fine, round, heavy breasts he

32

had been trying to imagine all evening. He made her stand still for a long moment, holding her by her upper arms, while he admired them. "Beautiful," he said at last. "Really beautiful." He held one in his hand, and bending down, kissed the nipple and licked it.

Her skirt came off next. He slid it down over her hips and tossed it aside. Tina's legs were excellent, sleek and golden in the glow of the lamplight. Continuing to move as slowly as possible, he pulled off her bikini pants and brushed his fingertips against the soft, crinkly black hairs on her mound. He turned her around and followed the curves of her lower back and buttocks with his hands. Then he kissed her neck and cupped her breasts, stroking them with his thumbs, feeling the nipples stiffen.

Tina's excitement had increased, but she stood still, accepting the role he had given her. Only her breathing and slight trembling revealed her desire for him, her response to his caresses.

Hendricks pulled the cover off the bed and sat her down facing him. He took off his own clothes then, standing close to her, the girl watching as he stripped shirt and trousers from his massive body. He was fully erect, and when he removed his shorts, his penis was inches from her face.

"*Mio Dio*," she whispered. "*E enorme.*"

He moved closer to her, and she held the shaft in her fingers, then touched the pulsing head with her tongue. Hendricks forced himself to keep from coming. He knew he wouldn't be able to hold back once he entered her, but he wanted to be inside her when he came the first time. He pushed his hips slowly forward, and she continued to flick her tongue over the tip of his cock. When he was on the edge, sure he couldn't control himself for a second longer, he pulled away and gently pressed her down onto the bed.

He began by sucking her toes, then licking the inside of her calves and her thighs, his mouth crawling slowly up the firm flesh, his fingernails tracing serpentine patterns on the sides of her legs. By the time he reached her mound, Tina was moaning softly, and her pelvis moved in a tiny circle. Hendricks explored the wet lips, his tongue darting, then took her clitoris into his mouth. He held it there, rolling it gently, and an instant later she cried out. She gripped his head with both hands, and the movement of her hips became frenzied as the orgasm swept over her.

As soon as her body relaxed, Hendricks mounted her. He

put his hands under her and held her open as he slid into her hot, streaming vagina. She tensed again, her hands clutching his back, and then he was coming, the exquisite sensation sending out an electric charge that reached to his fingertips and his toes. When he was completely spent, he let his muscles go limp but stayed on top of her and did not withdraw.

For two minutes or so Hendricks did not move, except to pull air into his lungs. Then he felt Tina contract a little, and in turn felt himself respond. His penis stirred and began to swell, and a moment later he was again erect. Now, he knew, he could last for a long time, virtually as long as he wished, provided he did not lose control. He began to move in and out of her in a slow rhythm, at the end of each thrust going as far into her as he could, until he could feel himself bumping against the top of the channel. Tina moaned again and brushed her tongue against his ear.

It was going to be a long night, he thought happily. And it would be exactly as he wanted it. He would be totally in command of this beautiful, sensitive girl, and he would use her in an endless number of ways. She would be his to enjoy, but in taking her, he would also be giving her much pleasure. It was the kind of sexual relationship he liked best, the one that was the most deeply satisfying to him. As he thought about this, a picture of Estelle Lemont came into his mind. He resolved once more never again to allow himself to become the property of a woman, any woman.

Tina arched her body, the small cry again issuing from her throat, and Hendricks smiled down at her.

chapter 7

He awoke to the aroma of coffee brewing. The small room was bright with sunlight, and he lay on his back for a time, staring at the cracked ceiling and breathing the pungent smell of the coffee. He heard a stirring and turned to see Tina sitting at the table, watching him. She was wearing a cotton robe, and her face was as serene as that of a very young girl. He yawned and stretched. "Hello."

34

"Good morning. Did you sleep well?"

He grinned. "Yeah. For a few minutes, when I couldn't think of anything else to do."

"Would you like some coffee?"

He stretched again. "In a little while. First I need to get kissed good morning. I'm very sensitive about that."

Tina smiled and stepped over to the bed. She bent over and kissed him lightly, and before she could straighten up, Hendricks grabbed her and wrestled her down onto the bed. She pretended to resist him, shrieking and giggling, but a moment later he had pulled the robe off and she was in his arms. He held her tight until her struggles subsided, and then his mouth was at her breast, sucking her nipple, and she was growing wet.

Her skin felt marvelous to him. Different from the night before, but warm and inviting against his body. He lifted his head and kissed her, and her legs opened and he was again inside her. They made love unhurriedly, almost languidly, but when he came, his orgasm was strong and intense and he wished it could last forever.

Later she lay with her head on his chest, her fingertips gently stroking his thigh. "That was beautiful."

Hendricks smiled. "Only way to start the day."

"Is it always the way you start yours?"

"If I'm lucky. I make it a point to try."

She pinched him. "I think it is what you try to do most of the time."

"Wrong. It's what I try to do all the time."

"Except when you are on a ship, and you have to settle for a, what do you call them, messboy?"

"Right. But I think I would rate you one or two points higher."

She tried to pinch him again, but he grabbed her wrist and slapped her backside with his open palm. He climbed out of bed and walked into the bathroom. "You got anything I can shave with?"

"Yes. There is a razor in the cabinet."

He showered and shaved, and when he had dressed, sat with her at the table and ate warm bread and drank the strong, thick coffee. The previous night's good food and the lovemaking and the sleep had been deeply restorative to him, and he felt wonderful.

"More coffee?" While he was in the bath, she had put on a blouse and pants. She looked bright and fresh and, he thought, quite beautiful.

"Sure, it's great. But hey, don't you have to go to work or anything?"

She shook her head as she refilled his cup. "I told you, I'm an actress. Right now I am between roles, as we say. I'm hoping for a part in the picture Morello is going to produce, but nothing has been settled yet."

"Uh-huh. Which reminds me, I have to check Antonio on when they're going to make that test."

"Would you like me to call for you?"

"No, I'd better do that. No sense telling the world where I spent the night."

She smiled. "It doesn't matter. I don't belong to anyone."

"I thought—"

"Matthew? No. We are just friends."

That was good to hear. He didn't want to do anything that would upset the relationship he had begun to build with the cameraman. "Okay, if you wouldn't mind. And ask if Weaver's face is okay."

Tina dialed a number and after a brief conversation put the phone down and turned back to him. "They will make the test tomorrow morning, and Matthew is fine."

"Okay, that's good." He drained his cup and held it out to her. "Any left?"

"Yes, there's plenty." She poured from the pot.

"Say, you know something? I've got a hell of a good idea."

"What is it?"

"Seeing as how neither one of us has anything to do today, how about you showing me Rome?"

She was delighted. "That is a lovely idea. I would enjoy it very much. But I must warn you that you will see only a tiny part of it in a day. There is so much of interest, a really thorough tour would take weeks."

"Then we'll see what we can."

"Of course. Do you have any idea what you might want to visit?"

"Yeah, the old part. I'm not much for museums and that stuff, but I would like to see some of the really early buildings and the ruins. I've done some reading about the Roman Empire, and it kind of fascinates me."

"What are we waiting for? Finish your coffee and we'll go."

They traveled by taxi, and the driver was as wild as the one who had driven Hendricks from the railroad station the night before. He drove flat out whenever possible, the Fiat careening through the narrow streets, and whenever the heavy traffic forced him to a halt, he leaned on the horn and cursed.

"Christ," Hendricks said. "Are they all like this?"

"Some are worse. An article in the newspaper last week said that Italy has the highest accident rate of any country in Europe, and Rome has the highest rate in Italy."

"I believe it."

They stopped before an ancient domed temple.

"The Pantheon," Tina said as they got out. "It is the best preserved of any of the old buildings in the city."

Hendricks stared at the massive reddish-gray stone colums supporting the portico. "How old?"

"It was built twenty-seven years before the birth of Christ, by Consul Marcus Agrippa. It was called 'the temple of the gods.' A hundred years later it burned, and then Hadrian reconstructed it in the second century."

"You seem to know its history pretty well."

"It is a national treasure. Every Italian schoolchild learns about it, along with many other points of archeological value in Rome."

"Those columns look as if each of them was made of a single piece of stone."

"They were. Of granite, cut in Egypt. They were brought up the river to this site on barges. They are the largest columns of their kind in the world. The doors, there, are bronze. They weigh twenty tons."

They walked inside the temple and stood gazing up at the aperture in the center of the dome. The interior was quiet and cool and peaceful.

"The opening is thirty feet across," Tina said. "The only light in the building comes through it."

Hendricks looked around in awe. "Amazing, that they could do work like this without machines."

"It is, isn't it? The reason that the proportions are so beautiful is that the diameter of the dome is identical to its height."

He shook his head. "Fantastic."

From there they went to the site of the Circus Maximus. It looked to Hendricks to be little more than a huge, oval-shaped depression in the earth, overgrown with a tangle of grass and weeds.

Tina pointed. "That is the course where the chariot races were held. There were marble tiers for the people to sit on, here, and all across there. It was common for as many as two hundred thousand people at a time to attend."

"That many?"

"Oh, yes. The greatest spectacles in Rome were the races, and of course the games. Both were exciting and extremely violent."

Hendricks studied the course. "Who owned the chariots?"

"The nobles. They had teams of horses and favorite charioteers, just as people own racehorses today. The difference was that these events were much more dangerous. Hardly a race was held in which horses were not killed, or men, or both."

"But it sure brought the people out, didn't it? Two hundred thousand? Some crowd."

"Yes, it did." She looked at him. "You're thinking that audiences have not changed that much, aren't you?"

"I'm thinking that people haven't changed that much. Just imagine, if the law would allow it, what you could do here now. If they got two hundred thousand here in those days, they'd probably pull four hundred thousand today."

Tina smiled. "And don't forget television."

"Yeah, you're right. I didn't even think of that."

They stayed there half an hour, walking around the course, until Hendricks realized that he was hungry again. He asked where they could have lunch.

Tina laughed. "I think your appetite is as big as you are."

"For all things, honey. But right now what I need is food. Lots of it."

They went to one of the cafés in the Piazza Navona. Their table was outside, shaded from the sun by a green-and-white striped awning, and from where they sat, they could see the water sparkling in the fountain and watch the flights of pigeons wheeling above the worn cobblestones.

Hendricks ordered insalata, canneloni, and a bottle of Verdicchio. He grinned at her. "You see? I'm getting to be an expert."

She returned his smile. "I think you are no stranger to Italian food."

He laughed. "You're right. It's always been my favorite. When I was a kid, there was nothing I'd rather eat than spaghetti."

"Where was that, where you grew up?"

"On the Chesapeake Bay, near Baltimore."

"And your father? What did he do?"

"He was a part-time fisherman and a part-time bum. He took off when I was twelve, and I worked on the oyster boats

38

until I was big enough to lie about my age and get an ordinary seaman's ticket."

"And you mother?"

"She died giving birth to me. From the bits and pieces I could put together, she was a waterfront hooker." He was quiet for a few minutes after that. His origins were nothing to be proud of, and he almost never spoke about them, but he liked this girl and enjoyed being with her, and besides, he had nothing to hide and no reason to pretend he was anything other than what he was. "How about you, Tina?"

"My father is a schoolteacher in Florence. He was scandalized by my desire to become an actress, so I ran away from home to come here."

He smiled. "And now you are a true Roman, right?"

"Right. Just as you will be."

Their food arrived, and Hendricks ate enthusiastically, as always. The canneloni was rich and flavorful, and the wine cold and crisp and delicious in the midday heat.

"How has the work been for you?" he asked.

"The way it is for most people in this business. You starve for a long time and then you are busy for a while and then you starve again."

"So you have to want to do it very much."

"Very much."

"What happens if no work comes along between the starvings?"

Tina shrugged. "There are always the porn films."

Hendricks paused, his fork midway to his mouth. "Yeah?"

"Not really." She smiled. "But maybe that's only because I haven't starved enough yet. I know plenty of people who work in them if there is nothing else."

"Then there's a lot of that stuff produced in Rome?"

"Oh, yes. This is one of the biggest production centers for it in the world. And most of the performers are out-of-work talent or just kids who will do it for the money."

"How does it pay?"

"Poorly. Even the so-called stars get no more than a hundred thousand lire for a picture."

Hendricks thought about it. "I guess if you're a kid and hungry, then getting a few bucks for doing what comes naturally wouldn't seem so bad."

"Exactly. But what is sad is that many of them think it is

39

somehow glamorous, and that it may lead to parts in legitimate pictures."

"Which of course doesn't happen."

"Almost never." She drank some of her wine. "Would you like to see one being shot sometime?"

"Yeah, I guess so." He grinned. "You could call it part of my education."

"Of course."

After lunch they visited the Colosseum, and this time Hendricks was truly awed. As they stood outside it, the vast amphitheater looked strangely anachronistic amid the traffic whirling past its crumbling walls. He gazed up at the towering edifice. "Did it look much like this when it was built?"

"Only in the most general sense," Tina said. "Originally it was finished in marble and travertine, and there were statues of emperors and senators in each of those portals."

"So what happened—were they stolen?"

"The statues were, but the marble and other fine materials were stripped away by later city officials who wanted to use them to build structures of their own. They wanted to erect monuments to themselves. But of course none of what they built was so important as this."

When they walked inside, Hendricks was surprised to see that there was no solid floor, but instead a labyrinth of subterranean passages.

"It is where the animals were held," Tina explained. "And the prisoners. The original floors were made of wood. The arena could even be flooded so that they could stage events like naval battles. Men would fight from boats, and sometimes there would be crocodiles in the water."

"But most of the time the games were held on sand, right?"

"Yes. Because the sand absorbed the blood. In Latin, the word for sand is *arena*. It comes from that time."

Hendricks looked up at the tiers of seats above them. "It's so much bigger than I thought it would be."

"It held almost ninety thousand people."

"That's a lot more than Yankee Stadium takes today."

"Yankee Stadium?"

"In New York. Where they battle Tigers and Indians."

"Are you serious?"

"Bad joke." He explained about baseball.

"I think that is a better kind of spectacle."

"Maybe better, but not nearly as exciting. How long did the games last here?"

40

"You mean each time they were staged? Usually for one full day, but later emperors tried to outdo each other and sometimes there would be an entire week of them at a time."

"There must have been a lot of killing."

"It was ghastly. First animals would fight animals. Bears against lions, and so on. Then men would fight animals, but the men were poorly armed, so that the animals would most often devour their victims. Then men would fight men, and in the end would come the real experts, the gladiators, who would battle to the death."

"Damn." Hendricks tried to imagine it through half-closed eyes, hearing the roar of the blood-crazed crowds, seeing the color and the pageantry as the slaughter took place.

"It is strangely moving, isn't it?"

"Yes, it is. And it's just like the Circus Maximus. Stage those games today, and you'd pack the place. People still love violence."

"You sound like Vicente Morello."

He laughed. "Do I? Good. You see? I have an instinct for show biz."

They stayed there a long time and then went back to Tina's apartment. The place was quiet in the late afternoon heat, and they made love, tenderly and without hurry, and went to sleep. When Hendricks opened his eyes, it was after nine o'clock.

The evening was balmy and pleasant. They went to Sabatini's, the charming restaurant in the oldest part of the city, and sat outside under the stars. Dinner was superb, antipasti and cioppino, and Hendricks got mildly drunk on Soave. He felt strangely exuberant over what he had seen and learned and in anticipation of the test he was scheduled to make the following day. Yet when they finally went home to bed, he was surprised to find that he could not sleep. He lay awake for hours, feeling somehow restless and apprehensive.

chapter 8

The Giandelli Studios were in the southeast part of Rome, an old section comprised of rotting tenements and grimy commercial buildings. The studios originally had been built as warehouses, but for the past twenty years had operated as a rental facility for any company that wished to use them. They were usually busy, for a variety of reasons. For one thing, there were perhaps a greater number of shoestring motion picture producers in Rome than in any other city in the world. For another, more and more American companies were shooting in Italy, partly for locations and also partly for tax purposes, and because there were no union problems as in the States. And finally, Giandelli's stages were relatively cheap. They were not air-conditioned, so that in the summertime the arc lights would often drive the temperature to over thirty-eight degrees Celsius. And in the wintertime, because they were badly heated and drafty, it was sometimes colder inside them than in the streets.

Vicente Morello rented office space at Giandelli's. In addition to the obvious attraction of economy, he did this because having his business headquarters there tended to associate him with whatever production activities happened to be underway at the moment.

To a visitor it would seem that if a company were shooting, it belonged to Morello. And giving the world an impression of constant industry, and hence prosperity, was vital to success in the business of producing motion pictures.

Despite his recent debacles, Morello's record of turning out moneymaking films was far above average. In a field in which four out of five such ventures failed, more than half of his pictures returned a profit. Moreover he followed the respected practice of using other people's money whenever possible. The trouble was, it was not always possible. Consequently, although he lived on a high scale, there were times when every lira he owned, as well as every one he could borrow, was on the line. On several such occasions he came close to losing everything, escaping only through the manipulation of Italy's vaguely written bankruptcy laws and the use by his accountant of two sets of books.

When Hendricks and Tina arrived at the studio, Antonio was drinking coffee from a cardboard cup as he watched a team of carpenters construct a flat. The men worked quickly, knocking together a frame of two-by-fours and covering it with plywood. He smiled. "Good morning."

Hendricks felt tense and ill at ease. He shook hands with Antonio and looked around. The interior of the sound stage seemed cavernous.

"Mr. Morello has not yet arrived," Antonio said. "In another day or two, perhaps."

"Uh-huh." Hendricks was wearing a fresh shirt, cotton with small blue-and-white checks, purchased in a shop near Tina's apartment just before coming here.

"You look fine," Antonio said to Hendricks. "Rome agrees with you, eh?"

"It's a beautiful city," Hendricks replied. "Tina showed me some of it yesterday."

"Good. I am glad you are enjoying yourself. You will be working on Stage Four." He pointed. "Through that door." He turned to Tina. "And you? Is anything happening with you? I hear they will be casting on Six. Something for television, to be shot next week."

"So I have heard," Tina replied. "I'm going over there."

"Before you do," Antonio said, "Stay around here for a little while, if you would. We may want you for this test. For our friend to play off."

"Of course." Tina smiled at Hendricks. "I would be glad to help."

"You can go on over to the set," Antonio said to Hendricks. "Weaver will be there, and he will get you started at once."

Hendricks walked across the huge empty floor to the door Antonio had indicated. On the other side was a stage nearly identical to the one he had just left. In one corner a dolly-mounted Mitchell 35 mm camera and two batteries of lights had been set up. Hendricks walked onto the set, continuing to feel awkward and out of place.

"Hey, man."

He turned to see Weaver approaching. "Hello, Matt."

The cameraman wore a piece of flesh-colored tape on his jaw. He held out his hand, and Hendricks shook it. "How you feeling?"

"Okay. I see you got your face put back together."

"Prettier than ever." Weaver waved toward the setup. "Right over there is where we'll be working. First off, we have to get some makeup on you." He cupped a hand to his mouth. "Hey, Rosa!"

A small, dumpy girl in a yellow smock came up to them. She carried a battered leather case. Weaver introduced them, and Hendricks sat in a canvas-backed chair while the girl worked on him. Rosa spoke no English, so Hendricks simply sat with his mouth shut, feeling sillier by the minute as she applied pancake makeup and a touch of lip blush.

Weaver studied the set, which consisted of nothing but a table and a chair. There was a door in the wall, stage right.

He instructed a technician to hit the lights and squinted through the viewfinder on the camera. He told the man to move one of the arcs in closer and to place a reflector near the table. Satisfied, he ordered the lights killed.

Antonio joined them, Tina trailing behind. He glanced briefly at Hendricks, who remained slumped patiently in his chair as Rosa continued to daub at him, and turned to Weaver. "You want me to direct?"

"No, I'll handle it. We don't need anything but the camera and lights."

"Okay. Just give us a few hundred feet of each setup—this one and the exterior."

"Sure."

Antonio raised a hand toward Hendricks in a languid wave. "Call me in a few days. We'll let you know how it turned out."

"Yeah," Hendricks said. "I will."

"*Merde.*" Antonio left the set.

When Rosa had finished with him, Hendricks stepped over to the cameraman. He felt like a clown in the makeup. "Say, Matt?"

Weaver was adjusting the lens on the Mitchell. "Yeah?"

"What did he mean by that—'*merde*'? That's French for 'shit,' isn't it?"

The cameraman looked up and laughed. "It's short for 'step in shit.' That's a traditional wish for good luck you give an actor before he goes on stage. The English say 'break a leg,' and the Germans are more thorough, of course. They say, '*hals und beinbreck*' which is break your neck as well as your leg."

"Uh-huh."

"Okay, come on in here, and I'll show you what I want."

The entire effort took less than an hour. Weaver gave Hendricks an entrance and a bit of business at the table, and after shooting that they went out onto the sidewalk in front of the studio for a piece of action that was even simpler. At the end of the exterior shot Weaver had Tina come into the picture to be embraced and kissed by Hendricks, and that was all.

When they were finished, Weaver seemed satisfied but somewhat preoccupied, explaining that there was something else he was working on and that he had to get to it. He grinned and shook Hendricks's hand. "*Merde.*"

"Yeah." Hendricks returned the smile. "Thanks for everything, Matt."

"Sure. Rosa will help you get the crap off your face. Be seeing you." He hurried off.

Tina left for her casting call, telling him she'd see him at the apartment that evening. When Rosa finished cleaning him up, Hendricks was alone. He walked down the street until he found a bar and went in and ordered a beer.

He felt empty and let down. The whole thing had been so much less than he had expected. A couple of simple moves and gestures, a few minutes in front of the camera, and that was all. He had been given no lines to speak, and even though he would have had to deliver them in English, he had thought that Morello would at least went to know how he would do if he had to talk.

Weaver, too, had seemed offhand and casual. A reading with his meter, a word or two of instruction, and then he had rolled film, and that was it.

But worst of all was his own conviction that he had performed like a robot. Stiff, clumsy, stupid, were the words that came into his mind as he tried to evaluate what he had done. The longer he thought about it, the more foolish he felt. All he had accomplished was to make a jackass of himself and to prove that his original reaction, back in Portofino, was the right one. He was no more an actor than he was a ballet dancer.

They all must have seen it, he decided. That was why Weaver had merely tossed it off, making no real effort, and why Antonio hadn't even bothered to stick around. He finished his beer and ordered a grappa. What the hell, he thought. He still had most of the money Morello had given him.

chapter 9

Vicente Morello drove the red Ferrari, Cecily beside him, to the door of the sound stage and stopped. He tapped his horn, which emitted a series of staccato blasts. A moment later the huge door rolled open, and he pulled the car into the interior of the stage. Two stagehands heaved the door shut again.

There was a parking lot behind the studios, but the Ferrari had cost Morello just over forty million lire, and he was not inclined to leave it there. Moreover he was the maestro, and parking his car on a sound stage was just one more expression of his status, a reminder to everyone of his importance.

He locked the doors of the Ferrari and headed for his office, carrying a slim Gucci attaché case of black crocodile, his favorite leather. He had driven down from Portofino the previous day, and he felt rested and relaxed from his holiday. His bald head was deeply tanned from the Riviera sun. He was charged with energy, as usual, and looked forward with enthusiasm to resuming work on the new picture. Cecily had to hurry to keep up with him.

In contrast to the shabbiness of the stages, Morello's private office was almost grand. It featured a huge desk, a conference table, sofas and chairs, and a bar. Framed photographs of many film stars, European and American, decorated the walls. Morello pointed Cecily to a chair and leafed through the pile of correspondence on his desk. His secretary, a plain woman in her early forties, brought a tray with a coffee service and china and poured coffee for them.

Morello sipped from his cup absently as he looked at his mail. "Send Antonio in, Maria."

"Si, Maestro." His secretary bowed and left the office.

Antonio seemed genuinely glad to see him and smiled as he entered the room. The assistant carried a bundle of manuscripts. "Good to have you back, Maestro. Good morning, Cecily. I hope you both had a pleasant holiday."

"Yes, yes," Morello said impatiently. "Are the others here?"

"Ready and waiting."

"Good. Those are the scripts for *The Hired Gun*?"

"Six sets." Antonio placed the manuscripts on Morello's desk.

"I will want them to read through it," Morello said, "but it's mostly for Caserta's benefit."

"I think we will have no trouble with him," Antonio said. "From what I can gather, he is in a tight squeeze for money."

Morello looked up. "Why is that? His last picture did very well, and God knows he will be getting enough for this one."

"It is a thing with his wife. She is pregnant, and she caught him with his mistress. There was a terrible uproar. Later the two women had a long talk together and decided that Caserta was to blame for everything. Now it seems that the mistress is pregnant as well."

46

Morello grunted. "So it is not only for money that he needs this picture."

Antonio did not understand. "There is something else?"

"This is a good time for him to be going on location outside of Italy."

The assistant laughed. "I see what you mean. Shall I bring them in?"

"In a moment. After the conference I wish to see Castarelli." He was Morello's chief accountant.

"Yes, Maestro, he is eager to have a discussion with you, also."

"Very well, Now bring in Livorno and Caserta."

When Antonio returned with the two men, there was an exchange of warm greetings and compliments among them and Cecily and Morello. Arturo Livorno was one of the new wave of Italian motion picture directors, young and intense. His thick black hair rose from his head in all directions, and he wore heavy horn-rimmed glasses. The other man, Carlos Caserta, was to be the male star of the picture. He was tall and very dark.

Morello instructed Antonio to pass out copies of the manuscript and told the group to read through them. While they did this, he busied himself with his mail and the telephone.

After about fifteen minutes Cecily tossed the mimeographed sheets aside. "This is shit. I cannot do it."

The others looked up in surprise. "What's wrong with it?" Morello asked.

Cecily waved her hand. "There is nothing to it. Scene after scene of shooting and killing, and a few in between with me in bed. You call that a story?"

"It has action, and it has sex," Antonio said. "What more do you want?"

"It has more than that," Livorno said. "It has the passions that people feel when they are oppressed. I think that the audience will identify with the villagers in hating the tyranny that the outlaws impose on them. They will see the killer as a kind of avenger. There are powerful social themes here."

Cecily wrinkled her nose. "You may call them social themes. I see only a madman who runs around shooting people."

The fact that Cecily was Morello's current mistress did not faze Antonio in the least. "What you would rather see," he said, "is more of you."

She turned a hand palm up. "There has to be character. How can it work if I am shown only screwing? That is not what makes drama."

"But it is what makes box office," Antonio replied.

"Nonsense," Cecily said. "If that were true, the greatest hits would all be pornography. There needs to be a development, a portrayal of what kind of person I am playing, so that the audience cares about me. Then when there are love scenes, they will have much more impact."

Caserta shifted in his chair. "There is something to what you say, but such things should not slow the story down. What makes this kind of picture is the action."

"Carlos is right," the director said. "Action is what this picture is all about. The villagers want to fight back against the outlaws, and so they do so in the person of the hired gunman. The pace must be very fast, and the scenes of the gunfighting are vital."

"Exactly," Caserta said. He was a big man whose film career had developed at the end of his span as a professional soccer player some five years earlier. His acting ability was severely limited, but he had been well known on the ball fields, having spent most of his playing years with the Naples team which had been one of Italy's more successful, and twice he had been named to all-star squads. He was getting a little heavy now, but women found him attractive, and his background as an athlete added interest and authenticity to his roles, usually as a gangster or a detective. Playing these parts provided an excuse for him to portray the tough character people expected of him.

Cecily looked at the actor, her mouth curling in an expression of contempt. "What do you know about this, Carlos? When have you ever appeared in this kind of a picture? This is a western. I think you will have enough to worry about, trying to keep from falling off your horse."

Caserta drew himself up. "Don't be concerned about me. The main reason people will pay to see this shit picture is because I am in it."

"That is not true," Livorno said. "As I pointed out earlier, there are social themes at work here. The emotions of the audience will be very basic. Anger. A desire for revenge."

Morello sat quietly, listening to the discussion. Each of the people in his office was behaving in character. Cecily was fighting to expand her part. Caserta wished to preserve his and to have everyone recognize him as the whole basis for the film's potential success. Livorno was torn between his loyalties to art and socialism, and he wanted to express a political message, as he did in any picture he worked on. Antonio was a realist who wanted to get the job done and to have the picture make as much money as possible.

As far as Morello was concerned, none of their opinions was of much interest to him. He was convinced that his concept would be eminently successful, and the kinds of squabbles he was listening to now were only to be expected. The producer raised his hand, and Antonio hurried over to him. As the others continued to argue, Morello asked his assistant the status of the screen test they had made of Hendricks the previous day. Antonio told him that the footage had come back from the lab earlier that morning.

"Set it up in the screening room," Morello said. "I want to look at it right away."

Antonio hurried out of the office, and Morello resumed listening to the discussion of the script. Caserta was now suggesting ways to add to the gunfighting scenes, and Cecily was sitting bolt upright, her green eyes flashing. Morello reflected that she was especially enticing when she was angry. He rose to his feet. "You will excuse me, but I have something I must discuss with Cecily. Another matter. We'll be back in a few minutes."

Cecily opened her mouth to protest, fearful of what the director and Caserta might agree to behind her back, but Morello took her arm and guided her out of his office.

The screening room was small and stuffy. It contained only a dozen seats. Morello and the actress sat in the rear, and Antonio signaled the projectionist to roll the film.

The footage consisted of a total of five minutes of two scenes, an interior followed by an exterior. In the opening part Hendricks walked into a room and approached a table on which a letter lay. He tore open the letter, quickly read its contents, and contorted his face in an expression of anger. Then he strode from the room. The exterior was a setup in the street outside the entrance to the studio. Hendricks appeared in the distance, came up past the camera, stopped, and returned. He stood still, looking intently at a point outside camera range. There was a zoom in to a close-up, and the camera held on his face for over a minute as he continued to stare intently at some faraway object.

Morello watched Cecily as much as he did the image on the screen. She sat totally still, not moving except to breathe, until Hendricks's face filled the frame in the close-up. Then very quietly she said, "Jesus."

The producer looked at the shot. The angle was from about

the level of Hendricks's chest, looking up at him. Hendricks's jaw was set, and his eyes above the high cheekbones were very blue. There was a slight breeze, and it ruffled the blond, sun-streaked hair. The mouth was strong and masculine, with a sensuous fullness of the lips. Hendricks held the expression for several moments, and then slowly his face broke into a broad smile, revealing large, extraordinarily white teeth. The camera pulled back, and a girl walked into the shot. Hendricks took her into his arms and kissed her passionately. The footage ended.

Morello turned back to Cecily. "Well?"

She continued to stare at the now empty screen as the lights in the room came up. "Another few seconds and I would come."

The producer threw his head back and laughed. "I think you liked what you saw, hm?"

Cecily turned to him. "I think it is stunning, what this man has. He is stiff and awkward, and he looks almost clumsy, the way he moves. But it does not matter at all. He has that quality of seeming even more exciting in a picture than he does in person."

Morello knew exactly what she meant. All great screen personalities, from the beginning of motion pictures as a medium, had that extra dimension that film somehow gave them. Partly, he knew, it was simply a matter of size, as the image of the actor or actress became magnified many times, especially in the close-ups. But it was also a matter of the camera seeming to find the essence of the subject's human force and illuminating it. To speak of cinematic portrayal as being larger than life meant much more than mere physical expansion on the screen. And oddly, it sometimes worked in reverse. Morello had seen highly competent stage actors come off like wooden dummies in motion pictures. When this happened, the subject seemed to shrink in size and to lose, rather than gain, the power of personality.

But as far as Hendricks was concerned, Morello had no doubt whatever. The man's impact was phenomenal.

"Dialogue," Cecily said. "It could be a problem, couldn't it? How do you know he can speak lines?"

Morello shrugged. "I don't. But what difference does it make? He knows no Italian, so I have to dub him anyway." He turned to Antonio. "Weaver shot this?"

"Yes."

"Get him in here."

The assistant returned a few minutes later with the cameraman in tow.

"Good morning, Matthew," Morello said. "You have seen the footage you made of this Hendricks?"

Weaver nodded.

"What do you think of it—of him?"

The cameraman scratched his beard. "I think he's maybe the best natural talent I ever saw. I gave him some moves to make, but there was very little I had to tell him. He just carried it out like he'd been doing it all his life. He's a little clumsy, maybe, but to me that just makes him seem believable."

The producer was silent for a moment.

"He seems to have no bad angle," Cecily said.

"You're right," Weaver replied. "The guy is amazingly photogenic. In the exterior, where I set up under him a little, shooting upward, he really was terrific. Made him look kind of heroic, you know?"

Morello looked at Antonio. "And you? What is your opinion?"

The assistant spread his hands. "I think he is a fantastic discovery. And for the western, perfect."

"In what role?"

Antonio thought about it. "Perhaps the sheriff. But I wish—"

"Yes?"

"No, it is impossible."

Morello smiled. "You were thinking of the role of the killer himself, eh? That would be taking too big a chance, and besides, Caserta is already signed for the part."

"A pity," Antonio said.

"Show this to Livorno," Morello instructed. "I'm sure he will agree. Then set Hendricks."

"At once, Maestro." He and Weaver started out the door.

"And Antonio?"

"Yes?"

"The girl. The one he kisses in the test."

"Tina Rinaldi. She is up for the part of the dance-hall girl."

"Set her too. She would be an excellent choice for it."

When the others had left the screening room, Morello looked at Cecily. "You are pleased, eh?"

"I think that he will be a great asset in what is otherwise shaping up to be a dreadful picture."

He laughed. "You have nothing to worry about."

"I don't?"

"Of course not. What you are arguing for makes good sense. I will be sure that your character has greater development."

She kissed his cheek. "I knew you would see it my way."

"Go back to my office," he said. "I will join you there in a moment."

When he was alone, Morello sat back in his chair and thought about the footage of Hendricks and of the others' reactions to it. As always, he was extremely pleased to see his judgment confirmed, but his instincts told him that this discovery of his had much greater implications than even he had thought. Potentially the young blond American was a highly valuable property. And that was of particular importance just now. He needed a success, and he needed one badly. His last two pictures had not merely failed, but had been fiascos of the worst order. He had no doubt as to why his accountant was so anxious to speak with him.

But seen in their proper perspective, his financial problems were mere trivia. He was convinced that he was on the verge of his greatest achievement. *The Hired Gun*. Even the title was thrilling to him.

chapter 10

Vito Castarelli had a bad case of ulcers. It was a malady he had suffered from for fifteen years and for which there appeared to be no acceptable solution. His doctor at one time had urged him to submit to a vagotomy, an operation in which the vagus nerve would be severed, thereby removing the direct link between Castarelli's emotions and his tortured duodenum, but this to him was not an acceptable solution. He would rather stay off alcohol and eat bland foods and bear pain than have his gut sliced open. As far as he was concerned, ulcers were simply an occupational disease, a hazard for any accountant, but especially for one in the motion picture industry.

This afternoon Castarelli's stomach was giving him particular hell. His whining, caviling wife had been urging him to move to a larger apartment in order that her mother could come to live with them, and his girl friend was threatening to leave him for a younger, more affluent man. Moreover his oldest son was in trouble in school again, and he was fairly sure that one of his daughters was having an affair with a married neighbor.

But these difficulties were nothing compared to the information he had for Vicente Morello. He had been trying to present the facts of the producer's fiscal situation to him for weeks on end, but Morello had continued to put him off. Finally, in desperation, Castarelli had telephoned his employer at Morello's villa in Portofino to tell him that the banks had suspended his line of credit.

Now, as he sat in his small, cluttered office waiting to be summoned, he could feel his belly cramp as if it were gripped in the jaws of a slowly tightening vise. A small, round man with a slim, carefully trimmed moustache, Castarelli prided himself on his professional standards. As well as his highly trained and experienced skills as an accountant, he brought to his job a remarkably developed ability to misrepresent the facts of the company's finances, whether to tax officials or to lending institutions. The trouble was, he could not fool himself. At the present time Vicento Morello Produzioni was in dire financial straits, and for the first time in his long association with the producer Castarelli could see no way out. He poured milk from a cardboard container into a glass and sipped it tentatively.

The phone rang, and Castarelli jumped. He lifted the instrument, and Maria told him that Morello would see him. The accountant belched, swallowed a little more milk, and gathered up the stack of ledgers before him.

Morello was on the phone, as usual. When the accountant knocked and was told to enter, Castarelli walked in and closed the door behind him. He stood diffidently before the producer's vast desk, his arms loaded with the books. After a minute or two Morello waved him to a chair. Castarelli sank into it and looked at his employer. From the end of the conversation the accountant could hear, Morello seemed to be arguing with a writer over a script. As in most such altercations Castarelli had no doubt as to what the outcome would be. Whatever Vicente Morello wanted, he almost inevitably got. Castarelli carefully placed the pile of ledgers on the desk as he continued to study Morello.

53

The man looked even more vital and healthy than usual. The sun had browned him, and the return to his business had obviously stimulated him. Morello appeared to be thoroughly enjoying the acrimonious exchange. For a moment it was reassuring to the accountant to see him in such good form. But then he thought about the financial problems he was there to discuss, and once again he felt the vise tighten around his belly.

Morello snarled a final expletive into the telephone and slammed it down. He looked across the desk and his face relaxed. "Vito. Good afternoon."

"Maestro, it is good that you are back. I hope your holiday was a pleasant one."

Morello inclined his head. "It was delightful, thank you. I judge from your telephone call to me at Portofino that we are experiencing a few difficulties."

Castarelli placed his hands palm down on the stack of books. For once he would not allow Morello to talk him out of the seriousness of a financial predicament. "Mr. Morello, I do not wish to alarm you, and you know that I would never overstate to you a problem when one arises."

"Of course."

"But the situation I must describe to you today is most grave." It was exasperating to Castarelli to see that a small smile played at the corner of Morello's mouth. "As I told you when I called, the banks have suspended our line of credit."

"It is not the first time, Vito. Nor probably will it be the last. Fortunately, however, the banks of the world are not confined to Rome."

The accountant shifted in his chair. "I do not refer, Maestro, only to the banks here. We are suspended also in Zurich, in London, and in New York."

Merello frowned. "What about Signor Fatasca?"

Castarelli raised his hands. "He says there is absolutely nothing he can do. Once the banks in Rome advise the others of the suspension, it is out of his jurisdiction."

"Then why have we paid the bastard a fortune over these years? A vice-president of the Banco de Roma, and he cannot be trusted?"

Castarelli shook his head.

Morello sighed. "Very well. I hate to do it, but we must deal again with the factors, those usurious shits."

"I have been to them, Maestro."

"And?"

54

"And they point out that we are in arrears on two loans we made in connection with *Death Watch*."

At the mention of the title of his most recent failure, Morello winced.

"Not only are we behind in payment of the principal, but even the interest has mounted. I do not have to remind you, Maestro, that they are very bad people with whom to fall into such a relationship."

For the first time, Morello's expression indicated that he was taking their discussion with the seriousness it deserved. "There must be an answer, Vito. I am in the process of launching what I am confident will be the most successful project of my career. It will make great amounts of money, more than any picture I have ever produced, I am sure of it. But you are as aware as I that to make money, one needs money. What I need to make this picture is two hundred million lire."

Castarelli sat quietly for a moment, as a small gaseous bubble rose from his stomach through his esophagus and burst sourly in the back of his throat.

"What I want you to tell me," Morello went on, "is how I am going to get it. Do you understand me? I do not wish to hear about where I have no credit. I wish to know where I can get the money I need to make this picture."

Castarelli opened one of the ledgers. "Maestro—"

Morello slammed the book closed. "Damn the books! I do not care to look at squiggles. I need a solution. I need money."

From a dull ache, the pain in the accountant's stomach turned into the burning of a white-hot needle. Forcing himself to remain calm, he folded his hands on his lap. "Mr. Morello, what I am trying to tell you is that at the present time, this very afternoon, we are in debt just over one hundred and three million two hundred fifty thousand lire. I have exhausted every source known to me in an attempt to borrow more funds—not to invest in the new project, but in order to stay in business. Our cash flow is a trickle. What little there is comes from second-run rentals on our old films running in other countries. The essence of the problem is that because of the rates we are obliged to pay on our past loans, the interest alone is growing faster than we can meet it."

"What about my properties?"

"There is already a mortgage on the house here and on the villa in Portofino. And on the apartment in Paris there is not only one mortgage, but two."

Morello rubbed the top of his head. "And my personal accounts? From what you are saying, I imagine there are some troubles there, too, eh?"

"I have stacks of bills, Maestro, that are long past due. Restaurants, liquor, food, your tailors here and in London, even the servants have not been paid in two months."

"What about the, ah—"

"The lady in Milano? I have managed to scrape together the money to pay her off. It seemed to me that it could become too great an exposure, not worth the risk."

Morello cleared his throat. "Yes, yes, you did exactly right."

"There are also the gambling debts, in Monaco, that cannot wait."

The producer suddenly seemed to have stopped listening. He sat back in his chair and was silent for several minutes. When he spoke again, his voice was flat, dispirited. "The personal investors, the people who have put money into my pictures in the past—have you spoken with them?"

Castarelli hunched his shoulders. "They are much easier to handle than the banks or the factors, Maestro. As far as they are concerned, they made highly speculative investments which failed. I have convinced them that nothing more could have been done."

Morello leaned forward. "In Christ's name, man, don't you understand me? I am not talking about past debts—I am talking about my need for *new* money. The solution is not to plug holes in a dike. It is to make a great success which will not only wipe out old problems but will make enormous profits."

Castarelli's hands trembled. "I do understand you, Mr. Morello. Believe me, I do. What I am trying to tell you is that I know of no way to raise such money."

"Four hundred million," Morello said.

The accountant stared at his employer. Sometimes, for all his genius, Morello acted slightly mad.

"If I had four hundred million, it would wipe the slate clean and give me enough to make *The Hired Gun* with something left for a cushion."

"In Sicily there is a proverb," Castarelli said. "If the cow ate cement, it would shit bricks."

But Morello was not listening. "What?"

"Nothing. I made a joke."

The producer's eyes narrowed. "There is one way."

"Pardon?"

"I said, there is one way to raise such a sum of money. It is hazardous, but there is a way."

Despite the late summer heat Castarelli felt a chill. From the look on Morello's face the accountant knew exactly what he meant. "With all respect, Maestro, I would say that way is no way at all."

Morello returned his gaze, his eyes bright in his strong, sunbrowned face. "I must have that money."

"Yes, Maestro." In God's name, Castarelli thought to himself, why did he have to work in this insane picture business? Why could he not work for the government, like his detestable brother-in-law?

The producer glanced at his watch, then reached for the telephone. "I will speak with you later," he said to the accountant."

"Yes, Maestro."

Back in his office Castarelli dumped the ledgers onto his desk. He raised the carton of milk to his lips and drank in long, thirsty gulps.

chapter 11

Club Rex was on the Via Sicilia, a block east of the Via Veneto. At three o'clock in the morning the club was at the height of its activity, and it would have been nearly impossible to squeeze one more body into its interior. The air was blue with marijuana smoke, and the sound from the giant speakers mounted high on the mirrored walls was an avalanche that poured down onto the guests who writhed on the dance floor or sat crushed together at the narrow tables.

Hendricks was dancing with a tall blond named Angela. She kept the lower part of her body in close contact with his while she bent over backward and dangled her arms, her head thrown back, her mouth open. If he had not already made love to Tina twice that evening and had not drunk a half liter of Scotch, the effect on him might have been more erotic. As it was, he merely moved against her and shook his hips and his shoulders in sync with the pounding beat of the music.

Angela gripped Hendricks's belt in her hands and increased the pressure of her pelvis while she slowly pulled herself upright. When she was tight against him, she put her arms around his neck and nuzzled against his throat. "I want you," she breathed.

"Terrific," Hendricks said.

"Take me somewhere."

"Sure. Maybe a little later."

She pressed herself closer, moving her breasts on his chest. "You will have to be very careful when we go out of here. My fiancé is crazy jealous."

"I'll watch it," Hendricks said. He had no intention of taking her anywhere, but the invitation, from a beautiful girl whom he had never seen until a short time ago, delighted him.

Angela looked up at him. "I love actors. Are you very famous?"

Hendricks laughed. "Not yet. But I will be."

"I know you will." She ground her hips into him and kissed the underside of his jaw with open, wet lips.

The record ended, and a new one came on, its tempo slower. Hendricks guided the girl over to where their group was sitting.

Matt Weaver looked up as they returned to the table. The cameraman was smoking an oversized reefer he had made by joining together two sheets of cigarette paper. "Hey, man. That was better than Travolta. In your next picture you ought to be a dancer."

"In my next picture," Hendricks said, "I'm going to be a cowboy." He looked over at Tina who smiled happily at him. She was sitting next to a thin, dark-haired young man, a set designer whose name Hendricks could not remember. The young man pawed at Tina and whispered to her, but she paid no attention to him.

"Have a hit," Weaver said, extending the joint.

Hendricks pulled smoke deep into his lungs and exhaled slowly. There was a pleasant buzzing in his ears. "I still can't believe it."

"The hell you can't," Weaver said. "Handled yourself like a pro, like you'd been in front of a camera for years. When Morello saw the stuff, he jumped up and started screaming, 'The greatest discovery since Rudolph Valentino. I am a genius.'"

Hendricks grinned. "I'll bet he did." He took another drag and passed the cigarette to Angela.

"Okay," Weaver said. "So you got the second male lead in your first picture. Not bad, huh?" His arm hung loosely around the neck of the girl beside him, a vapid-looking creature who seemed to Hendricks to be stoned on something other than grass or booze.

"It'll do," Hendricks said. "Antonio says we're going on location, but he wouldn't tell me where. What's all the mystery about?"

"No mystery," Weaver said. "That just means they haven't got one yet. You want a real mystery, try to figure out how they're going to finance this thing."

"What do you mean?"

"I mean El Cheapo has got his nuts in a grinder. The word is around that he's in hock up to here and having a hell of a time raising money."

This idea was hard for Hendricks to grasp, partly because he could not imagine a man of Morello's stature having financial difficulties of any kind, but also because he was experiencing a euphoria brought on by Scotch, pot, sex, and the staggeringly good news that his test had been so successful that he would have a part in the producer's upcoming picture.

"What kind of a deal did he make with you?" Weaver asked.

"Two hundred thousand lire a week when production starts."

"That's birdshit."

"What the hell do I care? It's a start."

"Did he give you a contract?"

"Yeah, I guess so. It was an agreement of some kind."

"You mean you signed it, and you don't know what was in it?"

"How could I? I can't read Italian."

Weaver shook his head. "Jesus Christ."

Angela slid her hands between Hendricks's legs.

"You better watch it," he said to her. "You get me too riled up and I'll put it to you right here."

"Good," she said, squeezing him. "I would love it."

"What about your fiancé?"

"He is busy." Angela indicated with a nod of her head, and Hendricks turned to see that the man she had come in with was pressing his face between the breasts of a girl with long dark hair and a lascivious, red-lipped mouth. He had opened her blouse and was slowly moving his head from side to side. The girl's eyes were half closed, and she moaned loudly enough to be heard over the reverberations of the music.

59

"This fucking place is too tame," Weaver said. "I know where there's a party. Let's get the hell out of here."

Continuing to feel extravagant over his good fortune, Hendricks paid the check. They rounded up the group, and when they emerged from the club, a man sitting on the fender of a car at curbside jumped to the sidewalk and bounded over to them.

The man carried a flash-equipped Nikon on a strap around his neck. "Hey, Weaver," he said, pointing at Hendricks. "Who's that?"

"You mean it?" the cameraman said. "You don't know?"

The man brought the Nikon to his eye and shot two quick exposures, just in case. "Who is it?"

"That's Hendricks," Weaver said. "You know, the American star?"

The paparazzo looked at the huge blond American. "Sure. Hendricks, eh?" He resumed popping.

They got into two taxicabs. Weaver and the stoned-out girl rode in the first one along with several others of the group, Hendricks and Angela among them.

"Hey, that was too much," Weaver said, laughing. "Wait till that jerk tries to peddle his pictures."

Hendricks grinned. Angela was sitting beside him, kissing his ear. "All he has to do is hang onto them for a while and they'll be worth a fortune."

"You're right, man." Weaver laughed again.

"How does he know you?"

"He knows I'm in the picture business. Paparazzi hang around anybody who has anything to do with movies. They figure I'm like the pilot fish, that I can lead them to the sharks."

"That's me," Hendricks said. "A shark."

Angela had unzipped his fly and reached into his trousers. "You're not a shark. You're a horse."

"You tell 'em, honey."

Weaver directed the taxi driver to an address on the west bank of the Fiume Tevere. They crossed the river and drove past the Palazzo Corsini to a townhouse from whose front door could be seen the lights of the Vatican City.

Their hostess was a woman of about fifty, introduced by Weaver as Contessa Coniglio. She was pale and cadaverously thin, with lank bleached-blond hair and oddly vacant eyes. "The contessa is the most famous groupie in Rome," Weaver said. "If you're a musician or an artist or in pictures, she loves you."

The blond woman kissed Weaver, a sad smile on her gaunt face.

"She's also very handy to know if it's late on a rainy night and you're lonesome or you want to blow some grass or you need to find a broad," Weaver said.

"Welcome to my home," the woman said to Hendricks, holding out her hand. Her tone was grave, her English heavily accented. She looked up at him. "I wish I were twenty years younger."

Hendricks had never seen this kind of opulence in a private house. The walls were hung with old oil paintings in gilt frames, and although he did not know that they were works by Titian, Fra Angelico, Bellini, and Giotto, he did realize that they were of the quality usually seen only in museums. The furniture also was impressive, even to his unschooled eye. It was a mixture of Italian and French antiques, the latter mostly Louis XIV. The rooms were illuminated only by candlelight, which cast a soft, ivory glow over the silks and damasks and the subtle patina of the ancient wood.

In marked contrast to the formality of the furnishings were the contessa's guests. They were all young and all either stoned or drunk or both. Equally incongruous was the acid rock that shook the place, surging from hidden speakers.

Hendricks wandered through the rooms, Angela staying close to him. In one of them a pair of delicate young men sat on ornate chairs playing backgammon while on the floor nearby a heavily muscled black man made love to a girl with flowing red hair. The girl moaned and writhed, her nails digging into the black man's shoulders, her legs pointed straight up in the air. Neither couple paid the slightest attention to the other.

In another room a naked young woman stood atop a table in a ballet position while a man painted her body in vivid colors. The artist had spread a drop cloth over the table, and he worked from a palette with great skill, using long-handled sable brushes. On his subject's skin he had created stripes and swirls and sunbursts in brilliant hues of red and orange and violet and green. A dozen people stood watching, smoking and drinking wine and offering comments and suggestions.

The painter cocked his head as he studied the girl's mound.

"Make it purple," somebody called out.

"Why purple?"

"Because I always wanted to see a girl with a purple cunt."

A laugh went up, and the artist dipped his brush into the palette and extended its point toward the girl with great care.

"Gregorio, you idiot," the girl said, squirming. "That tickles."

Angela seized Hendricks's arm. "Come on. I am sure there are other rooms in this house we will find more interesting."

Hendricks did not know where Tina was, nor Angela's fiancé. What was more important, he did not care. His enormous reserves of strength had restored him to the point that he felt almost no effects now from his earlier carousing.

He and Angela went upstairs. The first two bedrooms they entered were occupied. In one of them four people shared the same bed. Hendricks would just as soon have joined them, but Angela pulled him away.

The next room they tried was empty. In its center was an oversized four-poster from whose gracefully arched bow draped a canopy of lace.

Hendricks pushed the door shut behind them, and Angela was in his arms, her mouth open and hot against his, her hands stroking him. He reached for the buttons on her blouse, but she stopped him.

"No, let me," Angela said. Her cheeks were bright, and her fingers trembled with excitement as she opened his shirt. She removed his clothing slowly, deliberately, pausing to stare at the slablike deltoids, the smoothly bulging biceps.

The effect on Hendricks was highly stimulating. He could not remember having been undressed by a girl before, except for the times he had visited brothels in Yokohama and Singapore, and he found it extremely enjoyable, especially because the sight of his body was driving Angela to near frenzy.

When he stood completely naked, she walked around him slowly, her breath coming in short gasps, her eyes almost feverish as they moved over him. She reached out, her fingertips lightly brushing the short, finely curled blond hairs on his chest and belly and thighs, resting momentarily on the engorged head of his penis. She pushed him down onto the bed and quickly stripped off her own clothing.

The one aftereffect of the lovemaking Hendricks had experienced some hours before was to give him more control than he normally would have had in such a situation, and he was grateful for that. He lay sprawled out flat on his back, the nerves throughout his body responding to Angela's fluttering, teasing contacts with his skin. She licked his throat with her tongue, she bit his nipples lightly, she drew the ends of her long blond hair across his pulsing cock.

When Hendricks reached the point that he could stand no

more and was ready to pull her down onto the bed, Angela straddled him, and slowly, a centimeter at a time, eased her body down onto the thick shaft. When it was all the way inside her, she threw her head back and let out a low animal cry. Then she bent forward and began to ride him.

Their lovemaking lasted a long time. Hendricks lay as still as he could, letting her do everything, his mind filled only with an intense awareness of the joining of their bodies. When he came, it was thunderous, and the strength ran out of him as from an open drain.

At some point he dozed. He did not know for how long, or even whether he had in fact been asleep. When he opened his eyes, Angela lay curled beside him, her breathing slow and steady now in a gentle snore. Through the window he could see that the sky had gone from black to a leaden gray.

As quietly as he could, Hendricks got out of the bed, taking care not to disturb the sleeping girl. He pulled on his clothes and left the room. Downstairs the activity had abated somewhat, but people were still drinking and smoking and talking in various of the sumptuously furnished rooms. He walked out of the house and crossed the near empty street to the side of the river. He sat on a concrete abutment and stared at the slowly moving pewter-colored water. Upstream a barge passed under a bridge and slowly made its way down toward where he sat, on its way to the sea.

It had been, he reflected, a pretty good celebration.

chapter 12

The building was clad in white marble. It rose serenely from the tumultuous traffic of the Via del Babuino, its seven stories making it unusually tall for Rome. From the topmost floor one could see the Arco di Constantino and the Foro Romano, but the view to the northeast was the most charming, giving onto the Villa Borghese on the other side of the old Roman wall.

When Vicente Morello walked into the building, he felt as if he were entering a temple of power. There was a palpable aura of influence and money. The walls of the lobby were

Carrara, in muted shades of peach and beige, and the floor was laid in complementary darker tones of terrazzo. The heels of his handmade Buccellatis clicked sharply as he crossed the lobby, the sound an odd contrast against the steady roar of the street outside the heavy copper doors. He stepped into an elevator and punched a button. The car hurtled him silently to the seventh floor.

The reception area bore no sign of identification. It was constructed largely of chrome and smoked glass, one wall consisting entirely of windows which ran from floor to ceiling. The expanse of floor was covered in deep, thick chocolate-hued carpeting, and in the center of the area was a desk of polished white limestone. A girl sat at the desk. Her long black hair framed a face that reminded Morello of a portrait by Raphael that hung in the Musei Vaticani. He gave her his name and was asked to wait.

A moment later an equally impressive young woman, this one a blond, emerged from a door in a wall beyond the desk. She smiled pleasantly. "Mr. Morello?"

"Yes."

"If you will follow me, please, Mr. Braciola will see you now."

He walked behind her down a long, quiet corridor, admiring the swing of the girl's hips, the curve of her buttocks beneath the silk dress she wore. At the end of the corridor the girl paused before a door of bleached oak and knocked softly. She opened the door and gestured. Morello took a deep breath and walked past her through the door.

Mario Braciola got to his feet and greeted Morello warmly. He was taller than the producer, his dark face strong and square with a hooked nose and fierce black eyes like those of a hawk. Even when he smiled, Morello was aware, the expression in his eyes remained unchanged. He wore a gray sharkskin suit of a cut currently in fashion on Saville Row.

"Sit down, sit down," Braciola said, indicating a sofa. "Something to drink?"

Morello sank into the seat. "No, thank you. It is a bit too early in the day."

"For me, too," Braciola said. "So perhaps only a little *dell'acqua minerale?*"

"Very well."

Braciola lifted a telephone to order the refreshment, and Morello looked around. The room was more like a living room than an office. Its furniture was avant modern, in soft shades of the brown spectrum, ranging from parchment through burnt orange to near black. There was no desk, but only several intimate groupings of sofas and chairs and tables. On the walls hung a number of French Impressionist paintings. Morello recognized a Renoir and a Monet. Fresh flowers were everywhere, brilliant splashes of gladioli and zinnias in crystal vases.

"So, Vicente," Braciola said as he put the phone down. He took a chair opposite the producer. "It has been a long time."

"Very long."

"A dinner party, as I remember, in Cannes. You were there for the film festival, and you had with you Rita Cianelli."

"You have an excellent memory, Mario."

Braciola smiled. "How could anyone forget that? A famous producer and one of his most glamorous stars. It was a notable evening."

"Most enjoyable," Morello said politely. "You're looking well."

"It's the tennis." Braciola patted his stomach. "The one way to offset my penchant for the good things in life, such as pasta and aged wines."

"I can sympathize with such a weakness."

"Of course," Braciola said. "When I was a boy in Messina, we were so poor that even pasta was a treat. Often my mother did not have the eggs or the butter to make it. Today, when I could have anything in the world, it is still my favorite thing to eat."

"Mine also," Morello remarked. Actually he much preferred the North Italian cuisine of lean meats and delicate sauces, but he did not wish to upset Braciola's nostalgic reverie.

The door opened and the blond girl appeared, bearing a silver tray on which were glasses of mineral water and a plate of sliced limes. She placed it on the small table between the two men and left the room.

Morello squeezed lime into his glass and sipped the cold, slightly effervescent liquid.

"How is your business?" Braciola asked.

The producer was about to respond reflexively that everything was marvelous, but he caught himself. Mario Braciola was not one to whom you offered exaggerations, even if they were the product of optimism. Also Braciola probably already knew the state of Morello's affairs. "Terrible," he said.

The hawk-faced man nodded sympathetically. "It is such an unpredictable industry, eh? One of wild vicissitudes. All so dependent upon a fickle public that I do not know how you can cope with the kind of disappointment it must cause you sometimes."

Morello put his glass down. "It is because when a picture is successful, it is a gloriously thrilling experience. Everything a man would hope for is then satisfied. He is rewarded artistically, critically, and of course, monetarily."

"Yes, of course," Braciola said. "I can understand that. Especially the artistic reward."

"It is the best part." Morello thought of the more than one hundred and three million lire he was in debt.

Braciola crushed a slice of lime over his glass and dropped the rind onto the plate. "As you know, there was a time when I was most interested in the possibility of our joining you in the project of making pictures."

"I remember, Mario. In fact, that is what brings me here today."

Braciola tasted the mineral water. "Is that so? I had hoped that might be what you had in mind. So I took the liberty of looking into your financial situation. Just an overview, you understand. Nothing truly definitive."

Morello was glad he had told the truth when asked about the state of his business.

"You have some debts, at the moment. Fairly pressing ones, I would say. Is that correct?"

"That is correct."

"But surely you are not here simply to borrow money?"

Morello leaned forward. "Not simply that, Mario. I come to you with an opportunity for investment. My problem is that my debts prevent me from undertaking what I am positive will be my most successful venture."

"How interesting. And what will that be, this venture?"

"The picture I wish to produce," Morello said, "is based on a concept in which I have consummate faith."

"As a motion picture fan I find that fascinating. Can you tell me about it?"

"It is to produce an American-style western film here in Europe. But to produce one as the Americans have never done it."

"And how is that?"

"I intend to reduce the form to its fundamentals—to present the themes of hate and greed and lust in a story that will be savagely realistic."

"Ah." The black eyes glittered. "What is the title?"

"The Hired Gun."

A faint smile passed briefly over Braciola's face. "What happens in this story?"

Morello outlined the plot as Braciola listened intently. When the producer finished, he sat back on the sofa.

Braciola stroked his chin. "I do not pretend to know your business, but this sounds to me like a very exciting idea. It would be the kind of picture a great many people would wish to see."

"Exactly."

"What do you estimate it would cost to produce?"

"Three hundred million lire." Morello watched closely but saw no reaction. The dark features remained impassive as Braciola considered the information.

"That is the amount you would wish us to invest?"

Morello sipped some of the mineral water. "The amount I need is five hundred million."

"I see. The difference, of course, is what you require to relieve the pressure of your previous obligations."

"Exactly."

"And what might we expect as a return on such an investment?"

"One half of all profits."

"One half."

"That is correct. As you probably know, Mario, such a share would be considerably higher than that which could be expected by most investors. A bank, for example, would merely charge one or two points over its prime rate."

"Yes, I do know that." The hawk eyes fixed on Morello's face. "On the other hand, no bank would be willing to undertake such a risk, as your recent efforts to secure loans from those sources have revealed to you."

Morello exhaled slowly.

"Vicente, let me be frank with you. Five hundred million lire is no trivial sum. At the same time, it is modest, when compared to the positions we hold in various other enterprises, not only here in Italy but abroad. Today our dealings are virtually all in quite respectable businesses. Nothing like the old days." He gestured. "Oh, a few things here and there, the gambling, for instance. But by and large, we are highly legitimate."

"I understand that, Mario."

Braciola got to his feet. He pushed his hands into his trouser pockets and paced slowly as he spoke. "Truthfully, there are other ventures in which we could expect a far higher return on our money than this one, and at a lesser risk."

In Christ's name, Morello thought, am I going to get the money or not?

Braciola paused. "But what is most attractive to me about your proposal has not so much to do with a few hundred million lire. It has to do with the possibility of our entering what to me personally would be a challenging new field."

The producer studied his host coolly. He understood precisely what Braciola meant, perhaps better than Braciola understood it himself. Like no other area of human endeavor, more than trading stock or breeding racehorses or mining diamonds, the business of producing motion pictures was an irresistible magnet.

"Therefore," Braciola continued, "I think you may consider us your partners in this undertaking."

Morello stood up and held out his hand. "I congratulate you on a wise decision."

Braciola smiled as they shook hands. "I am delighted, Vicente. And I am sure it will be a mutually profitable relationship. Our people will contact you to work out the details of our agreement."

"Fine, Mario. I am very pleased."

"It is also customary with us that when we enter into a new venture, we assign a representative of our organization to work with you."

Morello hesitated. He had not expected this.

"Mainly it is for purposes of efficiency," Braciola said. "If you need to know our point of view on a given subject, or if it becomes necessary to make a joint decision, it will be convenient for you to have such a representative always at hand."

What a wonderful arrangement, Morello thought cynically.

Braciola stepped to the telephone and spoke into it briefly.

The door opened, and a man walked into the room. He appeared to be in his thirties, quite dark, dressed conservatively in a well-cut blue suit which failed to disguise extraordinarily wide shoulders and long arms. His face, above the thick neck, made Morello think of an ax blade. Braciola introduced him as Vito Zicci.

"A pleasure," Morello said.

Braciola detailed to the young man the nature of the undertaking in which his organization would have an interest. When he finished, Zicci regarded Morello appraisingly but said nothing.

"When do you expect production to begin?" Braciola asked.

"As soon as possible," Morello replied. "We are settling now on a location."

"And where is that?"

"Spain. Much of the area in the plains south of Madrid closely resembles the American West."

"Yes, of course," Braciola said. "That is quite ingenious."

"Another choice was Sicily, but Spain has the more authentic topography. Especially with the mountain ranges. They are much higher in Spain."

"I understand."

"Also the weather will be very good there at this time of year. Not much rainfall, and it will begin to cool off a little in September."

"Yes." Braciola turned to Zicci. "You see, Vito? A very good assignment. You travel to a beautiful country to work with an exciting group of highly talented people. You are fortunate, eh?"

Zicci looked at Morello coldly. "Very fortunate. How long do you expect that we will be there, making this picture?"

"It is my plan to shoot all the location work, which is most of it, in under five weeks. The rest, a few inserts, I shall make in Rome later."

The young man nodded.

"Thank you, Vito," Braciola said. "We shall discuss this project later, you and I."

Zicci bowed shortly and walked out, closing the door behind him.

"He is a very reliable man," Braciola said when they were alone.

"That was the impression he gave me," Morello remarked.

Braciola shook his head. "They become harder and harder to develop, these days. So many of them get caught up in communism or become terrorists simply for the sake of creating violence. So stupid, and so wasteful."

"Political ideology preys on the emotions of the young," Morello said.

"How very true. But fortunately we are blessed with some extraordinarily talented people. Many of them are from families who have been a part of our organization for a long time."

"I know your tradition."

The black eyes were cold and steady. "Do you?"

Morello realized he had made a mistake. He was suddenly aware that he was sweating. "That is, I—"

"Then if you know our tradition, you know that from this time on, you too are a part of our organization."

"I didn't, that is, I hadn't thought of it in those terms."

"Then think about it," Braciola said.

Morello pulled a handkerchief from his jacket pocket and wiped his forehead.

Braciola lifted his glass. "To our partnership, Vicente."

The producer raised his own glass and touched it against his host's. The elation he had felt a moment ago had become a cold lump in his belly. "To our partnership."

chapter 13

The location was a bull ranch three hundred kilometers southeast of Madrid. The company flew Alitalia's flight 366 from Leonardo da Vinci Airport, arriving in the Spanish capital just before noon, and then drove down to the ranch in a fleet of rented cars. The roads were winding and narrow, and the drive took over five hours.

Hendricks had never been in Spain before this. What he saw of Madrid looked as modern and as bustling to him as most of the world's major cities he had visited, but as soon as they left the suburbs, he observed that there were marked differences in the countryside. It was a land of farms and orchards and ranches somewhat like Italy, but it was much less heavily populated and its roads were traveled by far fewer vehicles.

He soon realized that Spain was years behind other countries in its use of machines. A road gang they passed employed many men with picks and shovels, but with the crew was only one mechanized road grader. The farms, too, appeared to be operated as they must have been for hundreds of years. Carts were drawn by oxen, and where he saw hay being gathered in the fields, the wagons were pulled by horses and mules. Occasionally they passed a peasant woman walking beside the road, her burden balanced precariously atop her head.

Their route took them through a few isolated towns and villages, through Ciempozuelos and Aranjuez and Santa Cruz, and then down into the great open plain country of La Mancha, the land of Don Quixote, with its scattered stands of walnut and scrub oak. In the distance Hendricks could see the craggy peaks of the Sierra Morena mountains. They stopped at a roadside café and had a lunch of sopa pescada and fried gambas washed down with icy bottles of superbly dry Valdepeñas, the famous wine of the region.

Antonio leaned back in his chair and waved an arm expansively. "It is beautiful, eh? A wonderful country."

"Just like Colorado," Weaver replied. "With maybe a little Nevada and northern New Mexico thrown in."

Antonio grinned. "The great American West."

There were just over thirty people in the group; the actors and actresses who would play the leading roles, the key technicians including the sound engineer and the lighting men and the prop man and the chief carpenter, the wardrobe mistress and the makeup people and a dozen others. They sat in the sunshine, enjoying the good food and the wine.

"Who's that with Morello?" Hendricks inquired.

Antonio looked over at the producer's table. "His name is Zicci. He is an investment banker."

"Where the money's coming from to finance this ratfuck, huh?" Weaver said. "They must trust our leader a whole hell of a lot if they have to keep a guy sitting in his pocket during the shoot."

Antonio drank some wine. "There is a great deal at stake here, a lot of money is invested in this picture. It is certainly understandable that they wish to see what goes on."

"What about the equipment?" Hendricks asked. "Where is all that?"

"It comes down from Madrid by truck," Antonio explained. "Some of it we flew in with us, and some of it we have rented there. It will arrive tomorrow."

They reached the entrance to the ranch in the late afternoon. A sign bore the name LA CUARTA LUNA and a crescent-shaped brand. A guard with a rifle slung over his shoulder met them at the gates, and after looking over the string of dusty cars, waved them on. They drove another ten minutes without seeing a building or another person.

Weaver stared out the window at the rolling landscape. "Who owns this place?"

"Juan Navarro," Antonio replied. "A former matador. One of the best in Spain in his time. He made millions in the ring. Now he is retired and raises bulls."

"How did you decide to come to his ranch?" Hendricks asked.

"Signor Morello has known him for many years. At one time he was married to Lois Peters, the American actress."

The main house was set in a grove of tall chestnut trees and surrounded by gardens. There were a dozen outbuildings, barns and stables. All were constructed in the Spanish style of plaster over beams and had red-tiled roofs.

Navarro was a lean, handsome man in his late fifties. His hair was still glossy black, with only a touch of gray at the temples, and his face was brown and wrinkled from years of living out of doors. He embraced Morello as the producer stepped from his car and then was introduced to each member of the company in turn; he welcomed them with great solemnity and paid special attention to the women. He wore leather chaps and a leather vest over a cotton shirt, explaining that he had spent the day working with the animals.

When he got to Hendricks, he smiled at the blond American and shook his hand in a strong grip. "So, a real cowboy, eh?"

Hendricks grinned. "Not me. I don't know one end of a horse from another."

"Then we will teach you. If you are willing to learn."

"Hell, yes, I want to learn. I'll take all the teaching you'll give me."

"Good, good. That is what it requires. Patience, and much desire."

Hendricks noticed that Carlos Caserta had watched this exchange with a smirk on his dark, heavy face. From the moment they had met, Caserta had made it clear that as far as he was concerned, Hendricks was little more than an extra. He, Caserta, was the star of this picture and would be so regarded by everyone. Well, screw him. Hendricks looked over at the big Italian actor and winked. Caserta turned away.

The company was deployed in living quarters according to rank. Morello and Cecily were given rooms in the main house, along with Caserta and Livorno, the director. Zicci was also installed there. The other actors and actresses, Hendricks among them, were lodged in a spacious guest cottage, and the rest of the crew lived in a bunkhouse. Extra tables were set up in the huge dining room in the main house where all meals would be served.

Hendricks looked into the room he had been assigned. He had bought some clothes before leaving Rome and a vinyl

72

duffel bag to carry them in. The bag was lying on the bed. He picked it up and wandered through the cottage until he found Tina's room.

She smiled warmly as he walked in. "I was afraid I might have to sleep alone."

He dropped the duffel bag and put his arms around her. "With all these horny guys around? Just the opposite. They'd be sniffing you like a bunch of hound dogs after a bitch in heat. So what I figured was, I'd stay here and protect you."

Tina flicked her tongue across his lips and pressed tight against him. "And how do you propose to do that?"

Hendricks slid a hand down between her buttocks. "Simple. As long as my cock is inside you, nobody else can get his in."

"It sounds ingenious. Why don't you give me a demonstration?" Hendricks reached a leg out and kicked the door shut. "That's sort of what I had in mind."

chapter 14

The closest Hendricks had ever been to a ranch before this was on those occasions when as a kid in Baltimore he had scraped up twenty-five cents to see a western in the grubby little theater on Water Street. From the moment he stepped out of the cottage early on the morning after their arrival here, however, he loved the life, taking to it naturally and absorbing with pleasure and interest everything about it he could. Hendricks had spent so many years in the open air at sea that La Cuarta Luna, with its vast expanses of rugged, desolate country, made him feel instantly at home.

The first thing he set about was learning to ride. The man in charge of the horses was a short, bandy-legged vaquero named Pepe who was very proud of the two gold teeth in the center of his mouth and displayed them constantly in a broad grin, not only because of his pride, but because he was a cheerful man who enjoyed his work. Hendricks learned that Pepe had first come to the ranch as a boy after his release from Franco's cavalry at the end of the Spanish Civil War. La Cuarta Luna had been owned by another man then, but Pepe had stayed on when Navarro bought it upon his retirement from *las corridas*. There were over two hundred head of horses on the 40,470,000 square meters Navarro owned, and working with them was as natural to Pepe as breathing.

Hendricks drew Levi's and boots from wardrobe, and Pepe assigned him a big gray gelding, explaining that the horse would be gentler than a stallion that still had *cojones* to make him ornery. The horse was called Humo. Hendricks insisted that Pepe show him how to saddle the animal so that he could do it himself whenever he wanted to ride and because he wanted to know as much as possible about horses and handling them.

When he first climbed up into the heavy working saddle, with its curving seat back and its high pommel, he felt awkward and uncomfortable, and Pepe laughed at him goodnaturedly. Even though the gray was relatively easygoing, he promptly threw Hendricks onto the dirt of the corral, and now Pepe doubled over. But Hendricks got up and after brushing the dust from his jeans again clambered onto Humo's back, and this time he stayed there.

From then on Hendricks rode everywhere. Pepe gave him some instruction, showing him how to get the horse to change gaits and how to guide him with his legs as well as his hands, and before long Hendricks began to get the hang of it. Navarro, too, offered advice and rode with him several times, and Hendricks was delighted with the progress he made.

A few others in the company occasionally took a horse out for a brief ride, but their interest was desultory. Mostly they played cards and lazed in the sun beside the swimming pool. As far as they were concerned, Hendricks was crazy. He in turn ignored them, except to catalog a few of the women and file them away in the back of his head for possible future reference.

Antonio had announced that they would not be ready to shoot for a few days, while locations were scouted and a schedule planned, and Hendricks made the most of the time, riding from early each morning until the light was gone in the evening. When he went into the dining room at night, he was almost too tired to eat dinner, and the muscles of his arms and back and shoulders and buttocks and especially his thighs were stiff and painful. But no matter how much he ached—and Tina pointed out to him the mottled blue bruises on his rump and his legs—he forced himself to get out to the corral at dawn each morning, his breath steaming in the cool, sharp air, lugging the heavy saddle as Humo whinnied a welcome.

There were a great many things of interest to see on the ranch. The business of La Cuarta Luna was to produce bulls which would be sold to promoters from among the hundreds of rings throughout Spain, and these animals were bred with expert care and knowledge by Navarro and his men. Altogether there were over fifteen hundred head of cattle, including the bulls, on the place.

The old matador was pleased by Hendricks's enthusiasm for the ranch and its activities and went out of his way to explain his methods and procedures. In his office in the main house Navarro had large, leather-bound ledgers in which records of every animal ever bred at La Cuarta Luna were meticulously kept. The entries showed each animal's bloodlines, and also to which ring it had been sold, and how bravely it had fought.

"It is very important," Navarro said, "to know that. You see, you cannot work a bull ahead of time, when he is young and first reaching maturity, because to do so would make him wise in the way of the matador. Then in the *corrida* the bull would perhaps ignore the cape and attack the man."

Hendricks wiped sweat from his face with a bandanna. It was cool in the house, with its stone and plaster walls more than a full meter thick, but the late morning sun had been hot and the outside air still. "So the first time he faces a man is when he's actually in a fight?"

"Almost. When he is still a calf, he is tested by a *vaquero* on horseback using a steel lance. It is to see if he will take the pain and still attack. If he will, then we know that he is a brave bull. Later, when he is sold to fight, we must know if he died so as to bring honor to the name of La Cuarta Luna. This also helps us to determine the value of his offspring."

"Then you breed them before they are sold to fight?"

"Yes," Navarro said. "You would like to see?"

"Sure."

They rode to the breeding pens, where young bulls were being mated with cows. Hendricks watched as the men forced one through a chute and into an enclosure where a cow waited. He was amazed and awed by the power and the spirit of the fighting bull. It was sleek and black and fierce and seemed to Hendricks to be like a huge bundle of compressed energy, ready to burst into fury at any provocation. He was also astonished to see how quickly and deftly the animal moved, and remarked on this to Navarro.

"Faster over a short distance than a horse," the Spaniard

said. "But that, too, is part of what we breed for."

Hendricks looked at the bull's magnificent head, crowning the enormous muscles of its neck and shoulders, and at the wide, curving horns which tapered to glossy needle points. "You ever been stuck by one of those?"

Navarro nodded. "Many times. Such a wound is called a *cornada*. It is most likely to be sustained in the belly or the thigh or"—looking at Hendricks—"in the groin."

The thought caused a tightening sensation in Hendricks's own crotch. "Christ, what a way to get it. Stabbed in the balls by a pissed-off bull."

Navarro laughed. "Fortunately it is not always fatal, or even permanently incapacitating. But for a time it can slow down one's activities."

"I would think so," Hendricks said, looking at the horns.

"It was worse before we had antibiotics."

They watched as the bull mounted the cow, the female docile and wide-eyed.

"She's not arguing," Hendricks said.

"A proper *mujer*," Navarro agreed.

"Is there some way you also test the cows? Besides that way, I mean." Hendricks smiled.

"Oh, yes. We cape them in the private ring here on the ranch. It is very important to know if a cow is brave. Only a brave cow, together with a brave bull, can produce an animal which will fight with distinction."

"Where do you keep the bulls while they're growing up—do they just run loose? I sure as hell wouldn't want to stumble onto one."

The rancher smiled. "They are allowed to run free, but in a large fenced-in area. Come, I will show you."

They rode out across the grassy plain, and even though he knew Navarro was taking it easy, Hendricks was proud and pleased that he could keep up as the horses moved at a brisk canter. His legs were still sore as hell, but Hendricks felt wonderful with the breeze from the ride on his face and his back warm from the noon-high sun. The air was clear, and there were white clouds moving across the high, blue Spanish sky, and on the horizon the mountains were looming shadows. It was easy to understand why, with all the money he had made in the bullrings, Navarro had chosen to spend the rest of his life on this ranch.

When they reached the barbed-wire fence, they reined in the horses, and the rancher pointed. Hendricks saw a number of young bulls on the plain beyond the fence. He guessed that there were as many as a hundred that he could see from where they were. Most of the animals grazed peacefully, but several pairs pawed the ground and charged at each other.

"Even at that age they're mean as hell, aren't they?" Hendricks remarked.

"They must be," Navarro said. "If they were not, they would be of no use to us."

"What happens when one turns out that way—with no balls?"

"He becomes meat for the poor families in the village."

Hendricks heard hooves pounding and turned to see a cowboy riding toward them. The man waved and pulled up close to them, and he and Navarro exchanged a few words in Spanish. Hendricks noticed that the man carried a pistol in a holster on his belt and that a rifle stock protruded from a scabbard on his saddle. The man waved again and rode off.

"Why the guns?"

"It is to keep anyone from getting near the bulls," Navarro replied.

"Who'd want to?"

The rancher smiled. "An aspiring matador. You see, a poor boy knows that to fight bulls is one of the very few ways he can escape poverty in Spain. He may even become rich and famous. The trouble is, it costs money to rent cows or steers for practice, and anyway caping a cow is not the real thing. So he sneaks onto a bull ranch and works with the bulls there."

"Which is good for the kid but bad for the bull."

"It is bad for the bull's owner," Navarro said. "And it can be especially bad for a matador who draws such an educated bull in a *corrida*."

Hendricks looked at the rancher. "So how did you learn— could you afford to rent cows for practice?"

Navarro grinned. "I was as poor as dirt. I learned by sneaking onto a ranch just like this one and working with the young bulls. But never in the daytime."

"You mean to say you fooled with those things at night?"

"I did it by moonlight," Navarro said. "Then there was enough light to cape the bulls by but not enough for there to be much chance of getting caught."

Hendricks watched as one of the animals challenged another.

"I'd like to see a bullfight. Are there any around now?"

"Of course. In fact, this is the height of the season. They are held every Sunday afternoon in cities and towns all over Spain. If you think you would enjoy it, I shall arrange an excursion for anyone in the company who might wish to attend."

"That would be great. I'm really very interested."

"It would be my pleasure."

"Is there a ring near here?"

"Yes, there is a very fine *plaza de toros* in Montillas, which is about thirty kilometers away. Bulls from this ranch are often fought there."

"Count me in," Hendricks said.

That night at dinner Antonio handed out copies of a shooting schedule, explaining that the first camera work would begin the next day in the tiny nearby village.

Matt Weaver leaned across the table toward Hendricks. "Okay, buddy—your vacation is over."

"That's fine with me," Hendricks said. "I figure I'm as ready as I'm ever going to be." He drank some of the rough and hearty *vino tinto*. The truth was, he reflected, that he had been looking forward to this for some time.

chapter 15

Cecily Petain kicked the covers off her bed and stretched her long, slim legs luxuriously. Then she lay quiet for a moment, thinking about the fact that today, like yesterday, there would be very little to do and that she was bored with this inactivity. The picture was already two days later getting started, which bothered no one else in the company besides her except Vicente Morello and Antonio Crescia and perhaps Livorno. The others would be content to lie around forever, soaking up the sunshine and growing fat on La Cuarta Luna's excellent food and wine. But for her, not to work was maddening.

It was not that Cecily did not enjoy the good life. She loved being in places like Portofino and Cannes and Capri and Monte Carlo, where there were beaches and yachts and casinos and endless numbers of important people to meet, people she could dazzle with her astonishing, catlike beauty. But she was here on this ranch to make a picture, a film which she believed could be a keystone in the building of her career, and she was eager to get at it.

She glanced over at Vicente's bed. It was empty, of course. He would have been up since dawn, out scouting locations with the director and Antonio. Ordinarily a producer would not be so deeply involved with detail in the pictures he made; but there was nothing ordinary about the way Vicente was approaching this production. He acted as if his life depended on its success. And perhaps, in a way, it did.

Cecily thought about Morello then for a bit. By and large she did not find him hard to tolerate, or to manage. Like most successful men, he had a much larger view of himself and his importance than sometimes seemed warranted, but she could put up with that. It was also true, she understood clearly, that a man had to have an ego if he was to be a man. And Vicente Morello's ego was huge. In a sense that was how they related. The producer needed her, with her youth and her compelling sexiness, to tell the world that he was still a vital, virile force, as devilishly effective with women as he was in making pictures.

The truth, of course, was something else, on both counts. Despite Morello's insouciance, Cecily knew that he had experienced absolute disaster with his last two films. The critics had bombed them unmercifully, which was not all that important, but the public had acted as if they were contaminated, staying as far away as possible. And that, she knew, was very serious. Nevertheless he had waved off any discussion of the subject whenever she had tried to pursue his thinking as to what had caused the pictures to fail, and except for a few superficial remarks, he would not respond. Nor would he ever give her the slightest reason to suspect that he had financial problems as a result of the failures. In fact he acted just the opposite, entertaining, traveling, gambling as if both films had been box-office bonanzas.

As far as his performance in bed was concerned, that was also something less than Morello's public image would suggest. Most nights the producer was asleep the instant his head touched the pillow, and he seldom made love to her more than twice a week. When he did, there was a fair amount of acting on both their parts, Morello playing the hungry, mature rogue who could not wait to ravish the lovely nymph, she pretending to be overcome by his all-powerful maleness. He would huff and puff and grunt and thrash about, and Cecily

79

would utter maidenly cries of passion, and then almost as soon as it had begun it would be over, with Morello issuing loud snores while she lay in the dark planning the next steps in her career.

He had even carried on a few clandestine affairs during the little more than a year that they had been together. Cecily had been amused to learn of them, understanding that they, too, were part of Morello's need to express to himself and to whoever else might be watching what an irresistible stud he continued to be.

Her own needs were another matter. She satisfied them with an occasional liaison, but she was meticulously careful not to let Morello have any knowledge that she did. It would have ended their relationship at once, she knew, and she was by no means ready to try her wings without the producer. As long as she needed Vicente Morello, she would be his loving, charming, loyal, companionable, beautiful mistress, and would consider herself indeed fortunate to have such a position. Getting there, at the age of twenty-three, had not been easy.

But speaking of needs, she had never felt hers more intensely than she did now. Partly it was a result of the inactive, relaxed life on the ranch, but also it was a consequence of being in the vicinity of a man who was as attractive to her as any she had ever seen. To Cecily, the big blond American with whom she had first made stunning contact that night she had gone aboard the *Chanteuse* was something that sooner or later she would simply have to have.

Cecily swung her legs over the side of the bed and stood up. She stretched again, observing with pleasure her image in the full-length mirror that hung on the wall at the opposite end of the room. She really did have a remarkable body, with its length and its firmness and its taut, ivory-colored skin and its marvelous pink-tipped breasts. Her face, too, was beautiful under the tumbling auburn hair. Not a line or a wrinkle anywhere. She smiled at the image with pleasure and picked up her watch from the dresser top. Nearly noon. They would begin serving a buffet brunch beside the pool in a little while. She went into the shower and covered her body with rich lather, staying under the warm water for ten minutes. When she emerged, she chose her favorite bikini from the pile in the drawer, a white string, and put it on. She pulled on a diaphanous short white beach jacket over that and went down to the pool.

There was a ripple of interest, as usual, when she appeared

on the patio. The women who were to play the parts of the dance-hall girls and the whores and the ranchers' wives looked up from their gin rummy and their gossip and expressed friendly greetings as she walked by. They also carefully studied her appearance as they pretended not to, she noted with satisfaction. The men, on the other hand, simply stared. In a film company, as in any other element of human society, there was a clearly defined status order. Cecily occupied the top rung in this one, without challenge, on three counts. One, she was the producer's mistress. Two, she had the role of the leading lady. Three, in a cast of sexy girls she was generally considered the sexiest. Any one of the reasons would have pleased her. Together they were something to relish.

She spotted Caserta sitting at a table by himself drinking coffee and went over to him. "Good morning, Carlos. May I join you?"

"Of course." He was wearing a black nylon bikini. A roll of fat girdled his middle, but otherwise he appeared to be in good condition.

Cecily sat down, and a maid brought her a steaming cup. Later she would eat something light from the buffet, but for now there would be only the thick, bitter Spanish coffee.

"Boring, isn't it?" Cecily said. "Sitting around, waiting for the shooting to start."

Caerta yawned. "It's all the same to me—I get paid anyway. So it makes no difference whether I swim or sleep or stand in front of a camera."

"But doesn't it bother you? Just doing nothing? We were supposed to begin two days ago."

"It is much like the army. Or a soccer team. The majority waits for the leaders to try to straighten out the confusion they have caused."

"I don't think that Vicente is confused. It is a matter of wanting to have exactly the right locations."

Caserta grinned contemptuously. "It is a matter of his being as fucked up as any other producer. The only difference is that he has recently made three of the worst pictures in the history of the cinema."

"Two," Cecily replied, realizing her mistake too late.

The grin widened. "Okay, two. Personally, I also thought the one before them was equally rotten."

"And I don't think you know as much about this picture business as you pretend to."

81

"I know enough to know that your friend is in a great deal of trouble."

Cecily suddenly felt uneasy. What information did this outsized oaf possess, if any? It would not be hard to find out. "Anything you believed to be a fact would only be a wild guess, Carlos."

"Is that so? Then tell me why the company has with it Vito Zicci on this location. An investment banker? That is a laugh."

"What is he then, if not that?"

"You really don't know?"

"I want to see if you are pushing steam out of your ears, as usual."

Caserta watched her face closely. "He is a member of 'the organization.' One of Mario Braciola's men in Rome."

Cecily was silent.

He laughed. "So you didn't know, did you? And now you are thinking furiously, trying to make all the connections. Well, I will tell you. And they are quite simple. First, it is the organization's money that will make this picture and that will keep your friend's head above water, at least temporarily. Second, as a result of that he now belongs to them, forever. Third, he is at the present busily making another gigantic error. But, of course, a man like Morello never does anything on a small scale."

"What error?" Cecily snapped.

The actor pushed a hand through his thick shock of black hair. "This picture. It will be at least moderately successful, of course, because I am in it. But it could be much better."

"How?"

"Obviously by expanding the key roles. Mine, for example. It is the title part, the foundation of the premise. It is what the people will come to the theaters for, what they wish to see. Instead that shit script has me in far too few of the scenes, even though it is my action, the violence, that is the major theme of the film. And does Morello understand that? Of course not. So little value does he place upon the script that he does not even have the writer here with the company. Not that I blame him for being contemptuous of the story. It should be printed on toilet paper."

"So your idea of a gigantic error is in his not making your role more important."

"I said the key roles. Not merely mine but yours, too. The picture would then have much more impact. Good God, woman, you saw that, the first time you read it."

Ah, Cecily thought, I see. You are proposing to make a deal. We offer mutual support, and thereby we both benefit. You will help me, if I will help you. She had already gotten Morello to agree to expand her own part, but this could be added insurance. Moreover it was true that Caserta was established, that he did have a certain following. It would be worth considering. But the other thing, the business of Zicci, was ominous. She wondered if Caserta knew what he was talking about. Unfortunately the answers it provided were far too plausible to dismiss out of hand.

"So? It makes sense, doesn't it?"

"Perhaps. I will think about it." She drank the last of the coffee from her cup and glanced across the patio. To her surprise she saw Hendricks approaching the pool. He was wearing a French tank suit, and it concealed nothing. Her eyes swept over the rangy, finely conditioned body, taking in the broad shoulders and deep chest, the hard, flat belly, the clearly outlined muscles of his thighs and calves. She watched as he strode to the coaming of the pool and dived in, cutting the water in a clean dive. He returned to the surface and swam steadily with an easy, unhurried crawl.

"It looks so refreshing," Cecily said after a few minutes. "On a hot day such as this." She stood up and dropped the jacket from her shoulders. "I think I'll try it." She stepped to the pool and dived into it.

Hendricks continued to swim laps, pulling himself effortlessly from one end of the pool to the other. Cecily pretended to pay no attention to him, floating and treading water. When he finally rolled over on his back, she drifted over to him.

"Hello, Hendricks."

"Hi. Oh, Cecily. Hello."

"I didn't think you liked to swim."

"Huh? Sure I do. Been busy, though, trying to learn how to stay on a horse."

"So I gather."

"Yeah, well. It's important, you know? I figure if I'm going to be in a western picture, I ought to look as if I knew what I was doing. At least a little bit."

"I think you know what you are doing."

"You do?"

"Yes. I think you know what you are doing at all times."

It was apparent to her from the expression on his face that he had no idea what she was getting at.

"Guess we'll finally start shooting tomorrow," Hendricks said.

"At last."

"You too? I've really been getting itchy."

Not half as itchy as I have, she thought. "You swim very well. I was watching you."

"Thanks. I ought to do more of it. Helps you stay in shape."

"You seem to be in very good shape."

"Yeah, I'm okay." He grinned. "And from what I've seen, so are you."

That was more like it. "Can you dive?"

"Dive?" He looked puzzled. "Sure. Why?"

"I was wondering. That's important too, you know. It's just like riding. An actor should be able to do as many things as possible."

"Oh, I see. Well, yeah. I can."

"Show me."

"What?"

"Do a dive for me. Any kind. Just a dive. I want to see it."

"Are you serious?"

"Of course I am. As I said, it really is important that you can do these things. Please?"

Still looking a bit skeptical, Hendricks swam to the ladder and pulled himself up out of the pool. Cecily watched as he stepped up onto the board and tested it. Just as he began his first step, she rolled over and swam quickly to the bottom of the pool.

An instant later Hendricks plunged into the water above her. Cecily giggled to herself as she saw the look of astonishment on his face when he spotted her. She reached out and slid her hand into his suit, her fingers closing on his cock. He continued to stare at her, his arms windmilling to keep him underwater.

To her delight Hendricks grew instantly hard, his penis becoming enormous in her hand. She pulled it out of his suit and closed her lips around the glans, her tongue working. Then she took in as much of it into her mouth as she could, slowly bobbing her head while with her other hand she caressed his balls. She expelled the air from her lungs gradually, all the while continuing to suck him, until pain seared her chest and colored lights began to dance before her eyes. When she could not stay down for another second, she let go and sprang to the surface.

A moment later his head appeared beside hers.

"That was a delightful dive," Cecily gasped.

84

Hendricks gulped air. "Hell of a way to end a jackknife. Ought to be worth ninety-nine points."

She smiled. "I think I will have some lunch. Will you join me?"

"I'm afraid I can't get out of the pool just now. Not for a few minutes, anyway."

"I understand. Later on, I'll be taking a siesta." She turned and swam to the ladder.

That afternoon, Hendricks did not ride his horse. He spent the entire time in the main house, and that night at dinner, to Cecily's immense satisfaction, he appeared more tired than he had on any previous day since his arrival at La Cuarta Luna.

chapter 16

Arturo Livorno was drenched in sweat. The heat of the Spanish summer had not yet begun to abate, which was in itself bad enough with the temperature hovering at thirty degrees Celsius, but what was worse was that he worried constantly about his work. These factors together caused his hide to exude water at an incredible rate. He wore jeans chopped off at mid-thigh and a T-shirt, and both were sopping wet. Around his head and his wrists were terry-cloth bands, and with these he could at least keep much of the stinging perspiration out of his eyes.

Thus far it had been a bitch of a morning, albeit not much different from most. Weaver was shooting Kodak 5247 Daylight ASA 100, and the first two batches had been spoiled by careless storage in the heat. But that at least had been discovered before the negative had been exposed, thus averting a far larger set of problems. They were now five days behind schedule, and Livorno could not afford to waste a day of shooting.

The director was no stranger to shoestring budgets and lira-squeezing producers, but he had rarely seen anyone as money conscious as Morello and his assistant. It was also clear to him that they were especially nervous because of the presence of Vito Zicci. The ax-faced one seemed always to be hovering on the edge of the work, scowling at their efforts to get the production on track. Livorno was not exactly sure of Zicci's position with the company, except that he obviously was associated with whoever was underwriting the cost of this production. Just who that might be was anybody's guess, and. such speculation was a favorite pastime of nearly everyone on the location. The Unione Siciliano, the Mafia, and the Black Hand were all obvious suggestions, and one rumor had it that the CIA was involved. Livorno thought the most original conjecture to date had been that the picture was being financed by Martin Bormann.

Livorno looked at his watch. Jesus Christ. Past eleven, and he had shot only a part of what he had planned to get this morning. They were in the little village ten kilometers from the ranch, and the scene they were working on was a running shot of Caserta riding into the village and the people reacting as they watched him enter. For this they would use the camera truck, panning with the big dark actor as he rode. Later they would pick up inserts of the villagers staring at the killer. They were held up now because Weaver was having trouble with his equipment.

"Son of a bitch," the cameraman muttered.

Livorno watched Weaver's hands as they worked. "What is the problem, exactly?"

"Wish I knew. Something in the swivel head here from what I can see. Can't get the mother to pan smoothly."

They were using an Arriflex for this work, because it was much lighter and easier to handle in an action shot than the rock-steady but cumbersome Mitchell. A product of the renowned Arnold & Richter of Munich, the camera was totally dependable, most of the time. This morning, as luck would have it, it was not. Livorno sat down on an aluminum-sided equipment case on the truck bed and silently cursed his misfortune.

Antonio Crescia approached the truck. "How is it going?" He addressed the question to Livorno, evidently knowing better than to bother the volatile Weaver at a time like this.

"He says it is a problem with the head, and he cannot make it pan properly," Livorno replied.

"How much longer, do you have any idea?" Antonio asked the director.

Weaver was working with a short spanner wrench. He carefully laid the wrench down on a stanchion bar and turned to the assistant producer. The cameraman was also sweating heavily, and the moisture ran down his sunburned cheeks and formed droplets in his beard. His voice was low and tight. "Maybe another week, Antonio. But you know what? I can always stick this camera up your ass and pan you by the hips." The low growl rose to a shout. "Now will you get the fuck out of here and let me work on it?"

Livorno took off his glasses as Antonio scurried away. He had nothing dry to wipe the lenses with. He put the glasses back on and thought about some of his other problems. On the far side of the street Caserta sat waiting in a chair, dozing. The chair was in the shade and the actor's hat was pulled down over his face and he looked as if he didn't care if they ever got started.

Actors, Livorno thought bitterly. What a far simpler business this would be if there were no actors in it. But then, he reminded himself, without actors there would be no business. Nevertheless, having to put up with their wheedling and their complaints and their arguments and their outbursts of temperament could be exasperating. That bloated football player, for example, constantly urging him to make even more of the part of the killer. As if it weren't already important enough. And now, curiously, even Cecily had dropped a few hints that seeing more of Caserta would help the picture. What could that mean?

A logical man, Livorno considered the possibilities. One, by helping Caserta, Cecily could stand to augment her own part as the female lead. And it was reasonable to assume that if she had suggested this to the director, she had already been working on Morello. Two, she was concealing a deeper, more devious motive that also was rooted in her self-interest. God knew what that might be, but it was apparent that Cecily was capable of anything. Three, she had begun screwing Caserta. Four, it was a combination of all of these. He decided that the likeliest answer was number four.

The sun had climbed higher. Livorno needed desperately to get out of the heat. He stepped down from the truck. "Back in a minute," he said to Weaver. "Got to take a leak."

* * *

Hendricks walked over to the equipment van. A gaffer sat in its cluttered interior, fanning himself with a piece of cardboard.

Hendricks smiled. "Hiya."

The man nodded.

"Hey, let me borrow one of those things, will you?" Hendricks pointed.

"What thing?"

"That. The frame there, with the black cloth on it."

"That is a scrim."

"Okay, a scrim. Let me have it, okay?"

The gaffer shook his head. "I cannot."

"Why?"

"It is for lights. Electrician's equipment. His responsibility."

"Where is he?"

"I do not know."

Hendricks smiled again, pleasantly. "Look, pal. Tell you what. I only want to borrow it for a little while. Soon as I'm finished with it, I'll bring it right back here, promise."

The man's face was impassive.

"And what's more, I owe you a bottle of wine."

The gaffer grinned and pulled the scrim out of its bin. It was about four by three feet. He passed it to Hendricks.

Holding the scrim under his arm, Hendricks walked across the street to where Weaver was working in the camera truck. He realized that he was beginning to learn the ins and outs of getting along with a film crew. When he reached the truck, he said nothing to the sweating cameraman but quietly went about fitting the scrim into one of the brackets that lined the railing on the side of the bed. Thus mounted, the rectangle of black cloth provided shade for the camera and for Weaver's upper body.

Weaver glanced up, but Hendricks merely looked at the camera without speaking. The cameraman wiped sweat from his eyes and returned his attention to the troublesome swivel head.

Hendricks's tone was calm, matter-of-fact. "It's stuck, huh?"

Weaver grasped the handle of the camera and swung the instrument back and forth. "No, it'll move all right. But the fucker ain't smooth. If I try to use it like this, it'll make a bitch in the shot. Look like hell when you see it printed."

"Have to use this camera?"

"No. I just prefer it. But if I can't get it to move right, I'll set up the Mitchell."

"They're all you have?"

Weaver went back to work with the wrench. "Can you believe it? I told you Morello was one of the world's great moneygrubbers. We're short on equipment and short on crew. You don't see an assistant cameraman around here, do you?

The one they brought down from Madrid isn't worth a shit. I sent him over to the saloon there, for a beer. Makes me nervous to have him around, staring at me like a goddamn monkey."

"Would it help to get this thing off and have a look inside the mechanism?"

"That's what I'm doing now. You lift it, will you, when I get it free?"

"Sure. What's next, after this scene?"

"A couple more running shots. You try to bunch them up. It's a more efficient way to shoot, you know?"

"Yeah."

"You're in some of the stuff we'll shoot this afternoon, I think. You and Caserta."

"That's nice."

Weaver smiled. "You better keep an eye on that big dago. He doesn't exactly love you, either."

"Uh-huh."

"Okay, I'll tell you when to lift it. I want to clean it out and give it a shot of silicone."

"Say when."

* * *

Carlos Caserta pushed his hat back on his head and stared across the dusty street at the camera truck. It took a moment to adjust his eyes to the glare of the sunlight. Weaver was still fiddling with his silly camera. And now someone else was with him. Christ, it was that yellow-topped shithead of an American, Hendricks. That one was a problem Caserta would have to handle, sooner or later. He was already hearing talk that the sailor was a great discovery, that he would be the outstanding character in the film. It was incredible. And he had thought he would only need to deal with Morello's cunt mistress who had indicated that she was dumb enough to go along with urging the producer and the director to expand the part of the killer. But Hendricks was something else. Caserta had not bothered to look at any of the dailies, but he had heard one of the girls chattering to another that the American looked like Apollo. Apollo, for the blood of Jesus.

Caserta got up from his chair and strolled slowly around to the rear of the building. The horses were tethered in the shade behind the structure, enclosed in a makeshift rope corral. Pepe sat leaning against the wall, his head resting on his drawn-up knees. He was asleep.

The actor ducked under the rope. He moved among the animals slowly, so as not to excite them. When he reached his own horse, a handsome chestnut, he dug into his jeans for a lump of sugar. The horse picked the sugar off Caserta's palm, and he scratched the animal's velvety nose.

He moved then to the big gray he had seen Hendricks riding and repeated the process with another lump of sugar. He petted the horse's neck and moved down the animal's left side. Keeping his back to the building, he quickly drew a short sheath knife from his belt. He lifted the stirrup strap out of his way and began to saw on the leather girth.

* * *

"It's okay?" Livorno asked anxiously. "You're sure?"

Weaver grinned. "Couldn't be smoother."

"Good, good. Let's go." He looked around. "Antonio?" There was no proper A.D. on this crew. Crescia was doubling, to no one's surprise. If there was some way to save a lira on this misery of a production, Morello would find it. One thing was for certain, Livorno reminded himself. When he had finally amassed a sufficient sum of money, that was when he would make a real picture—an honest-to-God portrayal of how the working class was exploited by capitalist scum. *That* would show Morello something, the gold-worshiping shit. "Antonio? Damn it, we're ready."

They had the shot in thirty minutes. Two good takes and a possible third. The next setup was on the road just outside the village. There were a number of scenes to be done there, one of them a running two-shot, Caserta and Hendricks together. He would get that after the lunch break, while the light was still good.

* * *

Hendricks sat astride the gray, Caserta on his chestnut alongside. The chestnut was a stallion, a lively, high-spirited animal much harder to handle than the more docile gelding. The Italian rode well, Hendricks would admit, but not nearly as well as he obviously thought he did. Caserta held his reins tight to arch the horse's neck, posing as usual as he maneuvered the prancing chestnut into position while they waited for Antonio's signal to begin their run. Hendricks was amused to note that Caserta had put himself between the gray and the camera, so that he would be upstage for the take. The fat fart.

Antonio trotted up to them. "All set?"

Both men nodded.

"Okay. This is to be a gallop, so you really want to make them step. The thing is to keep as nearly as possible always the same distance between the horses and the camera, you see? So we need to coordinate, you with the horses, we with the truck."

Caserta looked bored. "We will run the horses, you will run the truck. You must be a genius, to have figured that out all by yourself."

"Be alert for my signs," Antonio said. He turned and ran to where the camera truck waited, its engine running, with Livorno, Weaver, and his assistant already on board. Hendricks watched intently as Antonio clambered onto the truck. Livorno issued a command for camera speed, and a boy darted up to hold a slate before the lens of the Arriflex. Then the truck began to move, and Antonio swung his arm.

The big gray lunged forward as Hendricks dug his bootheels into its flanks. The chestnut quickly pulled ahead, but Antonio and Livorno both signaled frantically from the truck, and Caserta eased off a little, to bring the animals head to head.

They pounded along the dirt road, Hendricks going full out now. He kept his eye on the camera truck, letting Caserta worry about staying abreast of the gray. It would be more than enough for Hendricks to do to hold a steady distance between himself and the truck. He felt his horse straining, the huge animal lengthening his stride, head forward, ears laid back, and Hendricks realized he was enjoying this enormously. It was exciting as hell, the men and the horses and the camera truck all flying, and he grinned happily.

What occurred next took place so quickly Hendricks had no time to realize what was happening. It was as if the saddle had suddenly disappeared from under him. His right foot plunged downward and then he was between the horses and the road came up to meet him and he slammed into its hard surface with a numbing shock. His foot was caught somehow, and he was dimly aware that he was being dragged, and then there was only darkness.

chapter 17

Dr. José Borales hummed an aria from *Carmen* under his breath as he moved about his office. This was the busiest time of year, which made him very happy. It was not alone the increase in his case load that pleased the doctor, although he was a man who deeply enjoyed his work. More importantly, it was the underlying reason for the annual augmentation of the patient roster in the Montillas clinic, where he was chief surgeon, that put a special spring in his step. The clinic was crowded because it was the height of the bullfighting season, and Borales was a lifelong *aficionado*. Nothing made him feel more elated than to sit in his *barrera* seat each Sunday afternoon, studying with a highly knowledgeable eye the passes of a matador as he stepped through the ritualistic dance of death with a fighting bull.

But for the doctor the next best thing was to repair, when it was repairable, the damage done to human flesh by those terrible horns. During these months many of the clinic's beds were filled with wounded *toreros*. And thus for Borales the year was divided into two distinct halves. The spring and summer half was for experiencing the joy of the season of *las corridas*. The autumn and winter half was for waiting for the season to begin again.

As Borales watched, the radiologist placed his still wet pictures on the glass field and snapped on the illumination. Both men stood quietly for a time, hands in the pockets of white lab coats, squinting at the X-rays. Then the second doctor turned, waiting politely for the surgeon to express his opinion.

Borales hummed a few more bars as he peered at the subtle gray shadows. Finally he pointed to a picture. "I would say impingement syndrome. The rotator cuff, here, is being crushed between the acromion and the humerus."

The other man looked at the X-ray again. "Perhaps also there is damage to the deltoid."

The surgeon grunted. "Perhaps."

A nurse poked her head through the door. "Dr. Borales, excuse me, please. I do not wish to disturb you, but—"

"Yes, yes, woman. In God's name, what is it?"

The nurse was young and pretty and obviously unsure of herself. She blushed deeply. "I am sorry, but the friends of Senor Hendricks, the American patient—".

"Yes, what about them? I am looking at his X-rays now."

"They are threatening to kick the doors in if you do not speak with them at once."

Borales stared at the girl. "Call the police."

"Yes, Doctor."

"Wait." He sighed. "Tell them you will call the police unless they behave themselves."

"Yes, Doctor."

Borales returned his gaze to the X-rays, studying each picture with care.

A moment later the nurse reappeared. "I am sorry, Doctor."

"Dear Jesus."

The girl looked as if she were about to burst into tears. "One of the gentlemen said to tell you he was Senor Navarro, and could he see you, please."

Borales's heavy eyebrows arched in surprise. "Navarro? Juan Navarro, the matador? Why didn't you say so, woman—have you no brain whatever?"

"Doctor, I had no idea—"

He brushed past her and strode through the doorway.

The small waiting room was packed with visitors and ambulatory cases. Standing in the center of the room was a group of men, Juan Navarro among them.

Borales smiled broadly. "Matador."

"Doctor."

The two men embraced as other people in the room gazed at them curiously.

"You're looking fine," the surgeon said. "Not a day older. Perhaps you are about to resume your career, eh?"

Navarro threw his head back and laughed. "I would get through perhaps one *veronica*, and no more."

"I doubt that." Borales glanced at the men standing behind the old *torero*. "You are here to ask about Hendricks, eh? The American?"

"Yes," Navarro said. "I did not wish to impose upon our friendship, but we are concerned about his condition. No one here would give us any information."

Borales smiled. "He fell from a horse, true? You were teaching him to ride?"

"No, no—nothing like that. He is an actor, and these gentlemen are making a film with him, a *pelicula*. There was an accident, in the shooting. They are all my guests at La Cuarta Luna." He introduced Weaver, Morello, Livorno, and Crescia.

The surgeon shook hands with each man. He glanced at the other people waiting in the small room and asked the group to step inside with him. In the corridor beyond the swinging doors he addressed Navarro as the men crowded around him.

"I have just seen the X-rays," Borales said. "And there appear to be no fractures."

They issued audible sighs of relief.

"But there could be serious injury to his right shoulder," the surgeon continued. "One of the muscles, what is called the rotator, is being squeezed between the shoulder blade and the upper bone of the arm." He held up his hands, fingertips of one to the palm of the other, to illustrate.

"You will operate?" Navarro asked.

"Perhaps. The first thing is to keep him quiet for a few days. I will give him injections of betamethasone valerate, which is an anti-inflammatory drug. This may bring the swelling down and could obviate an operation. But first, he must rest in bed."

"Bed, my ass," a voice said.

They turned to see Hendricks standing in the corridor. His right arm was in a sling, and he wore a short hospital nightshirt that covered his legs only to a point just below his hips. There was a raw scrape on his jaw and another one on his nose and a piece of tape was stuck on his forehead. Both eyes were discolored. The young nurse was fluttering behind him.

Weaver spoke first. "Hey, man—how you doing?"

Hendricks grinned. "Terrific. I hope you got that shot. It's what I call my flying dismount."

The nurse seized his good arm. "Senor, you must return to bed at once."

He brought the arm down behind her, and she shrieked as he goosed her.

Borales hid his smile with his hand. "That will be all, nurse. I will take care of this."

"What happened out there?" Antonio asked. "The saddle came off while you were at full gallop."

"That's what happened," Hendricks said.

"You could have been killed," Livorno said.

Morello shook his head. "This will put us even further behind."

Hendricks looked at the producer and laughed. "The health and welfare of the cast always come first."

"I am glad you are all right," Morello said.

"Sure."

The surgeon cleared his throat. "It is too early to tell just what your condition is. I believe there is an excellent chance that you will be as good as new after a few days of bed rest here. I will also want the opinion of an orthopedist."

Hendricks smiled. "No way."

"I beg your pardon?"

"Look, Doc. I really appreciate it that you're concerned about me, you know? But it's my shoulder, and I think it's going to be okay, too. So if you want me to take it easy for a couple of days, fair enough. I will. But I'm not going to do it here."

Borales opened his mouth. "I think—" He closed his mouth and shrugged. "You are right. It's your shoulder."

"Yeah. So if you'll just give me my pants, Antonio will pay the bill and I'll get the hell out of here."

The surgeon shook his head. "At least come into my office so that I can give you an injection and some tablets. They will help to get the swelling down."

"Yeah, fine. And Doc?"

"Yes?"

"Say good-bye to that little nurse for me, will you?"

* * *

At the end of each day's shooting the exposed stock was driven by messenger to Madrid, where it was processed in the city's twenty-four-hour film laboratories. The following afternoon a slop print was rushed back down to the ranch, where the library had been set up as a temporary screening room. Every evening after dinner, Livorno and the others assembled there to view the dailies.

The director took a seat beside Weaver and looked around the room. Morello was already there, talking with Antonio. Vito Zicci sat with them, listening to their conversation but saying nothing. Several others of the crew, a few of the cast among them, lolled about waiting for the projectionist to thread his machine.

"We were lucky," Weaver said.

Livorno looked at him. "You mean with Hendricks?"

"Fucking right. He could have been killed."

"I am glad he wasn't. In everything we have shot of him so far, he looks very good."

"Christ, you're as bad as Morello."

Livorno shrugged. "I was relieved for him, of course. But we are already far behind schedule. I do not see how we could stand to have any more delays."

The cameraman sniffed. "Don't worry, pal. We'll have them. You know this business—it works just like an infantry operation. Nothing ever goes according to plan."

Livorno looked up as Carlos Caserta entered the room. The actor had not appeared at any of the other screenings, and Livorno was surprised to see him now. Caserta sat down on the other side of Weaver. Livorno nodded a greeting, but Carlos merely grunted in reply.

Unpleasant bastard, Livorno thought. In the beginning I was supportive to him and went out of my way to be friendly and cooperative, and for that I have earned nothing but more of his political maneuvering. Familiarity does indeed breed contempt, and with that baboon it is mutual.

The projectionist indicated that he was ready, and someone turned off the lights. Just before the room went dark, Livorno saw Hendricks step into the library and sink into a chair. The American carried his right arm in a sling, but he was fully dressed. Livorno decided that Hendricks was either very brave or very foolish, and probably both.

There were several thousand feet of film to go through, and as important as it was to him to review his work, the director had to fight to stay awake. He watched take after take of men on horses galloping along dusty roads in or just outside the village, and after a time he felt himself to be almost hypnotized by the flickering images on the screen. His day had begun, typically, at five o'clock that morning, and after hours in the blazing sun, struggling with a thousand complications arising from the perversities of actors and animals and technicians and balky equipment, he had been almost too tired to eat his dinner that evening. So he had picked at his food and drunk too much wine, and now his eyes burned cruelly as he forced himself to pay attention to the rushes.

Most of what he saw was acceptable, and much of it was very good. There was no setup thus far from which he did not have at least one usable take. In large part, he knew, he could thank Matthew Weaver for that. For all his irascibility the cameraman was the quintessential professional, and his work showed it. There was a fluidity, a smoothness, about the portrayal of the action that was never evident to the unpracticed eye, and that of course was the hallmark of the expert cinematographer. An audience should be riveted by what was revealed to it but should never be conscious of the existence of the camera.

A new scene loomed into view, and Livorno was instantly alert. He heard the sharp intake of breath among people in the room as they saw Caserta and Hendricks sitting astride their horses, waiting for the call to action. The audience knew what they were about to see, and the atmosphere in the library became suddenly tense. Livorno doubled his fists as he stared at the scene. The slate appeared for a second or two and was gone.

The shot began unsteadily, then settled down as both the camera truck and the horses accelerated. Caserta's chestnut pulled ahead a little, and after a few steps lay back alongside the gray.

The horses were really galloping now, and Livorno could feel a prickling sensation at the back of his neck as he anticipated what was coming. At the same time he was dazzled by the shot. Both animals were at full speed, eyes wild, hooves flying, their riders crouched forward as they urged them on. Hendricks's hat had blown off his head and was held by a cord under his jaw. The sunlight was glinting on his blond hair, and there was a huge grin on his face. Livorno could not take his eyes off the American.

At the instant of Hendricks's fall many of the men in the room shouted, and there were screams from the women. He disappeared into the dust between the galloping horses, and a moment later was again visible, dragging and bumping along the road behind the gray, his twisting body kicking up brownish clouds. It appeared to Livorno that one of Hendricks's feet was caught in a stirrup, while his saddle had fallen under the horse's belly. At that point the footage abruptly ended.

Someone turned the lights on, and for a few second there was a stunned silence in the library. Then every person in the room turned to Hendricks, who sat slumped in his chair, and spontaneously began to applaud. Livorno felt suddenly moved as he watched them. Cecily Petain had a look that approached adoration on her face as she beat her palms together, and Antonio yelled, "Bravo!"

Of them all, Livorno realized, the only one in the audience who did not join in was Carlos Caserta. The dark-haired actor stared at Hendricks, his mouth twisted in a sneer.

chapter 18

When the others had drifted out of the library, Vicente Morello sank back into his chair and thought about what he had seen. First of all, the footage had revealed the obvious. They were very lucky not to have lost Hendricks in that fall. The fact that the American had come through it with nothing more than what apparently was simply a painfully sore shoulder and some cuts and bruises was a small miracle. Morello had seen far worse damage done in accidents less spectacular than that one.

He was also gratified by the quality of the work they had done to date. Admittedly they were behind schedule in the production, and Morello was aware of the many cost-saving devices he had employed. Nevertheless he was convinced by what he had seen so far that *The Hired Gun* would be everything he had hoped. There was a rawness about it, an unpolished vitality, that made the film come alive with crackling authenticity. Except for the dialogue, even an American audience would believe this story.

He fantasized about that idea for a moment, envisioning the film with a dubbed American track being received with wild enthusiasm by fans in U.S. theaters. It was heady to contemplate. But it was also far into the future. The first task was to complete this production and then to launch it effectively in Europe. But that it would be highly successful he had not the faintest doubt. This picture would be hailed as Vicente Morello's masterpiece—the vehicle in which he would make a triumphant return to the pinnacle of the business.

His mind went back then to Hendricks. The blond actor was showing signs of becoming a genuine talent. In the beginning Morello had seen him only as a possibility, at best. The true reason the producer had wanted to give him a chance was that he was so obviously American, and therefore

Morello had felt that Hendricks's presence in the film would lend further credibility to it. The fact that Hendricks was also highly attractive to women was a bonus, an extra appeal that would have value at the box office. Now, to Morello's mild surprise, the man was actually displaying a growing ability to handle himself in front of a camera.

What was also interesting, the producer reflected, was that Hendricks's development was the result of concentrated work. It seemed that everywhere he looked, the former sailor was asking someone's advice or trying to learn some new aspect of film making. Hendricks talked to Livorno, of course, but also to Antonio and to Weaver and to virtually everyone else in the crew, absorbing information not only about playing his own part but about anything to do with the production. He seemed to have an insatiable desire for knowledge about how a film was made. And he prepared himself for his role very carefully.

As a result the basic appeals Hendricks had displayed in the test they had made in Rome were still there, but his actions on film were more natural, much less awkward. And in the scene Morello had just witnessed which had ended in Hendricks's fall from the horse, he had looked nothing less than stunning. As always when the producer had felt his own emotions rise in response to the image he was watching on the screen, he had looked about the room to see how others in the audience were taking it, the women in particular. He was gratified to see that each of them was enraptured. The girls were on the edge of their seats as they stared fixedly at Hendricks.

Especially Cecily. But then the actress all but drooled every time she saw him anyway. Morello wondered if they had been to bed together and decided that they undoubtedly had. It was, of course, perfectly all right with him, so long as Cecily was discreet about it. On the other hand, the one thing he absolutely would not tolerate from any woman was to be made a cuckold of publicly.

It had happened, a few times in his life, and Vicente Morello's retribution had been swift and savage. He thought back, briefly, to the aspiring Belgian actress he was living with ten years ago. He had caught her with the actor who was the leading man in a picture he was producing at the time. They were in the bedroom—Morello's bedroom, for the love of God—when he came home unexpectedly to find her lying there with the actor's shaggy head all but disappearing into

99

her vulva. He broke her nose with his fist, pulverizing it with repeated blows until he was sure that no plastic surgeon on earth could restore it, and that had been the end of her career. Afterward he naturally went right on working with the actor as if nothing had happened.

So as far as he was concerned, Cecily could do as she pleased so long as whatever relationship she might be involved in never became common knowledge among others, or news of it never appeared in a gossip column, or above all as long as she did not in some way, intentional or otherwise, make Morello aware of it herself. In fact her occasional dalliances were a relief to him, because while they were in progress, he did not have to be quite so attentive to her. And he could usually tell when she was having an affair.

Not that he did not enjoy Cecily in bed. She was extremely responsive to him, appreciative of his strength and his maleness. Which was understandable, he reminded himself. To a woman, probably just about any woman, he thought, he would represent everything desirable in a man. He was not only handsome and masculine, he was a famous figure in an exciting and glamorous business. And more than that he was powerful and rich. Or, at least, he would soon be rich again.

The producer got to his feet and stretched. It was late and he was tired and he wanted to get a great deal done in the morning. Perhaps he could make up for some of the time they had lost by rearranging the shooting schedule. He would also have to plan ways to use Hendricks in scenes which would not require him to ride, at least for a couple of weeks or however long it would take for the American's shoulder to heal. He walked out of the library, deciding he would have a nightcap of good strong Andalusian brandy before he went up to his room.

Vito Zicci was sitting on a chair in the hallway opposite the door. The young man sat stock still, staring at him, and Morello was startled. "I have been waiting for you," Zicci said. "I think we should talk, you and I."

From the first Morello had found Zicci faintly repulsive. There was something about that hard, narrow face, with its unblinking eyes and its slit of a mouth, that made Morello instinctively look away from it. "That would be fine, Vito. Why don't we have a drink together?"

There was a small sitting room off the far end of the great hall. They went into it and sat down and Morello pulled the bell cord. When a maid appeared, he asked her to bring them brandy. She hurried out, and he turned to Zicci with false joviality. "Well, what can I do for you?"

Zicci wasted no time in coming to the point. "I want to know what you are going to do about the money you are wasting in this production."

Morello was stunned. "Wasting? What money?"

"You have fallen far behind schedule in the shooting. At first it was days, and now it is weeks. Lost days cost money, and since it is our money you are using, it is also our money you are throwing away."

The motion picture business was a rough, amoral industry, and Vicente Morello had been in it for a long time. He did not scare easily. "So. You hang around a location for a few weeks and suddenly you are an expert? What do you know of schedules and shooting procedures or any of the other problems that have to do with making a picture?"

Before Zicci could answer the maid returned with a tray on which was a bottle of brandy and two snifters. She poured several ounces into each glass, bowed, and left the room.

Zicci stared at Morello coldly. "I know that you are nowhere near the point you had planned to reach by now."

Morello snorted. "And I tell you that you don't know what you are talking about. The schedule is merely an outline, not an exact timetable. It is the overall time I take to complete the filming that I am interested in, and as far as I am concerned, we are making excellent progress."

"It certainly does not appear that way to me."

Morello lifted his glass and held it under his nose. "Spanish brandy is superb, don't you think? I even prefer it to the French."

Zicci would not be distracted. "Earlier this evening, before we looked at the film, you told me that the footage you had made was excellent. From what I could see, it was a mere jumble, the same foolishness over and over and over again. And it has been like that every day."

Morello forced himself to hold his temper. This ignorant clod had not the faintest idea of what a production involved. "Vito, it is necessary to make several takes of each shot, so that we may be sure that we have at least one good one when the scene is cut together later on."

Zicci gave no sign that he understood this fundamental procedure.

"Cheers." Morello swallowed some of his brandy.

"What will you do about this American, now that he cannot work?"

"Livorno will shoot around him, until his shoulder is better. And then we'll begin by using him in scenes which don't require anything strenuous."

"What if the shoulder does not heal and he cannot ride at all?"

Morello snorted impatiently. "What if the sky fell down?"

The black eyes pierced him. "What did you say?"

"Vito, listen to me. I was at the clinic and heard what the doctor said with my own ears. Hendricks will be fine. He only needs to have some rest and the shoulder will be as good as ever. In the meantime the work will go straight ahead, and I am very pleased with what we are accomplishing."

"Everyone thinks he is much better, the blond one, than Caserta."

The producer stared at the younger man. "Better than Caserta? What do you mean?"

"I have listened to what people are saying. The women, especially, but the men, too. They say that this Hendricks looks very good, and that he should have a more important part in the picture than what he has."

Sweet Virgin Mary, Morello thought. On the one side I have that ape Caserta to contend with, forever pushing to expand his role, and even enlisting help from Cecily, who no doubt sees a way there to increase her own importance. Now on the other side it appears that I have a faction which thinks we should make more of Hendricks. And speaking for that group is this untutored hoodlum who would not know an aperture from his anus.

"What they are saying, I have decided, is the truth." Zicci lifted his glass and drank from it.

Morello could not believe his ears. "You have decided?"

"Yes. And that is what I shall report to Rome."

The producer felt a chill pass through his body. He thought quickly. No matter how much faith Braciola might have in this man, Zicci was sitll an underling. He raised his glass to the light and studied the clear amber of its contents. "When you do, give Mario my regards. And tell him for me that thus far I am pleased that you have done nothing to disrupt our work here."

The black eyes wavered for an instant as Zicci grasped the implication of the producer's words. He leaned forward. "I am not telling you how to run your picture."

"Good."

"I am only bringing to your attention a point of view which I felt you might find valuable."

Morello nodded with satisfaction. His shot had gone home.

Zicci poured the remainder of his brandy into the slitlike mouth and stood up. "Good night. I hope you have a productive day tomorrow." He left the room.

Somewhere in the house a clock chimed once. Morello looked at his watch and sighed. Twelve thirty, and he would be up at five. Normally he would never be so involved with every tiny step of making a film, leaving most of the detail of planning the action and the shooting to the director, with backup from Antonio, but he had staked everything in his career on *The Hired Gun*. He forced himself to put his conversation with Zicci out of his mind and to think about what he hoped to accomplish the following day. There were a thousand things to think of. After a time his mind grew numb from fatigue, and he realized that he could no longer concentrate. He poured one more splash of brandy into his snifter and drank it down. The brandy was fiery and clean and it burned its way into his gut, easing his tensions and relaxing him. He got to his feet and out of habit snapped off the lights before he left the room.

As he turned into the great hall, he saw two shadowy figures at the far end, near the foot of the staircase. They came together for a few moments and then parted. One of them melted away, and the other turned and began to ascend the stairs. As the figure on the staircase passed under a chandelier, Morello realized it was Cecily. He wondered who the other one had been.

chapter 19

Tina Rinaldi pulled open the bodice of the heavy, old-fashioned dress and shrugged the garment down over her hips. "God, that thing is like wearing a suit of armor."

The girl next to her glanced at Tina's image in the mirror. They were standing in the portable dressing room for women.

"At least you are finished for the day." The girl touched her upper lip with a makeup brush. "I wish I were. I still have a scene to do this afternoon."

"And I wish I weren't," Tina said. "I would much rather be here, working."

The other girl squinted as she continued to apply lip gloss. Her name was Maria Gambara. "I never should have been a rancher's wife. I would have been much happier as a whore."

Tina laughed. "That is what most women conclude, sooner or later."

The girl looked at her, puzzled, and then smiled as she realized what she had said. "You know what I mean, Tina. In this picture."

"Of course."

"As an actress I am already a whore."

"It's not that bad, is it? I don't really think we have all that much to complain about, either of us."

"You're right, we don't. Especially on this location. Except for the heat, some days, it has been very pleasant."

Tina dipped into a jar of cold cream and began to remove the thickly caked makeup from her face. "Perhaps we should exchange parts. Then each of us would have more of what we want."

"That's not a bad idea, although if I had your role, I would have to work with Carlos Caserta, which is a nauseating thing to contemplate."

"Really? I thought you two were pretty tight, together."

Maria sniffed. "We were, until I spent a night in his room. Once was enough. It was like sleeping with a pig, and not only because his body is covered with bristles. He really is a disgusting creature."

"Some of his appetites are a little unusual?"

"Not some of them. All of them. I thought I had seen everything, but he is a special case."

Tina looked at her. "Now you have my curiosity stirred up. What is it that he likes to do?"

"I couldn't tell you. It—well, if I *do* tell you, will you promise never to tell anyone else?"

"Of course I promise."

"Really, Tina. I wouldn't want other people to hear about this, even though it was not, you know, my doing."

"I will never tell anyone."

"Well. He took me into the bathroom, and made me lie on my back in the tub. Then he—ugh."

"Yes?"

"He urinated on me. All over me."

"How awful."

"Actually sprayed me with it. Standing there with that huge thing in his hand, howling like a madman. Like a madman? He is a madman."

"No wonder you were disgusted by him."

"It was horrifying. And then do you know what he had the gall to say, when I screamed at him to stop? He said that different people preferred different ways of making love. Can you imagine that?"

"Um. That is pretty odd. Is that all he wanted to do, the urinating?"

"Good God, no. That was later. He was fairly conventional, at first. But then more and more of the animal in him came to the surface."

"I see."

"And he is an animal, believe me. I think that is why he was so successful as a soccer player. All the people yelling at him, urging him on to be more and more savage, it must have affected him, you know?"

"Yes, you may be right."

"I'm sure I am. He is often very black in his moods. He spends a lot of time brooding, thinking about how to hurt people who get in his way. You have no idea."

"No, I'm sure I don't."

"Which is another thing."

"What is?"

"Perhaps I shouldn't tell you this either. But I owe no allegiance to that bastard."

"There is more?"

"It may be nothing, but then again it may not be."

"Yes?"

"It is the way Caserta feels about your American."

"Hendricks? What about him?"

"Caserta hates him. He is insanely jealous, of course, of anyone else he feels may be competitive to him. One night, after I had seen some of the first dailies, I said to one of the other girls that the American looked wonderful, like a Greek God. Like Apollo, I said. Carlos overheard me, and he was furious. Threatened to punch me if I ever said such a thing again."

"That's terrible."

"It is bad enough, but nothing compared to what I think he

is actually capable of. While he was carrying on over my remark, he said that he would take care of the American faggot. He said Hendricks would never finish this picture. Then a few days later there was the accident. That night at dinner, when Hendricks had been taken to the hospital in Montillas and there were all kinds of rumors, that he was paralyzed and even that he was dead, Carlos was actually smirking, he was so pleased. Can you imagine that?"

Tina thought about it. "After what you have been telling me, yes. But that doesn't prove anything. I mean, I don't doubt what you have said about Carlos's jealousy. But whether he had anything to do with the accident is another matter. That would be quite serious, you know."

"Of course it would. And so I have said nothing about it, to anyone. But later, when we saw the rushes, I wondered again. In the shot you could see them both riding so fast and so close together. I could not help but wonder if maybe Carlos had bumped him, or something, you know? I have heard that jockeys sometimes do things like that, and so I thought perhaps Carlos hit him and knocked him off his horse."

Tina shook her head. "No, it was nothing like that. I am sure of it. Hendricks told me that the saddle simply came loose and he fell to the ground. He had put the saddle on himself, and so he said that he was the one who was to blame."

"Um, I see. Well. It occurred to me, anyway. And I am relieved to hear that you think I was wrong. As I have told you, that animal is capable of anything."

"I don't doubt that," Tina said. "He sounds positively weird."

"He is worse than weird. Dear Jesus, I have the most incredible luck with men. You may think I am crazy, but sometimes I wonder if it is something I have done in my life, something terrible that I do not even understand. I mean, don't laugh at me, Tina, but perhaps I have blasphemed God, and I do not even realize it or remember what I have done."

"And you think that God is getting even?"

"It is possible, isn't it? We do not always pay for our sins after death, do we? Do we not sometimes receive punishment here on earth?"

Tina felt a little foolish, being thrust into this position of mother confessor, but as she had so often seen, people in show business could be such children. "You must not think those things. Fate has many unforeseen surprises in store for

106

all of us, but you must not blame yourself for the bad things that come your way."

The girl sighed. "Last year it was the masturbator."

"The what?"

"Another one of my fabulous lovers. He was a dancer in *Il Giorno Festivo*, you know the musical last season in Rome? I was mad about him. He would get us both worked into a frenzy, and then he would masturbate."

Tina hid a smile.

"And as if that were not bad enough, he did it in front of a mirror."

"You have had your share of bad ones."

"Haven't I? And now Caserta."

"So if your theory is correct, your next man will be a true prince charming, to balance things out."

Maria looked at Tina earnestly. "Do you really think so? Do you really think that is possible?"

Tina wiped the last of the cold cream from her face. "Of course I do. And it is what you should think, too. It is always much better to be positive about the world and what you are doing in it."

The girl put the brush down and impulsively kissed Tina on the cheek. "Thank you. You are a true friend. Ciao, I must run." She darted out the door.

Tina pulled on a shirt and jeans. Other girls came into the dressing room, chattering animatedly about the morning's work. She greeted them and went out into the sunlight.

Box lunches had been set up on wooden tables in a grove of trees. Members of the crew sat about eating the sandwiches and fruit, enjoying the midday respite. Tina picked up an apple and bit into it. As hungry as she was, she would not permit herself to eat more than this for lunch.

She looked across the grove and saw Carlos Caserta talking with Vito Zicci. The actor was dressed entirely in black: hat, shirt, trousers, boots, even his pistol holster. His eye caught hers, and a smile curled one corner of his mouth. Tina felt something close to a shudder as she turned away.

chapter 20

The company shuttled cars back and forth between the shooting site and the ranch several times a day. Tina got a ride in one of them and was back at La Cuarta Luna by early afternoon. The air was warm and pleasantly dry, and there were scattered white clouds drifting in sharp relief against the hard blue sky. She debated whether to go to the pool for a swim and decided against it. There would be several others there who, like herself, had nothing to do for the balance of the day, and the prospect of listening to their vacuous gossip was distasteful to her. After a time the expressions of petty jealousy and the endless discussions of who was screwing whom got on her nerves.

The conversation she had had in the dressing room with Caserta's erstwhile girl friend continued to trouble her. She resolved to tell Hendricks about it, conjecturing at the same time that he would scoff at the idea of Carlos being responsible for his fall and would dismiss it as simply one more of the wild rumors that circulated constantly through the company.

The trouble was, Hendricks never seemed to take seriously anything she said. The only exceptions to this, she reflected, were when she was stating a fact or imparting a piece of knowledge he found useful. He was unfailingly curious about anything to do with acting or film making, and when she spoke on these subjects, she had his complete attention. He seemed to absorb such information like a sponge. He was the same with everyone else in this regard, however, listening carefully to Livorno or Weaver or Antonio or anyone from whom he could learn something.

In contrast, whenever she tried to draw him into an earnest discussion on other matters, especially their own relationship, his response was invariably to joke with her or to tease her. As a result she felt like something between a child and a puppy toward whom he showed kindly good humor and tolerant affection. It was frustrating because it made her feel helpless and somehow deeply dependent on him. She saw herself as always hoping for a warm word or a pat on the head.

The underlying reason for this, she knew, was that she was in love with him. And although it was not the first time she had been crazy about a man, or even the dozenth, it was certainly an entirely new experience for her to find that she seemed to have no control over the situation whatever. But then she had never known a man who was anything like Hendricks. He was utterly without guile or pretension. And although he was so handsome it sometimes made her ache to look at him, he never showed any sign of conceit. Whenever the other women in the company flirted with him or looked at him hungrily, which was often, he merely appeared to enjoy it.

She wondered, then, as she sometimes did, if he might be having affairs with one or more of the other actresses. God knew it would be easy enough for him. Some of them did everything but send engraved invitations. Especially that witch Cecily, whose eyes crawled over his body constantly whenever she was around him.

Tina walked to the guest cottage and into her room. The real problem, she forced herself to admit, was that with Hendricks a relationship could never be anything but fleeting and impermanent. And thus the truth she found so hard to face was that sooner or later it would end, in all likelihood as casually as it had begun.

She stripped and took a shower, then dressed in tennis shorts and shoes and a white knitted top. She dug her racket out of the closet and went out to the courts, hoping to find a game.

No one was there. She sat down on a bench and closed her eyes, her face turned up to the warm rays of the sun. The heat soothed her and relaxed her and she dozed a little.

"Is this a private nap, or may I fall asleep too?"

Tina opened her eyes to see that Juan Navarro had sat down beside her. He was wearing tennis gear. She smiled at him. "I didn't mean to drift off. I was looking for someone to play with."

"You have found him, if you promise to go easy on an old man."

She laughed as she stood up. "I have a suspicion it may be just the other way around."

Navarro walked onto the court, carrying his racket and a basket of tennis balls. "Shall we just rally for a bit, at first? At my age you need some time to warm up."

Tina was amazed to see how gracefully he moved. There was no evidence of fat anywhere on the lean, suntanned body, and his legs seemed as resilient as a boy's. He stroked the ball easily, without wasted motion, so that the speed of his shots was deceptive. He never looked as if he were hurrying or exerting himself, but he was always in position, no matter where she put the ball. His footwork made it easy to see why he had been one of Spain's greatest matadors.

They played three games. Navarro won the first two, Tina the third. As she went back to the base line to serve, he held up a hand and grinned. "Enough. You're wearing me out. I surrender."

They walked to a patio in the garden and sat at a table there. A maid brought them a pitcher of sangria and glasses, and Navarro poured for them. The drink was made with Rioja and ice and oranges and limes and no sugar. It was very cold, and it tasted slightly tart and extremely refreshing after the tennis.

"It's delicious," Tina said.

Navarro drank from his glass. "And very Spanish. It was popular when the Romans were here, a thousand years ago."

Tina studied the slim features of his face, the dark eyes which were always so coolly alert. "You really love this land, don't you?"

He nodded. "Of course I do. But I would have to, wouldn't I? Stuck out here away from everything, with nothing to occupy me but raising bulls."

She shook her head. "No, it's really beautiful. And there is a great deal for you to do. This is the kind of life I would like to have myself, someday."

"Perhaps. But you would probably become bored with it in time. Most women do."

"Do they?"

"Oh, yes. My last wife, for example, thought as you do. Or at least she said she did. She was an actress, too, you know. After a couple of years she grew very restless."

"And you were divorced?"

Navarro smiled. "She ran off with another matador. One who had not yet retired. So you see, the lesson is, you would have to be very sure that you could be truly content before you would be happy to settle down to a life like this."

"But even then you never know, do you? As they say, nothing is forever. You just never know."

"That is correct," he acknowledged gravely. "You never know. And I think that lately you have done much thinking like this, about yourself and about what you are doing with your life."

110

She glanced sharply at him, surprised. "Why do you think that?"

"It's true, isn't it?"

"Yes, it's true. But I still don't know how you were aware of it."

He smiled. "That's not hard to understand. You are easily the most beautiful woman in all this group of beauties—"

She opened her mouth to protest, but he silenced her with an upraised hand.

"No," he continued. "I mean that most sincerely. Cecily Petain is flashier, I am the first to admit, and she so loves being the center of all attention. But what you have is true beauty, because it is inside you as well as out."

What a lovely thing to say, Tina thought. It is exactly the kind of thing I would give anything to hear from Hendricks. And it is just what he would never tell me.

"And so," Navarro went on, "I have paid a great deal of attention to you since you arrived here. I have seen that you are sometimes saddened because you know that you are giving greatly of your love, but you do not feel that it is being returned."

"You are quite perceptive," she said quietly. Tina liked this man very much, felt with sure intuition that he was being honest with her, but she was not ready to trust him completely.

"In some ways it is a problem of age."

"Age? What does age have to do with it? I assure you that whatever my problems are, immaturity is not one of them. At least I hope it isn't."

Navarro smiled. "Not yours, his. It is typical of a young man not to know what he wants. Not from his life, and least of all from his women. Even when he is making love, his mind tends to wander to other opportunities."

"That is terrible."

"That is truth."

Tina drained her glass. "And so what you are telling me, Juan Navarro, is that if I had any brains whatever, I would leave this insensitive brute at once and give my love to a man who appreciated me."

His smile widened. "Precisely."

"An older man, for example. Such as a retired matador who now raises bulls on his ranch in La Mancha."

Navarro laughed. "I was going to say that the other thing I find attractive about you is your sense of humor."

She looked at his strong brown face. "And I will admit that

111

it pleases me very much that you find me attractive. I hope you will be my friend."

"I am already your friend. What I want is to be much more than that." He leaned over and kissed her.

His mouth was warm and firm, and Tina was conscious of his strength and his maleness. To her surprise she found herself returning the kiss, responding to him, feeling a powerful reaction deep inside herself.

She stood up. "I must go. Thank you for the tennis and the drink."

He looked at her. "You will think about it, what I have said?"

"Oh, yes. I will think about it." Impulsively she bent and kissed him quickly. She picked up her racket and walked out of the garden and along the pebbled path back toward the guest cottage.

chapter 21

Hendricks ran lightly over the path that led from the pastures toward the barns. There were disk-shaped deposits of manure here and there, and he wove a little as he ran to avoid them. Cow flops, he had heard the farmers along the Chesapeake Bay call them, so many years ago.

The weather had finally broken, but still it was warm in the morning sun. Nevertheless he wore a sweater over his shirt and had wrapped a towel around his neck and he was sweating heavily. The run made him feel good. He came over a little rise and the barns hove into view, and he began to sprint, just for the hell of it.

Hendricks had never really been out of shape, but now he was in the best condition of his life, because for once he was consciously taking care of himself. He had been injured before, a number of times, but on those occasions he had simply waited for his body to knit, and then had gone on with whatever he had been doing before.

He thought back. On an oyster boat a wire seine line had fouled on a winch and caught his hand, and they had to cut the rusted wire out of his flesh. The doctor who sewed him up and gave him tetanus antitoxin shots told him he could easily have lost the hand. Off Rio, when he was older and sailing able seaman on a Lykes Brothers freighter, he had gone aloft on a king post to free a jammed block. When he got it loose, the boom swung and caught him in the back of the head, and he clung to the top of the king post, semiconscious, with the ship rolling on heavy ground swells, until they could rig a sling and ease him to the deck. He had hallucinated, and it was months before the headaches disappeared.

And then the fights. Christ, he couldn't begin to remember them all. He had been in brawls in joints and saloons and on decks and wharves and in alleys in Sidney and San Francisco and Caracas and Dar es Salaam.

This time, however, it was different. He had realized something, and its import had come home to him hard. His body was one of the main reasons he was here now, on this ranch, getting the opportunity to work in this picture. Therefore his body was a commodity and potentially a valuable one. It was something he had to look out for. Not that he would be timid after this, or that he would ever walk away from danger or a fight. But he would see to it that he was always in the best shape he could be in.

The pain in his shoulder was gone. The muscles were still a little tender, especially if he poked at them or inadvertently bumped them, but Dr. Borales's pills, along with the rest and swimming and calisthenics, had made the shoulder feel almost normal again. Today was Saturday. He had told Livorno he would be ready to work when they resumed shooting on Monday.

When he got to the barns, he slowed to a trot and then walked in a circle, letting himself cool down gradually. Across the way several vaqueros were working in the corral, gentling a horse. Pepe, the short, bandy-legged cowboy who had helped Hendricks learn to ride, sat on the fence watching them. Hendricks waved, and Pepe waved back. Then the cowboy climbed down and came over to where Hendricks, still breathing hard, continued to walk around.

"Hola, Hendricks."

"Hola, Pepe."

"How are you feeling?"

"Better every day. Very soon I will be as good as new."

The Spaniard smiled, sunlight reflecting softly from his gold teeth. "That is good to hear. Then hereafter you will be much more cautious, no?"

"No." Hendricks returned the smile. "Never."

Pepe dug into his shirt pocket and withdrew a crumpled package of cigarettes. He offered the pack, and Hendricks refused it. Pepe lit one of the cigarettes carefully and slowly exhaled a stream of blue smoke. He looked at Hendricks. "I have wanted to speak with you."

"Yeah? What about?"

Pepe glanced over his shoulder before he replied. "It is a matter you would call sensitive."

Hendricks was immediately curious. "Okay. This looks to be as good a place to talk as any."

"I think so." Pepe stepped to the wall of the barn and squatted on his heels.

Hendricks followed and assumed the same position, his head close to the vaquero's. "What is it?"

The vaquero dragged deeply on his cigarette. "It has to do with your—accident."

"What about it?"

The Spaniard's eyes were filled with sadness, but they looked at Hendricks without flinching. "It was my fault."

Despite himself Hendricks was astonished. "Your fault?"

Pepe nodded. The corners of his mouth turned downward, describing deep lines in the weathered face.

"How, Pepe? How was it your fault?"

"It was my fault because I had the responsibility for the horses. It was my task to guard them. And instead of that, on that day, I was asleep."

"So?"

Pepe thrust the butt of his cigarette into the dirt. "And so, afterward, when you had fallen and the ambulance came from Montillas and they drove you away, after that I took your horse and I gathered up your saddle where it had fallen."

"Go on."

"Senor Hendricks, the cinch had been cut."

A shout went up from the corral. Hendricks glanced across it and saw that the horse the cowboys were gentling had thrown one of them. The man was getting to his feet, a sheepish expression on his face, and the others were laughing at him.

"So you see," Pepe said flatly, "I was to blame."

Hendricks stood up, and the smaller man also rose. Putting his hand on the other's shoulder, Hendricks spoke slowly, his voice low and earnest. "Pepe, it was not your fault. Whoever cut that cinch would have found an opportunity to do it

114

eventually. If it wasn't that day, it would have been another one. And if it wasn't the cinch, it would have been something else."

The cowboy pursed his lips in an expression of doubt. "I do not believe Senor Navarro would agree with you."

"He might not," Hendricks said. "But he will never have the choice of agreeing or disagreeing, because I'm never going to talk to him about it."

"I appreciate what you are telling me. But I have also thought hard about whether I should tell him myself, just as I have told you."

"Yeah? And what did you decide?"

The smile crept slowly back onto Pepe's face. "I decided there was no reason to get him worked up over something he knew nothing about."

Hendricks threw his head back and laughed. He slapped Pepe's shoulder. "Goddamn. If there is one thing I admire, it's a practical man."

The vaquero's mouth was radiant with gold. "It is an honor to know you, Senor Hendricks."

Again a shout went up from the corral as the men turned the horse loose with another cowboy on his back. Pepe turned and walked quickly toward the corral. Hendricks watched him go.

It was nearly noon, but Hendricks had no need to look at his watch. His stomach was growling fiercely. He would have been hungry anyway, and the morning's exercise had made him ravenous. He pulled the towel from around his neck and mopped the sweat from his face as he walked across the patio toward the guest cottage.

There was some activity in the circular driveway that curved in front of the main house. Hendricks looked over that way and saw that a car had pulled to a stop there. It was a Mercedes, an uncommon make in Spain, and a big one at that. A 450 SEL, he would guess. In a land where most of the cars were Seats, built in Spain under license from Fiat, a Mercedes like that would cost 1,850,000 pesetas, he had heard. Therefore whoever was getting out of that car was someone of importance.

There was a cluster of people around the Mercedes. Hendricks recognized Navarro among them. There was a girl beside him, and Hendricks realized it was Tina. She looked across to where he was walking, and she beckoned to him to join them.

When he reached the group, Hendricks saw that Navarro was engaged in earnest conversation with two men he had never seen before. One of them was unusually tall for a Spaniard, perhaps six feet, and quite handsome. His features were fine and even, almost delicate, except for the square jaw. It was the face of a man with great poise and confidence. The other man was short and round and nearly bald. The few hairs remaining on his head had been combed straight across the top of his skull. He wore a thin moustache and waved a long cigar as he spoke.

Tina took Hendricks's arm. "It's Ricardo Zuelos, the matador. Juan was sure you would want to meet him."

Navarro turned and smiled as he introduced Hendricks to the taller of the two strangers.

It was Hendricks's experience that first impressions were usually the ones to trust. Although the matador's eyes were coolly appraising as the two men shook hands, Hendricks felt that there was a positive reaction between them, that Zuelos was the kind of man he would like.

The Spaniard's English was deliberate and heavily accented, but he spoke it well and with care. "You are a famous American actor, eh?"

Hendricks grinned. "You've got it one third right. I'm an American."

Zuelos returned the smile. "And you also know it is better not to take yourself too seriously." He gestured toward his companion. "May I present my manager, Jaime Gonzales."

The short, round man pumped Hendricks's hand. "A pleasure, a great pleasure, senor. You are coming to the *corridas* tomorrow?"

"You couldn't keep me away," Hendricks said.

Gonzales held up his cigar. "Wonderful. You are an *aficionado,* true?"

"Not yet," Hendricks said. "I've never seen a bullfight. But I want to very much."

Gonzales flicked ash from his cigar. "Then it is good that you will start by seeing a performance by the very best matador in all of the world. It will educate your taste, to see a *faena* as it should be."

"You must forgive my manager," Zuelos said. "Sometimes his loyalty and his enthusiasm distort his vision. I am by no means *numero uno* in my profession." His dark eyes glinted. "But I hope that if God is willing, someday I may be."

If you live that long, you mean, Hendricks thought. And

from what I've been told, fighting bulls is not the way to ensure a comfortable old age. He judged the matador to be in his late twenties. "I hope you have a great day tomorrow, for both our sakes."

Zuelos smiled. "Thank you."

"For everyone's sake," Gonzales said. "The entire town will be in the *plaza de toros*. When Ricardo Zuelos is on the card, it is impossible to find an empty seat."

Zuelos shook his head. "More exaggeration."

"Not at all," Navarro said. "I will conduct a large group from this film company to the *corridas*. It was all I could do to get tickets. I had to beg, argue, demand, and remind them of old favors long owed. Jaime speaks the truth."

"I'm glad to get the chance to go," Hendricks said.

"It will be a marvelous experience for you," Gonzales said to him. "One you will never forget."

"Come," Navarro said. "Let us have lunch. You can spend the night with us, I hope. I have had rooms prepared in the house."

Zuelos inclined his head. "That is very kind of you."

"Where is your *cuadrilla?*" Navarro asked.

"They drove on to Montillas," Gonzales replied. "They will be staying at the hotel there."

"It is just as well," Navarro said. "I'm afraid we are about out of space here at the moment."

The group moved en masse along the walk toward the patio where servants had laid out the usual sumptuous midday buffet. Hendricks was amused to observe that Ricardo Zuelos was looking admiringly at Tina.

As they approached the buffet tables, Carlos Caserta stepped up to them, and Navarro introduced the big Italian actor to the matador and his manager.

"Carlos is the star of the picture that is being made here," the rancher explained.

"I have seen some of your pictures," Zuelos said. "They were quite exciting."

Caserta drew himself up. "Thank you. It is very pleasing to think that they could be exciting to someone in your profession."

What a horse's ass, Hendricks thought. He recalled his conversation earlier with Pepe. So the cinch had been cut, and thus the accident was no accident. A few days before, when Tina had told him about the suspicions one of the girls in the cast had felt about Caserta's possible part in his mishap,

117

he had laughed it off as just another piece of foolishness from the mouth of a jealous woman. Now it was a different story. He wasted no time being shocked or surprised but thought only about the situation and how he would handle it. What it came down to, he realized, was how he would handle Caserta.

chapter 22

In the afternoon they went to the small ring on the ranch where the cows were tested for bravery. The weather remained sunny, but it was milder than it had been, and after the rich food and the wine there was an air of relaxation that reminded Hendricks of the atmosphere of a picnic attended by many people who were having a good time in the outdoors.

They stood beside the ring, watching, leaning on the fence rails, as the vaqueros ran each cow through a few passes. There was some good-natured joking with the cowboys, and then the bystanders coaxed Juan Navarro into getting into the ring. The old matador grasped the heavy cape in his strong brown hands, and Hendricks realized at once that he was looking at a man who was very special at what he was doing. Navarro was only half serious, obviously making gentle fun of himself as he planted his feet and shook the cape and took the animal past him, the onlookers shouting "olé!" with each pass. But the style was there, and the grace, and the sense of authority was unmistakable.

When Navarro climbed out of the ring, they urged Ricardo Zuelos to take the cape. The younger man finally acceded, and Hendricks wondered how the *torero* would conduct himself. To the delight of his audience Zuelos put on an act of a bumbling matador, making clumsy mistakes, getting his feet tangled on the passes, and once even hiding his eyes as the *vaca* charged. The performance was charming because in his self-deprecation the matador did not outdo Navarro, which Hendricks realized would have been bad form, but by making himself look comically inept was both amusing and ingratiating.

At the same time, Hendricks was aware, it took great skill to bring it off. For all the matador's cavalier attitude toward the cow, the animal was quick and brave and intent on causing harm to the man who taunted her. Again the shouts of "Olé!" rang out, and when Zuelos finally vaulted over the fence, there was a loud burst of applause.

Zuelos grinned. He pointed to Hendricks. "Now you."

The American looked at him in disbelief. "Me? Holy Christ, are you crazy?"

Matthew Weaver was standing nearby. He held what looked like a Bloody Mary in his hand, and he was swaying a little. "Hey, go on, man. Show everybody how they do it in Texas."

"Texas, my ass," Hendricks said. "I've never even been in Texas."

Weaver shrugged. "So fake it."

Tina caught Hendricks's eye and shook her head, an expression of alarm on her face. He saw her mouth form the words, "Your shoulder," but he looked away. With more cajoling and some pushing from members of the crew, he finally climbed over the fence. Zuelos followed him into the ring and showed him how to place himself and how to hold the cape.

"When she faces you," Zuelos explained, "you will be standing sideways, like so. You show her the cape, and you shake it a little, and she will charge. Then when she comes by you, the cape should be held thus. You see? That is the basic pass. It is called the *veronica*."

There were more shouts from those outside the fence, and after giving him a ceremonious pat on the back, Zuelos left Hendricks standing alone, the cape in his hands. A cry went up as the vaqueros opened the gate and a cow trotted into the ring.

From this perspective Hendricks was amazed at how big the animal looked. The cow pawed the dirt uncertainly, and he offered the cape to her as Zuelos had instructed him. The cow hesitated, and then she charged.

Hendricks held the cape too close to his body. In the fraction of a second as the cow's head passed him, he realized that he had made a mistake. He tried to correct it by backing away, but it was too late. He could smell the cow's hide and feel the heat of her and then her shoulder rammed into his belly and he was sprawling backward onto the sand.

A vaquero distracted the cow as Hendricks scrambled to his feet. He could hear the onlookers yelling, Weaver's voice louder than any of them. Planting his feet once more, he again offered the cape, and again the cow charged.

This time she actually took the cape and went completely past him. Hendricks knew he looked awkward and inept, but at least he had done it. With the shouts of "Olé!" still echoing, he turned toward the fence and bowed deeply, pretending to take the applause seriously, but in fact making a joke of it. The shouts of approval turned suddenly to shrieks of warning. Instinctively Hendricks sensed that the cow was lunging for his exposed back. He dropped the cape and sprinted for the fence, flinging his body over the top rail.

The crew gave him more applause and a stream of compliments, telling him he should forget the picture business and become a matador. After that a number of others tried their hands with the cows, and there was a great deal of laughter and kidding, until the wine and the fresh air and the excitement had done their work, and the crew members began to drift back to their rooms for a siesta.

* * *

At dinner that evening Hendricks made it a point to sit next to Ricardo Zuelos. He noticed that the matador ate lightly, and that he hardly touched his wine. He also noticed that virutally all the women in the room were watching the slim Spaniard with admiration clearly evident on their faces. Cecily was wearing her huntress look, and even Tina was studying Zuelos with interest.

Hendricks lifted his glass. They were drinking Almansa, and it was excellent, as bold and hearty as any red wine he had ever tasted. He swallowed half the contents, and as soon as he returned the goblet to the table, a servant refilled it. He turned to the matador. "You're the first Spaniard I've seen who didn't like wine."

Zuelos smiled. "On the contrary. I like it too much. It is only on the day before the *corridas*, and on Sunday before I go into the ring, that I am careful not to drink."

"Sure," Hendricks said. "I didn't think of that. I guess the last thing you'd need would be a hangover."

"That is quite right. We have a saying. When blood is mixed with wine, it spills faster."

"Yes. I'm sure that's true. And it would apply to just about any sport, come to think of it. If you could call bullfighting a sport."

"It has been debated," Zuelos said. "Some call it a sport, some call it a spectacle, some call it art. And some call it butchery."

120

Hendricks saw that there was a small, cynical smile on the Spaniard's face. "And what do you call it?"

When he replied, Zuelos spoke even more slowly than usual. "I call it a grand adventure."

"Ah," Hendricks said. "I understand that. Or at least I think I do."

"Do you?"

"Yeah. I think you're talking about the excitement, and taking the risks, and putting your life on the line, while at the same time you're getting all that fame and glory and money."

"Exactly," Zuelos said. "That is exactly right. The crowd is a whore, you see. But a savage whore. A vicious, murdering cunt. Together you and she make fantastic thrills, one after another, until you do not know how your senses can stand it. And for that, you pay her with everything you have. Sometimes with your life."

Hendricks drank more of his wine. "So I have to ask you the question you must get asked over and over again."

The matador smiled. "Yes. You are going to ask me, is it worth it? Is that correct?"

"Yeah. That's what I was going to ask."

"And the answer is, absolutely."

Hendricks grinned. "You get one shot on this earth, and the way to go is to make the altogether fucking most of it."

"Precisely."

The American raised his glass. "Here's to you, and to tomorrow." Zuelos lowered his head in acknowledgment, and Hendricks drained the goblet.

* * *

After dinner there was music in the great hall of the house, the playing of twelve-string Spanish guitars and a mandolin and tambourines, and even though there were many people there, the sound echoed from the stone floor and the vaulted ceiling. The evenings were cool now, and so logs blazed in the fireplace. The only light in the hall came from the fire and from torches set in sconces on the walls, and the flickering shadows and the music seemed to Hendricks to suit each other very well.

Navarro had brought in flamenco dancers for this occasion. They were dressed in the traditional gypsy garb, the girl in a low-cut red dress with a ruffled skirt which had a slit up the side, the man in a loose-sleeved white silk shirt, tight black pants, and heavy black boots. There was much clapping of the

121

hands and stamping of the feet as they danced, the music accented by the click of castanets on the girl's fingers. They were graceful together and handsome to look at, and although Hendricks was not familiar with the symbolism expressed by their steps, he understood that they were telling a mournful love story.

That was the purpose of most of these ancient dances, he reflected, regardless of which country you were in or whose customs were in force. Sometimes they were happy and sometimes, as now, they were sad, but almost invariably they described some kind of mating rite. He had seen a lot of them here and there around the world, but by far the best one he had ever witnessed had been performed on a beach in Papeete. The dancers that night had been naked, undulating wildly around a roaring bonfire of coconut logs, and when the dance ended, the performers and most of the members of the audience wound up fucking each other. He decided that this gypsy dance was more civilized, if not as much fun. Nevertheless it was beautiful to see, and it was setting a mood which the women obviously found romantic, and that was good. Maybe it would end up the same way after all, but not as publicly.

After the flamenco performance the music continued, segueing into European and American ballads, and people began to dance. It was nothing like what Hendricks was used to seeing in clubs and discos, with men and women twisting themselves into whatever individual contortions or gyrations turned them on, but rather it was like old-fashioned ballroom dancing. He watched Vicente Morello cut what the producer evidently thought was a dashing figure with Cecily in his arms, dipping and whirling, and he saw Matthew Weaver glide by with Maria Gambara, the girl who had spoken to Tina about her suspicion of Carlos Caserta. Weaver's dancing style was purposeful and direct. He held one of Maria's buttocks in each of his hands as he steered her about the floor.

Hendricks noticed that Ricardo Zuelos was also standing to one side, watching the dancers. He stepped over to the matador and stood beside him, his arms folded.

"There are some beautiful women in your company," Zuelos said.

"Yeah. But don't tell me that broads are something else you have to stay away from before a fight?"

Zuelos laughed. "No, thank God. In fact it is just the opposite. You never sleep better than after you have had a woman. I was just, how do you say, looking over the field."

"Sure."

"The one there, with the dark red hair. I met her earlier. Cecily, I believe she is called."

"You have a good eye," Hendricks said. "With that one, you might sleep right through till Monday."

"That is the producer she is with?"

"Right. Vicente Morello."

"They have an arrangement?"

"Something like that."

"Shame."

"Don't worry about it. Cecily will work something out."

"Oh?"

"Without fail."

"Excellent. And the other one there, dancing with Juan Navarro?"

"Tina?"

"Yes, that's it. Also very choice."

"Uh, yeah." To his surprise Hendricks had felt a twinge on hearing the matador's expression of interest in Tina. Jealousy was something he had never experienced, and he was not about to start now. You must be losing your grip, he thought. Nevertheless he was glad that Tina was occupied with Navarro.

The song ended, and Cecily approached Zuelos. "You are much too attractive to remain a spectator," she said to him.

He smiled. "Perhaps I was merely waiting for the right partner to appear."

Cecily clasped her hands behind her back in a way that thrust her breasts forward. She was wearing a gauze-thin blouse of her favorite pale green color, unbuttoned nearly to her waist. She smiled. "And has she appeared?"

Zuelos looked at her nipples and then into her eyes. "I am delighted to say that she has." He took her into his arms, and they moved off smoothly together.

A voice said, "I think tonight the women must ask the men to dance."

Hendricks turned to see one of the girls in the company smiling up at him. She was a pretty little thing, dark-haired with a full-lipped mouth, and well built. He could not remember her name or what part she had in *The Hired Gun*, but he had noticed her on the locations and around the ranch and had made a mental note of her. Rosalie, that was it.

"So, let's go."

She melted against him, and from their first steps together it was apparent to Hendricks that Rosalie had made some mental notes of her own. Whenever he gave her the opportunity, she slid a leg between his, and within seconds he could feel himself getting hard. He pressed her tight to him, and Rosalie laid her head on his chest, and he was aware of her warm breath coming through his shirt. He decided that old-fashioned ballroom dancing had its points, at that.

They danced through two or three more songs, and then Hendricks eased her out the door, and they were walking in the moonlight. He led her across the patio, where he could see other couples occupying chaises by the pool. The moon was enormous, a great ivory ball whose reflection shimmered on the water. There was a covered glider in the shadows near a cabana, and Hendricks guided her to it.

When they got there, Rosalie turned and kissed him, and Hendricks could feel her thighs and her belly moving in the suggestion of a humping motion as her tongue probed his mouth. He started to ease her down onto the glider, but she stopped him.

"No, wait." With a flicker of her arms her dress came up over her head, and she tossed it away from her. He saw that she had not worn anything under it. Then she lay down, hissing to him to hurry. Hendricks undressed in seconds. There was nothing, he thought, like a girl who didn't believe in formalities.

Rosalie turned out to be something more than that. The instant he was on top of her, she seized his cock and squirmed into position, trying to get him inside her. Her skin was warm, even hot, against his, and he could smell an animal muskiness from her that was a mixture of sweat and cunt, with faint overtones of perfume. She was running wet, and when he was all the way into the tight, juicy passage, she let out a primitive cry that startled him. He hurriedly clamped his hand over her mouth and held it there.

From then on it was like wrestling with a wildcat. Rosalie bucked and writhed and clawed and twisted and tried to bite his fingers. When he came, she kept right on moving, except that now she clenched her hands into fists and beat on his back to express her frustration until he was hard again.

It was a long time before Hendricks got up from the glider. When he did, his legs were weak and rubbery, and he felt as if it would be a great effort to walk back to the house. Instead he pulled his clothes on, except for his shoes, and stepped unsteadily to the pool. He sat on the edge and dangled his feet in the water.

Rosalie followed him and sat down beside him, and for a moment he was afraid she wanted more. But she merely leaned against him and put her head on his shoulder and made simpering noises. He resolved that hereafter he would keep Rosalie in mind for emergency purposes only.

In the moonlight Hendricks could see that there was a great deal of activity on the patio. He thought back once more to the night on the beach in Papeete and decided that this evening hadn't turned out all that differently, at that. And to his annoyance, he thought again about Tina. He wondered where she was, and what she was doing.

chapter 23

The *plaza de toros* was very old. Its circular walls were built of handmade bricks from the ancient kilns of Mantillas, and the wood of its doorframes and the windows through which the *billetes* were sold had been worn smooth by more than fifty summers of *la fiesta brava*. Today, however, it was resplendent with flowers and pennants, and it was trimmed with a fresh coat of red and white paint. In the streets outside it there was a sense of expectation and excitement mixed with an air of holiday as the people of the town milled about, dressed in their Sunday clothes. There was no more important event in the daily life of Mantillas than a running of the bulls, and there was no more important *corrida* this season than this one, which would feature one of Spain's greatest matadors. For all his modesty, many *aficionados* considered the slim young man who headed the *cartel* today to be the finest *torero* since Manolete.

Hendricks looked at the colorful posters adorning the walls outside the ring and felt a growing excitement of his own. It was pervasive, he realized, like the feeling you got when you arrived at a baseball stadium just before a big game, when the faces of the spectators told you that this was going to be a time to remember, and the mood was something you savored together, even with strangers.

RICARDO ZUELOS, the posters shouted. 6 TOROS 6 DE LA

CUARTA LUNA. The illustration was a painting of a matador passing a gigantic black bull. It was done in broad strokes of brilliant hues, and it was signed by an artist named J. Rues. Underneath Zuelos's name were printed those of the two lesser matadors who would appear with him.

True to his word, Juan Navarro had shepherded a large group from the ranch for this event. His guests had spent a relaxed day, enjoying the huge midday meal followed by a siesta and then had driven down here in a line of cars led by Navarro's Cadillac. In its way the Fleetwood was even more impressive to the *peones* who gaped at it along its route than a Mercedes, because it was bigger. In a land where cars were few and a luxury sedan *muy raro*, the long black Cadillac was something to see, *amigo*.

Their seats were on the shady side in the front row, directly on the *barrera*. Hendricks sat next to Navarro, Tina on his other side and Weaver beyond her. "You would like me to explain to you what is happening as it goes along?" Navarro offered.

"I would like that very much," Hendricks replied. "If it wouldn't be too much trouble for you."

The old matador smiled. "Not at all. It would be a great pleasure, especially because you are so interested."

High up in the stands a band began to play. It was a brass band, much like the kind you would hear at a circus, Hendricks thought. Leading the instruments was a trumpet, its notes sweet and clear and high above the rest.

"They are playing '*La Vergen de la Macarena*,'" Navarro said. "It is a tradition, as is everything else to do with the *corrida*."

The seats in the amphitheater filled rapidly, and the crowd was noisy and happy. Everywhere there were goatskin bottles filled with wine, and the spectators passed them back and forth, squirting the contents into their mouths in long red streams.

The band played louder now, martial music in quick march time.

"That is the *pasodoble*," Navarro said. "It means that the fight will begin very soon."

Some of the spectators stamped their feet in time with the beat. Hendricks looked up at them, seeing the faces browned and seamed from hours of toil under the summer sun. The band finished the march with a clash of cymbals, and as the echoes died away, a hush of expectation fell over the crowd.

Hendricks felt Tina's fingers squeeze his arm. At the topmost rim of the plaza even the flags were still against the deep blue Spanish sky.

The gate opened on the opposite side of the ring, and a mounted man led a parade of the participants onto the floor of the ring. The crowd burst into applause.

"He is the *alguacil*," Navarro said. "It is his responsibility to transmit the officials' orders to the *toreros*. He is dressed as in of the time of King Philip the Second, in the sixteenth century."

Following the mounted man, the three matadors walked slowly and proudly, smiling up at the cheering audience. Zuelos was in the center, flanked by the other two. He was wearing a dazzling suit of mahogany color, encrusted with heavy gold filigree. Under the short jacket was a ruffled white shirt with a red tie, and a cummerbund of the same color as the suit. A small black hat was perched on his head. The pants came to his knees, and they were so tight that Hendricks could see the Spaniard's genitals clearly outlined against his left leg. Thin white stockings and what looked like ballet slippers completed his costume.

"It is called the *traje de luces*," Navarro said. "The suit of lights."

One of the other matadors was dressed in blue, the third in silver. All three carried heavy capes. Hendricks was struck by how young they seemed; the one wearing the silver suit in particular appeared to be not much more than a boy. Behind the matadors came the rest of their *cuadrillas*, the *picadors* on horses, the *banderilleros* on foot.

After the *toreros* bowed to the officials' box, the matadors followed what Hendricks guessed was also a long-standing custom. Each of them selected a lady in a ringside seat and draped his cape over the *barrera* in front of her. Zuelos chose Cecily, and the baby-faced matador in silver shyly offered his cape to Tina, who responded with a dazzling smile as the spectators beat their hands and cheered.

The trumpet sounded, and a chute opened. The sounds of the crowd changed at once to a concerted cry of awe and fear as the biggest bull Hendricks had ever seen came galloping out onto the sandy floor. The animal was clearly furious. There was a stream of slobber from its mouth, and it snorted loudly as its black eyes sought a target for the murderous pair of dagger-sharp horns that curved out from its skull. Embedded in the bull's back was a small metal spike from which fluttered ribbons in the blue and white colors of La Cuarta Luna.

"This will be Zuelos's bull," Navarro said. "As senior matador he must fight the first and the fourth. Now he will take a look at this *toro*, to see his style and to learn whether he hooks with his horns or whatever other bad habits he may have."

Hendricks glanced down at the *torero*. He was standing behind the *burladero*, the inner wall of wood between the ring and the *barrera*, calmly studying the bull as one of his *banderilleros* tentatively approached the animal with a heavy fighting cape. When the man came nearer, the bull suddenly lowered its head and charged. The *torero* took the animal past him, extending the cape as far out from his body as possible. After several such cautious passes, the *bandrillero* turned and ran to the safety of the *burladero*, the bull in close pursuit, and ducked behind it. The animal crashed into the barrier, its horns splintering the wood as the crowd howled in glee.

As the bull continued to attack the wall, Ricardo Zuelos stepped out into the ring, carrying a fighting cape. He walked to the center of the ring, his steps an exaggerated mincing gait. When he arrived there, he shook out the folds of brightly colored cloth and shouted, "Hey, *toro!*"

At the sound of Zuelos's voice, the bull spun around and raised its huge head. It seemed not to believe its good fortune to find this impudent two-legged creature standing alone and unprotected only a short distance away. It trotted a few steps and then sprinted toward the *torero*.

Unlike the *banderillero* before him, Zuelos held his cape near to his slender, unyielding body, and when the gigantic animal thundered past him, it was so close it brushed against his suit of lights.

The crowd's "olé!" split the air like a pistol shot.

Zuelos turned and again planted his feet in an unmistakably defiant gesture, and again the bull attacked, his great horns chopping and probing at the tantalizing piece of empty cloth as the crowd roared its approval.

It was dazzling to watch, and Hendricks could not help thinking back to the previous day's playful *tienta*. If the cow had seemed fierce and dangerous then, what must it be like to stand down there now, inches away from the real thing, a monster intent on disemboweling you. After a number of passes, each one closer than the last, Zuelos whirled and strode arrogantly back to the *burladero*, leaving the bull staring at him in wonder.

The trumpet heralded the beginning of a new phase of the fight, and to groans and jeers from the crowd a *picador* rode slowly into the ring. The horse was blindfolded, and its body was covered by a thick, protective quilting. The rider's leg was encased in armor. He was a burly man, and in his right arm was crooked a heavy lance.

The bull charged this new enemy, and this time he was rewarded by finding a solid substance to rip his horns into. He dug at the padding, his enormous strength lifting the horse off its feet with each thrust as the *picador* rammed the point of his lance into the hump of muscle at the base of the bull's neck.

"It is to get his head down," Navarro explained. "The picing will weaken that muscle, and as we say, he will then not be so proud."

Three times the brave bull attacked the horse and rider, and three times the *picador* drove the thick steel shaft into the massive neck, while the crowd protested loudly. Then the horse and rider were led from the ring, leaving the bull standing alone, looking for another adversary, blood running down his shoulders from the pulpy holes in his black hide.

At the sound of the trumpet Navarro said, "Next comes the placing of the *banderillas*. It is beautiful to see."

As he watched, Hendricks decided that Navarro was right. If the phase of *picador* was brutal and clumsy, the one that followed was as graceful as a ballet. Rising up on tiptoes, holding the ends of the brightly ruffled barbed sticks in the palms of his hands, the *banderillero* ran swiftly on an angular course toward the charging bull, leaping into the air at the last instant, millimeters from the horns, to jab the barbs into the animal's neck. This was repeated twice, and each time the placing was done cleanly and with great skill. When the *banderillero* raced past the bull the third time, six of the multihued shafts hung from the beast's neck and shoulders. Applause swelled from the audience.

"What begins now," Navarro said, "is called the *faena*. It is the last of the three phases of the *corrida*. The matador must kill the bull, and he has only a few minutes in which he must do it."

Once more Zuelos stepped out into the ring. Now, instead of the large cape, he held only a small square of red cloth, the *muleta*, draped over his sword. What happened then was one of the most remarkable exhibitions of courage Hendricks had ever witnessed. Time and again the matador drew the great beast past him, each time closer, until he had to grip the bull's spine with his free hand to keep the animal's flanks from knocking him off his feet. His suit of lights smeared with blood, Zuelos spun the bull around him in a series of connected passes, man and animal moving fluidly together in a serpentine pattern, as if the two were one creature. The ring was awash with sound as the crowd's hoarse shouts of "Olé!" echoed one on top of the other.

"It is horrible," Tina said. "But I cannot take my eyes away."

Abruptly Zuelos stopped, and at that moment, so did the bull. It stood stock-still as if mesmerized by the matador's sheer willpower. Slowly, with disdain evident on his handsome face, Zuelos turned his back on the terrible horns and one stride at a time stepped away.

"Christ," Hendricks said. "How does he have the guts to do that?"

Navarro's expression was sober, knowing. "He has dominated the bull. This *toro* will fight more, and he will kill the matador if he can. But for this instant, Zuelos has imposed his will."

Now the matador stood before the officials' box. He raised his hat, then bowed.

"He asks permission to kill the bull," Navarro said.

Zuelos strode back to the animal which stood staring at him, its sides heaving, its neck and shoulders streaming crimson. Again he shook the small square of cloth, scant inches from the animal's nose, and again and then again the bull drove forward, hooking viciously with the daggerlike horns.

When the animal finally stood still once more, the matador slowly raised his sword in his right hand and sighted along it. "It is the moment of truth," Navarro said. "To kill cleanly and properly, he must expose his body."

There was an audible intake of breath in the stands. Holding the *muleta* low in his left hand, Zuelos went far in over the horns, plunging the sword to the hilt between the bull's shoulder blades. He sprang away, and the huge animal staggered, the steel blade deep in his heart. He coughed once, gouts of dark red blood spewing from his nose and mouth, and toppled dead at the matador's feet. The roar of the crowd shook the plaza.

The officials awarded Zuelos both the animal's ears. A *banderillero* cut them from the bull's head with a short knife and handed them to the matador, who made a triumphant tour of the ring, holding the hairy black tufts aloft as the audience pelted him with flowers and other gifts. Some of the men threw cigars and even money into the ring. As Zuelos walked slowly about the arena, holding the ears and smiling up at the cheering spectators, the *banderillero* scrambled behind him, scooping up the gifts from the yellow sand.

Matthew Weaver leaned over and handed Hendricks a goatskin. Suddenly aware that his mouth was dry, the American sent a stream of wine into it, grateful for the refreshing tartness after the tension caused by what he had just seen.

"Goddamn," Weaver said. "He like to scared the shit out of me. There ought to be some kind of a way to make a living easier than that."

Hendricks grinned and looked at Tina. She seemed dazed. He glanced at Navarro, and to his surprise, the old matador's face was frowning. "What is it?"

Navarro shook his head. "He was almost too good. Now the crowd will expect even more of him with his next one. And today he has one more bull to fight."

chapter 24

The performance of the second matador, the one who wore the blue *traje de luces*, was mediocre at best. His opening passes were lackluster affairs, a series of graceless swings of the cape which the crowd received with yawns. And when his picador leaned long and heavily on his lance, the point probing deep into the bull's neck muscles, the mood of the audience grew ugly. There were jeers and catcalls which became louder and more frequent as the *corrida* proceeded. The *aficionados* had seen near perfection, and what they wanted now was more, not less. Hendricks realized that he did not have to be an expert on bullfighting to understand what was happening down there.

Weaver turned to him. "Now I know what it means, a tough act to follow."

"And how." Hendricks drank again from the goatskin and passed it to Navarro. "There doesn't seem to be anything he can do right for them."

More epithets were hurled from the stands, until finally it came time for the hapless matador to kill the bull. Even this went awry, the first thrust missing its mark, the point of the sword bouncing off the animal's shoulder blade. The weapon skittered away onto the sand, and the matador suffered the further ignominy of having to run to retrieve it.

"I feel sorry for him," Tina said.

As the boos and curses of the crowd became a cacaphony, Navarro smiled cynically. "They are telling him to get a gun and shoot it."

By now the matador's confidence was totally shattered. He finally got the sword into the animal with a hacking sideways thrust, in the delivery of which he contorted himself to stay as far away from the horns as possible, but the bull did not die. Instead he stood looking dumbly at the humiliated *torero*, the handle of the sword jutting up from his back at a crooked angle.

One of the *banderilleros* ran out and grabbed the bull's tail. He pulled the animal around in a circle, and Hendricks realized that this would cause the sword blade to slice further into the creature's vital organs. The crippled bull still did not die but instead merely sank to its knees, its lifeblood dribbling out onto the sand. It raised its head and bawled piteously.

"Now they are yelling that even the bull must protest this miserable performance," Navarro said.

The *banderillero* stepped gingerly to the bull's back. He leaned over and jabbed his dagger into the animal's neck, just below the base of its skull. The bull kicked once, convulsively, and was dead.

Spectators rose to their feet and shook their fists, pouring their wrath down onto the disgraced matador, who hung his head as he walked from the ring. Twice he had to duck to avoid seat cushions that were thrown at him. The crowd did not quiet down until the mules had dragged the bull's carcass from the ring.

The third matador was something quite different, and the audience sensed it from the moment he stepped onto the sand. He was not quite as deft as Zuelos had been and not so technically brilliant. But he was incredibly brave, and Hendricks realized at once that with his apparent youth and his shy boy's face, he had the *aficionados* completely with him, their adulation growing with each pass.

Tina beamed and patted the cape the matador had left with

her, its gaudy folds spread out on the *barrera*. "He's mine. My sweet boy. Isn't he darling?"

"If he gets any closer," Weaver said, "that bull is going to gore his pecker off. Then you won't think he's so sweet."

When the *picador* entered the ring, there were the usual groans of protest. But the young matador knew how to turn this to his advantage, too. After the first powerful thrust of the lance, he stepped dramatically out from the *burladero* and ordered the *picador* to stop. If the crowd had loved him before this, they adored him now. Their cheers grew to a tumultuous roar as the heavily padded horse with its despised rider was led out the gate.

"That is very foolhardy," Navarro said. "A lightly piced bull is too strong, too dangerous to handle. This boy is pushing his luck to its limit."

After the *banderillas* had been placed, the matador began his *faena*. He whirled and strutted and took insane chances, and the crowd was delirious. They stamped their feet and shouted approval of the slim, diffident youth who seemed so casual in the face of death.

Tina was enthralled. "Look at him. He is beautiful, and he has such courage. I just want to hug him."

"So does that fucking bull," Weaver said.

When the boy killed, he went straight in over the horns, like a willow drawn to the vortex of a hurricane. He buried his sword in the animal's heart, and the bull collapsed, dead before it hit the sand.

Now there was no restraining the crowd. The matador was pelted with everything from whole bouquets of roses to straw hats, and to the delight of the audience even a pair of women's panties went sailing into the ring. These the *torero* picked up himself and stuffed into his jacket, to gales of laughter from the stands and more applause.

For his extraordinary performance the young matador was given both ears and the tail, an award which Navarro explained was quite rare. The boy paraded about the ring, smiling up at his admirers, and when he was directly below Tina, he paused and bowed to her with amusement. Both Navarro and Hendricks glanced at her with amusement.

"Don't laugh," Tina admonished. "I am truly in love."

Hendricks turned to Navarro. "You know, I think I see what you meant when you said that Zuelos's next bull would be tough for him."

The rancher nodded. "And after this boy's performance it will be doubly difficult. The crowd will demand everything from him that he can possibly give."

A few minutes later, when the dead bull had been removed and the sand of the ring swept smooth once again, the gates reopened and another ferocious *toro* thundered into the arena, the blue and white ribbons of La Cuarta Luna on its back. This one was even bigger than Zuelos's first bull had been, and it seemed to Hendricks to be faster and more agile. Strangely the spectators were rather quiet now, as if waiting to be shown what would happen.

What they were shown was amazing. If the boy had taken mad chances, the ones Zuelos took were impossible. If the boy had been breathtaking, Zuelos left the *aficionados* numb, their mouths hanging open as he passed the vicious animal again and again, unbelievably close, so slow and deliberate in his movements it was almost dreamlike as the man and the bull moved together in the ancient ritual. The people in the audience pounded their hands and screamed at what they saw, and Hendricks knew from looking at that proud face that Ricardo Zuelos would not be outdone, not outperformed, that day, no matter what it took. He was the senior matador, the master, and he would show them that he was *numero uno* or he would die.

As the boy had done, Zuelos also allowed only the briefest picing before haughtily ordering the picador out of the ring. The *aficionados* knew what they were seeing, and they loved it.

The trumpet announced the phase of the placing of the *banderillas*. The man reluctantly got into place, the shafts held high in his hands, and nervously eyed the huge, lightly piced bull. Before he could begin his run, Zuelos stepped alongside and took the *banderillas* away from him.

The crowd screamed in delight.

"They are thrilled," Navarro said, "when a matador places them himself."

Zuelos looked up into the stands. Then slowly, disdainfully, he broke off the brightly decorated wooden sticks, one at a time until each was no longer than a Las Palmas cigar.

Navarro leaned forward on the *barrera*. "He is crazy. He is absolutely crazy."

With the speed and mass of a locomotive, the bull attacked. Lightly, his ballet slippers kicking up tiny spurts of sand as he ran, Zuelos met the charge. He leaped into the air, the

134

horns slashing at his gut, and then was gone, and the stumps of the *banderillas* were home, their steel barbs embedded in the shiny black skin of the giant animal's neck.

As the cheers reverberated around him, Zuelos did exactly the same thing twice more. When he finished, the bull wore a collar of truncated *bandilleras,* and the spectators were limp from what they had witnessed.

"My God," Hendricks said. "What more can he do?"

There was a note of sadness in Navarro's voice. "There will be more. He will find it, and he will give it to them."

In the *faena,* the last stage of this monumental fight, the matador's work with the *muleta* was a thing of great beauty, and Hendricks knew that he would remember it for the rest of his life. As the man moved, the bull moved with him. Pass followed flowing pass, and the effect of watching it was hypnotic. The tension built until it was almost unbearable, because there was never a time that Ricardo Zuelos was not within the shadow of death.

Navarro's hands gripped the *barrera* in front of him. "Kill him. For Christ's sake, man, kill him."

As if he were chiding the crowd for having dared to find the boy matador worthy of comparison, Zuelos performed each *natural* with the classic control of a great artist. His passes became even slower, even more deliberate, and his slim, dark face was contemptuous as he showed the howling mob moves they could not believe.

When at last he raised the sword and sighted along the thin shaft of Toledo steel, the silence in the amphitheater was eerie. Then he went in, driving the sword one tantalizing millimeter at a time into the great beast, until the hilt was against its hide, and the blade had cleaved its heart.

But Zuelos had waited too long, and the bull had learned too much. Even as death glazed its eyes, the animal reared its head in one last vicious thrust and this time found its mark. The right horn plunged into the matador's groin. As thin and sharp as a needle at its point, the horn tapered out to the thickness of a man's wrist at its base. It went into the flesh until the bull's head slammed against Zuelos's belly, and then the matador was flung through the air like a rag doll.

The plaza was a maelstrom of sound. As the other *toreros* ran to where the matador lay beside the dead bull, two men leaped over the *barrera* into the ring. One was Juan Navarro. The other, Hendricks saw, was Dr. José Borales. Everyone in the stands was on his feet, screaming. Tina pressed her head against Hendricks's chest and sobbed. He saw Cecily Petain holding her hands to her pale face.

Down on the sand two men hurried in from the gates with a stretcher. One of the men carried a white box with a red cross on its side. As the men lifted Zuelos onto the stretcher, Dr. Borales reached into the box and withdrew a package of bandages. He tore it open and pressed a dressing against the matador's wound. Within seconds the white gauze turned black as blood pumped into it from the awful hole in Zuelos's groin. The matador's handsome features were twisted, his teeth clenched in agony. The two men picked up the stretcher bearing the wounded man and ran with it out of the ring, the others following.

Hendricks heard Matthew Weaver say, "It was the femoral, man. The fucking femoral. There's no way anybody's ever going to put that back together."

The roaring in the amphitheater continued. Hendricks turned and looked up into the stands. The people shouted and they howled and they wept. On their faces was pain and sorrow and misery. And as he watched, Hendricks saw something else on those faces, something he would never forget. It was ecstacy.

chapter 25

Hendricks bent Rosalie over backward and buried his face in the hollow between her neck and her shoulder. She was breathing hard, and he was aware of her breasts pushing against his chest. He lifted his head and looked into her eyes. They were dark and fiery and he could see the passion glowing in them. Her mouth opened, and her tongue flickered over her lips. Hendricks pushed her away from him, and as he did he brought his left hand up in a short arc. His open palm caught the right side of her face, and she spun away and landed in a heap on the bedroom floor. She stared up at him, her features showing surprise and shock which quickly turned to fury, and her full-lipped mouth spit curses.

"Cut." Livorno's order was weary.

Hendricks looked at the director, baffled. He was sure he had played the scene exactly as Livorno had instructed him. "What was the matter with that?"

The director wiped perspiration from his face with the sweatband on his wrist. It was after six o'clock, and he had not sat down since breakfast, thirteen hours ago. He put a hand on the American's shoulder. "The action was fine."

"So?" As hard as he was trying to be patient, Hendricks was a little annoyed. He was tired, too. They all were. But if he had played the action correctly, then what the hell did this ginzo want, anyhow?

"It was your expression," Livorno said. "There wasn't any."

There was a nearly inaudible snicker from someone in the crew, and Hendricks's instinctive reaction was to punch the director in the mouth. His fists clenched and his shoulder muscles tensed, and he felt the adrenaline pump. But he forced himself to relax, to take it easy. He had promised himself from the moment he had learned he'd be going to Spain on this shoot that he would be polite, cooperative, deferential at all times. He was there to learn, not to blow this opportunity by letting his emotions run away with him. He exhaled slowly. "What kind of an expression do you want?"

"Watch me." Livorno pulled Rosalie to him. "You stand over there," he said to Hendricks. "You are the camera. Now see. When you lift your face up from her neck, like this, you want her. You want to fuck her, right? But then, when you look at her, you get angry. You go from passion to wanting to knock her brains out." The director grimaced as he looked down at Rosalie. "You remember what she did to you, and the anger boils up. You bare your teeth like an animal. Then you hit her. You see?" He released the girl. "Okay. Let us try it again. Places."

But Hendricks did not move into position. "Arturo?"

"Yes? What is it?"

"Why?"

The crew was watching, Antonio and Weaver and the rest of the them, and it was apparent that Livorno was exasperated. The director wiped his face again. "Why what?"

"Why do I do that? I mean, I'm not arguing, but wouldn't that be kind of, well, overplaying it?"

Livorno opened his mouth and closed it. He gave Hendricks a funny look. "All right, listen. I will explain. You see, you have discovered that this girl has betrayed you. You have been screwing her, and it has been very good, and whenever

137

you see her, you get a hard-on, you know? But now a new emotion takes hold of you, even when you are in the process of pulling her clothes off. You remember what she has done behind your back, and you become furious, and you hit her. You see?"

"Sure, but—"

"So you must show the audience what you are feeling. You must let them see it, so that they will know why you hit her. When they see your face, and they know what you are feeling, then the blow, when you give it to her, will have much more impact on their emotions." He studied Hendricks curiously for a moment. "Okay?"

The American nodded. He felt sheepish, even stupid. Goddamn it, he should have seen that, should have understood it without having to ask. Livorno was absolutely right. He was an asshole and the director was a pro. Shit. He stepped to his marks.

"All right," Antonio said loudly. "Let's make another one. Slate!"

They ran through the scene again, and Hendricks carried out the moves precisely as Livorno had shown him, pulling his lips back over his clenched teeth and scowling fiercely before his hard slap sent Rosalie spinning to the floor. He stood over her for a few seconds, looking down at her, his face controted with hatred.

"Okay," Livorno said at last. "Cut." His voice was quiet, matter-of-fact. "We'll print that."

Hendricks felt let down. If he'd finally played the goddamn thing properly, why didn't Livorno say so? He flushed as he realized that he had expected a compliment or at least some indication of approval. But the director had turned away to discuss the next shot with Weaver and Antonio. Hendricks stretched and walked over to the table where the coffee urn stood. As he filled a cardboard cup with the steaming black liquid, he noticed that one of the gaffers was watching him. The man gave him a small, faintly superior smile and strolled away.

* * *

At dinner Hendricks didn't eat as much as he usually did. He also took it easy on the wine, which for him was also out of character.

Tina leaned over to him. "Do you feel all right?"

"Huh? Oh, yeah. I'm fine. Just thinking about something."

138

"Is there a problem? Do you want to talk about it?"

Hendricks glanced at her. If you had a problem, a real problem, you didn't discuss it. And if you ever did, you sure as hell didn't discuss it with a woman. "No, it's nothing. I was just thinking about something."

There was the customary animated conversation in the dining room as the crew, tired from the long, tedious day's work, eased their tensions with boisterous jokes and got a little high on the Almansa and the Valdepeñas. As usual a gray-blue cloud of smoke, a mixture of tobacco and cannabis, hung over the tables. Hendricks watched Livorno when the director got to his feet and wearily made his way out of the room. The American picked up a full bottle of the Almansa and two glasses and mumbled to Tina to excuse him.

He caught up with Livorno as the director was about to enter the library. "Hey Arturo, you got a minute?"

"Sure, what is it?"

Hendricks gestured with his head toward one of the rooms on the opposite side of the hall. "I thought maybe we could talk for a little bit."

Livorno gave him that somber, quizzical look again. His eyes were owlish behind the thick black-rimmed glasses. "Okay, but they will be showing the dailies soon."

"Yeah, I know. This'll only take a few minutes." Hendricks entered the small sitting room, the director following, and closed the door behind them. They sat down in comfortable chairs, and Hendricks filled their glasses with the Almansa. "Cheers."

Livorno raised his glass. "Salut."

The wine was robust and strong, the strongest of all Spanish wines, with an alcohol content of seventeen percent. The grapes from which it was made were grown in vineyards to the east of La Mancha, in the sweeping plains country that joins the Meseta to the coastal area of Alicante. In the short time he had been in Spain, Almansa had become Hendricks's favorite. He looked at the near black color of the wine and slowly drank half his glass. The Almansa was velvety and smooth on his tongue, its flavor a deceptive mask that disguised its power.

The director set his glass down on a small table. "So? What is on your mind?"

Hendricks's tone was respectful and earnest. "I wanted to talk about today. This afternoon, when we made the shot with Rosalie."

Livorno's face was expressionless. "Yes? What about it?"

Hendricks smiled. He readily understood why Livorno was wary. The director had to listen to a lot of crazy shit from actors all day long. "Well, it's just that, after you explained not only how you wanted the scene played, but why you wanted it that way, then I got it. I understood."

"Mm-hm." Livorno sipped his wine.

"What's bothering me is why I didn't get it before, why you practically had to draw me a picture."

The Italian shrugged. His face, under the wild mop of black hair, was deeply lined from fatigue. "That's what directors are for."

Hendricks leaned forward. "Sure, I know that. But what I'm asking is, doesn't a good actor, a really good performer, know those things himself?"

A small smile raised a corner of Livorno's mouth. "Sometimes. And sometimes not." He waved a hand. "Oh, the good ones, the really great ones, often know it better than the director does. But they are rare."

"Who are they, in your opinion?" Hendricks knew that the director would probably realize he was being flattered, being conned a little, but so what? He really wanted desperately to learn this, to understand this aspect of the profession.

Livorno sat up in his chair. It was apparent that the subject interested him. "I would say that the best of them, the number one in the world today, is Larry Olivier. The man can do anything, from Lear to a Scotland Yard detective. And the thing that is so wonderful about him is that he is always the character he is playing. He is never simply a charming British actor named Olivier who happens to be in a given role."

Hendricks was interested by the transformation that had taken place in Livorno. The director was suddenly wide awake and intensely involved in the conversation. "And after him, who then?"

"Mm. Perhaps John Gielgud. Or George C. Scott. That is another one who takes great pains to bring a character to life. His General Patton was fantastic. Patton was a man whose politics and character Scott hated, and yet he portrayed him with great faithfulness, warts and all. He even made you like the character, at least some of the time."

"What about Brando?"

Livorno drained his glass, and Hendricks refilled it. "Tremendous, but he is not so consistent. Also he is given to using tricks. He plays the character, but not like Olivier or

Scott. Brando cannot resist molding the part so that it is as much himself as it is the character. So what you get is not the Godfather, it is the Brando Godfather. Or the Brando Napoleon. Or the Brando Christian, as in *The Young Lions*."

"And others? Who are the good younger ones?"

The director snorted. "Younger ones? There aren't any."

"What about guys like Clint Eastwood or Burt Reynolds?"

"Clowns. Imposters. Eastwood lives up to his name by performing as if he were carved out of a tree in one piece. And Reynolds is a little boy who has stumbled into this wonderful joke. He gets to ride horses and drive fast cars and fuck pretty girls and all the while it is a great romp with his friends and he is making a fortune. It is what I call the Frank Sinatra approach to making a film."

"But there must be some young guys who are okay."

Livorno drank more of the Almansa. "Nicholson perhaps, sometimes. In *One Flew Over the Cuckoo's Nest* he was absolutely brilliant. And then there is Giannini. But he is another thing altogether. He is too much mesmerized by Wertmuller. She jerks the strings, and he dances around like a berserk puppet. Occasionally he is effective, but mostly he is a cow-eyed fool."

"I take it you don't really think much of Wertmuller, either?"

The director spat. "Her politics are ridiculous. She is all, how do you say, hung up on liberating women and the treatment of Jews and a lot of other nonsense."

"Uh-huh." Hendricks realized that asking Livorno about Wertmuller had been a mistake. Inquire about the Italian's opinion of another director's talent and what you got for an answer was a dissertation on politics.

"The real issues, the really important social problems, she gives the back of her hand. Or as in *Seven Beauties*, she turns them into a pathetic little satire, for the love of God." He waved his long fingers in a gesture of frustration. "What is one to do with such a cunt?"

Hendricks grinned. "The same thing you'd do with any other cunt, I guess." He was glad to see Livorno laugh. It gave him an excuse to get the hell away from this dreary subject. He leaned forward, his face again sober. "Of course, what I'm really getting at is, what can I do to improve myself? What can I do so that I'll know better about how to handle a scene like today?"

Livorno peered at him with his magnified owl eyes. He

smiled. "You really are serious about this acting, aren't you, Hendricks?"

"Serious? Christ, I've never been more serious about anything in my life. Do you know what this means to me, working on this picture?"

Livorno's expression continued to show amusement. "Yes, I think I know."

The American raised his hand. "In one shot, I went from a seagoing bum to a guy who might, just might, make it as an actor. Shit, I know it's a long shot, that I don't know fuck-all about this business, but I sure as hell am trying to learn."

The director's face grew serious. "Yes, I'll give you that. You have tried as hard as anyone I have ever worked with."

"Okay, and what I'm getting is a mixed reaction. When they run the dailies, a lot of people in the crew say I look pretty good. But then, like today, when I show how fucking ignorant I am, I'm nothing but a joke. Arturo, what the hell can I do to learn?"

Livorno slumped back in his chair. He stared pensively at Hendricks for a long moment before he replied. "I cannot teach you. That is, I can help, a little, but the real learning you will have to do yourself. When you are back in Rome, you should go to a drama coach. There are several good ones there, and I will give you some names. You should also see as many movies as you can. Good ones, bad ones, any kind. All of them will help you."

Hendricks nodded. "Sure, I will. But what can I do now, while we're on this shoot, to improve myself?"

Livorno sipped Almansa. "For one thing, you should continue to learn everything you can about the technical aspects of making pictures. That is very good. And incidentally, you should also learn something about editing."

"About what?"

"Editing. The cutting together of all these miles of shit we have been shooting. On a decent picture, with a decent budget, the editor would be here, watching the filming, making suggestions, consulting with me, planning how he will cut together the shots to make the scenes as effective as possible. Naturally there is no editor here because of that cockhead Morello and his niggardly budget." His face darkened. "That money-grubbing, art-exploiting eater of shit."

"Sure. But what else? I mean, aside from the technical stuff?"

The director drained his glass, and again Hendricks refilled it. When Livorno replied, he spoke very slowly. "You must make yourself become much more sensitive. That is the secret, the real secret, of becoming a great actor. Technique is something the drama coach will give you. And what experience will help you to learn. But the most important thing of all is how you look at life and everything that goes on around you."

"Can you explain that—be more specific?"

"Yes. I will tell you exactly what I mean." Livorno rested his head against the back of his chair and stared at the ceiling. "The ordinary things in living are of no moment. That is, brushing your teeth or reading a newspaper or taking a shit. They are nothing. But the relationships between people, the motives, the loves, the hatreds, the jealousies—they are everything. You must train yourself to be constantly aware of them. Over and over again you must ask, why? Why did he do this, or she that? Why did a man think as he did or feel as he did in a certain situation? What was he trying to achieve, and above all, why? How did he look when this or that was happening? How did he move? What were the emotions you could read on his face? Then, for a few minutes every day, you should stand in front of a mirror and practice facial expressions. Run the entire gamut, from surprise to rage to suspicion to fear. Make yourself laugh, and make yourself cry." Livorno brought his gaze down to Hendricks's face. "And then learn to read a script."

Hendricks's mouth opened. "Read a script? Jesus Christ, there hasn't been a day since I've been here that I didn't know the scene cold when I came to work."

Livorno smiled. "That is exactly my point."

"What is?" Hendricks wished the director wouldn't talk in fucking riddles.

"You memorize the scenes, and it is true that you know your part every time you come onto the set. But you haven't the faintest idea of what the scene is really all about or what it will do to move the story forward. It is obvious that you try hard to prepare yourself, and for that I commend you. Most actors are lazy shits who want the director to do all their work for them. But what I am telling you is that if you really want to become a great actor, then you must dig deep under the skin of the character you are playing. You must burrow like an animal all the way down into that character's soul. You must know precisely why he is doing a certain thing and precisely how he feels while he is doing it and why. And then you must determine carefully just how you are going to reveal this information to the audience.

"You see, motion pictures are really a very subtle medium. Most people, and especially theater snobs, do not understand that at all. They consider live performances art and movies pop culture. But that is absurd. The fact is that the theater is very restrictive in the limitations it imposes on the playwright. He is handicapped by the fact that all the action must take place within the confines of that small, shallow strip of stage. And all the actors must project their lines so that each speech is clearly audible in the last seat in the last row of the balcony. But with film, the screenwriter and the director can do anything. They can have an actor whisper, or show a close-up of his hand on a lady's tit, or bend time forward or backward, and do a thousand other things that give new dimensions to drama as no other medium every has. Can you imagine what Shakespeare would have done with film? Or Chekhov or Molière? Christ, it makes your mind whirl to think about it."

"Yeah, but you were saying—"

"Yes, I know. I was wandering. What I am telling you is that you must do everything you can to develop sensitivity to the point that you know why the character you are playing does something better than the writer himself knows. And then you must learn to give that understanding to the audience. Do you follow?"

"Yes. I follow." Hendricks was aware of a strange, growing excitement. He could feel it in his chest, as if he were involved in something thrilling and a little dangerous. It was a feeling he did not understand and could not analyze, but it was there.

Livorno smiled. "So. I didn't mean to give you such a lecture, but you asked."

"Hey, listen. That's exactly the kind of thing I wanted to hear. I—"

The door opened and Antonio thrust his head into the room. "Arturo! I've been looking all over hell for you. Signor Morello wants you for the screening. He's furious that you've kept everybody waiting."

Livorno looked calmly at the assistant producer. "Fuck Signor Morello."

Antonio grinned. "No thank you. I can do better than that."

The director got to his feet slowly. "I doubt it."

Antonio winked at Hendricks and left the room, Livorno following.

"Say, Arturo?"

Livorno turned back to Hendricks. "Yes?"

"I just wanted to say thanks. I really appreciate your telling me those things."

"Hm? Yes. You're welcome." The director seemed preoccupied. He blinked behind the thick glasses. "Don't forget what I said about sensitivity. And one other thing."

"Sure. What is it?"

"You should try to remember everything that is exciting or interesting that happens in your life, including the things that have happened in the past. You should think about those times and try to recall them as scenes. And not just things that happen to you, either. Sometimes the most valuable occurrences are ones that have happened to someone else, and then the person tells you about it. Seeing those stories, recreating them in your mind, is fantastic training."

Hendricks felt the excitement rise again in his chest.

Livorno was speaking very slowly. "You see, that is where it must all happen, in the end. If you are to become an actor, a real actor, it must happen in your mind." The director walked out of the room and across the hall into the library.

chapter 26

The room was fairly well filled with people. They sprawled on the folding chairs and looked at the takes flashing one after another on the screen, whispering among themselves and occasionally oohing and ahing over the flickering picture.

Hendricks sat among them and saw nothing. Instead he felt his excitement rise even higher as he thought about what Livorno had told him. He was positive that he had learned something of enormous value, if only he could harness and control the concept the director had expressed to him.

Jesus, what a wild idea. It was like making a theater—or better still, a movie screen—out of the inside of your head. It was dizzying to think about. You took your emotions and your memory and your awareness and you put them to work for you and that helped you to become—what? An actor, a

145

real actor, as Livorno had said? No. It was something bigger than that. A lot bigger. Hendricks felt a sense of awe as he realized that what he was begining to get hold of was the thought of becoming a creator on film.

Holy shit. Where did he come off screwing around with something like that? One minute waking up with a head-busting hangover, out of a job on the beach at Portofino, and the next minute he was going to become another De Laurentiis. He laughed out loud at the absurdity of it. One of the members of the crew sitting nearby glanced curiously at him, but Hendricks was unaware. He felt ebullient, almost giddy, as he ruminated on the concept. He went back over the things Livorno had told him, and the more he thought about them, the more exhilarated he felt.

Livorno had said that some of the best experiences were the ones that were related by other people. All right, that made sense. You were taking the story you had been told and you were making pictures out of it in your mind. You were building what the words told you into a drama. Who had told him stories like that, and when?

* * *

It was one bell on the four-to-eight morning watch. The tanker *Fort Cumberland*, bound for Bayonne, New Jersey, with a million and a half barrels of Arabian crude, pitched heavily into the black waters of the North Atlantic. Her bow dug deep into the roiling swells, flinging salt spray over the foc'sle head and the foredeck all the way to the midships house. On the starboard wing of the bridge Hendricks stood alongside the chief mate, who had relieved him a half hour earlier. Hendricks was off now until noon, when he would again stand the twelve-to-four, and he had nothing to do but go below for breakfast and then crawl into his bunk for six hours or so. But he was in no rush. The sky in the east was beginning to turn gray, and he loved this time of the morning, when the predawn air was fresh and clean and the only sounds were the steady beat of the ship's engines and the roar of the ocean as the big tanker dove through the heavy seas.

And besides, the mate was good company. He was a burly man, thick in the chest and shoulders, with a square-jawed face and a shock of black hair. His name was Elmer Johnson, and he was from Eagle Island, Maine. Like Hendricks, he was a deep-water man who had spent virtually all his working life

146

on the sea, from the age of eight when one of his chores was hauling the family lobster pots into his dory and harvesting the catch. He was about fifty now, Hendricks judged, and he had been shipping out in tankers ever since his discharge from the navy at the end of World War Two.

"It's a funny thing," Johnson said. He had a strong Down East accent that Hendricks liked to listen to. "But I hate cold weather. I grew up where it was so cold winters I'd get up in the morning and the piss would be frozen in the pot under my bed. You'd think I'd have got used to it by now, but I never did."

Hendricks pulled his cap lower on his head. He felt a fine encrustment on the visor, and when he touched his lips with his tongue, he tasted salt; both were a residual from the incessant spray. He was wearing a fleece-lined oilskin and under that a thick, white wool turtleneck and long underwear and dungarees and wool socks and felt boots and seaboots over those, but he was chilly nevertheless. It wasn't only the cold but the rawness that sank deep into your flesh at night on the North Atlantic.

"Give me the Pacific any time," Johnson went on. "That's the kind of weather a man can really live in."

Hendricks smiled. "So why don't you go down there?"

The chief mate snorted. "And do what? There's no jobs there, except maybe on some shitbox freighter running copra. No thank you. I'll take tankers any time. Even where it's cold."

"You spent much time in that part of the world?"

"The Pacific? Some. Enough to like the climate."

"Was that during the war?"

"Yep. I was on a destroyer most of the time, leastwise till we got hit."

"Where was that?"

"Off the Solomons. We were a three-ship screen for a light cruiser. All three cans went down."

"What happened?"

The mate hunched his shoulders against the cold. "It was early morning, a little later than this. We were running near a fog bank, maybe a mile off of it, when out of that fog come a Jap battleship. I damn near shit. Turned out she was part of a good-sized force that had sneaked down there during the night. Radar was pretty crude in those days, and we never knew a thing about them until we saw that battleship. She must have been just as surprised as we were."

147

"And then she sank you?"

Johnson shook his head. "Our lead destroyer was skippered by a lieutenant commander named Buck Conroy. The captain of our ship was Frank Nelson. I forget the third guy's name. Anyhow, all three of them had played football together at the Naval Academy. I was just a kid striker at the time, but my station was on the bridge, so I could hear and see everything that went on. When that Jap sailed out of the fog, Conroy's voice come over the radio. He said real quiet, 'Jesus Christ.' You see, there was no way the light cruiser we were screening was any match for the Jap wagon, and at that range she was too close to run for it."

Hendricks felt the hairs prickle on the back of his neck. "What did you do?"

"Well, in an action between capital vessels, the book says that destroyers are expendable. A second later Buck Conroy's voice come over that radio again as calm as could be. This time he just said, 'Let's go, Navy.' And Nelson said back, 'All the way, Buck.' And then the three cans swung right for that fucking battleship."

"Good God."

"Yeah. I was never so shit scared in all my life. We were zigzagging, the three of us, and firing and dropping torpedoes, but it was like hound pups snapping at a bear. The Jap just depressed those sixteen inchers and started blasting. The shells were so big you could see them coming, like fiery blue balls flying through the air. One of them hit our three-inch-fifties on the foredeck and just cleared the turret right off. One second it was there and the next there was only smoke and fire. But we kept right on going. Conroy's ship got it first. She must have took one in the magazine. Went up with one big boom, and when the smoke cleared, she was gone. I couldn't see the third can, and by this time our ship was in pretty rough shape too. She'd slowed down a lot, and we were on fire everywhere, but we kept on. When we were only a hundred yards or so from the Jap, I realized what Nelson was going to do. He said to the helmsman, 'Come hard right,' and when we were dead on the battleship, he said, 'Steady as she goes.'"

"Jesus."

"Yeah. Nelson was a big guy. He played tackle at the academy, I think. Anyhow, I can still see him standing in that wheelhouse, his legs wide apart, his cap shoved back a little. He said, 'All the way, Navy.' And then we rammed the Jap wagon."

Hendricks shivered a little as he saw in his mind the scene Johnson had described. "What happened then?"

"I'm not sure, exactly. Except that our can sank and somehow I got free."

"What about the battleship?"

"The last I saw her, she was on fire too, and she had a hell of a port list and was turning back into the fog."

"So your cruiser got away?"

"Yeah, she made it. I spent twenty hours or so in the water hanging onto a piece of wreckage, and the next day a PT boat came by and picked me up."

"Christ, were you lucky."

"Don't I know it? Most everybody else on that destroyer is still with her, including Frank Nelson."

Both men were quiet for a moment, and then the chief mate turned and spat into the lee. "You know, I did a lot of thinking in all that time I was in the water. I thought about what had happened and how those skippers had acted, and why. And I think I figured out something."

"What's that?"

"Well, when Conroy said 'Let's go, Navy,' he wasn't being some asshole gung-ho shouting 'Hurray for the U.S.A.' or any of that shit. I figured out that what he was really doing was leading his old teammates, just like they were going down the field against Notre Dame or Army."

"Yeah. I can understand that."

"Sure. Being on a team does that to a guy, you know? And later on, when I grew up, I thought about it some more, and I realized that playing with a team is really man's nature. You think about it. We started out hunting together, in packs. We had to fight together as a team, and we had to protect each other, and sometimes, up against a mammoth or a saber-toothed tiger or one of those things, some of us got killed. But it's the instinct of man to band together in a hunting pack, and that's part of why playing on a team means so much to a guy, and why once he does, he carries a great pride with him for the rest of his life, and he never forgets it."

"You're probably right, Elmer."

"Yeah. I'm pretty sure I am."

Hendricks suddenly felt tired. He wished the mate a good morning and descended the ladder from the wing of the bridge to the catwalk that ran aft to where the messroom was. The ship rolled under his feet, and on the horizon he could see yellow fingers of light streaking the leaden sky.

149

Matthew Weaver stood looking down at Hendricks. "Hey, wake up. Movies are over. You don't want to sit here the whole fucking night, do you?"

Hendricks smiled. "Not exactly."

Weaver scratched his beard. "What do you say we go get a booze?"

"I say that sounds like a good idea." Hendricks got to his feet and stretched. As he walked out of the library, he was aware of a continuing sense of exhilaration. He was a man who had discovered a fabulous secret.

chapter 27

In the history of the tiny village, there had never been anything like the production of *The Hired Gun*. Thirty years earlier, during the civil war, there had been excitement too, but that was different. That had been a bad time, when the Fascist regiment came marching along the dusty road, led by two armored cars, and seized the squalid little settlement. The soldiers were there only a few days, but their retribution against those villagers who had opposed Generalissimo Francisco Franco was terrible and swift.

Now, however, with the filming of this *pelicula*, it was a good time. In a village where the passing of an automobile was something special to see, the antics of the production company were a never ending source of fascination to the inhabitants. The villagers watched the crew roar around in a whole fleet of cars and trucks, as if petrol were no more valuable than water. They watched the staging of galloping posses and stampeding cattle and of gunfights and saloon brawls. They saw beautiful women parade about in shamelessly brief costumes that were a blasphemy against God but a delight to look at, although the sight all but produced a myocardial infarction in the heart of Father Pedro, priest of the church of Santa Maria. They gazed upon wondrous pieces of equipment that cost millions of pesetas, including a crane which could whisk three men and a camera high into the air at the mere touch of a button. And best of all, they watched the crew spend money as if it were so much confetti.

At first those in the village who had something to sell, whether merchandise or services, were hesitant about increasing their prices when crew members came to buy. But then they observed, to their astonishment, that doubling, or even tripling, the charge for a bottle of *cerveza* or a piece of *queso* or the hourly rate for running errands was of no moment to the crew whatever. Soon these entrepeneurs were enjoying unheard of profits for their time and wares, albeit on the basis of two price structures: one for the members of the film crew, and another uninflated one for their fellow citizens.

Moreover, for the first time in anyone's memory, this was a period of one-hundred-percent employment for the inhabitants of the village. Any person who could walk or crawl or be carried in his mother's arms was hired as an extra for the filming. The work itself was ideal. Most of the time one was required only to stand or sit about and wait, while the technicians struggled with their equipment or the director and the producer and the actors conferred among themselves. Even this could be amusing, for frequently such discussions became loud arguments, and several times the participants came close to blows. Then it would finally be time to shoot, and the extras would be involved in a few minutes of action as the camera rolled, after which there would be more paid idleness. The only flaw in this employment was that the man who oversaw the hiring had none of the generosity of the other members of the crew. This one's name was Antonio, and he paid the lowest wages he could. Still there were jobs for all, and for every single person in the village to be earning money was beyond their wildest dreams. The people concluded that all those of the film industry were millionaires, not grasping that many of their extravagant customers were themselves often unemployed, and that even though inflation was rising fast in Spain, it would be some time before the nation's inept government could catch up with the runaway spiral which blighted the other countries of Europe.

The presence of the crew also had a corruptive influence on the morals of the young women in the village. There were not many of them who had passed pubescence and were not yet married, and those few had been subjected to the strictest kind of Catholic upbringing, as well as to the customs imposed by centuries of Spanish tradition in which the virginity

151

of an unbethrothed female was guarded like the crown of Isabella. Nevertheless these young ladies were not about to miss the opportunity to consort with the carefree, glamorous, rollicking, hell-raising members of Vicente Morello's company. It would be, they knew instinctively, an experience they would cherish for the remainder of their otherwise drab lives. So in defiance of their parents' admonitions they crept from their beds at night and they danced and they ate and they drank wine and they sang songs and they made love until the sky in the east turned yellow and the cocks began to crow.

Thus for the tiny settlement the time of *The Hired Gun* was a good time indeed. In fact, virtually the only person in the entire village who was not pleased by the largesse of the film company was Father Pedro. To be sure, the wages earned by the villagers were reflected in a dramatic upturn in the offerings collected by the priest when he conducted mass in his ancient church. But the padre knew that this was but a small and temporary swelling of his coffers. What bothered him far more than the public drinking and carousing, more than the heathenous revelation of the actresses' flesh, more than the sexual congress he suspected was taking place between the girls of the village and the crewmen, was that the film company had vast amounts of money and what his church was seeing of it was a mere pittance. The priest thought about this, and he fretted, but he was fundamentally an optimist and so he bided his time. As he saw it, the proximity of the film company represented an opportunity which, in one way or another, would eventually present itself.

That presentation came in the form of a fight which occurred one day among Morello, Antonio, Livorno, and Matthew Weaver. It was late afternoon, and the company had been working for most of the day in the café. The men were standing outside it arguing, their voices growing louder and their tones more heated. Father Pedro had been walking by when the argument erupted, and he stopped now and stood quietly among a small group of villagers who were listening to the quarrel. The men's differences, the priest inferred, centered around the fact that there were very few buidings in the village which were more than one story high.

"I don't give a damn," Livorno snarled. His sweating face was red with emotion. "If I must direct this dog's cunt of a picture, then there must be integrity in my work."

Morello leaned toward the director. "And I say what in hell difference does it make?"

"It makes a great deal of difference," the director shouted. "Don't you see? I cannot stage a fight on a rooftop and have a man fall to his death when he is one ridiculous story above the ground. The audience would be hysterical at such a farce. It would be more believable if he were to drown in a pile of cowshit."

Morello rolled his eyes skyward in disgust.

Antonio tried a conciliatory approach. "Listen, Arturo. Of course you want the scene to be believable. We all do. But it is not our fault that no tall buildings are available."

"The barn down there," Morello pointed. "What about that?"

The director shook his head. "No good. We have looked at it. The pitch of the roof is too steep. There is no place to stand on it."

"What we should do," Antonio said, "is fake it." He turned to Weaver. "You can do that, can't you? You shoot the action from a low angle, looking up at the men silhouetted against the sky. Then the audience will never know that the men are not so far above the ground."

The cameraman spat into the dust. "Won't work. We've got to show them in an establishing shot. And as a matter of fact, the right way to do the scene is to cut back and forth with the action. Close-ups with an occasional long shot of them slugging each other on the roof. No way you can fake that."

Livorno waved his hands. "The answer, in God's name, is to change the script. Is there anything so complicated about doing that?"

"No!" Morello's jaw jutted forward. "We will not change the script. This fight is essential to the story. It is how the killer destroys the sheriff, and it must stay in."

"So the killer destroys the sheriff," Livorno snapped. "But where is it engraved in stone that he must destroy him by knocking him off a roof?"

The producer exhaled through clenched teeth. "I want the scene because it will be different. It is the one time the killer uses his fists to kill an enemy instead of his gun. And it is the one time the action takes place on an elevation other than ground level."

Livorno's voice rose again. "But there is no drama, I tell you! I cannot make the action work with these miserable squat hovels."

It was at this point that divine providence gave Father Pedro inspiration, as he had believed with consummate faith

153

it sooner or later would. He stepped forward and spoke shyly. "Please excuse me."

"Not now, Father," Antonio said.

The priest stepped closer. "But I have a suggestion," he persisted.

Morello stared at the shabbily robed cleric. "What is it?"

Father Pedro turned and extended his hand. "The church. It is taller by far than most of the other buildings here in the village. And along the ridge of the roof it is flat. Would it not serve your purposes?"

The producer squinted against the rays of the setting sun. "I will be goddamned. Forgive me, Father." He turned to the others. "He's right, do you know that?"

Antonio was excited. "Perfect. A perfect solution. Falling off that thing, anybody would be killed instantly."

"I don't know," Livorno said. "What would they be doing on top of a church?"

"The same thing they would be doing on top of any other building," Morello replied. "The sheriff is up there trying to shoot the killer, and the killer goes up after him. If they could be on top of the saloon, as in the script, why not on top of the church?"

Livorno was unconvinced. "How do they get up there?"

"There is a stairway in the bell tower," the priest said.

Antonio hopped up and down. "You see? You see? It would work beautifully. Matthew, what about it?"

The cameraman shielded his eyes with his hand. "Yeah. It could work. It's even kind of nice, you know? I mean, it's supposed to be a holy place and everything, and those two cocksuckers are up there trying to knock each other's brains out." He spat. "I like it."

Morello looked at his watch. "Let us get over there and see."

As the priest had suggested, the church was the ideal building on which to stage the scene. It would open, the film makers decided, with the sheriff crouching in the bell tower as the killer rode into town. The sheriff would attempt to snipe the killer with his Winchester and fail, whereupon the killer would make his way to the roof, and the fight would commence. The longer they studied it, the more pleased they became with the crumbling old building. Even Livorno grew enthusiastic. Most of the close-ups they would shoot from the crane, and Weaver and Livorno worked out an additional angle they would get by positioning the Arriflex in the bell tower.

The director wiped sweat from his face. "It's good. Really very good. And the fall will look beautiful. He can bounce once, off the edge there, and we'll catch him sailing through the air on the way down."

"Sure." Weaver studied the roof. "For one take, we could even put the camera here on the ground, looking up, you know? Then you'd see his body twisting as he came down."

Livorno glanced at the sky. "Too bad it is so late in the day. If the light were better, I would attempt to shoot some of it now."

"Impossible," Weaver said. "We'd never get it to match in the morning."

"Yes. But it is so good I am anxious to get at it."

"Sure."

"What about Scalzi?" Antonio asked.

Livorno turned to the assistant producer. "What about him?"

"I would like to hear what he thinks," Antonio said. Scalzi was the stunt man they had brought with the company from Rome. On Morello's budget, they could afford only one, and Scalzi thus far had been photographed while doubling as a dance-hall girl being punched in the face by a cowboy, as a rancher falling from a wagon, and as a drunk being kicked by a horse.

"Sure," Antonio said. "Let's get him over here."

The stunt man was a trim, compact former athlete. He looked up at the church roof with an experienced eye. "No problem. I could even do a flip, if you want. After I hit the edge there."

Livorno grinned. "Lovely. Just lovely."

"You want me to do the whole fight?" Scalzi asked.

The director shook his head. "No. All of the action on the rooftop must be with Caserta and Hendricks. When Caserta finally knocks Hendricks off the roof, we cut away for a long shot. That's where we pick you up."

The men discussed the scene a few minutes longer, and then Morello ordered Antonio to have the crew strike their equipment for the day. They moved off toward the cars, still talking animatedly about what they would do in the morning.

No one said anything more to Father Pedro before leaving, not even to thank him for his suggestion. But he did not mind. One of the priest's stock-in-trade was forgiveness and another was understanding human nature. What Father Pedro needed to do next, he knew, was to have a discussion with

155

Aldo Jifero. A good friend of the pastor, Jifero was the owner of the village café. He was also the only man in the entire settlement who had ever received any training in the law.

chapter 28

The bed dated from the time of the Moors. It was a four-poster, built entirely of ebony, and its intricately carved columns were tall and graceful. Juan Navarro lay quiet on the cool white sheets, his brown body sprawled out comfortably. He put his arm gently around the girl's shoulder and held her close to him. Her skin was warm and smooth to his touch, and her hair smelled sweet to him. It was early afternoon, and the air was mild and pleasant, and the sunlight filtering through the lace of the draperies cast a dappled pattern of gold and black shadows on the far wall.

Tina turned her face and looked up at him. "I'm glad you are back. It must have been very hard for you."

"No funeral is a pleasant thing," Navarro said. "It is simply something you must go through, at various times in your life. In mine, because of the profession I was in for so long, I have perhaps attended more than the usual number."

"Were you in the funeral?"

"Yes, a pallbearer. With his brother and his manager and the members of his *cuadrilla*."

"The television news said it was one of the largest funerals ever held in Madrid."

"I'm sure it was," Navarro said. "Grief is an infectious emotion, and also a noble one, because it gives us the opportunity to display to each other how much we care."

"That sounds cynical."

Navarro shrugged. "Perhaps. But the funeral had nothing to do with Zuelos. I said good-bye to him in Montillas, in the clinic, when I held his hand and felt his life slip away from him."

She shivered a little, and he stroked her shoulder. "The television said he was very great, perhaps even greater than Manolete."

156

"Mm. That is another advantage of a hero's death. It tends to elevate one's niche in history."

"You shouldn't speak that way. He was your friend."

Navarro smiled. "And he would have been the first to agree with that statement. Who are the top matadors in the annals of tauromachy? Joselito, Manolete, and now Ricardo Zuelos. All dead on the horns."

Tina touched her finger to a ridge of scar tissue on his chest. "You sound as if you envy them."

"Not so. In Spain we have a proverb. No man would die young, but no man would grow old. It does not apply to bullfighters."

Her voice teased him a little. "And what about you, Juan? Are you growing old?"

"Of course I am. By the day."

"I hadn't noticed."

"That's good. But I am not surprised. The last thing a matador loses is the rigidity of his sword."

She pushed him playfully. "And which have you conquered more of with it—girls or bulls?"

"I really can't say. I would have to consult my book of records."

"That's dreadful," Tina said. She was quiet for a moment. "How many times were you married?"

"Twice, officially."

"And where are they now, your wives?"

"The first one lives in Barcelona. She remarried and has eight children, I have heard."

"But none by you?"

"No. We were married when we were little more than children ourselves. Her family was horrified."

"Because you were a bullfighter?"

"Because I was an unsuccessful bullfighter. At the time I was just starting out, and all during the long season I was never home. Most of the time I lived in the back seat of my manager's car as we drove back and forth across the country. I fought terrible bulls in shabby little rings in towns whose names I have mostly forgotten."

She touched the scar again. "And you were often injured?"

"Often. When you fight bulls, there is only one way you learn from the mistakes you make."

"And what happened, then, with your wife?"

"When I was gone, her family worked on her. They were merchants, and they looked down on me as if I were vermin.

157

One day I came home from the hospital in Valladolid. I had been gored in the ring there. When I got to our tiny apartment in Madrid, she was gone. There was a letter there, waiting for me, from her family's lawyer. It said that our marriage had been annulled. Divorce is illegal, you know. But as with anything else, when one has money, a satisfactory result can be achieved."

"Yes. An unfortunate truth."

"Not unfortunate. Merely a truth."

"And the second one, the actress. What happened to her?"

"She ran off with a matador, I think I told you. I was retired, and he was at the very top of his career."

"Is she still with him?"

"No. He also faded, in time. And then she moved to someone else."

"And then what?"

"And then the years grew heavy for her also, and she found one day that she was no longer either young or pretty. It is the surprise that all beautiful women believe they will never experience, but always do."

"How did she take it?"

"Badly. She began to drink. Or rather, she began to drink more heavily. And instead of the drinking being a part of the long celebration she deluded herself into thinking she was making of her life, it became her life. The alcohol hastened the aging and the ugliness. And so of course in self-pity she drank more."

"Did you ever see her?"

"A few times. The last occasion was in a restaurant in Barcelona. I hardly recognized her. But she knew me."

"Did you speak with her?"

"Oh, yes. We exchanged a few meaningless words."

"Was she sad?"

"You would prefer that, wouldn't you? It would be fitting to the kind of sorrowful story of lost love women fashion when they try to imagine such things. But in reality she was only bitter. Oddly, she blamed me for her misfortunes. But I suppose that was because it would be much easier to do that than to blame herself."

"Lois Peters," Tina said.

"Yes."

"I have seen some of her old films. She was really very beautiful. When she was young."

"Very. But she was not talented. That was the trouble, you

see. When the beauty was gone, there was nothing left. When there is talent, as with some of the older stars, then they have something with which to cross that bridge. But Lois did not have it."

"It is the rarest thing," Tina said. "Talent. I hope I have it."

Navarro kissed her hair. "From what I have heard, from Morello and Livorno and the others, you have a great deal of it."

"I hope so."

"There seems to be only one person in the company who believes that you do not."

Tina turned her head to look up at him. "Who is that?"

There was a suggestion of a smile on his mouth. "Cecily Petain."

"Oh, you." Tina slapped his belly lightly and returned her head to its former position on his shoulder.

Navarro stretched and lay quiet. He dozed, for a time.

*   *   *

Tina listened to the steady beating of Juan Navarro's heart. Its rhythm seemed very slow to her, and she recalled reading somewhere that all great athletes had low pulse rates. After what she had seen that day in Montillas, God knew that to be a ranking matador, one had to be a great athlete indeed. She thought about the awful events she had witnessed in the *corrida* and shuddered involuntarily. Life was so short, and so full of unexpected twists and turns.

It was also often hard to fathom, especially your own role in it. She was deeply in love with Hendricks, more passionately than she had ever believed she could be with any man, and yet now she was in bed with someone else. What was more, she did not feel at all guilty about it but only a little sad. Why was that? She tried to analyze her emotions and concluded that there were two reasons for them that she could identify.

The first was that it was actually possible to compartmentalize how you felt about one person, so as to keep it from affecting the way you felt about someone else. And in a totally different way from her feeling for Hendricks, she loved Juan Navarro. He was steady and kind and wise, and he seemed to understand so much. Not only about how people thought and acted and why they did, but about Tina herself. He knew her hopes and her anxieties, and he knew when to react seriously to the problems she described to him and when to joke with

159

her to change her mood. He knew when to suggest and when to comment, and when to say nothing, which was also important. And when he did speak to her, what he said invariably helped her to see what she should do. He was the kind of man a woman dreamed of spending her life with.

The second reason was her growing conviction that Hendricks would never be hers. At first she had pretended to herself that it was possible that he would change, and that in time he would return her love as strongly as she gave it. But that, she now forced herself to admit, was a beautiful illusion, one she had fashioned to comfort herself. Instead of growing closer to her, he was now just so much more casual. And the longer they stayed at La Cuarta Luna, the more the big blond American became the hero of the company, which she decided also had a direct bearing on their relationship.

To nearly everyone's growing admiration, Hendricks was developing what appeared to be a genuine talent for acting. Astonishingly photogenic from the start, he now had learned a good deal in the relatively short time they had been in Spain. Watching the dailies was like seeing the development of his skill recorded on undercranked film. Each day he seemed smoother, more poised, and most important of all, more natural. He also, she perceived with bittersweet awareness, had learned the most difficult trick of all, the ability to project onto film the essence of his slightly picaresque, self-effacing, who-gives-a-damn good humor that women, including herself, found so irresistible. He would be, she was convinced, not only the success he hoped, but far more of a success than even he could imagine. If Hendricks would be hard to hold onto as a penniless sailor who had been fired from his job on a yacht, what would he be like as an exciting new talent in motion pictures? The answer was not hard to imagine, and as Tina thought about it, she felt her sadness deepen. She wanted so much for him to have the success he was struggling hard to achieve, but she had no doubt that the achievement would take him farther and farther away from her.

Navarro stirred in his sleep, and Tina pulled herself up a little and looked at him. In repose the strong brown face seemed younger, less hard. She tried to imagine what this man had looked like when he had been a great matador, as great in his time as Ricardo Zuelos had been in his. She decided that he must have been remarkably handsome. He would have been not quite as fine featured as Zuelos, but slightly more coarse. And that would only have made him seem more masculine. Even now, nearing sixty, he was powerfully attractive.

She looked at his body, finding it also appealing. The skin was still firm and taut over the ropy musculature. Only the scars were there to suggest the life he had led as a bullfighter. And what a life that must have been. The curving patches of shiny tissue were everywhere on his torso and his legs.

As her gaze drifted over Navarro's dozing form, Tina's eyes stopped on his penis, and she felt herself respond. Flaccid now, it was still long and thick, curling against his leg as if it too were asleep. A pearlescent drop hung at its tip. Reacting to an impulse, she reached down and touched her fingertip to the drop. The fluid was thin and slightly sticky as she pressed it between her thumb and forefinger.

As she watched, the penis twitched and began to swell. It thickened and grew longer and moved away from his leg, increasing in size until it was almost twice as big as it had been at rest. It seemed to her to act as if it had a life and a will of its own. Within seconds it was fully erect, standing stiff at an angle down his belly.

Tina suddenly realized that she had become extremely excited. There was something doubly erotic about causing this to happen while Navarro slept, as if she were keeping an illicit tryst between herself and the matador's cock. She drew herself up onto her knees and crouched over his still form, moving her face close to his penis. She touched the shaft lightly with one hand, feeling the blood course through it, each pulsebeat throbbing in the distended, purplish glans. With the other hand she reached down and stroked herself.

When she was very near to orgasm, Tina brought her face closer, and as gently as she could encircled the tip of the penis with her lips. The skin was hot and smooth, and the head seemed to fill her mouth. The matador's heartbeats were much more perceptible to her now. She forced herself to take more and more of him into her, feeling his cock press against the back of her throat. It tasted strong and slightly musty and she was reminded that every man's was different, as individual as he was himself. She moved her head up and down and up again, slowly and steadily, in an exact rhythm, the glands in her mouth exuding saliva, her tongue sliding from side to side on the underside of the shaft.

Navarro groaned, and Tina felt a warmth spread from between her legs along the nerves and tissues and muscles of her body, the orgasm seizing her and holding her in an exquisite tension. She quickened the movement then of her bobbing head as she heard the sounds issue from deep in his chest. His body tensed. "Jesus God, woman. Don't stop now." Tina moved her lips and her tongue, tightening her grip on him, her excitement now all but unbearable as she sucked him, her head dipping and rising faster and faster, urging him, exhorting him.

Navarro's cock jerked convulsively, and a scalding stream of semen spurted into Tina's mouth. She could feel it spilling into her, onto her tongue and running from the corners of her lips. She swallowed once and held her head still then, conscious that almost immediately the penis had begun to relax, as if it had made an effort so supreme as to have given up its life, and it was dying now, diminishing once more to a limp flaccidity.

Her own heart pounding, her breath coming in gasps, Tina fell over beside him on the bed. She lay quiet, listening to the intermingled sounds of their breathing in the large, shadowy room. A slight breeze had risen, and it stirred the lace draperies. They billowed gently inward from the windows.

Navarro's voice was soft and slightly hoarse. "That was beautiful."

She did not answer.

His hand touched her back, stroking it lightly. "I love you, Tina."

Still she made no response. Her sadness had deepened. The French had a term for it, she reflected, as they did for everything. Something about sorrow after making love. In her mind's eye she saw Hendricks, and the ache in her grew stronger.

chapter 29

The sun rose at shortly after six o'clock, but it was not high enough to shoot by until nine. By that time the crew had done much work. The area around the church of Santa Maria was clustered with vehicles. The equipment van, the camera truck, the crane, the portable dressing rooms, the toilets which in film-makers' parlance were called honey wagons, the carpenter shop, and a scattering of automobiles, including Morello's Ferrari, which had been shipped in from Rome, were all parked nearby. Livorno was excited about the scene they were to shoot, and his enthusiasm was both contagious and inspiring. He raced around the location, shouting and giving orders.

Hendricks also felt very good. In fact, he realized as the makeup man worked on his face, he felt better than he had at any point in his entire adult life. For the first time in his memory, he was employing a regimen which combined a moderate diet with regular exercise. He ate high-protein foods with very little sugar or salt, restricting his carbohydrate intake mostly to that provided by fresh fruit. His drinking was confined almost entirely to wine, which he seldom drank except in the evening. And he now smoked no more than a handful of cigarettes a day, rather than the customary two or three packs. About the only thing he did not enjoy in moderation was sex, and that he took in as large quantities as he could. He was in absolutely superb condition, and this, he had discovered to his delight, not only increased his capacity for lovemaking, it sharpened his already powerful interest in it.

Antonio called to him that Livorno wanted to run through the scene, and after a final dab from the makeup man's sponge, Hendricks stepped over to where the director, the cameraman, and Carlos Caserta waited.

"We will block the action here," Livorno said. "On the ground. Then we'll shoot it up there on the roof."

Hendricks hitched up his jeans. "Okay."

Livorno pointed at the church. "We'll do the scene backward, starting with the fight, because it will be the most difficult part to make. The other stuff, the sniping from the bell tower and all that, we'll get later." He put one hand on Hendricks's shoulder, the other on Caserta's. "Listen closely, both of you, and I will explain to you exactly what I want to see in this fight."

To Hendricks's surprise Caserta was cooperative, even pleasant, as the director began to take them through his plan for the action. At first the American relaxed, assuming that Caserta had perhaps decided to be a little more human, for once. But then he thought back to his fall from the horse, and his instincts told him to raise his guard. If anything, he realized, the big Italian actor would be doing this to get him to think that a truce had been effected. And that would be precisely when Caserta would make his next move. There was still the possibility that Hendricks's suspicions were baseless, of course. He had no proof that the secondhand gossip he had heard from Tina had any foundation in fact or that what Pepe had told him about the slashed girth assigned guilt for the act to Caserta. It was all so much supposition and guesswork. Nevertheless it sure as hell would pay to keep his eyes open.

"The trick," Livorno said, "is to come as close as possible with a punch without actually striking the other man. Carlos, I realize you know all this, but for Hendricks it is new."

Caserta set the black hat on his head. "Sure. No problem."

"Later," the director explained, "when we mix the track, we will dub in the sounds of fists hitting. You see?"

Both men nodded.

"Now, the other thing to remember is that when you are the one being hit, you must give us a very big reaction. As the other's fist passes you, you must snap your head back, and if the action calls for it, you must fall down hard. All of this must be done with some exaggeration, because on film it will add to the appearance of great violence in the fighting."

Matthew Weaver glanced at the sky. He held a Westrex meter in his hand. "Beautiful. Couldn't ask for better light."

Livorno looked at the meter. "Good, good. We'll be ready to go in a few minutes." He turned back to the actors. "The first shot we make will be the master. After that we will go for the close-ups. We will be shooting from the crane, and the action calls for the killer to chase the sheriff out onto the roof from the bell tower. The sheriff has dropped his empty gun, and he realizes there is no escape; he must stand his ground and fight. Understood?"

"Where should I stop," Hendricks asked, "to make my turn?"

"About midway along the roof," Livorno replied. "I was up there a few minutes ago. It is not very wide, but the footing is good."

Weaver indicated the crane. "We'll be up in the cherry picker. It'll help to mark your position for you."

"Right," Livorno said. "The fight should begin right in front of us. Now, let us run through the action here before you go up onto the roof."

They rehearsed the fight until the director was satisfied, and then both actors entered the church and clambered up the winding staircase that led to the bell tower. When they got there, Hendricks stepped out onto the narrow ridge that ran along the roof of the church, Caserta following. From there, the roof seemed much higher than it had from below.

The crane was still at ground level. As Hendricks looked down, he saw that some kind of discussion was going on. Antonio shouted up to them to take a few minutes break. Hendricks sat down on the roof, and Caserta responded as he usually did in such situations, stretching out full length on the roof tiles and placing his hat over his face.

*　　*　　*

Father Pedro had waited patiently for more than two hours, Aldo Jifero at his side. The priest had discussed his plans with his friend the café owner until the small hours of this morning, and that, added to his excitement, had prevented him from getting much sleep before conducting the first mass of the day at six o'clock. Now, however, he felt fresh and rested and confident, more optimistic even than usual as he contemplated what he would do today.

It was endlessly fascinating, Father Pedro reflected, the way God did His work. As a young man in Barcelona he had looked forward to what he believed would be a steady climb in the hierarchy of the church, but all that changed abruptly when he was discovered in the basement of the rectory with Sister Theresa. After that his assignment to Santa Maria, here in this humble, remote village, had been a kind of banishment. But he had never given up hope, nor wavered in his conviction that better things would eventually come his way. Now at last, in the form of Vicente Morello and his rich film-making company, they obviously had arrived. Father Pedro watched the busy preparations with interest, waiting for precisely the right moment before stating his position.

Standing beside the priest, Aldo Jifero wiped his face with a handkerchief. The air was mild, but the café owner was also excited, and besides that he was attired in his Sunday suit, a well worn but fine garment of wool which included a vest in addition to a jacket and trousers. He had owned the suit for more than ten years, during which time he had inexorably gained weight, until now the suit was quite tight, and he was sweating profusely.

"Let me see the paper once more," Father Pedro requested.

Jifero reached into his inside jacket pocket and withdrew the agreement on which he had labored so painstakingly for most of the night. He handed it to the priest.

For the third time since Jifero had joined him earlier that morning, Father Pedro placed his wire-rimmed spectacles on his nose and read the flowery legal language with great care. The priest was far better educated than his friend, and even to his eye, untutored in the law, the agreement was rather verbose and awkward, but it would do. He returned the paper to Jifero.

High up on the church, silhouetted against the sky, the two actors emerged from the bell tower and made their way along the roof. On the ground, as Father Pedro watched, three other men of the crew climbed into the cup-shaped receptacle at the head of the crane in which the camera was mounted. The priest decided that the time had come to announce his proposition. With Jifero following, he stepped briskly over to Vicente Morello, who stood beside the crane.

Father Pedro bowed. "Excuse me, please."

The producer glanced at him. "Later, Father."

Father Pedro bowed again. "But it is a matter of some importance."

"Can't it wait?"

"It concerns the filming," the priest said. "It would be better if we were to have our discussion before it begins."

Morello sighed. "Very well." He turned to the crane. Livorno, Weaver, and Antonio were already inside. "Hold it a minute. Father Pedro wants to tell us something."

Antonio stepped out of the crane and joined the producer and the other two men.

"I would like to present to you my *abogado*," the priest said. "My lawyer."

Aldo Jifero smiled proudly.

Suspicion formed in Morello's mind. He stared. "Your lawyer? He is the café owner. What is this shit?"

Father Pedro clasped his hands before him. "He is also my counselor-at-law."

The producer looked at Jifero, who continued to smile broadly as sweat coursed down his face. "All right, he is your lawyer. Now what is it you wish to discuss?"

Father Pedro cleared his throat. "First, I must tell you that I am deeply honored that you have chosen to give our simple church of Santa Maria a position of importance in the grand *pelicula* you are making."

Morello glanced at Antonio. He spoke to his assistant in rapid Italian, assuming that the Spaniards would be unable to follow. What he did not suspect was that Father Pedro, with his many years of study in Latin, had no difficulty whatever in understanding his words.

"It's a holdup," the producer said. "The usual crap. He thinks that because we want to use his broken-down church, he can hit us up for a fortune."

"I'm sorry," Antonio replied. "It's my fault. Ordinarily I would have gotten a release before this started, but with a priest? Christ, you can't trust anybody."

"A priest is also a human being," Morello said dryly. "Despite his divine connections. Let's see what the bastard wants. We'll haggle, of course, but the ceiling should be somewhere around twenty thousand pesetas. And even that is robbery."

Antonio folded his arms. "Yes, Maestro."

The producer turned to Father Pedro. "What is it you are proposing?"

"It is a modest request," the priest replied. "Senor Jifero will present to you the agreement I would like us to make."

With a flourish, Aldo Jifero withdrew the piece of paper from his jacket pocket. It had become somewhat limp now from the moist heat his body generated. He held it before his face. "I shall read it."

"Spare us that," Morello said. He held out his hand. "I'm sure I can understand it well enough."

Crestfallen, Jifero looked at Father Pedro. The priest smiled reassuringly. "Let him read it, Counselor."

The language was filled with wherefores and whereases, and parties of the first part and parties of the second part, but the thrust of it was clear enough. Morello read through it slowly, his face reddening, as Antonio peered at the dank paper from over the producer's shoulder.

When Morello finished, he looked at the priest, who returned his gaze benignly. "This is a fucking outrage."

The priest did not change his bland expression. "I beg your pardon?"

"Forgive me, Father," Morello said. "But this is impossible. We use your church in a few minutes of film, and for that you want it practically rebuilt?"

The priest held his hands before him in an attitude of piety. "Not at all. I request only that you pay for a few simple repairs."

Morello's eyes returned to the agreement Jifero had drafted. "A few simple repairs? You want the church to be completely refurbished inside and out, with new stained-glass windows and not merely a new bell but a set of carillons from Antwerp?"

The priest inclined his head. "That is somewhat extravagant, I know, about the bells. But the very finest ones in the world are made in Belgium. It is something I have had my heart set on for such a long time."

The producer's voice was hoarse. "This is absolutely out of the question. Do you understand me? It is utterly impossible for me to comply with these demands."

Jifero drew himself up. "Perhaps you wish to consult your own legal counsel—"

Father Pedro raised his hand. "Of course, Senor Jifero. An excellent suggestion. Then perhaps we can resume our discussion in a few days' time."

Morello's mouth opened slackly. "A few days' time?"

The priest smiled. "Next week, perhaps."

"The thieving son of a bitch," Antonio hissed into the producer's ear. "What about the *guardia civil?* We've paid him enough. Maybe we can get him to help us make this holy crook back off."

Morello glanced over to where the policeman lolled against the fender of the equipment truck. "No. It would never work. No matter how we bribed him, we could never get him to work against the church."

"Then let me see if we can't find another location."

"Are you crazy? We looked at every structure in this entire whore's nest of a village before stumbling onto this one."

"We did not stumble onto it," Antonio reminded him. "Our friend here presented it to us."

Morello gritted his teeth. "The bastard. Even then he must have been planning this."

"I know what we can do," Antonio said. "I will drive into Montillas and have a look. There must be a place there we could use."

The producer sighed. "No good. The background would never match. This jackal has us by the balls."

And that, Father Pedro thought to himself, is the time to squeeze. "Gentlemen," he said aloud. "I would appreciate it if you would remove your equipment now, please."

Morello looked at him. "If we would do what?"

"Your equipment," the priest said patiently. "I would like you to remove it from the church property until we have our discussion next week."

Air escaped slowly from between Morello's clenched teeth.

Livorno approached them, frowning. "Hey, what's going on

here? I don't have all day, you know. The light is perfect now. What's the holdup?"

"It's a holdup, all right," Morello replied.

The director squinted quizzically. "What?"

"Nothing." Morello turned to Jifero, his face the color of old mahogany. "Give me a pen."

"Maestro—" Antonio began.

But the producer knew when he was beaten. "Shut up."

Smiling radiantly, Jifero handed Morello the agreement and a pen. The Italian scratched his name on the paper furiously.

"I will have a copy made for you," Jifero said.

"Yes, yes." Morello turned away. "Okay, let's get this going."

"About time," Livorno muttered. He scrambled back to the crane.

The priest looked up at the cloudless sky, his lips moving in a silent offering of thanks to the Holy Father as Antonio cupped his hands and shouted to the figures on the roof. "All right, you two. We're ready for the fight!"

chapter 30

"Okay, everybody," Livorno shouted. "Let's make it a good one. Action!"

Hendricks stepped quickly along the roof toward the rear of the church. He could hear Caserta's boots clattering on the tiles behind him, and from the corner of his eye he could see the camera platform at the head of the crane, with the director, Weaver, and Antonio crouching inside it. When he was at a point directly opposite the camera, Hendricks stopped. As the director had instructed him on the ground, he was now making his decision to take a stand against the pursuing killer. He tensed his body, crouched, and spun around to face Caserta.

The Italian grimaced as he approached, hunching his shoulders and doubling his hamlike fists. Christ, Hendricks thought, but you are one ugly guinea son of a bitch.

The action called for Hendricks to throw the first punch.

He brought his right around in a wild roundhouse swing, missing Caserta's jaw by a half inch. The Italian's head snapped back, and the big man staggered several feet backward along the roof. Hendricks followed, setting his body as if readying himself to strike the next blow.

Now it was to be Caserta's turn to punch Hendricks. The dark actor's teeth were bared in a snarl as he looped his left hand up from his boot tops. Hendricks's gaze fixed on the other man's eyes, and that was where he found the answer. In the split second as Caserta's fist hurtled toward his face, Hendricks grasped what the Italian intended. Instinctively he pulled his head back.

If the blow had landed flush, Hendricks would have been knocked clean off the roof. As it was, the grazing punch still had great force as it hit the point of his jaw. He went over backward, twisting his body and clawing for a grip on the tiles as he felt himself fall from the flat surface and begin to slide down the steep incline below it. He could hear the men in the crane shouting.

Hendricks's fingers caught the tiles and arrested his slide. He tightened his grip on the rough terra-cotta and scrambled his legs in an attempt to climb back to safety. He looked up and saw Caserta bend over and reach down as if to help. But the savage expression continued to burn in the Italian's eyes.

Caserta's heavy black boot stomped down onto Hendricks's right hand. He felt bones crunch, and fiery pain shot through his wrist and his elbow to his shoulder. Continuing to hold desperately to the tiles with his good hand, he pulled his mutilated right free and hooked it around the heel of the boot. The move was agonizing, but Hendricks forced himself to jerk the hand forward. Caserta flipped over backward, and Hendricks could hear a long scream trailing from the Italian's mouth and the clatter of tiles on the far side of the roof. A few seconds later there was a loud thud, and the scream stopped abruptly.

The pain in Hendricks's hand nauseated him. He pulled himself back up onto the flat surface atop the roof, inching his way by squirming with his knees, toes, and elbows until he lay facedown on the tiles, fighting for breath.

* * *

The connection was poor, and Castarelli's voice faded in and out, his words obscured by a distant roaring that reminded

Morello of an ocean storm. The producer shouted into the telephone. "What did you say?"

"I said we cannot stand to have this trouble."

"Jesus Christ, I know we cannot stand it. Do you think I wished it upon us?"

"No, no, Signor Morello. What I mean is that our budget cannot stand it. We are halfway through October, and the shooting should have been nearly finished by now."

"It is not finished. It is nowhere near finished, and now with Caserta gone, we must reshoot much of what we had."

"How much, Maestro—can you tell?"

"No. Livorno and Antonio are checking that now. But everything with that gorilla in it must be scrapped."

"Isn't there any way you could save it? Perhaps work the script around, somehow?"

"No, impossible. We must throw out every bit of it."

A new sound emitted from the receiver. It sounded to Morello like hiccuping. "What is that? Is that you?"

Castarelli's voice faded in again. "Forgive me. My ulcer."

"I need to know our position," Morello shouted. "Do you understand me?"

"Of course I understand. The problem is, I cannot tell you our position until I know how much more shooting you must do. All I can promise you now is that we will need more money."

Morello felt a sinking in his own belly. "More money? Good God."

"I know, but I cannot perform miracles. Besides the filming there is the editing, and the music, and the dubbing, and the inserts you planned to make back here, and—"

"Shit! I know all that."

"If you could let me know, when you have a better idea as to how much new footage you must shoot and what your schedule will be, I could tell how much more money we will need."

"I will call you back tonight, or tomorrow."

The accountant's voice was nearly unintelligible. "I beg your pardon? I cannot hear you clearly. The connection—"

Morello slammed the phone down. He clasped his hands on the desk before him and tried to think. It was late afternoon, and he was sitting in the small first-floor study. There was a sound behind him. He turned and saw that Vito Zicci was slumped in a chair, staring at him.

The producer felt a flash of anger. "Are you in the practice of listening in to private telephone conversations?"

"Private?" Zicci's slit mouth twisted in a sneer. "You have no privacy in matters of this picture. It is business, and therefore it is also our business."

Morello started to reply but thought better of it. He had enough difficulties to deal with, without exacerbating his already strained relationship with this man.

The black eyes regarded him coldly. "Did I hear you say you would need more money?"

Morello swallowed. There would be no point in lying now. And anyway, as much as he hated to face the truth, he had known before telephoning Castarelli that they would be into heavy cost overruns. He forced himself to appear calm, almost casual. "It is only to be expected. After all, one cannot anticipate an act of God."

"God, my ass. First the American falls off his horse, and now this other idiot falls off a roof. Do you expect me to think there was no way that these stupid accidents could have been prevented?"

Morello felt sweat pop out on his forehead. He could use a drink, but instinct told him that ordering one would be seen by Zicci as a revelation of weakness. He said nothing.

"Why were there no safety nets around the roof?"

As he replied, the producer realized his tone sounded strained. More weakness. "They would have spoiled the shot. You would have seen them." His voice trailed off.

"I have already spoken with Rome," Zicci said. "Signor Braciola's patience is wearing very thin."

Yes, Morello thought. You would not make that mistake again, you bastard. First you state your case to Rome, so that you are then forearmed when you turn to deal with me.

Zicci leaned forward. "How much more shooting will be required to finish this piece of shit?"

Morello sighed. Axface was now a film critic. He decided that he might as well deal with the situation. "We must reshoot every scene in which the killer appears."

"And the killer? Who will play that part now?"

The producer shrugged. "Hendricks, of course. There is no one else."

A trace of a smile crossed Zicci's features. "And so your act of God has forced you to do what you should have done in the first place."

Morello felt his anger rise again, but he managed to maintain his poise. "And in turn we must also reshoot everything in which we now have Hendricks as the sheriff." There, cunthead, he thought with bitter satisfaction. You didn't think of that, did you? Aloud, he said, "Together those two problems will require us to remake a little more than half of what we have shot so far. Antonio and Livorno will report exactly how much."

"I am not sure," Zicci said slowly, "whether it would be worth it to us to put any more money into this fiasco."

"No? I think it would. Because otherwise, everything you have invested thus far would be wasted. Leaving the picture at this point would be like having enough petrol to fly three quarters of the way to New York. You would have a nice ride, but in the end, nothing."

Zicci got to his feet. "Perhaps. But I will tell you this, Signor Morello. There comes a time when our support can be exhausted." The half smile flickered again. "That is when we must decide whether to write off our mistake." He turned and left the room.

Morello sighed and again clasped his hands before him. He toyed with the thought of flying back to Rome to present his case directly to Braciola but finally dismissed the idea. To do that would make his problems appear even more severe than they already were. It would look better if he were to remain here, throwing all his energy into coping with the company's difficulties firsthand. Jesus God, what a business. How could any endeavor swing so quickly from burgeoning success to disaster?

"Maestro?"

The producer turned to see Antonio standing in the doorway, holding a sheaf of papers in his hand. "Yes, yes. Come in here and close the door behind you. Are those the scenes?"

Antonio handed the papers to him, and Morello quickly scanned the shot list. Each of the scenes they would have to reshoot was marked in red. It was sickening to look at.

"Livorno and I have a plan," Antonio said.

Morello looked up. "Yes?"

"There are cuts we could make, here and there, in the script. Also some of the action could be abridged. It would at least save us from having to remake every one of those scenes."

The producer slowly shook his head. "No. I cannot back off now. This picture must be as good as I can possibly make it. And if it is as good as I believe it can be, then even this disaster with the excess costs will not matter. If it is not good,

173

then I am dead anyway." The implication of his words suddenly occurred to him. A Freudian slip, he thought ruefully. "Therefore, there will be no more shortcuts."

Antonio sank into a chair. "Dr. Borales says Hendricks can work in a few days."

"A few days? Shit. He will work tomorrow. We will shoot around the hand until the cast comes off."

"He is in some pain."

"So am I." Morello consulted the shot list. "Tell Livorno we will start with the first saloon scene in the morning. Also tell makeup to paint Hendricks's cast a flesh color. And tell Weaver I wish to discuss with him this problem of shooting around the hand."

The assistant got up and started out the door.

"Antonio?"

"Yes, Maestro?"

"What about Caserta?"

"He will live, but his back is broken. He is paralyzed from the neck down. Dr. Borales says it is too early to make a prognosis of whether his condition may improve."

"I see."

"It is fortunate that we are so heavily insured."

Morello did not answer. His mind was already occupied with other matters. He studied the shot list carefully.

chapter 31

At dinner on the evening of the incident on the church roof Vicente Morello got up and announced to the company that the part of the killer would be reassigned to Hendricks. This was no surprise to anyone, but nevertheless the assembled crew members burst into loud and prolonged applause. Morello then told them that although Caserta had been badly injured, the doctors in the clinic at Montillas had every hope that he would make a complete recovery. The producer phrased his words carefully, because he did not wish to impair the company's morale. What exactly the crew thought of this news

174

was hard to ascertain, however, since they displayed no reaction to it at all.

The following day they began the tedious efforts of remaking the scenes, and to the gratification of Morello and Antonio and Arturo Livorno, the effect on the company of having Hendricks in the lead was galvanizing. Instead of drudgery the work was a pleasure. A feeling of confidence and excitement and soaring enthusiasm permeated the production activity. The actors and the technicians were relaxed and happy and enjoyed themselves, buoyed by the conviction that the quality of their new footage would be excellent.

"It's like having the first string in there," Matthew Weaver said. "The number-one quarterback is now running this fucking club, and we are moving!" He drained the contents of his bottle of *cerveza* and wiped his beard. They were finishing lunch in the shade of a grove of walnut trees.

Livorno looked puzzled. "The number-one what?"

Weaver belched. "Never mind. Just the number one."

The company's confidence was given a further boost the following evening when the first of the new rushes came back down from Madrid. The library was crowded, and as Morello looked around, he realized that more of the crew members were here for this screening than at any time since production had begun. Waiting for the projectionist to thread his machine, Morello felt tense and nervous, and it came home to him just how much he had riding on the few thousand feet of acetate they were about to review.

Then the room was dark and the images were flickering on the screen, and as the producer looked at the first scene, he felt the familiar prickling sensation at the back of his neck. It was a reaction to his work he had learned to trust more than he did any other, more than comments from members of his crew or from others in the business, more than the acclaim of critics, or even the stirring of a theater audience, because above all else Vicente Morello had faith in his own taste, his own emotional response to a piece of film. If Morello believed in anybody in the world, he believed in himself, and what he saw now made the hairs at his nape stand on end.

In the first scene Hendricks strode into the saloon and swept the room with his gaze. He then made his way to the bar, where the awed and intimidated patrons fell back to make a place for him. To Morello's delight, the rangy American displayed the exact quality that had first excited the

175

producer in the screen test they had made in Rome, except that there was now added to it a poise and a self-assurance that made him not only believable as the killer but which gave the character great force. The quality was clearly evident in each of the subsequent scenes they looked at, and for the second time since the company had come to the ranch, there were spontaneous cheers at the conclusion of the screening. The crew had something very good going here, and they knew it, and they were proud of it.

Because of his youth and his excellent physical condition, the broken metacarpals and jammed knuckles in Hendricks's right hand mended quickly. At Morello's urging, Dr. Borales removed the cast after only two weeks but kept the hand heavily taped. Within days after that, patient but steady exercise had the fingers reasonably limber once again. The injuries sustained by the opposite ends of the actor's arm did, however, leave behind evidence of the damage the limb had suffered. From that time on, Hendricks carried his right shoulder higher than his left one. Borales noticed it, and commented on it, but Hendricks merely shrugged off the physician's attempts to determine whether its cause was physical or psychosomatic. Whatever the reason, the slight, uneven hunching became a permanent characteristic of Hendricks's carriage. And although neither he nor anyone else knew it at the time, that characteristic was to become famous.

The scenes the company made first were the easier ones, at least from the standpoint of the athletic demands imposed upon Hendricks. But as time went on, and the condition of his hand improved, they shot more and more difficult action. Hendricks rode, and rode with skill, having switched to Caserta's chestnut stallion. He learned to quick-draw and fire the heavy single-action .44-caliber Colt pistol so fast the eye could hardly follow, his hands dangling at his sides one instant, fanning the hammer of the roaring weapon the next. He fought with his fists and swung a beer bottle in a rough-and-tumble brawl in the saloon. And he chased, tackled, and then raped Cecily in as erotic a sequence as had ever been photographed.

They also remade the scene of the battle on the roof of the church, and this time Morello saw to it that heavy pads were laid on the ground on either side of the building before the actors went up the stairway into the bell tower. To the producer's relief the pads were not needed, however, and the work went smoothly. In fact it was one of the most exciting scenes in the entire filming, and Morello's satisfaction would have been complete had it not been for one attendant incident which occurred on the morning they shot it.

This involved, predictably, Father Pedro and his *abogado*, Aldo Jifero. When Morello looked up to see them approaching, he became livid. "Not one fucking peseta more," he shouted. "I don't give a shit if you have me excommunicated, I will not be screwed again!"

"Calm yourself," Father Pedro said soothingly. "I have no wish to be unfair, even though it is obviously not my fault that you must once again feature our lovely Santa Maria in your *pelicula*."

"Not once again," Morelly snapped. "It is the first time. The other footage was no good because of the accident, and you know it."

Aldo Jifero leaned forward. "We rent the church by the day, not by the scene."

"You stay out of this," the producer said.

Jifero set his jaw. "How can I stay out of it, when I am legal counsel to Father Pedro?"

The priest raised his hand. "If you will examine the agreement we signed, Senor Morello, you will see that it clearly states that the rental period was for that day and that day only."

Morello opened his mouth in a snarl.

"However," Father Pedro continued hastily, "it is certainly not my desire to take advantage of anyone, least of all a man of your faith and generosity." He waved a hand toward the church. "As you can see, the work you so kindly made possible is nearly complete, and by the time our new carillon is delivered from Antwerp, our Santa Maria will be the most beautiful church in all of La Mancha." And when the bishop sees it, he thought, and realizes what I have accomplished, he will surely decide to transfer me from this flea-infested village and to elevate me to a place in the diocese more suitable to a priest of my obvious talents.

"So what are you getting at?" Morello demanded.

Father Pedro brought his hands together before him in a gesture of supplication. "In acknowledgment of your previous generosity, and as an act of compassion for your misfortune, I make but one small request in exchange for this additional use of our church."

Morello's eyes narrowed in supsicion. "What is it?"

"I humbly suggest that you donate a statue of our patron,

Santa Maria, which would occupy a niche there." He pointed. "Over the front door."

The producer stared at the church. "What niche?"

Father Pedro shifted his feet. "As you can see, such a niche does not now exist. It would be necessary to construct one. But of course, that would be but a small project."

Morello turned back to the priest, frowning. "How much?"

The cleric shrugged. "A few hundred thousand pesetas."

"A few hundred thousand pesetas?" Morello's face darkened again. "For the love of Christ."

"Of course."

"How many hundred thousand?"

Father Pedro pursed his lips. "I cannot say, exactly. Seven, perhaps, or eight. Plus, of course, the niche."

Morello looked at the church, and at the crane and the trucks and the cars and the actors and the technicians, and his shoulders slumped.

Antonio approached, his face registering immediate understanding of the situation. "Oh, no. Not again."

"It's all right," Morello said resignedly. "At least this time it is not a total rape."

In response to a gesture by the priest, Aldo Jifero reached into the inside jacket pocket of his suit and withdrew the inevitable piece of paper. He held it before him and cleared his throat. "Whereas the church of Santa Maria, hereinafter known as the party of the first part—"

"Stop!" Morello commanded.

Jifero looked at the producer, startled.

The producer stepped closer. "Just see to it that your goddamn paper puts an absolute limit of nine hundred thousand pesetas that I must pay for this new rental, and that I have the right to reshoot as much as I please if that becomes necessary. Do you understand me?"

Jifero returned Morello's gaze with dignity. "It already says that, senor. I was about to read it to you."

Morello turned to Antonio. "You read the infernal thing. And be sure you read it with care before you sign it."

"Yes, Maestro." Antonio took the paper from Jifero, who looked crestfallen.

Morello marched off toward the crane, waving his arms and exhorting the crew to get moving. Father Pedro watched him go and then rolled his eyes heavenward. As if God's original message to him had not been clear enough, the Holy Father had now underlined the statement.

178

As the shooting went forward, a phenomenal change became evident, one that is rare in the industry, but which, when it occurs, gladdens a producer's heart. Whereas previously the company had fallen farther and farther behind Morello's schedule, they now actually began to move ahead of it. They were working seven days a week, saving most of the interiors for the evenings, so that they could stretch their hours to fifteen and sixteen a day. The effort was backbreaking, the timetable exhausting. But, strangely, their productivity became inspirational, so that the more work the crew turned out, the more pride they took in it, and the more they tried to accomplish.

Matthew Weaver stood up from the toadstool-shaped metal seat behind the Mitchell and stretched. It was nine o'clock in the evening, and they had decided to go for one more take before ending the day. Pain from his fatigue laced the cameraman's shoulders. He turned to Livorno. "You know what Vince Lombardi used to say, 'When the going gets tough, the tough get going.'"

Livorno looked at him, mystified. "Who is Vince Lombardi?"

Weaver was disgusted. "Never mind. He was just another wop ballbuster. Jesus, you don't know any fucking thing, do you?"

Three weeks after they had begun work on the new schedule, and one full week ahead of it, they were finished. Late on a Tuesday afternoon the director completed the third take on a scene in the main street of the village. He looked at his watch, and then glanced at Weaver. "That one okay for you?"

Weaver spat into the dust beside the dolly. "Hell, yeah. Couldn't do much better."

"Yes." Livorno brushed sweat from his forehead with a wristband. He looked across the street. Morello was standing there, talking with Antonio. Vito Zicci was nearby. The director took off his glasses. Shit. He never had anything to wipe them with. He set them carefully back onto his face and walked over to where Morello stood.

The producer looked up as Livorno approached. "How goes?"

"That's it," the director said.

"That's it?"

Livorno suddenly felt very tired. "That's it. We are finished. Last scene, last take. Done. Over. *Finito*."

The producer smiled broadly. He put his arms around Livorno and kissed him tenderly in the middle of his unshaven,.

179

sweating cheek. *"Molto bene. Senza dubbio, tu hai fatto il tuo capo di lavoro. Io sono fiero di te."*

The director nodded.

Morello turned to Antonio and shook his hand. He looked at Zicci disdainfully, then strode to the center of the street. "Listen to me, everybody," he shouted. "That's it. A wrap. We have finished shooting. Except for a few bits I will make back in Rome, *The Hired Gun* is complete. I want to thank each and every one of you for doing great work. You are by far the best crew I have ever been associated with. To all of you, I give my love and my gratitude."

A roar went up. Actors hugged each other, and then everyone was slapping backs and embracing and kissing. Most of the women were crying, and some of the men.

Morello held up his hands. "One moment, please. One moment. I have one more announcement. Tonight, we shall have a celebration at La Cuarta Luna. I promise you, it will be a party you will never forget."

This time the cheers were even louder.

chapter 32

They were all drunk. Gloriously drunk. And most of them were stoned as well. They sat at the tables in the dining room and drank wine and champagne and passed the joints back and forth and told each other anecdotes about the shooting they had just finished and laughed until the tears ran down their faces.

Morello had imported a rock band from Montillas. There were four instruments, a lead guitar, a rhythm guitar, bass and drums, and although the musicians were inept, they were also enthusiastic, and the sound pouring from the big amplifiers was so loud it made your ears buzz. The band's repertory was entirely eclectic, a collection of imitations of records by The Beatles and The Rolling Stones, and the effect of a group of young Spaniards trying to sound like Englishmen trying to sound like Tennesseans was highly comical. But nobody cared, because the beat was steady and spirited, and the work was

180

over, and tomorrow the crew would be going to Madrid and from there they would fly to Rome, and this chapter in their lives that was *The Hired Gun* on La Cuarta Luna in the lovely rolling plains country of La Mancha would be closed forever, and so tonight, who could give a shit about anything? There was only to get drunker and to get higher and to have as good a time as it was possible to have.

Cecily Petain raised her glass and sipped champagne from it. Of all the people in the huge room, she was perhaps the least affected by the alcohol and the cannabis. Cecily was enjoying a different kind of high, largely inspired by her emotions. For some weeks now she had perceived with growing conviction that the picture would be not only good, but perhaps even great, a classic of its kind. This was due principally, she believed, to the fact that with the assumption by Hendricks of the male lead, the film had become the vehicle in which a powerful new screen personality would emerge. Fundamentally, as far as audiences were concerned, she knew that *The Hired Gun* would be Hendricks's movie. And although there was no more ruthlessly ambitious female in the business, an industry which had spawned women who would make Lucretia Borgia look like Mary Poppins, Cecily Petain was not stupid. The force and the power and the inevitable box office appeal she felt so surely that Hendricks would generate had to make this picture a hit, and for her to be the female lead in a hit would be the realization of her penultimate dream. After that, she told herself, the greatest objective of all would be within her grasp. She would become a major, full-fledged star. Cecily sipped more champagne and smiled at Vicente Morello.

The producer looked about the room, an expansive expression on his tanned features. "It's wonderful, isn't it? To sit here and contemplate what this picture will mean to us?"

"I think about it all the time," Cecily replied.

"More than anything else, it will mean freedom. Its success will mean that I will again have the freedom to do anything I choose. Do you understand that?"

"Clearly." Because it will give me exactly the same thing, she thought. And perhaps, dear Vicente, it will even give me freedom from you.

Arturo Livorno felt marvelous. He was exhausted, he knew, his muscles and his nervous system having been sapped of their resources until there was very little energy left in either. He had lost fifteen pounds during the shooting, and his usually smooth features had become gaunt and furrowed. More than anyone else involved in the production of a motion picture, more than the producer or the cameraman or the actors or any other single member of a company, the responsibility of shaping the action, of telling the story on film, falls to the director. The task was demanding, leeching, nerve-shredding in any circumstances, but the problems posed by this one had been even more difficult than most. Strapped by a lean budget, beset by accidents, driven by an impossible schedule, Livorno had been virtually forced to make the picture twice, once with Caserta in the lead, the second time with Hendricks. As a result he was now totally worn out, unable to find the strength to do much more than swallow *vino tinto* from his glass or inhale smoke from his joint. Yet emotionally he was soaring. *The Hired Gun* was finished, and it was good, and an enormous burden had been lifted from his aching shoulders.

"Have a hit," someone said.

Livorno looked up to see Matthew Weaver smiling down at him. The cameraman was glassy-eyed, and a broad grin was spread across his face. He was smoking a huge cigar-shaped joint which he now extended toward Livorno.

The director held up his own roach. "Thanks, I have one."

Weaver sneered. "Not that shit, man. That's corn silk. This here is hash. From Marrakech. Guaranteed to destroy your brain. Try it."

Obediently Livorno took the thick joint from Weaver and inhaled deeply. The hashish was harsh and powerful and burned the membranes of his throat. Almost immediately he felt the buzzing in his head increase in intensity, while simultaneously he became aware of a numbness in his fingers and his toes. He handed the joint back to the cameraman. "Very nice. Somewhat like being shot dead."

"I told you you'd like it," Weaver said. He was silent for a moment. "You know, you're really not a bad director."

"Thank you."

"I mean it. I've worked with all kinds, from good to terrible. I think you took on one hell of a tough job and did okay with it."

"I tried."

"Yeah. We all did. How about that fucking Hendricks, huh? Son of a bitch is a born winner."

"Yes. He has a remarkable talent."

"So do you, you know it? If you'd forget about all that political crap."

182

Livorno smiled. "What next, for you?"

"Hell, I don't know." The cameraman exhaled a stream of blue smoke from the hashish cigar. "Winter's coming, so I'll probably look for something when it's warm, you know? Last year I was in Africa for a couple of months."

"Africa? Not for me. Insects and disease."

"Nah, we were in Nairobi most of the time. Wasn't hard to take. No shortage of cunt, either."

"What color?"

"Every color. Every color you ever heard of."

"That is exploitive, to use black women."

"Bullshit. And anyhow, the insides of all pussies are the same shade. Pink. Damn, if I could find one big enough, I'd go live in it."

Livorno laughed and drank more of his wine.

The cameraman moved on, stopping here and there to exchange a word with a crew member. When he got to where Maria Gambara was sitting, he elbowed his way into a chair beside her. "Hello, baby. Have a hit."

"I am already high, Matthew."

"So get higher, for Christ's sake. I can't stand conservative broads."

Maria took the proffered cigar, inhaled, and coughed. "Dear God, what is in that thing?"

"Ground up monkey gonads. Smooth, ain't it?"

"You are crazy."

"I am crazy about you." Weaver carefully unbuttoned her blouse and reached inside, cupping a warm, full breast in his large hand. "And you know, you've got the absolute best set of jugs of any girl in the whole goddamn world."

"Do you really mean that, Matthew?"

Weaver stroked her nipple with his thumb. "Of course I mean it. You know I'd never tell you anything that wasn't true."

"That is very sweet of you."

"Yeah." He pulled the blouse open and bent down, very gently encircling her nipple with his lips.

Maria giggled. "Your beard. It tickles."

"Mmmmm."

"And if you keep that up, you will have to take me to my room."

"Mmmmm."

"Matthew, I am starting to get very excited."

He looked up at her and grinned. "We could do it right here. On the table."

"I don't think so."

"We might even win a prize."

She reached down and gripped him. "There is only one prize I want."

"That's another thing I like about you, Maria. You've got taste." Weaver got to his feet and took her hand. "Come on."

Maria's room was in the bunkhouse. On their way through the great hall, they passed a number of couples dancing. The band was now playing "Yesterday," and the lead guitarist was rendering a phonetic version of McCartney's lyrics. One of the couples was Juan Navarro and Tina. Weaver slapped Tina on the ass as he walked by.

"He is a wild character, that one," Navarro said as he watched the cameraman lead Maria out the front door.

"Everybody in films is a little mad," Tina said. "It is a necessary qualification if one is to do this kind of work."

"It is amazing to me that suddenly your picture is finished."

"I think it is amazing to all of us."

"It is also very sorrowful."

"I know."

He held her tight against him. "In a way it has been like so many other things you find in this world."

"How is that?"

"A few short weeks ago I did not know you existed. Now it is as if I have known you and loved you all my life."

"I feel the same way, Juan."

"Do you?"

"Yes. You know I do."

"Then you must not leave, Tina. This place has become your home. I want you to share La Cuarta Luna with me, forever."

"Juan, darling, you know I can't do that."

"Because of your American?"

"Partly because of that, even though I know he does not really belong to me, and perhaps never will."

"Well, then?"

"But there is a chance, if only a small one."

"And there is something else, as well?"

"You know that, too. I want to find out if I can be a successful actress."

He smiled. "That is an easy question to answer. You simply take my word for it. I have no doubt that you would be one of the greatest stars that motion pictures have ever seen. There, you see? Now you don't have to go through all that terrible agony trying to find out."

"But I do, Juan. I do. I have to go through it because I have to learn the truth about myself. If I did not do that, I would be unhappy forever, thinking about what I might have become and never finding the truth."

"Is that really so important?"

"To me it is. As the poet said, 'Of all sad words of tongue or pen, the saddest are these: it might have been.' "

"Who wrote that?"

"John Greenleaf Whittier."

"Well, I must say that I agree with him. If you leave me now, I will think those words for as long as I live."

She kissed his cheek. "Then it will be hard, for both of us. But seeking answers is how we spend out lives."

Navarro gestured with his head. "There is one answer you don't have to look very far to find."

Tina turned her head to follow his gaze. She saw Hendricks walking out the front door. His arm was around the waist of Rosalie La Sorda.

chapter 33

The Ferrari sputtered to life, then emitted its characteristic savage roar as the five-liter V-12 caught fully. Rosalie threw her head back and laughed with delight. "Do you think the maestro would mind if we took his toy for a little spin?"

Beside her in the passenger's seat, Hendricks shook his head. "Hell, no, he wouldn't. Kindest, most generous man in the world. He'd probably be really thrilled if he knew you were driving this piece of shit." He laughed and dragged on his joint. For the first time since he had fallen from Humo's back, the big American had broken his rules on moderation. He was drunk, and he was high, and he was very happy.

"Then we shall do everything we can to please him." Rosalie found reverse and eased the bright red Boxer out of its parking place on the circular drive in front of the house. She stopped, fumbled again with the shift lever, and then moved forward down the drive.

Hendricks looked up at the clear night sky. "Hey, look at that. There's a quarter moon up there. That's a good sign, you know it? A quarter moon on La Cuarta Luna. Jesus, I ought to be a songwriter."

"I know, Hendricks. You are truly a genius."

"Fucking right."

Rosalie drove at moderate speeds until she reached the gates of the ranch, and then she wound the Ferrari through the gears, revving the big engine almost to the red line, dropping finally into fifth. "I'm getting the hang of it."

"Sure you are, baby. Rosalie Louda Peterson Stewart Andretti."

"I love it. It makes me feel like I am flying. Almost as good as making love."

"Don't get carried away, now. Nothing else feels that good."

"Are you sure?"

"Hell, yes, I'm sure."

"Maybe we should make a determination."

"That would be some trick, lovey. If you could do that and drive this at the same time, you'd have to be a contortionist."

She laughed again. "Fortunately, it is not necessary to do both at the same time."

There was a grassy knoll beside the road. Rosalie pulled the car off the blacktop onto the knoll and shut down the engine. She turned to Hendricks. "Now we shall see." She put her arms around his neck and covered his mouth with wet, sloppy kisses. As always, she was instantly aroused, like a race horse that moves from the starting gate to a full gallop in the first stride.

"Maybe we should get out of this thing," Hendricks said.

"No. All my life I have wanted to have a car like this and a man like you. Now I am going to have them together."

"Well, at least to get our clothes off."

"Okay."

They climbed out of the car and stripped. The air was cool, and the thin moonlight reflected on drops of dew in the tall grass. When they got back into the Ferrari, Hendricks was struck again by how hot this girl's skin always seemed to be.

Rosalie continued to work on him with her mouth, at the same time stroking him and brushing his chest with her heavy, swinging breasts. When she was nearly frenzied, she crawled up on top of him, facing him, and slid her body down onto his penis.

"*Dio, Dio,*" she shuddered and whipped her head from side to side.

"Christ," Hendricks said. "I haven't done this since I was a kid in Maryland." He held her buttocks in his hands, watching her bucking, heaving body and admiring her breasts with their broad nipples that looked almost black in the moonlight, seeing the curve of her hips and her belly, the patch between her legs rising from him and then slamming down again as she rode his cock.

He had slid forward in his seat and cranked the backrest rearward, but Rosalie continued to bump her head on the low ceiling of the car. She moaned, low growling noises issuing from her throat. Her motion became more and more rapid until her body suddenly went rigid and she gripped his neck with her fingers, her nails digging into his flesh, and her moaning turned to a loud cry. She held him that way for nearly a half minute, and Hendricks could feel her hot juices pouring down onto him. Then she collapsed against him, and Hendricks was coming too, holding the lovely hot buttocks in his hands and spurting into her.

Afterward he fell asleep. He had no idea how long he dozed, but when he awoke, he was cold and stiff, and the door of the car was open and Rosalie was standing outside, pulling his arm.

"Come on, Hendricks," Rosalie urged. "Get dressed."

"Huy? Yeah. What time is it?"

"I don't know. It's late."

He looked at his watch, but he could not make his eyes focus properly. Rosalie pulled at him again, and he saw that she was dressed. He crawled out of the car and put his clothes on. His shirt and trousers felt clammy against his skin. He glanced up at the sky. The moon was down, and the night had turned from black to gray. He could see his breath.

Rosalie shivered. "Let's go."

"Want me to drive?"

She shook her head. "No, I want to."

Hendricks was asleep again as soon as he sank back into the deep leather seat. Rosalie started the engine, revving it until the V-12 settled into its steady snarl. She moved through the gears surely now, delighting in the immense power the engine generated. The car hurtled forward, faster and faster,

187

snaking along the winding blacktop. When she reached fifth gear, she glanced at the speedometer and felt a thrill as she saw the needle climb past two hundred twenty kilometers per hour.

She was right, she told herself. This was almost as good as making love. She was flying and it was wildly exciting, and holding this beautifully sleek and powerful thing in her hands was like holding a man in her cunt. A strong, handsome man like Hendricks. The thought pleased her, and she laughed happily. She was becoming aroused again and she could feel the slippery wetness between her legs. She glanced down at Hendricks's blond head, slumped against the seat back, and reached down to touch him.

The V-12 was now producing close to 7,000 rpm, and the blatting roar had modulated to an eerie high-pitched scream. The Ferrari was covering the road at two hundred sixty kilometers per hour, and at that speed no more than the lightest touch on the padded leather steering wheel was required to flick the big red two-seater through the twists and turns of the serpentine highway.

Rosalie was on the brink of orgasm. She held the Boxer's wheel in her left hand, Hendricks's cock in her right. She squeezed both, tighter and tighter, until the rush of ecstasy spread through her body. She arched her back and closed her eyes.

The right front Perilli caught the soft sand shoulder of the road, and the Ferrari went into a long, sickening left-hand skid, covering a full two hundred meters in seconds, until the can ran out of straightaway and flipped over. With the first impact the right door sprung open, and Hendricks was thrown from the cartwheeling vehicle. The fact that he was asleep and totally relaxed undoubtedly saved his life. He went skittering and rolling through the wet grass, half stunned and unable to comprehend what was happening to him.

He came to a stop, finally, on his belly, and when he lifted his head, he saw the Ferrari some distance from him smash into an outcropping of rock, and then its tank exploded and it burst into flames.

Hendricks pulled himself to his feet. His body ached and there were sharp pains in his legs, but he didn't seem to be badly hurt. He tried to run, yet he could produce no more than a hobble from his battered legs. He forced himself forward, staggering toward the wreck, but when he was still fifty meters away, the heat from the fire seared his face and he could get no closer.

Rosalie La Sorda's funeral pyre was a billowing tower of orange flames that leaped and soared high into the night sky, crackling and bursting as a series of minor explosions shook the twisted mass. Thick, oily black smoke roiled from it, trailing off on the wind and rising hundreds of meters above the ball of fire that had been the red Ferrari.

An acrid stink bit into Hendricks's nostrils. It was a mixture of burning petroleum and melting metal and flaming rubber and leather and plastic and cloth. There was something else, too, and he realized it was the odor of cooking meat. He turned away, and his stomach heaved and he vomited into the grass at his feet.

The vomit was hot and bitter and it stung his throat and his mouth. What a hell of a way for it to end, he thought. This trip to Spain, this new beginning in his life, was the best thing that had ever happened to him, and he knew it as surely as he knew the sun would rise a few minutes from now, over the Universales Mountains to the east, where the sky was already streaked with yellow. Yet from now on, whenever he thought back to it, he would think of this, and he would remember the flames roaring and the thick black smoke, and he would think of crazy, passionate Rosalie, her body alive and writhing with passion one minute, a charred black cinder the next.

He wiped the vomit from his mouth with his sleeve and hobbled back toward the road. The wind was stronger now, and it was carrying the stink toward him and he could feel the heat of the flames on his back.

His voyage to Spain was over.

chapter 34

The Hotel Albero was a crumbling four-story *pensione* in the southeastern section of Rome. Most of its guests were whores who engaged the small, drab rooms by the hour. When they

189

brought a customer to the desk, the clerk charged the man twelve thousand lire for one night's lodging. After the customer had been serviced, the hotel changed the towels, and occasionally also the sheets, and rented the room again. In the morning the management paid the whores a commission for each of the customers they had steered to the place. Business was brisk in the summer, when Rome's streets were thick with tourists, but slow now, in the winter months, and much of the time the Albero was not more than one third occupied, its dreary interiors damp and cold and smelling faintly of urine and disinfectant.

Although the Albero catered mainly to transients, a few of its inhabitants were permanent residents. One of these was Guiseppe Scozza, who occupied 3 D. A Neopolitan by birth, Scozza had come to Rome while in his early twenties, hoping to find glamour and excitement and to associate with famous people. He achieved his goals, but not as he had envisioned. For the next ten years Scozza was self-employed as a paparazzo, a profession many people considered a cut below that of the Albero's other tenants.

Now thirty-two, Scozza looked much older. He was chronically overweight, and his nose had been broken several times, and there was a nervous tic in his right cheek. During his career he had been beaten and stabbed and threatened with death, and on two occasions subjects he was attempting to photograph had tried to run him down in their cars. He had been spat upon, kicked, clawed, and punched in the balls. And he had spent more nights in Rome's jails than any of the girls who trafficked the Albero.

At the end of this decade Scozza was as poor as a rat, although he always made considerable amounts of money in his calling. Some of this was paid to him by editors of newspapers and magazines in Rome and other Italian cities, and even by editors in such foreign metropolitan centers as Paris and Munich and London. What these journalists wanted principally were pictures of famous people, and most of all informal shots of them at play. So Scozza crept through bushes and skulked behind doors and slipped onto patios and brazened into nightclubs, and although he sustained much physical punishment, he also got results, for which his clients paid dearly. He shot Jackie O and Anthony Quinn and Sophia Loren and Carlo Ponti and Anna Maria Alberghetti and Frank Sinatra and Raquel Welch and dozens of other lesser personalities, and there was always a ready market for his work.

Others of his fees came from people he had photographed who, for one reason or another, did not want their pictures to appear in print or on TV and who were therefore eager to buy the negatives from him, usually for large sums. More often than not this was the more lucrative source of Scozza's income, but it was also the more hazardous to come by. Once he climbed a tree on the Via Boncampagni and spent hours crouching on a limb, patiently shooting seventy-two frames with a Nikon F2 mounting a 200 mm lens, the first roll ASA 400, the second ASA 1200, just to make sure he had stopped all the action. His subjects on that occasion were the wife of a member of the House of Parliament and her chauffeur. The pictures were splendid, razor sharp and finely detailed and even, in Scozza's opinion, artistic.

A week later he met the lady in an obscure cantina on a side street off the Via Nazionale. She was chic and mysterious in her black hat, veil, and dark glasses, and she actually chuckled when she looked at the contact prints. She paid him every lire he asked for without haggling, although his price was even more outrageous than usual, and Scozza assumed that this was because her husband, a prominent Christian Democrat, was up for reelection. After Scozza counted the stack of bank notes and put them carefully into his inside jacket pocket, they burned the negatives, one at a time, in an ashtray on the table before them. Then the lady said good-bye pleasantly and left the cantina, taking the prints with her.

Scozza lingered over a glass of Strega, thinking of what he would do with the money. He looked up when a man in a black suit sat down beside him at the tiny table. It was the chauffeur. Before Scozza could react, the man plunged a stiletto into the paparazzo's leg. The blade was nine inches long, and it passed completely through his thigh and pinned him to his chair. The chauffeur got up and walked out of the cantina as calmly as his employer had done, and Scozza fainted from the pain and the shock. But even after he had bribed the proprietor not to notify the police and had paid his hospital and doctor bills, he still had made a handsome profit.

The trouble was, Scozza spent money faster than he made it. Whenever he collected a large fee, he immediately rented a lavish suite in a first-class hotel, such as the Hassler or the Grand, and gave himself a party. He installed three or four of the best prostitutes in Rome, really elegant girls of taste and breeding who were nothing like the riffraff that infested the Albero, and for as long as the money lasted, he lived and ate and drank and whored like a king. Unfortunately Scozza was also a gambler, and sometimes roulette and chemin de fer in clubs like the Rex or Nero's consumed sizable amounts of the sums he made, so that he was unable to pay his other obligations, and he was forever rushing from one debtor to another, like a demented Hollander plugging holes in a dike.

For a long time Scozza deluded himself with a secret plan by which he would lay aside a few million lire and retire to a villa on the Riviera. But finally he faced the truth that in every aspect of his life, in the pursuit of his photography, in the gouging of editors or the blackmailing of subjects, in the burning his nose with cocaine or filling his belly with pâté de fois gras and champagne, in his use of women and in his gambling, he was a compulsive, and the only way he would leave Rome would be in a pine box. After reaching this understanding of himself, he was not happier, but at least he was more at peace.

The air outside Scozza's window this morning was cold and raw, laced with tiny drops of rain. He made his breakfast on the hot plate which stood on the table beside his bed; a slice of toast, a cup of filtered coffee, and three fingers of Fernet Branca, and thought about what he would do that day. It was nearly noon, and a man from *Mädchen*, the semipornographic magazine published in Hamburg, was due to meet him at one in the lobby of the Excelsior to discuss the purchase of some photographs. Scozza despised Germans, remembering the stories his family told of the occupation during World War Two, when Wehrmacht soldiers raped his sister and looted his home, but he held no prejudice against their money. Besides, he found them less demanding than Italian or French editors, and less critical than the English. The Germans would often accept shots of second-rank personalities, and they always paid promptly and well.

Scozza downed the last of his Fernet Branca, dropped his cigarette into his coffee cup, and pulled on a light raincoat. He stuffed a manila envelope into his pocket. As he was about to walk out the door, the telephone rang. He answered it.

"Scozza?"

"Yes?"

"Galupo here, of *Il Mondo*. I would like to see you. We have an assignment I think you would be right for. Can you come to my office?"

"When?"

"As soon as possible. This afternoon?"

"I have an appointment. How about tomorrow?"

"Better that we do it today, if you can work it out. This is something big, and there is a time factor. Every day is important to us."

Scozza looked at his watch. *Il Mondo* was a slick, gossipy news magazine that made heavy use of photos of jet setters and show-business personalities. Something big to this publication would mean big money to him. "I could be there later. Say, around six?"

"Okay. See you then."

Scozza took a taxi to the Via Veneto. Even in the wintertime the lobby of the Excelsior was crowded. The stately but somewhat garish hotel on the east side of the wide street, just a few hundred meters from the ancient wall, was perhaps the most famous in Rome. It catered to a broad range of clientele, from tourists to businessmen to celebrities, and was often correctly accused of being more American in its style than European.

Despite the throngs, Scozza had no difficulty locating the man from *Mädchen*. The white-blond hair and moustache were a dead giveaway, but even without them the squarish features and the arrogant manner labeled him German. His name was Schmidt. Scozza shook hands with him, and they sat down at a table in the north end of the lobby and ordered coffee.

The paparazzo dumped cream and sugar into his cup. "How was your trip?"

Schmidt spoke Italian slowly and deliberately, with a heavy accent. "It was all right. Lufthansa is the best airline in Europe, of course, but even with them you sometimes have delays in the wintertime. The weather is a problem, over the mountains."

"Perhaps you should try Alitalia on the way back," Scozza suggested innocently.

"Alitalia?"

"A fine airline, with much experience in flying the Alps." And also a terrible safety record, Scozza thought. With any luck, you could fly into a mountain, you Hun bastard.

Schmidt sipped his coffee. "I think I will stay with Lufthansa."

"Whatever you think best, of course."

It was apparent that Schmidt felt they had wasted enough time on pleasantries. "You have the pictures?"

"Oh, yes." The paparazzo withdrew the manila envelope from the pocket of his raincoat and laid it on the table.

193

The German affected boredom. "How did they turn out?"

"In a word, they are sensational."

Schmidt took a package of cigarettes from his pocket and extended it toward Scozza. "Smoke?"

"No, thanks."

"They're very mild. *Krone Zigaretten*."

German, Scozza thought, so I should appreciate them. "I have my own."

Schmidt lit one of the cigarettes and exhaled slowly. "So. Let us have a look."

"Certainly." Scozza picked up the envelope but made no move to open it. "The girl is Anna Cirelli, as we agreed."

"Yes."

"I'm sure you can appreciate how difficult it was to get pictures of this kind of a major motion picture star."

The German flicked ash from his cigarette. "Pictures of what kind? I haven't seen them yet."

Scozza had been in situations like this one more times than he could remember. "Frankly they are even more explicit than I promised you I would try to get."

Schmidt said nothing. His eyes, Scozza noticed, were a pale blue.

"She is with a young man, also an actor. He is her newest lover, and there is a lot of talk in Rome that he will become more famous than she, in time."

"Yes?"

"He is extraordinarily handsome. To get these, I took a terrible risk. I bribed her butler and hid in the closet of her bedroom."

There was a glint, now, in the blue eyes.

"I used a Leica M5, which is virtually silent."

"I know," Schmidt said impatiently. "They are made in Wetzler."

"Even so, I could have been discovered. I might be in jail now, or worse."

The German stubbed out his cigarette. "Let's have a look."

"Not all of them are perfectly clear. Some are much better than others."

Schmidt held out his hand. "May I?"

"Of course." Scozza opened the envelope and withdrew a stack of eight-by-ten glossies. "They're not in any particular order." The truth was that he had spent almost a half hour arranging them.

Schmidt stared at the first photograph. It was slightly out of focus, and there were heavy black lines running down both sides. The subject was not clear, but it appeared to consist of two naked bodies on a bed.

Scozza pointed to the black lines. "I am sorry about these, but I did not dare to open the door any wider."

Schmidt grunted and studied each print in turn. As he went through the stack, the photographs became clearer, and the action portrayed in them more and more bizarre.

"Beautiful, isn't she?" the Italian said.

The blue eyes glinted as Schmidt peered at the pictures. "She is attractive, yes."

More attractive than the clapped-out Prussian whores you are accustomed to looking at, Scozza thought. Aloud he said, "And the boy. Do you see what I mean?"

"Yes, I do see." Schmidt lingered over a shot in which the young man's buttocks were prominently displayed.

Aha, the paparazzo thought. You reveal yourself. An Aryan queer.

The last three photographs in the stack were incredibly filthy. Schmidt carefully placed them side by side on the table before him.

Scozza shook his head in wonder. "No accounting, is there, for some people's tastes?"

The German stared at the pictures. "They are quite, ah, interesting."

"Yes."

Schmidt picked up the photographs and put them back into the manila envelope. He casually lit another cigarette, not bothering to offer the package to Scozza, who lit one of his own.

Scozza looked at his watch. "I don't mean to rush you, but I have another appointment."

"Yes? Well. The photographs are acceptable." Schmidt reached into his inside jacket pocket and withdrew a thick leather billfold.

The tic in Scozza's cheek began to work, causing the muscle to flutter slightly. "There will have to be an adjustment in the price, of course."

Schmidt froze. "An adjustment? What do you mean?"

The paparazzo cleared his throat. "Certain things have changed since you telephoned me with this request."

"What things?"

"Why, ah, the boy, for example."

"What about him?"

"He is famous in his own right. Or soon will be. His name is Armand Grasso. You should write it down."

"I will remember it."

"So in effect, you have photographs of two screen personalities, not just one."

"Mmm."

"And also, you will admit that what the pictures show is quite amazing. Can you imagine what Signorina Cirelli would give to have these back?"

The blue eyes narrowed. "You are thinking about becoming a blackmailer?"

Scozza was indignant. "Never. Such an idea is repulsive to me. I am a journalist, and one of the best in my field."

"A journalist." There was a hint of irony in the German's tone.

"Exactly. And I am very proud of my work. These pictures, for instance. You and I both know that they will cause an absolute sensation when they appear in your magazine."

Schmidt lit another of his Krone. "Frankly, some of them are too bizarre, even for *Mädchen*."

"Oh? I didn't realize that. Perhaps you should cull out the ones that are unacceptable. I'm sure I would have no trouble finding a market for them elsewhere."

"Impossible," Schmidt snapped. "This was an exclusive. We had a clear understanding."

The Italian shrugged. "Then pay me what these are worth. That's all I ask of you, Signor Schmidt. Is that so unreasonable?"

"It depends." Schmidt's stare was icy. "How much more do you want?"

Scozza turned his palms upward. "Only a little bit extra, to compensate me for the risks I took and for the extraordinary value of this work."

"How much more?"

"I thought perhaps, ah, an additional fifty thousand lire, over and above the base price, of course."

There was no change whatever in Schmidt's expression. His features might have been carved from stone. "Out of the question."

Scozza sighed.

"A small increment I could perhaps work out."

"And what would that be?"

Schmidt opened his billfold. "Ten thousand."

"Forty."

They settled, as Scozza had known they would, on an extra thirty thousand lire.

When the paparazzo had counted and pocketed the stack of bank notes, the German picked up the envelope. "And the negatives?"

"All there, in the envelope."

A frosty smile appeared under the white-blond moustache. "I'm sure you won't mind if I check them?"

"Of course not. I would expect you to. After all, they are your property, and they are extremely valuable."

Schmidt pulled a small magnifying glass from his pocket. It took fifteen minutes for him to examine the strips of acetate. When he was finally satisfied, he thrust the envelope into his pocket and stood up. He shook hands with Scozza and bowed stiffly. "It has been a pleasure to do business with you."

The Italian smiled. "For me also. I wish you a pleasant flight home. Over the Alps."

"Yes. *Auf wiedersehen*."

"*Buon viaggio*."

Scozza slumped back down into his chair and watched as the German strode through the crowded lobby. He waited for a few minutes, then strolled casually to the elevators. He got off on the seventh floor.

A soft voice answered his knock. "*Avanti*."

The paparazzo opened the door and closed it behind him. He locked it and dropped the chain into place.

Anna Cirelli was sitting on the bed. Her large, dark brown eyes were fixed on him, their color a striking contrast to the pale skin of her face. She licked her lips. "Did you get the money?"

Scozza took off his raincoat and tossed it over a chair. "I got it, but not as much as the bastard promised me."

The large eyes looked frightened. "Not as much? Why not?"

"Because the rotten Hun jewed me down, of course. You know you can't trust those lying turds."

She licked her lips again. "How much did he give you?"

Scozza pulled a sheaf of bank notes from his pocket. He peeled off a number of the bills and dropped them onto the bed.

Wordlessly, her fingers trembling, Anna Cirelli picked up the money and counted it. When she finished, she looked up at the photographer, her eyes wide now with fear. "There is only twenty thousand lire here. You promised me—"

"I promised you?" Scozza's tone rose. "I promised you? What about what was promised me? What about that cheating piece of German dogshit? Do you think I like being screwed?"

The girl's voice broke. "But I really need that money. I told you the—the problem I have. I—"

"You are not the only girl in the world who has a habit to feed."

Anna bowed her head. Her shoulders shook.

"Jesus Christ." Scozza pulled the sheaf of bills from his pocket and counted a few more of them. He threw the notes down onto the bed. "There's another ten thousand. I hope you realize that cuts even deeper into my own stinking little share."

She looked up at him and wiped her eyes with the back of her hand. "Thank you."

Scozza grunted. He unbuttoned his shirt and pulled it off. "It wasn't easy, you know, for me to sell the damned pictures to him anyway. He wanted someone better known. The truth is, Anna, he'd never heard of you."

"But that is understandable, isn't it? He is German, and I don't think *Neve Profonda* was ever released there. In Germany, I mean."

Scozza stepped out of his trousers and threw them after the shirt onto the chair. "So what if it had been? One part in a small picture? That hardly makes you a star. Incidentally, I think I can get you a part in a porno a friend of mine is going to shoot next week."

The girl picked up the bills and put them into a drawer in the night table.

Scozza looked at her. "Now there is the other part of our agreement."

"Yes." She got up from the bed, her face solemn, and pulled her dress over her head.

When Scozza was naked, he lay down on the floor on his back. His skin was the color of camembert, and his belly sagged to one side like a pouch filled with thick liquid. He was excited, and his heart was beating rapidly. "Come on, hurry."

Anna unhooked her bra and removed it, and slid her pants down over her smoothly curving hips.

She really does have an excellent body, Scozza thought. Fortunately the drugs have not ruined it. Yet. I should have gotten more money from that filthy Hun.

198

The girl stood over him with her legs apart, her feet on either side of his head. She was facing his feet.

Scozza looked up at her, his eyes shining. "Now. Do it now."

Slowly she brought herself down into a squatting position. Scozza's breath was coming in short, hot gasps. He could feel his pulse pounding in his temples as he watched her sphincter muscles work and saw her anus begin to open.

chapter 35

Il Mondo's offices occupied the third floor of a modern office building on the Via Lombardia. Framed covers of the magazine hung on the walls of the sleekly furnished reception room. It was six-thirty in the evening by the time Scozza arrived, but the place was bustling. A number of visitors sat waiting in the deep leather chairs. Scozza took off his raincoat and shook water from it onto the large black and white tiles of the floor.

The receptionist was not bad, he decided. A little long in the nose, but good tits. Round and full, they would photograph well. "I'm Scozza," he said pleasantly. "The photographer. Signor Galupo is expecting me."

The girl smiled and spoke into a white telephone. When she put the instrument down, she said, "Signor Galupo will see you in just a moment. Would you care to have a seat, please?"

Scozza returned her smile. "I prefer to stand. Been lying around all day."

"I know your work," the girl said. "It's very good. I've seen your credits often. In the magazine."

He was pleased. "Have you? That's very kind of you."

"Must be exciting, to be a famous photographer."

That was a little heavy, Scozza thought. Probably she was angling for something. "It has its moments. Although most of the time it's simply a lot of damned hard work." This afternoon, for example, had been exhausting.

"Oh come on, now," the girl teased. "You get to take

pictures of all those pretty girls. That can't be too hard to put up with."

So that was it. Scozza composed his face so as to look sincere. "You've done modeling yourself, I suppose?"

She seemed surprised. "Me? Model?" She laughed. "Oh, no. That is, just some amateur stuff, back home."

"And where is that?"

"Agrigento. Do you know it?"

"Sure. It's in the south, near Taormina."

"Right."

"You ought to think about it, you know."

"About what?"

"Modeling. I have a hunch you might do very well."

"Are you serious? With my nose?"

"That's nothing. It makes you seem real, believable. And that's what could make photos of you quite interesting." He looked at her breasts, his expression sober, professional. "I couldn't really tell, of course, until I shot some tests in my studio."

The girl was wide-eyed. "Where is that, your studio?"

"In the Hotel Albero."

"Do you think we could—"

The phone rang. The girl answered it and looked up at him. "Signor Galupo will see you now. Do you know where his office is?"

"Sure. Thanks." He smiled again. "Maybe we could talk more, later."

"Yes, of course. I'd love to."

I'll bet you would, he thought. And so would I. He tucked her away in his mental file and walked through the door behind her desk, his wet raincoat draped over his arm.

The editorial offices of *Il Mondo* were a shocking contrast to the modern chic of the reception room. It reminded Scozza of the time when, as a boy, he had worked in a hotel restaurant in Naples. The dining room was quiet, and the guests sat at tables covered with crisp white linen, and then you went through the swinging doors into the kitchen and there was squalid, steam-clouded bedlam, the cooks cursing and the heat and the noise insufferable and the floor strewn with bits of food and other slop.

This place was like that. There were paste-up and layout tables and drawing boards and glass-walled writers' cubbyholes haphazardly crowded together, and all of it was littered with pieces of paper and photographs, and men and women, most of them young, were running in all directions. Scozza wondered how a magazine could ever be produced in such confusion.

Not that *Il Mondo* was a work of art. But it was generally considered the best of its genre in Italy, and its pages were invariably jammed with advertising, and it had a circulation of over two million. The magazine also paid top rates for photographs. Scozza was curious as to what Galupo had in mind. He took a deep breath and knocked once on the white door of the managing editor's office.

"Come in!"

The paparazzo stepped inside and closed the door behind him. Galupo's office was as disheveled as the area he had just left.

"Hello, Scozza. You're late." Galupo was about fifty, but he tried to emulate the young men on his staff. His gray hair hung down over his ears, and he wore his shirt open, a gold chain gleaming at his neck. His trousers were tight, and the waistband cut into his gut.

Scozza dropped his raincoat onto a chair. "Sorry. You can't get taxis in this damned town when it rains."

"Sit down, sit down," Galupo said. "Drink?"

"Sure."

The editor reached into a drawer of his desk and produced a bottle of Hennessey Three-Star and paper cups. He filled the cups and handed one to Scozza. "Cin-cin!"

"Cin-cin." The photographer knocked back the fiery liquid, enjoying the spreading warmth as the cognac coursed into his fat belly.

Galupo emptied his own cup and shuddered. "Good stuff."

"Perfect for a night like this." Scozza waited politely for the editor to get down to business.

Galupo leaned forward and squinted at him. "Before we discuss one word of this, I must have your solemn promise that this subject will remain absolutely confidential, whether you take the job or not."

Scozza raised his right hand. "On my mother's grave."

A cynical smile etched the corner of Galupo's mouth. "In your case, that may or may not be an acceptable vow."

"I will say nothing."

"Okay. Here is the deal. A certain motion picture producer will open a new film here in Rome in a few weeks. From what I have heard, this will be the best work this man has ever done, and it will almost surely be a huge hit. Now. The star of

201

this movie is somebody new. An American. There is some controversy surrounding him. His personal life, love affairs, that kind of thing."

Scozza sniffed. "And you want pictures of him. With his women, or whatever."

"More than that," Galupo said. "Much more than that. When the film opens, we want to break a complete story on this man. The making of the movie, some of the controversial things that have happened to him, and yes of course, his affairs. But all of it must be done in absolute secrecy."

"And that is why you want me to do this work, rather than one of your own staff photographers?"

Galupo smiled. "The reason you asked me that question is because you wanted to set the stage for our discussion of your fee. That's right, isn't it, Scozza?"

The photographer's expression was one of bland innocence. "Fee? We have said nothing about my fee."

"I know, but we shall. The reason I want you, my friend, is that you are without question the tops in your entire whorey business. You are the nonpareil, the champion. Okay? I tell you that right off, so that we do not have to waste time fucking around in an argument over money. I will pay you handsomely for your work. But what is much more important than the size of your fee is that I must determine whether you can do this. The assignment will take time, and it involves travel, and it will not be easy. And I must be certain that you can give me outstanding results. You see, this is not to be merely a few sensational photographs, although I want the most sensational photographs you have ever taken. It is to be much more than that. It is to be an outstanding piece of photojournalism."

As he listened to the editor's words, the lira signs in Scozza's head doubled and then tripled. He wet his lips. "Is there any more cognac in that bottle?"

"Sure." Galupo refilled their cups. "We can't fly on one wing, eh?"

Scozza sipped his drink this time, savoring it. "If the film has already been shot, how would I go about getting pictures of these incidents, whatever they were?"

"I will tell you, if you take the assignment. I assume you want it?"

"Of course I do." The photographer pulled a cigarette from his pocket and lit it.

"And you understand that you must give this one hundred

fifty percent of your effort until the job is finished?"

"I understand that clearly. And to be frank with you, I am intrigued by what you are telling me."

Galupo swallowed the contents of his cup. His eyes watered, and he wiped them with his shirt-sleeve. "Good, I'm glad you are."

Scozza smiled. "And now, as much as I hate to bore you with such a mundane subject, I need to know the fee you are offering."

The editor paused dramatically. "Your fee, Scozza, will be six hundred thousand lire plus expenses."

Despite himself, the paparazzo's mouth opened and closed. That was even higher than the top figure he had audaciously hoped for.

"And that's not all," Galupo said. "If you bring me really great stuff, do a really outstanding job, there's a fat bonus on top of that."

Scozza drained his cup. Jesus Christ. A scene appeared in his mind. He was in the royal suite on the top floor of the Hotel Grand, surrounded by spectacularly beautiful girls. One of them was brushing his hair, another held a tiny spoon to his nostril, another was manicuring his fingernails, and still another sucked his cock.

"Well?" The editor watched him closely. "How does that sound?"

"It sounds acceptable."

"Yes. I thought you would find it so. Now what about it—could you positively deliver what I am asking for?"

Scozza blew a stream of blue smoke toward the ceiling. He spoke slowly. "What I will give you, without any question, is the finest work I have ever done."

Galupo slapped the desk with an open palm. "That's what I wanted to hear." He extended the hand to the photographer who shook it warmly.

"Now can you tell me who these people are?"

"Yes, of course. The producer is Vicente Morello."

Scozza grunted. "No problem. I have shot him before."

"I know you have. And also his mistress, Cecily Petain. She is the female star of the movie."

"Who is the man, this American?"

"His name is Hendricks. He is a huge blond oaf whom women seem to find beautiful. Also there is a very pretty Italian actress in the film named Tina Rinaldi."

"Never heard of her."

"Neither had I. But I'm told she may make it big."

"What was the controversy?"

"You know Carlos Caserta?"

"I know who he is, sure."

"Originally he was to be the star of the movie. But then he was injured badly while they were shooting in Spain. He's still in a hospital there."

"Ah. I think I read something about that in the newspaper."

"Yes, the papers were full of it a few weeks ago. Also there was an accident with a car. Morello's Ferrari, in fact. This Hendricks was in it, and a girl. The girl was killed."

"Interesting." Scozza stubbed out his cigarette in the ashtray on the editor's desk.

"Yes, you can see that there is plenty to work with."

"Was that the travel you mentioned—you want me to go to Spain?"

"Exactly. An interview with Caserta would alone be worth the trip."

"Yes. Where is the hospital?"

"I'll give you all that."

Galupo opened a file drawer beside his desk and withdrew a packet. "This contains a list of the people I want to feature, along with addresses and so forth. It also will give you an outline of how I want the story developed. Although you're to see it only as an outline. I'm sure that other ideas will occur to you as you go along. The thing is, of course, always to overshoot."

"Yes, of course, I know that. I always do."

"Okay. What I would like you to do is to take this along and study it. Any questions, call me. But I want you to put your own thinking against this too. With your experience there must be a lot of ideas of your own you could give me."

"I'm sure there will be." Scozza took the packet from the editor and put it on his lap. "What's the timetable?"

"The premiere is scheduled for Easter week. They do it that way because holidays are always the biggest periods of the year in the movie business. We're timing this so that the story will break just as the film opens."

"So this is for what, your April issue?"

"Exactly."

Scozza drummed on the packet with pudgy fingers. "Doesn't give me all that much time, does it?"

"You'll have a couple of weeks, which should be more than enough."

"Uh-huh. I hope so."

Galupo pulled an envelope out of the file drawer. It was filled with lira notes. The editor slowly counted out a stack of them onto his desk. He handed Scozza the stack. "One hundred thousand lire. That is your retainer. You get the balance upon completion of your work."

"And my expenses?"

"You'll draw them as you go along. We'll take care of your reservations and the tickets for your trip to Spain."

The photographer withdrew a billfold from his jacket pocket. He carefully inserted the lira notes into the billfold and returned it to his pocket.

"And if you would sign this, please." Galupo slid a receipt and a ball-point pen across the desk to the photographer.

Scozza scribbled his name on the piece of paper. He looked up. "Okay. Is that it?"

The editor stared at him. "Almost."

"So? What else?"

Galupo folded his arms and leaned forward, placing his elbows on his desk. "Just this, Scozza. When you take this job, you understand something. This is a one-shot proposition. The story must break when the film opens for us to get the maximum impact. Otherwise our story will be just one of many after the movie is running. Therefore there are no second chances. From our end, we're paying you a hell of a lot of money. From your end, you deliver. No excuses, no fuck-ups, no nothing. Just great pictures, on time. Understood?"

Something in the editor's manner made Scozza feel distinctly uncomfortable. "Yes. Understood."

Galupo continued to hold the photographer in an unblinking stare. "And if you don't deliver, you go floating down the Tiber, along with all the other pieces of shit."

"You don't have to threaten me."

"Who's threatening? I am merely stating the terms of our agreement. That way, nobody has any misconceptions about what is expected. Now if you'll excuse me, I've got work to do. Study that stuff and call me tomorrow." He stood up and extended his hand. "*Bona sera*."

The photographer got to his feet and shook Galupo's hand. "*Bona sera*." Holding the packet under his arm, he picked up his raincoat and left the office.

On his way out Scozza smiled at the receptionist once more and promised to telephone her. Outside it was still drizzling, and the sky was filled with the raw, cold rain that was typical of winter in Rome. The paparazzo stood on the sidewalk, his shoulders hunched against the wet, and tried unsuccessfully to flag down a taxi.

chapter 36

Vicente Morello sprawled on the squashy brown leather sofa and chatted amiably with the producer of *Rome At Night*, one of Italy's most popular television talk shows. The TV producer was a man Morello had known for a long time. His name was Giorgio Serrani, and he had begun his career as an aspiring actor. After failing to win anything but minor roles on the stage, Serrani had turned to movies, where he had won no roles of any kind. He then stumbled into television, where he quickly perceived that whereas he probably would do no better as an actor in that medium than he had in the others, even an idiot could succeed in the management end of TV. Serrani started as a gofer on a soap opera running on R.A.I. Corporation, the government-owned two-channel station, and from there caught on as an assistant producer. Three years later he was producing *Rome At Night*.

"What are your plans for foreign distribution?" Serrani asked.

Morello adjusted the massive gold ring on the third finger of his right hand. "I'm going to wait until after the film opens before I get down to serious negotiation."

Serrani smiled. "Pretty sure of yourself, eh?"

Morello regarded the other man as he might a fly on a pile of horse droppings. "It is by far the best picture I have ever made. Better than *The Orphan*, better than *The Jewel Robbery*, better than anything. I would be a fool to make a deal on foreign rights before the premiere."

Serrani had an oily face and a mass of carefully groomed hair. He touched a lock of the hair. "It must be wonderful, to know you have something that good."

That was more like it. Morello expected inferior beings to keep a respectful tongue in their heads at all times, even when, as in this instance, he was manipulating them to do his bidding. "It is satisfying, yes. But only because it means that my grand plan is proceeding as conceived."

Serrani twisted the lock of hair round a pudgy finger. "Your grand plan?"

"Yes." Morello glanced casually at the large round electric clock on the far wall. "How much time do we have? I would like more coffee."

Serrani leaped to his feet. "More coffee? Of course, at once." He snapped his fingers, and a harassed-looking girl scurried into the room. She wore glasses and tight-fitting jeans. "Bring us a fresh pot of coffee, quickly," Serrani ordered. The girl spun around and hurried out. With affected casualness the television producer slumped back down into the chair opposite Morello. "We have plenty of time. The commercials will be on for another ten minutes or so."

Morello nodded. In Italy, TV commercials were all shown at once, rather than sprinkled through the programs as in the United States. They were aired at the same time each evening—eight o'clock—for twenty minutes. Partly because the quality of the programs on the national network was so bad, and partly because the commercials were quite good, more people tuned in to the advertising than to the so-called entertainment.

"Go on, Vicente," Serrani said. "About your grand plan."

"Mm? Oh, yes." Morello smoothed his elegant silk Charvet tie. He looked tan and fit, as usual, having returned only a few days earlier from two weeks of winter sunshine on the beaches at Tenerife. "This film will not only be extremely successful in terms of the business it will generate. Far more important is what it will mean to the history of the industry."

Serrani's eyes widened.

Morello spoke slowly, for effect. "*The Hired Gun*, you see, will be epochal."

"Epochal?"

"Exactly. It will mark the beginning of a new era in the production of motion pictures. Not only here, but in the States, as well."

The girl reentered the room, carrying a pot of coffee. She refilled their cups and set the pot down on the low table between the men. Morello studied her snugly encased buttocks as she left. Serrani leaned forward. "You were saying?"

Morello sipped coffee. "The picture is a western, as you know. And good westerns have always made money. They have been a staple since the days of the silent one-reelers."

"But a western made in Italy?"

Morello fixed the television producer with an imperious gaze. "Why not?"

"Well, it's just that—"

"This country has a tradition of creating innovations in films. *The Bicycle Thief, Satyricon,* the list is endless. Now I have done an entirely new kind of western. And the genre will never be the same again."

A page poked his head into the room. "Two minutes, Signor Morello."

Serrani looked at the clock. "Then in your, ah, grand plan, you see this as only the first of its kind? You intend to follow it with others like it?"

Morello smiled. "You have a quick mind, Giorgio. I like that."

"Thank you, Vicente."

"My organization is growing, of course. Perhaps you might be interested in joining me, at some future point."

Serrari's pink tongue moistened his lips. "That is very flattering. I would like such an opportunity very much."

"Of course. Motion pictures are where the money is, you know. In our business," he added fraternally.

"Oh, I know that. I know that very well."

"And I appreciate the publicity you are giving *The Hired Gun.*"

"Not at all," Serrani said quickly. "It is an honor to have you on our show."

The page reappeared. "Time, Signor Morello."

"There will be more," the television producer went on. "The entire country will be very interested in your movie. We'll have you on again soon, perhaps with members of the cast."

Vicente got to his feet. "Wonderful, Giorgio." He shook the other man's hand and followed the page out the door.

There was a burst of applause as Morello walked from the wings onto the stage. He loved this, a live appearance before a live audience, people beating their hands and cheering. It reminded him of his days in the stock companies, when he lived out of a wicker suitcase and ate unspeakable food and found that it was worth every hardship the instant he went before the footlights. He smiled broadly and waved to the audience. His already brown skin had been darkened further by pancake makeup, and with his gray sideburns and his white teeth and his tan silk gabardine suit by Peckham's of London, he looked wonderful, he knew.

The hostess of *Rome At Night* was Angelina Lucati. A one-time assistant editor of Italian *Vogue* magazine, she had started in TV as a reporter and had talked R.A.I. into giving her a shot as the duenna of a gossip show in which she tried hard to copy the personal style of David Frost, tapes of whose British as well as American programs she studied diligently. At first her show was only moderately successful, but then as she attracted more and more celebrities and show business guests, probing their personal as well as their professional lives with wide-eyed ingenuousness, *Rome At Night* pulled larger and larger audiences, and now it was one of the top shows in Italy, at least in terms of viewership. Angelina was not the prettiest girl on television, but she was voluptuous and likable and it was obvious that one of the chief reasons for her popularity was that the average young woman could identify with her.

Tonight Angelina was wearing low-cut orange silk pajamas, and she looked almost glamorous. There were two large cup-shaped modern chairs in the center of the stage, and she lounged in one of them. As Morello waved and grinned at the audience, Angelina smiled adoringly at the producer and held her hand out to him. He crossed to where she sat and held her hand in both of his while he kissed her cheek warmly. The applause swelled, and at last Morello flopped into the other chair, directing his smiling gaze now at the lens of the camera whose red light told him it was taking.

Angelina's voice was rich and throaty. "Vicente, welcome to *Rome at Night*. It's wonderful to see you."

"Thank you for having me, Angelina. Believe me, I'm delighted to be here."

"Even though we obviously had to tear you away from a beach and lots of sunshine and bikinis and all those wonderful things?"

"Well now, I have a confession to make."

"Good. Is it nice and juicy?"

"No, not really. In fact, the opposite. I have to confess that after a few days of that life I get very itchy and can't wait to get back to work."

"Vicente! What would Cecily Petain say if she heard you make such a remark?"

Morello smiled slyly. "I don't know. I'll have to ask her later tonight."

The audience snickered its appreciation. It was common knowledge that the producer and his star lived together, and this kind of oblique reference to their relationship was titillating, a fact Morello understood far better than they did.

Angelina leaned forward. "Speaking of Cecily, I hear that she has gone absolutely mad over your new leading man."

Again the audience stirred. This was exactly the kind of gossip they loved about Angelina and her show.

Morello's face was somber. "To tell you the truth, Angelina, that is something I cannot deny. Cecily and I have had several long talks about it. She has confessed that she simply cannot help herself."

"As a man, don't you find that humiliating, or even infuriating?"

"I did at first, but I have been around beautiful women for a long time, and I understand them."

"Who is this new actor, and what is so attractive about him?"

"His name is Hendricks. He is an American, and his own life in many ways has been more fantastic than any role he could play in movies. He was a cowboy in Texas, and after something happened, I don't know what because he won't talk about it, but I think it was a shooting over a woman, he left and went to sea."

"To sea?"

"Yes, he was a ship's captain when I discovered him."

"A captain! How fascinating. And what made you realize he could become an actor?"

"I knew immediately, from this man's great personal force, from his magnetism, that he could be not only an actor but a tremendous screen personality."

"And so you cast him in the lead of your new film?"

"Oh, yes. At once."

"From sea captain to the starring role in a Vicente Morello production in one jump. How marvelous. That's the kind of thing all we ordinary mortals can only dream about."

"He is an extremely unusual young man."

"I'm sure that's true, Vicente. He must be some hunk of *pesca dolce*."

The audience roared, and Morello grinned. "Women seem to think so."

"What about his acting?"

"Tremendous. He has great natural talent, and of course I

210

had him schooled by some of the best dramatic coaches in Europe."

Again Angelina leaned forward. It was a trick she used to signal the audience that she was about to bore in on her guest with a tough question, and it was very effective. "Isn't it true that Hendricks and Carlos Caserta were hot rivals for the part of the leading man, and that Hendricks got the part only because Caserta was injured and could not complete work in the picture?"

Morello looked uncomfortable. "Who told you that?"

The hostess's mouth turned upward in a sly smile. "You can't keep secrets when you work with a film crew, Vicente. You should know that better than anyone. Now what about it. Isn't that what happened?"

"Well, in a way you could say so." Morello shifted in his seat.

Angelina's tone became even lower, even silkier. "How was Carlos Caserta injured?"

A fine bead of moisture appeared on Morello's forehead. He reached into his pocket for a handkerchief and patted his head with it. "He, ah—fell."

"Fell? How?"

"We were shooting a scene on a roof, and he, ah, fell from the roof."

"Fell from the roof? How awful." Angelina's eyes glittered. "Tell me, Vicente. Was he alone at the time? On this roof?"

Morello swallowed. "No. He was not alone."

"I see. And who was on the roof with him?"

The producer again mopped his forehead.

"Well?"

When he finally answered, Morello's voice was hoarse. "Hendricks."

The audience gasped.

"But don't go jumping to any wild conclusions," Morello said quickly. "It was an accident. He fell. And that is all there was to it. Carlos was badly hurt, but he is coming along nicely, and the doctors tell me he will be home soon."

Angelina sat back in her chair and smiled sweetly. "All right, Vicente. Just as you say. Now I understand you have a treat for us."

Morello looked distinctly relieved at having the subject changed. "That is correct. I have a clip from the picture. Just a few feet of one scene, but I think it will tell you much more about *The Hired Gun* and my new star than I ever could."

"Wonderful." Angelina swung her gaze out to the audience. "And here it is, ladies and gentlemen, the first peek anyone has had at the picture all of Italy and in fact all of Europe is awaiting so eagerly."

There was a monitor just offstage. Morello watched it as the network fed in the clip from *The Hired Gun*. It was a scene in which Hendricks entered the saloon and looked disdainfully at the local cowhands and ranchers as they hastily made room for him at the bar. He ordered whiskey and leaned casually on the battered mahogany planking, one booted foot on the brass rail. He was taller than any of the others, and his blondness made a startling contrast against their dark, Latin features. He knocked back the shot of rye, and as he did a man in one corner of the room surreptitiously slipped his pistol out of its holster. The camera was angled so that you could see Hendricks was not oblivious to the danger, as his attacker thought, but was calmly watching the man in the mirror behind the bar. When the man raised his gun, Hendricks whirled rattlesnake fast, and the big .44 Colt roared and bucked in his fist.

The man slammed backward into a poker table, and cards and chips and whiskey glasses flew in all directions. The table collapsed, and the man lay spread-eagled in the midst of the wreckage, gouts of dark red gore pumping out of a hole in the front of his shirt. Hendricks holstered the Colt and dropped a silver dollar onto the bar. He strode past the cowed patrons and through the swinging doors out onto the street. A girl stood there, a look of terror on her face. Hendricks glanced down at the girl and smiled. He put one arm around her and gave her buttocks a reassuring pat. As he held her, the girl's expression went from fear to wonder. There was a cut to a reverse angle close-up of Hendricks from her perspective, looking up at him. Hendricks's sideburns were long, and they were bleached out from the sun. There was a red bandanna tied around his neck, and his large, even teeth were incredibly white against his tan skin.

Morello heard women in the studio audience gasp as they looked at the tight shot of Hendricks, and the producer chortled to himself. It really was a hell of a good scene, and the American was phenomenal. The clip ended, and the audience burst into cheers and applause.

When the hand clapping finally died down, Angelina smiled warmly at Morello. "I want to thank you, Vicente, for being our guest this evening. And after what we've just seen, I don't think there's any question in anyone's mind that *The Hired Gun* will be a tremendous hit."

At that the audience applauded once again, and Morello grinned out at them. He thanked Angelina and kissed her cheek and bounded off the stage.

*   *   *

Later, in Angelina's dressing room, Morello lounged in a chair and puffed on a cigar as the show's hostess wiped makeup from her face.

She looked at his reflection in the mirror before her. "Well, what did you think?"

Morello tapped the ash from his Havana. "Not bad."

Angelina was surprised. "Not bad? What do you mean, not bad? I just gave you the biggest hype you ever saw on television, and all you can say is, not bad. Vicente, you are an ungrateful bastard."

The producer smiled. "You could have built up the bit about Hendricks and Caserta on the roof a little more."

Angelina dabbed cold cream on her face. "Oh, nonsense. The audience was panting over it, and you know it."

"Maybe you're right." Morello knew better than to appear too grateful to a woman for favors done, no matter how munificent. He studied Angelina's ass. She really was a well-rounded piece. Maybe he would fuck her tonight, just to be nice.

Angelina's dark eyes were fixed on his reflection in the mirror. "Do you know what you're going to do for me tonight?"

"I was just thinking about it."

"You're going to buy me the most fabulous dinner in the most fabulous restaurant in Rome."

Morello looked at her ass again. "Okay. I'll do that, too." He pulled gently on the long, fragrant cigar.

chapter 37

On spending money, Scozza was schizoid. When he was flush and indulging himself, the paparazzo threw it away on whores and cocaine and food and champagne and gambling as if the bills were tainted and he could not get rid of them fast enough. But when he was on business, and especially on those rare occasions when he was operating on an expense account, he was as penurious as a starving miser. This was not because Scozza wished to save his employer money. It was because he wished to have as great a difference as possible between what he spent and what he could claim to have spent. That difference, of course, would go into his pocket.

When he got off the plane at Madrid International Airport, Scozza carried a camera bag containing two Nikons, film and filters, and a canvas satchel in which were his shaving gear, a couple of extra shirts, and some socks and underwear. After passing through customs, he bought sardines and fried peppers from a street vendor and then rented a car. The cheapest available was a 950 cc Seat, and Scozza haggled with the clerk over the rate before taking the machine, an underpowered little piece of junk he could barely stuff his bloated body into.

The drive south took four hours, good time for the trip, and especially in light of what Scozza was driving. The day was sunny and pleasant, with spring much in evidence in the Spanish countryside. The olive trees were green, flowers were in bloom, and farmers with ox-drawn plows drew deep furrows in the rich black earth. But the paparazzo hardly noticed. He was too busy scheming, considering angles, weighing one move against another. The fee *Il Mondo* was paying him was enormous, greater than any he had ever received for a magazine assignment, and yet his crafty mind was working hard to invent means by which he could force the publication to increase the sum.

One of Scozza's intellectual strengths was that he assumed everyone was as amoral as he was. He therefore saw anybody with whom he had dealings of any kind as an adversary who was out to screw him. Hence his modus was always to strike—or screw—first. Do unto others before they do unto you. A useful motto. And thus it had immediately occurred to him upon learning what his fee for this job would be that something was awry. The premise that *Il Mondo* would pay such a stupendous amount—six hundred thousand lire, for the love of God—simply because they thought they could build a scandalous story around this new picture Morello was producing, would not hold up. There had to be something else, something furtive and probably even bizarre that Galupo did not want the photographer to know about. Well, the hell with that. Scozza would learn the editor's secret, and then he

214

would devise ways to use the information. And along the way, as he worked, he would find other opportunities to gather facts as well as photographs that he would hold back to use, as he had so often and so lucratively in the past, for himself.

When he arrived at the clinic in Montillas, Scozza asked for the doctor who was treating Carlos Caserta, explaining that he represented one of the most important periodicals in Europe, whose editorial staff had assigned him to do a story on the medical man in charge of the case. Scozza knew from long experience that there was no better ploy than this one to open official doors and to cut red tape. Appeal to a man's vanity, and he was yours. Accordingly, and as expected, he was shown in to Dr. José Borales within a few minutes.

Scozza repeated his story to the doctor, throwing in a few unctuous comments on Borales's skill and growing fame as a result of his treatment of the actor and was rewarded by a warm and expansive reaction from the surgeon.

The paparazzo's tone was earnest and respectful. "What is your prognosis, Doctor?"

Borales folded his large hands before him on the desk. "I am pleased that the patient is making good progress. For a time, you see, it was questionable whether he would walk again."

Scozza inclined his head sympathetically. "You must have employed enormous skill, as well as knowledge, to repair such damage. It is like a miracle."

The doctor was obviously flattered. He cleared his throat. "Well, I would not go quite so far as that, but I certainly will admit that it has been an extremely difficult case." He followed this with a long, technical explanation of Caserta's injuries and the methods he was employing to treat them. His comments were full of arcane phrases to do with lumbar regions and motor response and a lot of other mumbo jumbo. Scozza did not understand any of it, but he pretended to take extensive notes. He also made sure he asked Borales questions about the doctor's personal background and medical training.

Borales outlined his background, remarking that he was probably best known for his work with *toreros* who had suffered *cornadas,* wounds on the horns.

"Of course we knew that, Senor Doctor," Scozza assured him. "Your fame from such work has spread all across Europe." That was heavy, but Borales seemed to be buying it. "And now, with your kind permission, I would like to take a few photographs."

The doctor expressed surprise. "Photographs? Of me?"

Scozza unzipped his camera bag and pulled out one of the Nikons. "Yes, of course. *Il Mondo* is a photo magazine, you know."

"Um. Yes, of course. I understand."

The paparazzo shot a dozen or so exposures, coaching Borales on various poses at his desk and also standing beside the X-ray scanner. When Scozza finished, he returned his camera to its bag and remarked almost casually that he now wished to look in in Caserta.

Borales was laconic and firm. "See the patient? Out of the question. We've allowed no visitors, and especially none from the, ah, press."

Scozza's fat face sagged in disappointment. "That really is a shame. I mean, without perhaps just one or two pictures of Senor Caserta, the story on you would be, you know, incomplete."

The doctor blinked. "It would?"

"Of course. Our editors would feel that we did not have you fully covered if we failed to include at least something on him."

"Yes. Um. I see."

Scozza drew the strap of the camera bag over his shoulder. "But of course, you have your rules."

"Yes. Well. Perhaps there could be an exception, just this once."

"Really? Honestly, Doctor, that would be wonderful. And you can see how it would make the feature on you even more interesting."

"Yes, I understand. But mind you, no more than a few minutes."

"Certainly. Whatever you say."

A moment later Scozza was led by a nurse to Caserta's room. The paparazzo had seen Caserta a number of times during the years he had been in Rome, on the first occasion when Caserta was still playing professional soccer. He had also photographed the big man three or four times more or less routinely after he had become an actor, and once during an altercation with a headwaiter outside a nightclub when Caserta had beaten the man's face to a bloody pulp. That shot had been worth thirty thousand lire from *Il Messaggero*, the morning newspaper. As a result, even though he knew Caserta was in this clinic because he had sustained a serious injury, Scozza was startled by the changes in the actor's appearance.

Caserta was wan and very thin. Even his skin seemed to have changed, its color a waxy gray instead of its usual swarthy olive. He was sitting in a chair beside his bed, wearing a bathrobe over his pyjamas, and slippers. His hands, folded on his lap, looked slim and fragile. He glanced up when Scozza walked in, the movement of his head slow and deliberate, as if it caused him great pain to make the slightest movement. His eyes seemed to have sunk deep into his head, and there were black patches under them. Scozza had the unpleasant impression that he was looking at a dead man.

Caserta's voice was small and distant. "Yes? What is it?"

"Signor Caserta, how good to see you. I am Scozza, journalist from *Il Mondo*, in Rome."

The actor appeared not to comprehend. "Journalist? From Rome?"

Scozza extended his hand. Caserta took it with apparent effort, and there was no strength in his grip. "Yes, *Il Mondo* sent me. You know, the picture magazine? People from all over Italy, all over Europe even, are eager to know how you are coming along, praying that you are recuperating."

"They are?" Caserta's face registered confusion. "But I have heard very little—"

"Hospital rules." Scozza drew up another chair and sat down on it. "They are afraid here of getting you too excited. But your fans are clamoring for news of you. So great is their interest, the clinic finally had to give in. My story may even be syndicated to other publications."

Caserta nodded.

"Here, I've brought you something." Scozza dug into his camera bag and withdrew a gaudily wrapped package. "May I open it for you?" He tore away the paper and held up a book. "There, you see? The complete history of this past soccer season. All the records of every team in the world. All the scores, everything."

Caserta made no move to take the book. "That is very kind of you."

"Yes, I'm sure you will find it fascinating. Here, let me put it on your bedside table, where you will be able to reach it easily."

"Thank you."

"Not at all. Well, Signor Caserta, how are you feeling?"

"Not good. I am in considerable pain."

"Ah, I am sorry to hear it. But I must say, you look wonderful. A trifle thin, perhaps, but outside of that, very fit."

217

"I do?"

"Absolutely. And Dr. Borales tells me you are making a marvelous recovery."

Caserta stared at his feet. "Each day I try to take a few steps. But it is very hard, and that is when the pain is at its worst."

Scozza pursed his lips in what he hoped would pass for an expression of sympathy. "I can imagine. But of course, you have always been noted for your bravery. Going back to when you were a great soccer star. Tell me, when do you expect to return to Rome?"

The actor's voice was weak and distant. "I don't know. A few more months, perhaps."

"What a shame. You will miss the premiere."

"Premiere?"

"Of *The Hired Gun*. The picture you were working in when you were injured. It is scheduled to open in Rome in a few more weeks. There has been a lot of talk about it."

"What talk?"

"That it will make this Hendricks, the American, a star."

Caserta's tone suddenly seemed stronger. "That son of a whore."

Ah. This was more like it. "It is criminal, that he should be in the picture, in a role that is rightfully yours."

"He planned it, the bastard. All of it."

Scozza dove back into his camera bag and pulled out a Nikon. "Planned it? What do you mean?"

Caserta grimaced. "Just that. He wanted my part in the picture from the beginning. Yelled and screamed to get Morello and the director to give it to him. And when they would not, he—did this to me."

"No. You mean deliberately?"

"Of course deliberately, the American shit. He tried to kill me."

"Incredible." Scozza pulled a floor lamp closer to Caserta's chair. "I want to get a little more light, so I can take a picture or two." Actually, he had plenty of light, having loaded the Nikon with Ilford 800. What Scozza wanted was effect. With the light now glaring harshly over Caserta's shoulder, the actor looked like a ferocious death's head. Scozza was delighted with the result. He began shooting rapidly.

Caserta gritted his teeth. "I will get revenge, no matter how long it takes, or what I must do."

The paparazzo fired away, cocking the F2 with his thumb,

releasing the shutter with his index finger, all the while goading Caserta to make more savage exclamations of what retribution he would exact from Hendricks when he returned to Rome.

A nurse appeared in the doorway. She was squat, broad, and wore a moustache on her upper lip. She glared at Scozza. "That is all, senor. Time is up."

The photographer went on shooting. "But Dr. Borales said—"

She folded her arms, the gesture unmistakably asserting her authority. "Dr. Borales said you could have a few minutes. You have been here for twenty."

Scozza snapped even more rapidly. "Very well. Just as soon as I—"

The nurse's voice rose. "You will go *now*."

The paparazzo got to his feet. "I was just leaving." On impulse he took a shot of the nurse, then shoved the Nikon back into his bag. "Arrivederci, Signor Caserta. It's wonderful to see you coming along so well."

Caserta nodded weakly. "When will the story appear?"

"Very soon. We'll let you know."

Outside the clinic it was already dark, and the air was cool and fresh. The moon had risen over the mountains to the west, and it hung in the velvety Spanish sky like a great orange lantern. Scozza stuffed his bulk into the tiny Seat, wondering where he could find a meal, a bottle of wine, a room and a girl, each to be had as cheaply as possible.

chapter 38

The next day the paparazzo rose early and returned to the same small, greasy café in which he had had dinner the night before. He breakfasted on *huevos, café con leche,* and a shot of *aguardente*. The notes Galupo had given him were in his inside jacket pocket, but Scozza had no need to look at them. He had committed every detail to memory and knew exactly what he had to do. He lingered over his brandy and coffee, smoking cigarettes and going over his plans for the day.

Upon leaving the café, Scozza asked directions to the office of the *guardia civil* and drove there. In the office he asked a few questions and bribed a clerk one thousand pesetas to give him two glossy eight-by-ten-inch photographs from a file.

From there Scozza drove northwest to La Cuarta Luna. It was midmorning when he arrived, and the warm spring sun felt good on his back as he got out of the tiny car and approached the rifle-carrying guard at the gate of the ranch. He explained what he wanted, and the man telephoned from the tiny guard house beside the gate. The guard then opened the heavy gate and waved Scozza through.

To his surprise the paparazzo found Senor Navarro polite but very cool. The rancher did not even invite Scozza into the house, but instead stood outside the front door. He answered Scozza's questions patiently enough, but limited his replies to providing only the barest amount of information. What was further puzzling was that he appeared to have no reaction whatever to the photographer's attempts to flatter him with fulsome references to his career as a matador.

Scozza's suspicious mind told him that something was behind this, but he could not fathom what it was. Not until he had almost given up and was about to leave did he get a hint of what had inspired Navarro's aloofness. It was a casual reference Scozza made to Tina Rinaldi that caused a flicker of interest to appear in the rancher's eyes.

On seeing this, Scozza immediately jumped to several conclusions. He decided to test them. His tone became even more offhand. "Beautiful girl, Signorina Rinaldi."

"Yes. Very beautiful."

"A lot of people think she is much more appealing than Cecily Petain, the star of the picture. And that she is a better actress."

"Much better. And certainly more appealing because her beauty is so much more . . . natural."

So he had been right. Scozza glanced at the mild blue sky, his manner now of a man who was merely making conversation. "Too bad they are no longer together."

"Who is that?"

"Signorina Rinaldi and Hendricks, the American."

Now Navarro could not hide his interest. "They're not together?"

Scozza shook his head. "I don't know what happened, but I have heard that they split up and that she plans to leave Rome."

"Have you heard anything about where she intends to go?"

"No, but I could find out for you, Senor Navarro, and let you know."

The rancher would not bite. He reverted to his earlier coolness. "Not necessary. It's really not important to me."

Nevertheless Scozza knew he had stumbled onto an interesting angle. "Well, I won't take any more of your time. You've been very helpful. Mind if I take a few pictures?"

Navarro shrugged. "One or two, if you like."

From the ranch Scozza drove to the little village, where he took many more photographs and spoke with a number of people, among them Father Pedro and Senor Jifero. At the end of the day he drove back to Madrid, where he ate a meal of fried squid washed down with a bottle of Valdepeñas. He then drank half a liter of brandy and engaged the services of a whore, whom he took to a fleabag hotel on the Avenida Rosas. The girl was reluctant to accommodate him in his requests, proclaiming that never in her career had she encountered such bizarre preferences, but he finally persuaded her by doubling her fee. When she had serviced him, he threw her out and drank the remainder of the brandy, after which he fell into a drunken sleep.

In the morning Scozza returned the rented Seat and then boarded Alitalia's first flight to Rome. As the jet climbed out of Madrid International and turned to the east, the paparazzo adjusted his porcine body as well as he could to the cramped economy-class seat and reflected on his trip. A smile formed on his thick lips. He had been in Spain less than forty-eight hours, and what he had accomplished was far beyond what even he had hoped for. Now the task was to determine how he could use what he had gathered not to the best advantage of Galupo and *Il Mondo*, but to the best advantage of Scozza. The more he thought about it, the more exciting the possibilities became.

chapter 39

The girl's name was Anna. She was young, probably no more than eighteen, but she was already at that point when Italians say, *la prugna e pronta a cadere*, the plum is ready to fall. In less than a year the firm pink flesh of her hips would swell with fat, and her full breasts would begin to sag. But tonight, God—she was something. Hendricks grinned happily as he watched her pour two glasses of champagne from the bottle on the sideboard and bring them back to the bed. He plumped up the pillows and took one of the glasses from her, and she climbed onto the bed beside him.

Anna touched her glass to Hendricks's. "To the return of your good health."

"The return?"

Her smile was sardonic. With her free hand she reached down and flicked a finger against the head of his limp penis.

Hendricks chuckled. "Hey, what do you want from me, woman? Three times in only a couple of hours. That's not bad." His Italian was awkward and crudely accented but a hundred times better than it had been only a few months earlier. Most important, he could converse in the language with ease and was able to discuss nearly any subject with clarity if not eloquence.

Anna sniffed, pretending to be hurt. "If you really loved me, you would find the strength."

He laughed. "Jesus, I do admire a girl with a sense of humor." He sipped champagne, its icy effervescence teasing his throat as he swallowed. "How'd you get into this business, Anna?"

"Just lucky, I guess."

He laughed again at her delivery of the punch line of the old gag. "Men always ask that question in whorehouses, don't they?"

She shrugged. "Only if the girl is very beautiful, like me."

"So how did you get into it?"

"The truth?"

"Of course."

Anna drank from her glass and gazed at the ceiling for a few moments. When she spoke, her voice was quiet, subdued. "My father was a very rich man. He owned a leather factory in Padova, and we lived on a beautiful estate. A huge house, many servants. He was a great sportsman and taught me to ride before I was six." She paused, rocking back and forth a little, her knees drawn up, the expression on her round, childlike face distant and sad as she remembered.

Hendricks stroked her back. "Go on."

Her tone was even softer now. "My horses were hunters, wonderful animals. I went to only the best schools, and when

222

I was at L'Ecole Greuze in France, my mother and my sister died suddenly of typhoid fever. It was an epidemic that killed many people. A year later my father remarried. His new wife was a hussy, a mean, spiteful woman many years younger than he."

"And she was cruel to you?"

The girl's black eyes glittered. "She was vicious. Insanely jealous, and the most selfish woman I have ever met. Around my father she was sweet, cloying. But when he was away on business, which was often, she abused everyone. The servants, and especially me."

"You couldn't let your father know?"

She shook her head. "In matters to do with her he was totally blind." She sighed. "My father was in his late fifties, and all he could comprehend was that he was married to a sensuous young woman. She had quite an appetite."

"How do you know that?"

"First from how my father mooned about after her when he was at home, like a dog after a bitch in heat. And then one day—he was in Milano, as I remember—I went past the potting shed, and I heard whispers. I crept close and looked inside, and there she was on a pile of burlap, her legs in the air, the gardener on top of her." She twisted her mouth in revulsion.

Hendricks was fascinated. "Did she discover you?"

"No. She never knew."

"Then how—"

"At the end of that summer, my father suffered a stroke. He was paralyzed, but he lived almost a year after that. When he died, his will left everything to her, nothing to me. I knew the will was fishy, of course. My father loved me and would never have done such a thing, but what could I prove? Before he was cold in the ground, she turned me out. I had only a few lire and a suitcase with my clothes from school. I came to Rome, and when I had no more money, and nothing to eat, a man brought me here." Her gaze returned to the ceiling, and her voice trailed off.

Hendricks stroked her back again, and they both sipped champagne in silence for a few moments When he spoke, his voice was low and tender. "Anna?"

"Mmmm?"

"You're full of shit."

She spewed champagne from her mouth in a golden spray and guffawed.

"You know what killed it?"

Her mouth curved in delight. "What?"

"The bit about your stepmother fucking the gardener. Right out of D. H. Lawrence."

"Who is D. H. Lawrence?"

"Never mind." He pinched her nipple. "You going to tell me the straight story now?"

She smiled. "Nothing to tell. I never knew who my father was." The smile widened. "I don't think my mother did, either. She was from the river slums just south of here. A drunk with a whole bunch of kids by different fathers. I was the only one pretty enough to become a whore in a good house like this one."

"Then you really were just lucky, huh?"

"Damn right. It is *fantastico*." She waved her arm at the room, festooned with velvet draperies and stuffed with plush, old-fashioned furniture. "Imagine getting paid for working here."

"How'd you learn to talk so well?"

She raised her shoulders. "I have been here since I was fourteen. The *signora* teaches us good manners, and I am often in the company of rich men."

"And the story? Where'd you get the crap about your stepmother and all that?"

"From movies, mostly."

"Ah, movies."

"You like them?"

"Sure. I go all the time. In the early afternoon, usually, when it's not so busy here."

"And then when men ask you why you work in this place, that's what you tell them?"

She pursed her full lips mischievously. "Oh, I vary it, from time to time. Once in a while I am like a Sophia Loren, and I have run away from the stepmother to defy her."

"Loren is good, isn't she?"

"Terrific. A real *affascinatrice*."

"You ever seen Cecily Petain?"

"Who?"

"Cecily Petain. Young French actress."

"Oh, that one. She fucks the producer, what's-his-name, Morello, right?"

"I've heard that."

"She is nothing. Just another cunt."

Hendricks drained his glass and handed it to her. "How about some more of that good stuff?"

Her voice took on a different tone. "Only if you do something nice for me."

"Jesus, baby, I told you. It's worn down to nothing."

"But you want more champagne?"

"Uh-huh."

"Okay. I'll give you some." She took his glass from him and put it on the bedside table. She emptied her own glass into her mouth but did not swallow. She put her glass beside his and then bent down over him.

The effect was like nothing Hendricks had ever experienced. Her mouth was incredibly soft and at first cool with the champagne but then quickly warm. At the same time the tiny bursting bubbles tingled and played at the nerves in his cock, and to his astonishment he could feel the thing grow instantly larger, as if showing him that it could, even if he didn't think so, its desire and enthusiasm far ahead of his own.

Sensing the result of her efforts, Anna increased both pressure and tempo, until she was sure Hendricks was ready. Then she quickly climbed astride him, facing his feet. She rode him slowly, the position and the muscles of her passage clamping him in an exquisite hot vise.

The feeling was deep and nearly painful, producing an excruciating pleasure in his body. He lay against the pillow, not moving, watching the ripples in the girl's back and in her marvelous buttocks as she writhed and twisted in the dim light.

When he came, Hendricks cried out involuntarily, and his fingers and toes fluttered convulsively. To his further amazement the orgasm was even more intense than the earlier ones had been, and it squeezed what seemed to him surely the last vestige of energy out of his spent body. Feeling it, Anna threw her head back and shuddered as she joined him in an ecstatic climax, the juices of their bodies mingling in a fetid, viscous mixture that flooded the hairs of his pubis and ran down his scrotum.

Hendricks could not stir. His body was totally limp, as if the bones and sinews had turned to rubber, and he had no control over any part of himself. It required a conscious effort just to breathe. It occurred to him that he was as exhausted emotionally as he was physically. The French views on his condition passed through his mind, what they called the little death of orgasm, and the *tristesse* that follows lovemaking, and he decided that it was all bullshit. He was incredibly drowsy, unable to feel glad or sad or any other goddamn thing, and all he wanted now was to sleep. Just as he felt himself going under, a flicker of movement in a shadowy corner of the room caught his eye, and one small, barely conscious part of his brain registered amusement. If anybody was trying to hustle him, they'd be disappointed. He'd already given the whore nearly all the money he had, and only a few crumpled lira notes remained in the pocket of the trousers he had tossed over a chair. A moment later he drifted into unconsciousness.

chapter 40

"Hey! Hey, big boy, wake up!"

"Mmm, what—"

"Get up, you hear me? Time to go."

Hendricks made an effort to focus his eyes. The girl was leaning over him, her long glossy black hair tickling his shoulders, her heavy breasts pressing against his arm. What the hell was her name? Anna. "Hello, Anna."

She grasped his jaw in strong fingers and squeezed. "Hey, come on. I let you sleep almost an hour. Got to go now, or I'll get in trouble."

He yawned. An hour? Christ, he'd barely closed his eyes. "What time is it?"

"After four. Come on." She tugged at his arm.

"Yeah, yeah, okay. Where's Weaver?"

"Your friend? He's downstairs, waiting for you."

Hendricks swung his legs over the side of the bed. The rubbery feeling was still with him, and something new had been added: his head hurt. That was the trouble with champagne. The goddamn stuff tasted like something between white wine and soda pop, then when you looked the other way, it snuck up and blew the back of your skull off. Of course the Bardolino and the beer he had consumed before coming to this joint hadn't helped matters a whole hell of a lot either

He and Weaver had gone through two bottles of the fruity red wine at dinner, and then afterward they'd each downed a dozen or so bottles of Heineken. He hadn't drunk that much in months, not since he had returned from to Spain. He was in excellent shape, and except for the hitch in his right shoulder, there were no residual traces of the batterings he had twice sustained, compliments of Carlos Caserta.

But his head—Jesus. Every pulsebeat was like a pistol shot going off between his ears. He pulled his clothes on as quickly as he could, while the girl stood nearby, fidgeting. He suddenly remembered the movement he thought he had seen in the room just before he'd gone to sleep and thrust his hand into his pants pocket. The lira notes were still there, so he must have imagined it. Still the idea that he would doze off under those circumstances was a little disconcerting, whether or not he had been mistaken. Rule one, he had learned in Rio more than ten years ago, was never close your eyes in a whorehouse, señor. It was a good rule not to forget, and yet he'd gone right ahead and ignored it, just like some greenhorn ordinary seaman going ashore on his first trip.

Downstairs in the parlor Weaver sat on a sofa smoking one of his cigarlike joints while he fondled the left breast of a thin but pretty girl with dark, snapping eyes that darted about like those of a ferret. When Hendricks entered the room, the girl's eyes lit momentarily on his face, snapped to his belt buckle, and then fixed on his crotch. Look as hard as you like, baby, Hendricks thought, but you won't see a thing there. Not tonight, anyway.

On the opposite side of the room another whore and a fat man with a thick moustache and a bright red face were drinking champagne and talking animatedly. There were no other people in the dimly lit parlor. A stereo softly poured Scott Joplin into the smoky air.

Weaver waved his joint toward the stereo. "It's a hell of a thing, you know? Progress fucks everything up. Even the whorehouse piano is canned nowadays."

Hendricks sank into a chair. "Cuts down on the overhead."

The cameraman scratched his beard. "Overhead? What the hell do I care about their overhead? Place costs a fortune anyhow. Sixty thousand lire for a piece of ass, for Christ's sake." He looked at the thin girl, still stroking her breast. "Shit, that's almost a hundred bucks."

The girl's voice was husky. "Nobody ever complains ahead of time. Only after."

Hendricks laughed. "It's a function of the economic laws of supply and demand. After a man gets supplied, his demand goes down."

Weaver exhaled a cloud of acrid marijuana smoke. "Down? Hell, mine fell clean off."

The thin girl looked at Hendricks's crotch again. "Would you like to do something?"

He laughed. "Sure I would, honey. But unfortunately I am not able."

"Supply and demand," Weaver said. He crushed out his roach in an ashtray and stood up. "Hey, what do you say we get out of here and go someplace for a drink? A real one, not that fucking giggle water."

Hendricks got to his feet and the pounding in his head increased its tempo. "I'm not sure if I'm able to handle that, either."

"Sure you are. Good for you. And anyhow, this is a farewell celebration." He bent and kissed the thin girl. "So long, sweetheart. Promise me you'll be faithful forever."

Anna walked into the room. She was wearing a low-cut dress, and she had applied liberal amounts of lipstick and eye shadow to her proud young face. Interesting, Hendricks thought. She looks more like a whore now than she did in the sack.

Anna looked at Weaver and then at Hendricks. "You'll come back soon?"

"He will," Weaver said, "but I'll be gone for a while."

They said good-bye to the girls and walked out onto the street. The air was clean and fresh and the night was turning to the gray that comes before dawn. A cab was parked nearby, its driver slumped behind the wheel. When he saw them he flicked his lights and Weaver signaled him to pull up to where they stood.

"This guy knows where to find the late fares," Hendricks observed.

Weaver opened the door of the cab. "Fish where the fish are."

They went to a small cantina near the Piazza Navona. A few sleepy drunks crouched over their glasses at the bar, and at one table two men were playing cards.

Weaver talked Hendricks into a cognac. "Go ahead, it'll straighten you out. And anyhow, this is my going-away party. You wouldn't want me to have to drink alone, would you?"

Hendricks climbed onto a barstool. "I wouldn't give a shit.

But if it'll help me feel better, I'll have one. Ireland, you said."

Weaver ordered brandy for both of them. "Ireland. Most beautiful goddamn locations you ever saw."

"Better than Spain?"

"Different. But yeah, I'd say so. Because it's lusher. So green you can't believe it. And of course, you don't get that in Spain."

"Seems like a long time ago, doesn't it?"

"It sure as hell does. You still with Tina?"

"I moved out, couple weeks back. Got my own place, a two-room apartment on Via Giulia."

"What happened?"

"With Tina? Oh, you know how it is. She started to get too serious. Never said so, but I could feel it. I'd sleep someplace else once in a while, and she'd mope."

"Well, that's women. They pretend they're like men, that they think the same way, need the same things, but it's bullshit. Inside every one of them is a picture of some romantic, perfect guy who loves only her and who only wants to stay home and make babies and rock by the fireside."

Hendricks raised his glass. "Here's to motherhood."

"My ass."

The cognac was liquid fire, but Weaver had been right. It soothed Hendricks, made him feel better. And to his surprise the mention of Tina had produced in him the same twinge of nostalgia it always did. He saw her beautiful face in his mind's eye and experienced a strong desire to see her, to talk with her. Christ, there he was, acting like some dumb kid again.

Weaver wiped his mouth with the back of his hand. "You take the way a man uses whores. Women can't understand that."

"The whores can."

The cameraman laughed. "Okay, but I mean other women. To them, it's incomprehensible that a man would pay to fuck a stranger who's only doing it because she wants the bread."

"Yeah."

"But you take a good hooker, not some broken-dowm bimbo you see in the street, but a real good one like in that joint tonight. Hell, to a man, she's an artist."

"I would say Anna was more of a destroyer."

Weaver grinned. "Same thing, isn't it?"

"I guess so, in that line of work, anyhow."

"What's the best joint you were ever in?"

Hendricks shrugged. "I don't know. We talked about Madame Pauline's in Saigon, remember? I guess that was about as good as any. Or maybe one in Tokyo. The Oriental places are more elaborate, wouldn't you say?"

"Absolutely. They make a much bigger production of taking care of you, and the girls are trained to do all those far-out things."

"Yeah."

"You ever get to Hungry Lil's in Singapore?"

Hendricks shook his head.

"Now there was a place. Every one of those broads was a falling-down knockout, and they had all kinds. Not just Orientals, but Eurasians, Russians, every damn thing. And before Lil would let any one of them work, she personally put the girl through a special training course."

"Is that right?"

"Yeah, unbelievable. A finishing school for pussy. She even taught them the Chinese love rope."

"What the hell is that?"

"You never heard of it?"

"No."

Weaver signaled the bartender for more brandy. "Goddamnedest experience I ever had. The girl has this cord made of silk. It's about two feet long, and every couple of inches there's a knot in it. Before you make it with her, she sticks the cord up your ass."

"What?"

"Yeah, really. But she leaves the end hanging out."

"Christ, I hope so."

"Okay, then, just at the precise instant you start to come, zango! She pulls the mother out." Weaver demonstrated with a violent swing of his arm.

"What does that do?"

"Do? Man, every one of those knots gives your prostate a little tickle. Jesus—I couldn't believe what it did. The tears came out of my eyes, the wax came out of my ears—"

Hendricks roared with laughter. "God, now I've heard everything. The Chinese love rope."

"I'm telling you, it's sensational."

"I like my ladies a little more conventional."

"Don't knock it if you haven't tried it."

"Fair enough. When you leaving?"

230

"Tomorrow afternoon at two. Fly to London, then connect to Dublin."

"You said it's a war picture?"

"Yep. With James Brady. Hell of a break for me to get to work with him. And John Ford's the director, no less. Reason we're shooting in Ireland is because it's a World War One story, but that's what Europe looked like forty, forty-five years ago."

"Really?"

"Sure. Think about it. Today Western Europe is one big jam of towns and cities and superhighways. But Ireland is still meadows and trees and farmland, with quaint little villages here and there, just like France was in 1917, 1918."

"Yeah, I guess you're right. I mean, I've never been there, but I see your point."

"Uh-huh." Weaver drank some of his cognac. "So by the time I get back, you'll be a big fucking star."

"Bullshit."

"I'm telling you man, you can't miss. The picture's got it, and so have you."

"I'll settle for not being embarrassed."

The cameraman swallowed some brandy. "You really that nervous about it?"

Hendricks looked into his glass, and then at Weaver. "I'm about as nervous as I've ever been about anything in my life."

Weaver stroked his beard and spoke with great solemnity. "Remember this. The worst can happen is, you fall on your ass." He threw his head back and brayed laughter.

Hendricks drank the last of his brandy. "You son of a bitch."

The cameraman waved for another round. "Tell you what. We'll drink to success."

Outside a horse-drawn cart rattled by, the clopping of the horse's hooves on cobblestones echoing hollowly. Through the window of the cantina Hendricks could see a few people moving in the thin light, earlygoers hurrying to work. He wondered how he would feel a few days from now. Christ, anything would be better than the tension he felt whenever he thought of the opening.

chapter 41

Vicente Morello studied his appointment book. He glanced up sharply at his secretary who sat across from his desk, her steno pad on her lap. "This doesn't give me enough time." He stabbed the book with his forefinger.

The woman had worked for the producer for five years, a record for the job. She was plain, highly intelligent, and meticulous in her attention to detail. She was also always in control of her emotions, which somehow irritated Morello. She tapped a pencil against her steno pad. "The appointments are exactly as you asked me to make them. Lunch at Bella Fontana with Signor Vache at one o'clock, then your siesta here. You audition Signorina Triano at five, then the columnist from *Paris Match* interviews you at five thirty. At six thirty—"

Morello's voice was harsh. "Damn it, I know what is in the book. It's too crowded." He sat back in his oversized leather chair and pursed his lips. The girl coming in at five was a fireball, he was sure of it, the type who made no bones about her willingness to do anything for a part in a Vicente Morello production. He would have her on the sofa within minutes after she walked in the door. But he hated to rush a situation of that kind. It was too delicious, too precious. Something like that deserved to be savored, languidly.

The secretary's homely face was impassive. "I could push the *Paris Match* interview back to six o'clock."

Jesus Christ, could she read his mind? Sometimes he thought she must be a witch. "No. Too important. See if you can get the Triano girl in a half hour earlier."

"Yes, sir." She made a note on the pad.

Morello leafed through the stack of correspondence on his desk. "There are a number of calls I wish to make."

"Signor Castarelli has been waiting to see you for an hour. He says it is urgent."

"Not now. I have too much to do."

232

Her tone was flat, patient, but quietly insistent. "You have been promising to speak with him for three days."

The producer sighed. The truth was, he knew, that he detested these discussions with his financial man. The only things worse were the meetings with his lawyers. Having to listen to Castarelli drone on, whining about shortages of funds here and overdue amounts there and threatened lines of credit, and all the rest of that accountants' crap—goddamn it, he was a creator, an artist. Becoming burdened with Castarelli's woeful whimpering leeched the producer's energies, sapped his creative strength. Shit. He was a man of brilliant vision, and Castarelli represented ugly, mundane reality. "All right. I'll give him a few minutes. And get me some more coffee, please."

When the controller had seated himself across from the desk, the phone rang. Morello's secretary informed him that Riccini, a director Morello was considering for an upcoming picture, was on the line. Morello was about to take the call when he glanced at Castarelli's face. The man looked even less healthy than usual. He was chewing on something, probably an antacid pill. "No," he said into the instrument. "I'll call him back. And hold all calls until I've finished speaking with Signor Castarelli." He hung up.

The controller held the inevitable stack of folders on his lap. "Thank you, Maestro."

Morello inclined his head graciously. One thing about Castarelli, at least, he was always properly respectful, in contrast to that officious lump of a secretary. "You wanted to see me?"

"I'm sorry, Signor Morello. But I must always bother you with these problems."

"Problems? I thought the additional money we got from Braciola's people put us in an excellent position."

"It did, Maestro. At the time. But now we are again under a considerable strain. The finishing costs on *The Hired Gun* far exceeded estimates, and the commitments to the new projects have caused a further drain."

Morello slapped his desk with the palm of his hand. "Why wasn't I told of this sooner?"

"You were, Maestro. I wrote you two memos." He shuffled through some papers. "The first one was dated February third, and the second—"

"All right, enough. I'm sure you sent them."

Castarelli belched. "Excuse me, Maestro, my stomach."

"And now we have cash flow and credit problems once again."

"I am afraid so."

The producer leaned forward, his eyes hard. "This won't affect my plans for the premiere, will it?"

Castarelli raised his hands. "Oh no, Maestro. I have double-checked everything myself so that we have no problems with anything you have ordered. Although, I must say—"

"Yes, what is it?"

"Well, frankly, Signor Morello, the costs of the opening and the festivities you have planned will be somewhat, ah, exorbitant."

"Exorbitant? Exorbitant? For the love of Christ, man, do you realize what I have invested in this picture?"

The controller gripped the folders on his lap in an effort to control the trembling of his hands. "Believe me, Maestro, I do realize what is invested. I know to the penny, and it terrifies me. Excuse me, I should not have said that."

"And so you are telling me that I am opening a picture that could bring in fifty or sixty million, perhaps more, and because I wish to make its premiere an important event, I am being *exorbitant*?"

Beads of sweat dotted Castarelli's gray, doughy face. "Forgive me for a poor choice of words, Maestro. I only meant to say that the party will be, uh, suitably lavish." His voice trailed off.

Morello's manner abruptly changed. He relaxed in his chair, a faint smile on his suntanned face. "You should look on the positive side, Vito."

"I try, Maestro, believe me. I try."

"Yes, well. Concentrate on all the good things we have developing, and you will feel much better. I am confident that *The Hired Gun* will be one of the great box-office attractions in the history of motion pictures. Its success will certainly finance, or complete the financing, of both of the new pictures I am working on."

"If it is all you hope, then outside financing will be readily available to us once again."

"Yes, and not the kind we had to turn to last time."

"I hope not, signor. As it is, I regret that we have them involved in *The Hired Gun*."

Morello toyed with a pen. "Don't worry about it. Remember that this is our business, not theirs. There is a great deal they do not know about the process of making money with motion pictures, and I see no reason why we should teach them."

"I beg your pardon, Maestro, but I don't quite follow—"

Morello gestured impatiently. "What I am saying is that they invested a few million at a time when we needed it, and that the money was very helpful to us. Very well, they shall have their investment back, plus a handsome profit. That is all they need to know about it, and it is eminently fair, no?"

Castarelli shifted uneasily in his chair. "It is fair, Maestro. That is, if you are asking me or any other reasonable man, it is fair. But the trouble is, you are not asking them. From what I have heard of them, they are not usually known to be reasonable. I do not believe they expect only to make a profit."

The producer's face darkened. "If they get back a large and generous return, then goddamn it, that is enough, do you understand me? What more can they ask for—blood?"

Castarelli popped another pill into his mouth and ground it between his teeth. "They have been known to ask for exactly that."

"Bah!" Morello swung his chair away in disgust. He stared for several moments at the handsome leather-bound volumes in the bookcases that lined the wall. When he turned back to the controller, his expression was again benign, and his tone was what he might have used in attempting to explain arithmetic to an idiot child. "In the first place, the only records they will see will be the same ones you prepare for the government tax agents. And if you have been able to keep those jackals at bay for all these years, then you should have no trouble with Braciola's people, who have no familiarity whatever with this industry."

Castarelli made no reply but continued to chew slowly, as if transfixed by his employer's words.

"And in the second place," Morello went on, "that is only part of the solution I have worked out to this problem. The major step is one that even I must admit is pure genius."

The controller pushed another pill into his mouth. "And may I ask what that is, Maestro?"

Morello smiled pleasantly. "Of course you may. What I intend is that our friends' investment in *The Hired Gun* must be restricted to the picture's domestic exhibition. What business it does here in Italy will be considerable, of course, but nothing compared to what I expect it to do worldwide."

"You mean, you intend to sell the foreign rights without Braciola knowing about it?"

Morello's smile was smug. "Exactly."

"But, Maestro, I think that could be a very, uh, risky thing to do."

"Risky? My dear man, all my life I have taken risks. In every venture there are risks. But it is the bold, intelligent man who knows exactly how to assess them and then determines how he must proceed. Do you follow me?"

There were flecks of white at the corners of Castarelli's mouth. He wiped them away with a handkerchief which he then applied to the droplets of sweat on his forehead. "I follow you clearly, Maestro. Only in this case I think it would be especially wise to use caution."

"Yes, yes. Of course. I shall be most discreet." He glanced at the wafer-thin gold Gerard Perregaux on his wrist. "And now that's all I have time for. If you'll excuse me, there are calls I must make."

The controller indicated the stack of folders on his lap. "But, Maestro, there are a number of important matters here we should discuss. And the details of the party. You sent word that all of them had to be reviewed with you."

Morello sighed. "Not now. We'll simply have to meet again later. I must make these calls, and I have a very important luncheon at one o'clock. My secretary will be in touch with you later about another appointment."

Castarelli nodded mechanically. "Whatever you say, Maestro."

The producer glanced again at his appointment book. He would have to hurry to make his one o'clock luncheon. Which reminded him; he was voraciously hungry. And the luncheon was important because his companion was the publisher of *Republica*, one of Rome's leading daily newspapers. Later there was the more interesting part of the day, when Signorina Triano would arrive. But first, his calls. He riffled through the stack of letters on his desk and reached for the telephone. As he picked up the instrument, Morello noticed that Castarelli had left the office. Strange, he had not even heard him go.

chapter 42

Estelle Lemont was bored. It was a condition that sometimes lasted for weeks and which invariably caused her to feel restless and irritable and then depressed, until finally she would force herself to take some action which would effect a change of mood. Once when she had been in these doldrums, she came out of them by giving one of the most lavish and exciting parties Paris had seen in years, with guests jetting in from as far away as New York and Rio and San Francisco. Another time she had instructed her furrier to design a floor-length golden mink cape which she later had worn exactly twice. Several times she had changed lovers, and once she had taken up with the husband of her best friend. That had been one of the more interesting ways in which she had emerged from ennui, because the friend had confided in Estelle daily that she suspected her spouse of a liaison but was unable to catch him. Estelle had counseled her with wisdom and understanding while secretly diddling the husband into a state of befuddlement. This time, however, her discontent seemed much deeper, and her bitterness tasted even more brackish.

Above all, there was the problem of her own slug of a husband. Claude Lemont had suffered a major coronary occlusion back in November which had resulted in her spending as dismal a winter as she could ever remember. They had been forced to cancel their holiday cruise aboard *Chanteuse*, and the big yacht had remained moored at Cannes, freshly outfitted, its hull white and gleaming, its brass and bright-work polished and shining, with no place to go. As a consequence Estelle had spent the ensuing months in their apartment on the avenue Foch feeling like a caged animal, listening to Claude's whimpers of self-pity and wishing that she could be almost anywhere but here.

This morning she opened the doors that led onto the terrace and walked out onto the red-tiled surface. The sky was gray and brooding with the threat of rain, and the early spring air was chilly and oppressive, with no hint of warmth, even though there were buds on some of the plants in the boxes which lined the parapet. Estelle folded her arms against the cold, and her gaze swept the Paris skyline listlessly. The city was bustling, as usual on a weekday, the streets clogged with snarling streams of traffic. The tallest feature of the view was the Tour Eiffel, of course, and nearby were the intricate scrolls of metal laticework on the balconies of the Plaza Athenée. She looked at the Arc de Triomphe and at the naked trees standing like sentinels along the Champs-Elysées, and she saw a tug slowly hauling a barge up the Seine.

She saw, but none of these images registered on her brain. She was thinking about Claude and what his illness was doing to her life. A soft and self-indulgent man, he had always been a hypochondriac, forever administering pills and medicines to imaginary ills, endlessly deploring the condition of his health. Now that he actually did have a serious malaise, it was as if he had entered a state of living death. He flatly refused to leave their penthouse, even though his doctors had told him it was not only permissable but would do him good to spend some time outdoors and to take some mild exercise. His days were spent in the library, his feet propped up on a leather hassock, his body swathed in blankets, a nurse, a maid, and his valet in constant attendance. For a time Estelle had pleaded with him to get out for some fresh air and a change of scenery, perhaps a visit to their country estate in Bordeaux, but he would not budge. Instead he read or watched television or dozed, or simply sat and complained that he was not being cared for properly.

Estelle wondered, as she often did, when Claude would die. She had become so involved in that possibility after his heart attack that she had read up on coronary disease and had learned to her dismay that he could go on like this for many years. She was thirty-six now, and the thought of living in this shadow until she reached her mid-forties or even her fifties was appalling to her. She had been thinking seriously about divorce before his illness, but that was no longer possible; any court would consider her a pitiless monster to leave poor defenseless Claude when he needed her most, and a settlement would be reduced accordingly. She walked back into the drawing room and closed the terrace doors behind her.

A clock on the mantel chimed softly. Eleven thirty. The prospect of another empty, pointless day made her grind her teeth. She would do her calisthenics and bathe and dress, and then what? Perhaps a late lunch at Chez Garin or Café Flore with one of her friends, and then a visit to the art galleries or a couturier or the cinema. Then possibly she would meet André, her current lover, at his apartment for a tryst of an hour or two. Then home to listen to Claude whine about her having left him for the entire afternoon. It hardly seemed worth it.

Even the idea of going to bed with André did nothing for her. He was a lawyer, a partner in a prestigious Parisian firm, who lived with his family in Neuilly but kept a flat in the city. He was charming, an intellectual in his early forties who could converse knowledgeably on virtually any subject and who had perfect manners, but who had begun to bore the hell out of her. The trouble was, André was too polite, too courtly, too nice. His performance between her legs, which she had at first thought outstanding, she now considered barely adequate, if not perfunctory. It was, she knew, the repetition of a familiar pattern. A man was at first wildly exciting, and she might even fall in love with him. Then he would become comfortable, pleasant to be with, a dear friend. And one day she would look at him and realize that she detested him and could not comprehend how she had ever thought him attractive.

With one or two exceptions they had all been like that, even when she had chosen a man simply because there had been a purely animal appeal about him. And the exceptions, she knew, had in fact only been variations on the same theme.

Except one. She entered her dressing room and took off her peignoir and thought about the tall young blond American who had served as mate on the *Chanteuse* for a few weeks the previous summer. God, what a man that one had been. She lay on her back on the thick, pale beige-colored silk pile carpet and began her routine.

First, the bicycling. Her trunk thrust into the air, one hundred revolutions of each leg. Then one hundred push-ups. Was there another thirty-six-year-old in Paris who could do them? Her friends thought such strenuous exercise was crazy, warning her that she would produce bulges with these exertions, but Estelle knew better. What the calisthenics produced instead were taut muscles, a flat belly, and firm, round buttocks. And best of all, the breasts of a teen-ager—full and erect with no hint of sag. No, it was she who was right and her friends who were developing wrinkles and cellulite and loose folds of flesh. Even in the days of her brief but moderately successful career as a motion picture actress, Estelle had understood that a youthful condition was a blessing a woman had to work at to retain, and time had proven her correct. After the push-ups, she did one hundred sit-ups, an effort which left a leaden ache in her gut and in the small of her back but which made her exult in her accomplishment. Then came the toe touches and the knee bends.

What was the American's name? Hendricks? Yes. She thought of him naked, the shoulders wide and heavily muscled, a light golden mat of hair across the tight pectorals. In her mind's eye she saw the narrow hips and the sharply defined quadriceps, and the great red cudgel of a cock. Ah. She imagined herself opening to receive him, seeing the crown of sun-bleached hair, the blue eyes, the adorable half smile as he entered her. Christ, it was torturous to think about. She wondered what would have happened if their brief affair had not ended so abruptly. Would the relationship have gone the way of all the others? Perhaps. In fact, she forced herself to admit, it probably would have. And yet he just might have been the man she had sought so hungrily all these years.

She paused a moment, hands on hips, thinking about it. What made the question so tantalizing, of course, was that she would never know the answer. She looked at her reflection in the mirror, her breasts heaving from her exertions, a light film of perspiration covering her skin. She was still a little tan, but not nearly as dark as usual for this time of year. Customarily they would have made their annual cruise to Tenerife and Marbella and Marrakech, and her skin would be a delicious coppery shade that contrasted sharply with the narrow white bikini line across her pubis. Goddamn it.

There was a knock at the door.

"Yes?"

To her surprise, Claude's thin voice answered. "May I come in?"

"Yes, of course." She opened her door.

Her husband entered the dressing room slowly, placing one foot in front of the other with the deliberateness of a very old man. Estelle realized that she hated even this about him, a halting gait which in truth was just one more plea for sympathy. He was wearing pyjamas, slippers, and a paisley silk gown. It occurred to her that he had not once been dressed since he had suffered the coronary. His gown was printed in bright hues of red and gold, and the lively colors made his pale face

240

look all the more wan. The miserable son of a bitch had undoubtedly chosen it with great care.

Claude hesitated. "I was wondering."

"About what?"

"That perhaps, I mean, it just might be that the doctors could be correct."

"Correct?"

"Yes. In their theories." As he spoke, his eyes ranged slowly over her body. "I would be taking a chance, of course, but it just might be possible that it would be good for me to go out. Nothing strenuous, naturally, but Jean could take us for a drive along the river."

A number of reactions flashed through Estelle's mind. The first was one of distinct disappointment. She grasped that this was because Claude's querulous suggestion could mean that he was getting better. And that, she suddenly understood, was something she did not want to happen. If his condition improved, it could mean that his life would be extended for God only knew how long.

"Perhaps we could even go down to L'isle Adam for lunch." He continued to gaze at her body, first studying her breasts and then her crotch.

"Mmmm, perhaps." Another thought occurred to her, a half-formed idea that quickly built itself into a plan so simple, so clear, so brilliant that it was as if she had spent months working it out.

Claude fingered the lapel of his dressing gown, his eyes remained fixed on the dark triangle of hair below her belly. "I believe I may actually be feeling just a bit stronger."

"That's wonderful, darling." She moved one leg so that her weight rested mainly on it, at the same time bending her other leg and tilting her pelvis a little so that she looked sexy and provocative. If Claude had not been out of the house in all this time, then he had had no opportunity to visit a mistress or one of the elegant Parisian prostitutes whose apartments she suspected it had been his habit to drop in on occasionally during the years they had been married. And if he had seen no one else, and since he had not been in her bedroom since the day of his coronary, that meant that the randy old bastard had not been laid in months.

His eyes moved slowly back to her nipples. "But I have to be careful, you understand."

"Of course I understand." She stepped close to him and

gently kissed his cheek. "But at the same time, it could be good for your spirit for you to resume doing some of the things you really like."

"You could be right."

"Of course I'm right." She undid the front of his robe and slowly slid her fingers inside, moving them lightly, expertly, her touch as delicate as the fluttering of a bird's wings.

Claude's breath came a little faster now, and there was a faint flush on his cheeks. "The doctors have been very specific about no . . . sex . . . until I am much better."

"Yes, naturally they know exactly what is best for you." Her fingers moved on him, and her tongue brushed his earlobe. "But now that you are feeling stronger, a little love would surely be wonderfully uplifting."

"Do you really think so?" He cupped one of the fine round breasts in his hand and stroked the nipple with his thumb, tentatively.

Excitement, which had nothing whatever to do with erotic urges, caused Estelle's pulse to pound in her ears. "I know so. And you must also realize, Claude darling, that it has been pure torture for me to go all this time, being around you, wanting you," her voice grew husky, "and not being able to have you."

He licked his lips. "Yes, I can understand that."

"Come." She grasped his wrist firmly and led him into her bedroom.

Estelle's bed was a Louis XIV four-poster. In all its years it is doubtful that the venerable antique had ever seen a performance like the one she put on now. She coaxed Claude, and teased him, and aroused him, and provoked him, and each time he was ready to climax she squirmed away from him, returning a few minutes later to urge him to new levels of frenzy, heights he had rarely attained. For more than an hour she kept at him, fondling, squeezing, licking, nipping, until his tongue protruded from his open mouth and he panted like a rabid dog. When at last it was obvious to her that he had reached the point where nothing could keep him from ejaculating, she sank her teeth into his neck and plunged her finger into his anus and bucked like a wild mare. At the same time she clamped her thighs about her husband's soft hips with all her strength.

Claude Lemont's body shuddered. His body arched and a low, half-strangled cry rattled in his throat. He twisted his head, his eyes popping in their sockets, and his face took on the color of cordovan leather. Then suddenly he was limp.

Estelle lay quiet for a moment, breathing hard. She pushed Claude off of her, and he flopped over onto his back. She climbed out of bed unsteadily and looked down at his inert body before she turned and went into her bath. The tub was constructed of Carrara marble, sunken into the tile floor. It was fitted with Jacuzzi jets, and it held over two hundred gallons. Estelle shook liberal amounts of Joy bath oil into its depths and turned on both faucets. While the water poured in and the air became redolent with a warm, steamy fragrance, she lay on a chaise lounge and forced herself to be calm.

She remained in the bath for a long time, occasionally replenishing the hot water, and now and then engaging the Jacuzzi. When at last she stepped out, she felt marvelous, totally relaxed, alert and confident. She pulled a thick, rough-textured towel from the heating rack and rubbed her body until her skin tingled. Then she pulled on a terry-cloth robe and went back into the bedroom.

Claude Lemont remained exactly as she had left him, lying on his back, his arms at his sides. His jaw hung slack, and his half-opened eyes were glazed. The skin of his face was mottled with bluish blotches. There was a strong stench in the room, and Estelle realized that his bowels had loosened.

She looked down at him for a long moment, and finally she turned and tugged sharply at the bell cord which would summon her maid.

chapter 43

Spring comes early to Rome, and it comes in a rush. Through the winter the air is raw and cold with the wind out of the northeast, and then one day the wind becomes a warm breeze from the south, and at once there is a flood of brilliant sunshine and the skeletal branches of the trees are softened with an emerging green haze, and in the Piazza Navona and on the Via Veneto vendors hawk bunches of flowers in riotous colors, and it seems that lovers are everywhere. Hendricks emerged from his apartment building in midmorning, en route to the studio because he had nowhere else to go that day, and as he opened the lock on the chain that held his motorcycle to a lamppost in front of the building, he was aware that suddenly it was springtime.

The machine was a Moto Guzzi, ten years old and not in the best condition, but it was much cheaper than a car and more exciting transportation than anything else Hendricks could afford. He stowed the chain in a saddlebag and swung a leg over the motorcycle. The first kick of the starter produced nothing, but on the second try the engine caught and broke into its characteristic throaty howl. He pushed off into the thick traffic, enjoying the sunshine and the warm air and the sense of excitement that spring never failed to produce in him. There was also, he realized, the growing tension that coiled within his chest, reminding him that now the opening of the picture was little more than hours away.

The flood of cars and trucks and horse-drawn carts and motorcycles roared along with no seeming order, the drivers whipping in and out of the stream, shouting and cursing as they took absurd chances and asserted their masculinity in a mad game of outdaring and outmaneuvering each other. Hendricks enjoyed this sport, aware that on the Moto Guzzi he had a special advantage, with the bike's acceleration and its darting quickness. He turned south on the Via Arenula, then ran along the Via dei Lungaretta for a short distance at full bore, just missing a lorry which turned without warning directly into his path. On the Municipio he could see the flags snapping brightly in the breeze, and above them the sky was a clear, bright blue that made him think of Spain.

At the Piazza di Porta Portese he was caught by a traffic light. He braked to a stop and waited for the light to change, his legs straddling the Moto Guzzi, feet flat on the cobble-stones. On the sidewalk beside the curb there was a news-stand, its shelves bright with magazine covers, many of them adorned with photographs of naked girls, and Hendricks's eyes drifted over the sea of flesh. His gaze was suddenly arrested by something that seemed familiar, and to his astonishment he realized that he was looking at a photograph of himself. He whistled shrilly through clenched teeth and pointed, and the vendor scooped up a copy of the magazine and hurried over to him. Hendricks shoved a bill into the man's hand just as the light changed. He thrust the magazine between his buttocks and the seat of the motorcycle and pulled away with the traffic.

There was a sidewalk café a few hundred meters down the street. Hendricks parked the Moto Guzzi and sat down at a table. He laid the magazine flat in front of him and stared at the cover. The picture showed him prominently in its center, surrounded by other people in less important positions, all gazing at him. He was wearing a shirt and bandanna as in costume for the picture. The others were Cecily Petain, Tina, Carlos Caserta, and Rosalie La Sorda. At first he could not imagine when the photograph had been shot. But then as he studied it, he realized that the situation it depicted had never really existed, that it was a cleverly assembled composite.

"Prego, signor?"

Hendricks looked up. A waiter was standing beside the table. "Huh? Oh. Bring me a beer." He returned his attention to the magazine. Above the photograph a headline screamed in yellow type, IL FUCILE AFFITTATO E UN UCCISORE Even with his clumsy Italian, that wasn't hard to translate: THE HIRED GUN IS A KILLER Jesus Christ. He flipped the pages until he came to the story.

At first he couldn't believe what he was seeing. He felt numb, as if he were looking at something that did not really exist, and his mind could not absorb it. There were a great many photographs, all in black and white, and the story ran across six pages. In one shot Hendricks held Cecily in his arms; in another he was kissing Tina, and in a third he clutched Rosalie. There was also a photograph of him fighting with Carlos Caserta, and he surmised that most of these were the work of the still man who had been with the crew in Spain to shoot publicity pictures. But on another page was a close-up of Carlos Caserta in hospital garb, looking like death incarnate. Then there was a picture of a mangled wreck of what had once been an automobile, smoke still rising from its charred remains.

The waiter returned with his beer. Hendricks paid him and absentmindedly gulped down most of the contents of the glass, not tasting it, as he continued to pore through the pages of the story. There were pictures of Morello with Cecily, and more of Hendricks, one showing him riding a horse. There was a shot of Dr. Borales and one of Juan Navarro. And Mother of God, on the next page was a picture of himself in bed with some girl. He squinted at the photograph and recognized the whore he had been with the night before Weaver had left for Ireland. So there had been someone else in the room that night after all, and that someone

245

had not intended to rob him. At least, not of his money.

Hendricks sat back in his chair and looked around him. The café was moderately crowded with people drinking coffee and wine and taking in the sights and sounds and smells of spring. At a table near him a girl wearing a red shawl was feeding crumbs to a jostling crowd of pigeons, and the warm breeze was playing in her long, glossy black hair. He returned his gaze to the magazine, feeling as if he had been kicked in the gut.

When he had studied each of the photographs, Hendricks began on the text. He was far more accustomed to speaking Italian than he was to reading it, but he had no trouble deciphering this story, written as it was in near-moronic prose. He read very slowly and deliberately, the feeling of numbness increasing as he absorbed each word.

This week a new motion picture has its world premiere in Rome, and the city has never been more excited about the opening of a movie. *The Hired Gun* tells the truth about the savage American West, and its hero is a newly discovered actor named Hendricks, a real-life killer who did not stop at attempting murder to get the starring role.

Originally the part was given to Carlos Caserta, the man who was once one of Italy's greatest soccer players. But while the picture was being shot in Spain, Hendricks knocked Caserta off the roof of a church during the filming of a scene, very nearly killing him.

Was this an accident? In an exclusive interview at Caserta's bedside in a hospital in Spain the actor, still within the shadow of death, told *Il Mondo*, "This Hendricks is a mad dog. He tried to murder me to get the part. It is a miracle I survived, but the doctors say I will never walk again."

The movie also stars the beautiful French actress Cecily Petain, who has long been romantically linked with the producer, Vicente Morello. Rumors abound that Cecily and Hendricks have been carrying on a red-hot affair. Meanwhile Hendricks has been involved with lovely Tina Rinaldi, another major actress in the film, as well.

Is Hendricks really a killer, out of bed as well as in it? In still another scandalous episode during production, the American wished to shed himself of Rosalie La Sorda, a bit player he had been sleeping with, in order to clear the decks for more action with Cecily and Tina. When Rosalie piteously begged Hendricks not to drop her, the Yankee actor's response was in keeping with his character. He borrowed Vicente Morello's Ferrari and took the poor girl for a late-night high-speed run along the twisting back-country Spanish roads. There was a hideous crash, and Rosalie died in the flames, her tender flesh charred to a cinder. Hendricks, of course, emerged without a scratch. Another accident? Perhaps.

Where did he come from, this half-civilized animal who will stop at literally nothing to get whatever he wants? *Il Mondo* has learned that Hendricks was an American cowboy, an authentic gunfighter who fled to the sea from his native Texas to escape a murder charge. Not surprisingly the crime was committed in a battle over a woman. Once he became a seaman, Hendricks employed his usual brutal tactics to help him rise quickly to the rank of ship's captain. Producer Morello spotted him in Portofino last year and knew at once that the man had that rare charisma that could become star quality.

"He was plainly irresistible to women," Morello said, "and at the same time men were fascinated by the way he seemed to live outside the law, answering to no one but himself. I saw him as an authentic throwback to the days of the Old West, an American version of Attila the Hun, a hard-riding, hard-shooting barbarian who would as soon blow an enemy's head off as he would drag a lady into bed."

Physically the American's looks match his swagger and his aggressiveness. He is tall, well over six feet, and heavily muscled. His hair is long and blond, his eyes as blue as the oceans on which he spent more than ten years. Women invariably have a powerful reaction to his even features and his swashbuckling ways. It is rumored that his sex drive is so strong he must be serviced by a woman every few hours or he becomes angry and irritable.

Isn't it an unusual idea for a western to be produced in Europe, featuring mostly Italian actors? "Absolutely," says Vicente Morello. "But *The Hired Gun* tells the truth about those times, in a way that American films never do. Instead of the usual sugar-coated pap, this picture portrays the blood and the sex and the brutality with shocking fidelity. Unlike the Americans, we had nothing to hide."

Sweet screaming Jesus. Hendricks's mouth suddenly felt dry, and he gulped down the last of his beer. There was more to the story, mostly about the extravagant party Morello was giving after the premiere and the feverish anticipation the opening was generating in Rome. Hendricks skimmed through the remainder of the piece and looked once more at the pictures. Then he closed the magazine and sat back in his chair. He glanced again at the other people sitting at the tables in the sunshine, and at the dusty swirl of traffic moving by in the street. Anger was building up inside him like molten lava about to blow the top off a volcano.

He stood up and shoved the magazine into the back pocket of his jeans. "Goddamn sons of bitches." He spit out the words in English, and the girl who had been feeding the pigeons looked at him curiously. What the hell could he do? He felt like kicking somebody's head in. One thing was for sure, he wasn't going to let that shit-paper rag get away with it. He strode to the Moto Guzzi, swung a leg over the saddle, and fired the engine. In a blue cloud of exhaust smoke he took off into the traffic.

chapter 44

The summons to the white marble-clad building on the Via del Babuino had been curt and peremptory. On entering the spacious terrazzo and Carrara lobby, Morello felt, as he always did when he came here, that he was in the presence of power so tangible he could smell it. He took the elevator to the seventh floor and was shown almost immediately into Mario Braciola's suite.

A change had occurred in the relationship between the two men. It was a subtle thing, barely perceptible in the small

248

gestures, the slight differences in manner exhibited by Braciola, but it definitely had taken place. Morello was no longer the honored guest, the man who was a respected and accomplished figure in a field which Braciola found foreign and somewhat mysterious. Instead the producer had the distinct feeling that he was now an employee, and at that one with whom the tall, hawk-faced man was not especially pleased.

"Sit down, Vicente." It was more of an order rather than an invitation.

Morello sank into one of the deep, nubby-textured chairs. "You're looking well, Mario."

"Yes. I wanted to talk to you about the picture."

"Of course. I am looking forward to having you see it. I think you'll be delighted, frankly. It has turned out even better than I had hoped."

The black eyes were cold and steady. "The cost overruns have caused us great concern."

Morello made a conciliatory gesture. "In this business, you must understand, there are invariably unexpected twists and turns, little emergencies of one kind or another one cannot anticipate."

Braciola waved a hand impatiently. "I understand that very well. But what I do not understand is how such little emergencies, as you call them, could possibly result in virtually doubling the cost of the production."

The producer shifted uncomfortably in his chair. "Surely you realize that we could never have known that we would encounter such a problem as we did with Carlos Caserta. That made it necessary to practically start over again. We had to scrap almost everything we had shot before he was injured."

"And thereby to risk everything on this American, this Hendricks, a man who has had no acting experience before this."

Morello leaned forward. "Mario, to tell you the absolute truth, I find this turn of fate to have been very much in our interest."

"What do you mean?"

"I mean that as unfortunate as it was for poor Caserta to have been hurt, I truly feel that it was fortuitous that we were forced to put Hendricks into the lead."

A flicker of interest passed across the ripe-olive eyes. "I have heard that he has done surprisingly well. But that does not give us the certain appeal that we would have had with an established performer like Caserta."

Jesus Christ. What did this bastard want? It certainly was not Morello's doing that Caserta had been injured. Nor would he have wished it to happen in a thousand years. But, as it was, he had come up with a solution that had turned out to be a fantastically good one. So the reshooting had been expensive. So what? They could just as easily have been set back by an earthquake or a fire or the plague or any other goddamned unexpected act of nature. "I am confident, Mario, that in this American I have discovered a genuine new star, and that the picture will be not only a success at the box office but a major hit." He smiled. "In fact, I think the profits on your investment will be handsome."

Braciola folded his arms. "I think they had better be, Vicente. I am not accustomed to being made a fool of in matters involving our money."

The producer turned both hands palm up. "I swear to you, Mario, the rough cut is fantastic. The picture is everything I had wanted it to be and more. And as you must be aware, the advance publicity we are generating has been senational. The picture has not yet opened, and it is already the talk of Rome."

"Yes. I have seen some evidence of that."

Morello's mouth curved in a sly smile. "Then you must also be aware of what I am doing to create an aura of excitement and mystery around the American. Television, newspapers, and magazine articles. Perhaps you read the story in *Il Mondo*?"

"It was brought to my attention."

"Wonderful, didn't you think? The women in this city can't wait to have a look at this man, and neither can the men. I don't ever remember a picture causing a bigger stir before it was even released."

Braciola continued to fix the producer in a cold, steady gaze. "Perhaps. But as I say, we are holding you to all your rosy predictions." He glanced toward the windows for a moment. The spring sunlight entering the huge room was filtered by gauzelike draperies. When he looked back at Morello, it was as if he were seeing him for the first time. "There is another matter I had wished to discuss with you today."

Morello tensed, wondering what was coming now. He forced himself to sit back in the deep chair, to appear as casually unconcerned as possible. But his antennae were up. "Yes, Mario, what is that?"

Braciola's tone became more deliberate, the cadence of his words more measured. "When we first spoke of this venture, and our participation in it, I told you that you had, in effect, become part of our organization."

"So you did."

"But I doubt that you realized what that meant, exactly, and what its implications might be."

Morello sensed that his mouth was going dry, but he tried to maintain his confident air. "I understand very well that we were establishing a true partnership."

"Yes? Well, that is correct. In part. But there is a great deal more to it than that. From now on, Vicente, we are not only your partners in this picture. We are your partners in everything. Do you understand that? Whatever pictures you make from this time onward, you must first clear with us, you must get our agreement. Moreover, there will be a change in our financial relationship."

The dryness in Morello's mouth was beginning to make it difficult for him to speak. "What kind of change do you have in mind, Mario?"

Braciola studied the producer's face for a moment before he replied. "As you are aware, our organization is involved in many different businesses. Some of these are viewed with a somewhat different attitude by the government than others." He gestured. "As you perhaps also know, we are careful to have people in key postions of influence. Tax collectors, judges, politicians at every level of importance. Nevertheless, it is not always possible to keep the wrong noses out of our activities and the wrong eyes from looking into our records." He smiled, a slight stretching of his lips. "Therefore it is necessary for us to use various means of maintaining our privacy, of ensuring that the nature of our various enterprises be kept secret. And particularly those aspects of our undertakings which involve the extent of our investment."

"I'm not sure I follow you, Mario."

Braciola continued to speak in a flat, measured tone, as if he were reading a speech. "Your industry, Vicente, is a relatively clean one. Moreover it involves large sums of money, often in constant flow. You require considerable capital to make pictures, and the revenue produced when a film is successful can be sizable. Therefore your company represents to us an excellent means to obscure funds we may have coming in from others of our activities."

Morello got it then. He had to swallow twice before he could reply. "What you are saying, then, is that you want to use my company to launder your organization's money."

Braciola stared at the producer. "I would be careful, if I were you, of the use of such suggestive terminology."

Morello felt a cold trickle down his sides.

"Be aware that it will be necessary for you to work very closely with us with regard to what properties you wish to produce."

This didn't seem to be quite so clear. "What difference would that make? What I wish to produce, that is?"

"It makes a great deal of difference. Sometimes, you see, as in the case of *The Hired Gun*, we shall be investing on the basis of an unexpected return on our capital. You make a good picture, financed by us, it turns a profit, and we all benefit. Other times, however, it may be necessary that a film lose money. A lot of money. Or to be more precise, so it will *appear*."

Morello was beginning to feel drained, as if his energy were running out of his body through an unstaunchable wound. "And what advantage could that have for me?"

"My dear Vicente, such a paper loss would of course take place with the clear understanding in advance that you would be amply rewarded for your seeing to it that our objectives would be met." There was a glass-topped table between the two men. Braciola tapped his forefinger on the smooth surface as he spoke. "But at the same time, you see, an enormous advantage will be accruing to you."

"And what would that be?"

"It will mean that it will never again be necessary for you to worry about financing. You will have all the capital you need to produce your pictures, and you will have a foolproof guard against any damage to you when a film does not do well. Of course, you will not have so great a profit opportunity for yourself personally as you have had in the past, but neither will you be so exposed to the possibility of failure."

Morello took a deep breath. "Let me see if I understand exactly what you are telling me. First, I must clear any picture I wish to make with your organization."

"Correct."

"Second, all financing of my pictures will come from your organization."

"Also correct."

"And according to my books, sometimes my pictures will succeed, but perhaps much more often they will not."

Braciola nodded, as if he were a teacher acknowledging the

252

work of a bright pupil. "I think you have an excellent grasp of how we shall work together."

"May I . . . think about all this, Mario?"

"Of course you may. Think about it as much as you wish. But at the same time, you realize, as far as I am concerned, we have reached an agreement."

When Morello left the tall, cool white building and plunged back into the clamor of Rome's streets, he was sharply aware that, for the first time in his life, he was caught in a trap he was not sure he could get out of. He thought about it as he drove south through the usual dense traffic, and the more he thought, the angrier he became. It was one thing to have to go to Braciola, hat in hand, for the financing he had desperately needed for *The Hired Gun*, even if that had meant giving away an enormous chunk of the profits the picture would earn. But it was quite another thing to turn himself into a mere manager of one small part of Braciola's organization. It was as if he had suddenly been relegated to run a division of some conglomerate. From now on, according to what Braciola expected, the producer would be allowing the organization to use his film company to screw the government, just as Morello himself had been doing for years. Only now it would be done on a much grander scale, and most of the benefits would go to Braciola and his people. It was outrageous.

Morello was driving a new Ferrari. It was a blood-red coupe, like the one that had been destroyed in Spain, but one of the new four-liter superlight models, capable of attaining even greater speeds than his old one. The interior had the rich smell of newly tanned leathers, and there was a sensual pleasure in the feel of the padded steering wheel and the polished walnut of the shifter knob. Even with the roar of the city's traffic, Morello was conscious of the distinctive notes of the Ferrari's engine, snarling haughtily above the mundane sounds produced by lesser machines. As he drove, he forced himself to concentrate all his mental powers on his problem.

For one thing, he knew that he was up against a vast structure, one whose tentacles spread throughout Italy, and which in fact had connections all over the world. Morello even knew some of Braciola's counterparts in other cities. There was Lotacci, for example, in Milano, and the Chizzano brothers in Napoli. Yet he was reasonably sure that they were not associated with the banking interests in Switzerland, organizations every bit as secretive and as shadowy as Braciola's, and equally ruthless. Now what Morello had to do was to find a way to use his Swiss connections to sell off the foreign rights to *The Hired Gun* without Braciola's knowledge, however risky that might be. At least it would give him the wherewithal to make his move, to extricate himself from the situation he was in now. With the money that would bring him, he could leave Italy altogether, perhaps go to the States and begin there anew. Plenty of others from the Italian film industry had done it successfully, and therefore there was no reason that a man of Morello's reputation and talent could not do as well, or better. The trouble was, how could he do it? He thought of the conversation he had had with his accountant on this matter and how Castarelli had seemed terrified by the prospect of the producer making such an audacious attempt.

All right, he would admit that such a plan was hazardous. But then he had only to consider the alternative. And living life as a vassal, a flunky taking orders from Mario Braciola, turning his studio and his own creative genius into tools at the disposal of the organization, was to live no life at all. He downshifted, snapping in the clutch, and was rewarded by the screech of rubber and the throaty howl of the Ferrari's twelve cylinders.

chapter 45

By the time Hendricks reached the Giandelli studios, his anger had turned into a cold, barely controlled fury. He chained the Moto Guzzi to a tree and strode directly into Vicente Morello's suite. He was on his way into the producer's private office when Morello's secretary spotted him and blocked his way. An argument ensued, and when Hendricks's tone became a roar, the door opened and Morello appeared.

At the sight of Hendricks the producer's face broke into a broad smile. "Ah, good morning, my boy. Do come in." He glanced sternly at his secretary. "You know my door is always open to this young man." He led the American into his office and closed the door. "Please sit down. And calm yourself. You seem agitated."

"Goddamn right I'm agitated. Have you seen this?" Hendricks pulled the rolled-up copy of *Il Mondo* from the back pocket of his jeans and waved it at Morello.

"What is it? What do you have there?"

"It's a copy of some pornographic fucking magazine, that's what it is."

Morello took the copy from Hendricks's outstretched hand and unfurled it. "Ah, *Il Mondo*. It is one of our more successful magazines here in Italy. And I see they have done a cover story on you. How nice."

"Nice? Jesus Christ, wait till you see what that cunt rag is saying about me."

"Here, here, relax. Sit down and let us get you some coffee. Go ahead, sit down."

Reluctantly Hendricks sank into a chair. He glared at the copy of *Il Mondo* which lay on Morello's desk as the producer picked up the telephone and instructed his secretary to bring coffee for them.

When Morello put the instrument down, he riffled through the magazine. "Quite a spread. Let's see . . . six pages. That is a tremendous piece of publicity."

Hendricks leaned forward, his jaw muscles working. "Vicente, you don't understand. That thing is calling me everything from a sex maniac to a murderer."

Morello's manner was benign. "Is that so? Hmmm. Some of these pictures are fascinating. Tell me, is this one really you?"

The American flushed hotly as he saw that Morello was pointing to the photograph of himself in bed with the whore. "It's . . . I was . . . yes, goddamn it, that's me."

Morello chuckled. "Well at least they didn't get it entirely wrong, did they?"

"They didn't get it right, either. Hell, I'm no murderer."

The door opened, and Morello's secretary entered the office carrying a tray on which were coffee and pastries. She set the tray down on the desk, and Hendricks fidgeted while the woman went through the ritual of filling the cups and offering cream, sugar, and little cakes. He took only a cup of black coffee.

Morello indicated the pastries. "Are you sure you won't have one of these? They're really delicious."

"No, no, I don't want any." Hendricks watched impatiently as the secretary backed out of the room. When she had closed the door, he turned to Morello. "I think you ought to get your lawyers into this right away."

The producer seemed surprised. "My lawyers? For what reason?"

Hendricks voice rose. "For the reason that this is, what do you call it, libel, for Christ's sake. And invasion of privacy and a lot of other shit. Nobody can just make up a pack of lies like this and hang it on somebody and get away with it. The editor of this thing ought to be in jail."

The telephone rang and a moment later the intercom buzzer sounded. Morello spoke briefly with his secretary and then took the call.

Hendricks drank some of his coffee and put the cup down on the desk. From what he could hear of Morello's end of the conversation, the producer was in some sort of argument over a rock band that was supposed to be flying in from London to play at the party following the premiere of *The Hired Gun*. Hendricks picked up the copy of *Il Mondo* and looked at the story again. So what the hell if he had been in bed with that bimbo? That didn't make any of the rest of that crap true. He dropped the magazine back onto the desk and finished his coffee.

Morello put the phone down. "What were we saying? Oh, yes. This story."

"I was saying you ought to call your lawyers."

"Mm, yes." Morello placed his fingers together. "You realize, of course, that the difficulty in a situation like this is to prove that harm has been done."

Hendricks was dumbfounded. "Prove harm? Prove harm when somebody's calling you a fucking murderer in print?"

The producer stood up and walked over to a painting which hung on the far wall. He straightened it a fraction and turned back to the American. "Hendricks, let me explain a few things to you. First, you are going to have to understand that your life from this moment on is never going to be the same again. As of now, you are public property. There can be no invasion of your privacy, for the simple reason that you have no privacy. You wanted to become an actor. Very well. From the beginning, back last summer in Portofino, I saw talent in you. I saw a quality that I knew I could mold and develop, which could make you a great star. In a very short time all of Rome, and then all of Italy and all of Europe will be talking about you. Soon, perhaps, even America will want to know everything about you. Because in one sudden, stunning burst, I will have made you a personality."

Hendricks stared in silence as the producer spoke.

Morello paced slowly back and forth, his hands thrust into the pockets of his elegant brown cheviot suit. "You must realize that there is no figure more interesting to the public than a motion picture star."—

"Star? Hell, I'm no star. I—"

"No, but you will be. The point I am making is that the public is endlessly fascinated by screen personalities. Much more so than by politicians or musicians or writers or anyone else who could be called famous. Why? Because the motion picture star is entirely an illusion. A kind of superhuman who can do anything, who is rich and beautiful and who is free to go to the places and do the things that most people can only dream about. Do you see?"

"No, I don't. I don't see what that has to do with this rag writing lies about me."

Morello sighed. "Hendricks, what I am trying to explain to you is that it is all part of the illusion. The kind of thing that is in that story is all part of the mystery, the glamour, the excitement that the public wants to believe about you. No one stops to ask whether such things as the story describes could be true, or how it could be that if they were the police did not arrest you."

"Exactly. Everybody just assumes that it's the literal goddamn truth."

"Perhaps. And perhaps not. What is far more important is that people will talk about you, and discuss you, and be curious about you, and even become infatuated wth you. And that will add a great deal of brilliance to your image." He paused. "It will also make them want to go to the theaters to see you. And sooner or later you will learn that, in this business, that is everything."

Hendricks snorted. "You may think so, but I don't. I say we ought to sue the shit out of this bunch of grave robbers."

Morello appeared mildly amused. "Sue? Because this story helped to make you and the picture a success? Believe me, the court would find your complaint to be something of a joke. To say nothing of the difficulty you would have in establishing your credibility."

"What do you mean?"

The producer gestured toward the magazines. "That picture. The one of you in bed with the girl. You said that was indeed you, did you not?"

"Yes, but—"

"And how would you prove that the other things in the

257

story did or did not happen? The girl did die in that wreck, didn't she? And Carlos Caserta is in fact in a hospital in Spain, is he not?"

Hendricks exhaled slowly.

"And what is more, you will find that the popular press has a remarkable amount of freedom in this country, especially when it comes to running stories like this one about people in show business." He smiled. "You should see what they ran about Gina Lollabrigida a few months ago. Same magazine."

Hendricks looked at his hand. His anger was still with him, but now it was mingled with a growing sense of frustration.

The phone buzzed and Morello answered it. When he hung up, he glanced over at the American. "I have the publicity people here for a meeting on *The Hired Gun*. Perhaps it would be instructive to you to listen to the discussion."

Hendricks got to his feet. "No, I don't think so. I've listened to all the publicity talk I want to hear for today."

"As you wish."

The door opened, and two women entered, both carrying thick folders. Hendricks said his farewells as quickly as possible and slipped out of the studio. He felt like an utter, absolute horse's ass.

chapter 46

Two police motorcycles led the black Cadillac Fleetwood limousine through the evening traffic, their sirens shrieking. From his seat in the back of the big car, Hendricks could see searchlight beams probing the sky in the distance ahead of them. It was just like the Hollywood bullshit he had seen in the movies. He fingered the clip-on batwing bow tie at his neck and shifted uncomfortably. This was the first time in his life he had worn a tuxedo, and he felt stiff and awkward in the strange black suit. Morello's wardrobe department had issued the thing to him, and it was perhaps one size too small, binding his chest and shoulders slightly. And as if that weren't bad enough, the shirt had ruffles down the front and at the cuffs. Christ, he must look like a pimp.

Beside him Ceciy Petain was humming under her breath as if her excitement were an electric current escaping in little waves from her half-open mouth. She reached between Hendricks's legs and squeezed him. "Isn't it marvelous?"

He grunted.

"Oh, come on, Hendricks. You know you're just as thrilled as I am. But you are being the big strong man who refuses to let anybody see he has emotions."

"You think so?"

"I know so. Men are really just as emotional as women, but they are desperately afraid that somebody will find out about it and think they are weak. So they pretend to be cold and aloof and above such things."

"It so happens you're wrong, Cecily. The truth is, I'm scared shitless."

She laughed. "I don't believe that either."

"You don't, huh? Well, you better believe it, because that's exactly how I feel. In fact, I can't really get hold of the idea that this is happening to me."

"Ah. I can understand that. You are thinking things like how less than a year ago you were on some boat, right?"

"Exactly. One year ago today I was on the *Panama City*, running from Abadan to Bayonne. I keep expecting the ordinary to call me for the four-to-eight watch."

"And now you have entered a wonderful new world."

"Not yet I haven't. What I'm going to find out in a couple of hours is whether the door is going to get slammed in my face."

"Stop worrying. You are going to be the biggest thing ever to hit Rome."

"Uh-huh." Cecily had continued to work on him, squeezing and stroking, and Hendricks suddenly realized he had become fully erect. He turned and looked down at her. Even in the dim light she was stunning. She wore a green lamé dress, cut so low it barely covered her nipples, and a white ermine stole around her shoulders. Her auburn hair tumbled thickly around her face, and her eyes were shining. He understood that her excitement had affected her sexually, that she was even more aroused than he was.

As if she knew exactly what he was thinking, she rubbed her leg against his. "I wish we could do it right now, here in the car."

"You keep that up and we'll have to."

She giggled and squeezed harder.

259

As the Fleetwood pulled up to the sidewalk under the marquee of the theater, Hendricks pushed Cecily away from him. He sure as hell couldn't get out of the car in front of all those people while he was in this shape. He looked ahead and saw that another limousine was discharging its passengers in front of them. Split-second timing. The publicity people must have really sweated on all this.

The car ahead was identical to the one Hendricks and Cecily were in. He recognized Morello, looking resplendent in a beige tuxedo with black piping. Police were holding the crowd back and flashbulbs were popping. Hendricks could see a mobile television unit parked beyond the marquee, its crew operating a camera from the roof of the vehicle. There were also several trucks mounting searchlights nearby, their huge lenses sending enormous columns of brilliant light thousands of feet up into the night sky. There was music, too, coming from somewhere, but he couldn't tell whether its source was a band or a recording. As he watched, Morello waved to the fans who were straining against the ropes held by a line of cops and then turned back to the Cadillac. The producer reached in and helped Tina out of the car.

Damn. She looked wonderful. She was also wearing furs, a luxurious gray-white cape that Hendricks guessed was lynx. Her dark hair gleamed under the lights, and her smile was dazzling. Morello took her arm, and both of them waved as they moved into the theater. Hendricks realized it was the first time he had seen her in a couple of weeks. A loudspeaker was booming, but he couldn't make out the words.

A doorman opened the door of their limousine, and Hendricks got out. He smiled widely, as the publicity people had instructed him to do, and then he heard the loudspeaker echoing, ". . . the star of *The Hired Gun*, ladies and gentlemen, the fantastic new American actor, the man all of Rome wants to toast, Hendricks!"

The crowd roared, and Hendricks waved at the sea of people, continuing to grin idiotically. He turned and helped Cecily out of the car, and she stood for a moment, exultant, thrilling to the moment as the flashbulbs exploded like a string of firecrackers. "And here she is," the loudspeaker intoned, "the staggeringly beautiful and talented costar of the picture, Signorina Cecily Petain!"

The cries were not as loud this time, but Cecily seemed not to notice. She raised both hands and beamed in all directions.

Hendricks took her arm and guided her toward the entrance of the theater lobby.

As they made their way between the cordoned-off walls of people, a dark shape suddenly detached itself from the crowd and hurtled toward them. Before Hendricks understood what was happening, he felt a searing pain in his cheek and turned to see someone ripping and clawing at him. It was a woman, apparently a young one. She was spitting curses at him as she tried to tear his face with her nails. Instinctively Hendricks backhanded her in the mouth, knocking her to the sidewalk. A policeman grabbed her and hauled her to her feet.

Hendricks stared at the girl in astonishment. She was dressed all in black, and he saw that she was quite pretty, even though her face was contorted in rage and blood was welling from her split-open lower lip.

The girl twisted in the cop's grip, her large dark eyes continuing to glare at Hendricks. "Killer! Murderer! Cheating bastard!" She kicked backward at her captor's shins, and then she was dragged away.

Cecily touched Hendricks's arm. "Your face—it's bleeding."

He touched his cheek with his fingertips and saw that they came away red.

Cecily thrust a handkerchief at him. "Here, use this."

Hendricks dabbed at his face, and Cecily linked her arm with his and pulled him toward the lobby. As they moved inside, it occurred to him that the flashbulbs had been popping the whole time.

Cecily looked at his cheek. "She really scratched you. Who was she?"

"Beats the shit out of me. I never saw her before in my life."

"Really? Are you sure?"

"Of course I'm sure, for Christ's sake. I'd never laid eyes on her, and she came at me like I was her worst enemy."

The lobby was crowded with people wearing evening clothes, a number of reporters and photographers among them. Hendricks spotted various members of the cast and crew, including Livorno, who looked bored. Morello and Tina made their way over to the American and Cecily, inquiring solicitously about his face. As they talked, two reporters materialized at Hendricks's side. One of them pushed in close. "We understand that young lady on the sidewalk was your mistress until you became famous. Would you care to comment on that?"

Hendricks jaw dropped. "What? That's a lot of crap."

The second reporter elbowed his way in. "Why did you hit her?" This one reeked of garlic. He clutched a pad and pencil, staring expectantly.

Hendricks felt a wave of anger rising in his chest. "Hey, listen, buddy—"

Vicente Morello put his hand on the American's shoulder and spoke softly. "Easy. Don't lose your temper. Just answer pleasantly."

Hendricks took a deep breath. "I don't know who she was. I never saw her before."

Garlic-mouth persisted. "Then why did you knock her down?"

"I didn't. That is, it was an accident. She came at me, and I instinctively raised my hand to protect myself. I didn't mean to hit her."

"How long had you been together?"

"Hey, listen, goddamn it, I told you—"

Morello tugged at his arm. "Come. There are people who want to meet you." He smiled at the reporters. "Excuse us, please."

The producer guided Hendricks through the crowd in the lobby, introducing him to elegantly dressed men and women. The American was a head taller than nearly else in the huge open area, and that, together with his blond hair, made him stand out like a beacon.

It occurred to Hendricks that most of the people he met reminded him of the guests he had seen on the *Chanteuse* during the weeks they had cruised the Mediterranean last summer. The men were older, many of them apparently in their sixties, and there was about them an aura of power, a sense of confidence and strength, as if they were much at home in positions of command.

The women, too, were familiar, even though he had never met any of them. They were nearly all in good physical shape, most of them younger than their men, and their clothes and their jewels were extravagant. There was from each of them a cool gaze of appraisal, quick glances at his face, his chest, and his shoulders, as if they were looking over a thoroughbred stud at a horse auction. Then would follow a warm smile, an expression that made clear that the invitation was there, if Hendricks wanted it. He had seen that expression often enough, so that it was unmistakable.

A gong sounded, and the crowd began moving into the auditorium. Morello led Hendricks and the women down an aisle to their seats, which were in the center of the orchestra, a little less than halfway back from the stage. The theater was large, with a capacity of nearly three thousand, and it took twenty minutes for it to fill up. Hendricks tried to keep up a running pattern of small talk with the others, as much to hide his nervousness as for any other reason. At one point he turned around in his seat and glanced at the glittering array of people in the orchestra behind him and in the balcony and boxes above. It occurred to him that facing a crowd like this from the stage must put a tremendous demand on a performer, and he decided that he could never become a legitimate actor. The wait seemed interminable, and then the house lights dimmed and the curtain parted.

The opening scene was a long shot in which a lone rider trotted along a trail through open plains country. The man rode tall in the saddle, and even at a distance you could see that he and his mount were worn and dusty, as if they had been traveling for a long time. They moved at an easy pace along the trail, until they came to a small, shabby, sun-baked village, the kind you would expect to find in south Texas, near the Mexican border. As the man rode into the village, the scene revealed that two men were engaged in some hell raising in the main street of the settlement. They were drunk, and for sport were tormenting a whore who apparently worked in a nearby saloon-bordello. They pushed the girl into a horse trough, and as she emerged from the water, alternately sobbing and cursing, one of the men grabbed the front of her sodden dress and tore it open, leaving her bare breasted as the men jeered and taunted her. The girl climbed out of the trough and tried to strike one of her tormentors, but he punched her in the jaw and knocked her back into the water. As this went on, the lone rider dismounted and quietly approached the action involving the two drunks and the whore. He stood silent for a moment, then called out. The closer of the two men turned and spat at the stranger. The tall rider grinned, revealing large, perfect white teeth in his tan face. His voice was low, almost lazy. "Looks like you're ready to die, asshole." The drunk who had spat at him went for his gun, but before it had half cleared its holster, the tall stranger's pistol belched flame and black smoke, and the drunk slammed into the dirt, his face a gory mass. The second man moved as if to draw, but stopped, obviously realizing he had no chance. Calmly, deliberately, the stranger swung his pistol on this one and shot him in the belly, leaving him twitching in the dirt

263

near the horse trough. The stranger then smiled at the terrified whore. "Better get out of there, ma'am. You could catch cold." He slid his pistol back into his holster and walked into the saloon as the titles came up, accompanied by a thunderous burst of music.

To Hendricks's surprise the audience burst into applause. He was aware that his fists were clenched and that he was sweating profusely. He forced himself to relax and slumped down in his seat. As familiar as he was with every frame of this picture, having seen the dailies, and then having worked ten and twelve hours a day assisting with the editing, he could not keep from being amazed by the enormous images of himself on the screen. It was as if he were watching a total stranger move through the antics in the scenes. At the same time he was acutely critical of his performance and embarrassed by it. He looked stiff and wooden and clumsy, and his lines sounded hollow and phony. Jesus, he couldn't act to save his ass. The acclaim he had been given by the crew was all a lot of bullshit. Now, tonight, when it counted, in front of this hip, cool, sophisticated crowd, he would be stripped naked and revealed for what he was: a stumblebum seaman who had fallen into a bucket of shit and come up with roses in his teeth, but whose luck had finally run out. The ball was over, Cinderella, it was past midnight, time to get your ass back to the scullery. He began to wish fervently that he could sneak out of this goddamned theater.

At one point about a third of the way into the picture, Morello leaned over and whispered to him, "Do you hear this crowd's reaction? Sensational."

Sheepishly, Hendricks grasped that he had been aware of the noise from the opening titles on, but had not related it to what effect the picture was having on the audience. Now he began to observe more closely, finding that every scene was getting a big reaction. Bits that seemed to him to be overplayed, or too obvious, or clichéd, were nevertheless producing gasps or murmurs or laughs or shouts from the crowd. Two hours later, when the movie finally ended, he felt drained.

The house lights came up, and the applause was a roar. People all over the huge theater were standing, clapping their hands and whistling and yelling. And to Hendricks's utter astonishment, they all seemed to be looking directly at him.

chapter 47

The palazzi was twenty minutes drive from the theater. Originally built by Mussolini for his mistress, Claretta Petacci, the elegant blue-white villa stood high atop Monte Mario, and the views of Rome from its broad terraces were magnificent. When the Fleetwood bearing Hendricks and Cecily arrived, the parking area was already crowded with cars, all of them sleek and powerful. There were Rolls-Royces and Mercedes, Ferraris, Alfas, Lancias, Maseratis, Aston-Martins, and several other makes Hendricks could not identify.

Inside, the villa was alive with music and laughter, as if the party had been going on for hours. There was not one band, but three, one on each of the floors, the music from them producing a jarring conflict of sound. Waiters bore trays of elaborate canapés and glasses of champagne, and buffet tables were heavily laden with an almost infinite variety of dishes.

When Hendricks moved through the reception room and up the steps opening onto the main salon, people called to him and applauded and toasted him. Well-wishers clapped his back and shook his hand, and the women gushed and a couple of them kissed him. He made his way through the mass of humanity to the bar and ordered a Scotch.

"So you got what you wanted, huh?" It was Livorno. The director looked as rumpled in his tuxedo as he did in his working denims. His eyes were hugely magnified by his thick glasses and under his wild shock of black hair his face wore a faintly cynical smile.

Hendricks drank half the contents of his glass. "Sure. They seemed to like the picture."

"That's not what I meant. I was talking about you. Bang. One shot, and you are instantly famous. All the beautiful people want to kiss your ass."

He decided Livorno was a little drunk. "I've got a lot to learn, if I'm going to be a real actor."

"Yes, you do. But it was obvious tonight that you have enough equipment to get by." He laughed. "To get by? Hell, to be a roaring success in this shit star-system business."

So that was what was eating the director. He was viewing everything, as usual, in terms of social protest. "All the audience sees in the picture is the handsome, brave, adventurous cowboy. All the things that are really important, they are not even aware of."

Hendricks finished his Scotch and signaled the bartender for another. "Why don't you have a drink, Arturo?"

"Thank you. I will."

"You know, that picture is a hell of a lot more the product of your work than anybody else's, including mine. I'd think you'd be pretty happy about the reaction it got."

The director shrugged. "The picture is so much crap. What I wished to express is sublimated by the role of the killer."

"Uh-huh." And you, too, Livorno, are envious, whether you've got it sorted out in your head or not.

"Hendricks, you were marvelous." A very pretty blonde in pink silk evening pyjamas pressed against him on the other side. He had never seen the girl before. A large young man was standing behind her, apparently not overly pleased by her fawning over the actor. The girl put her hand on Hendricks's arm and brought her face close to his. Her eyes were deep blue and almost imploring in their expression of sincerity. "Honestly, I've never seen such a fabulous performance. Will you dance with me?"

The band was playing bossa-nova rhythms, and the blond pressed herself against Hendricks and ground her pelvis into him. She told him she was an American living in Rome with her Italian husband who was a manufacturer of women's shoes, and that she found the life there dull as hell. She said she lived for the few trips to New York she made each year and that Hendricks was the most wonderful actor she had ever seen. She told him her husband was leaving on Monday for a few days' visit with his leather suppliers in Trieste and invited him to spend some time with her. She gave him her phone number and made him promise he'd call, and Hendricks said he'd do his best.

Later he danced with the wife of a member of Parliament and then with an Israeli singer who was enjoying a big success in Europe. Both of them made more or less the same pitch that the blonde had, and Hendricks began to understand what the groupie syndrome was all about. He had been propositioned by women before; there was nothing new about that. But what made this strangely different was that these people were acting as if he were something unique simply because he had been in the picture. It was flattering, but at the same time it was somehow degrading.

He touched a handkerchief to his face. The scratches on his cheek weren't bleeding, but they burned like fire. He looked around and saw that the other principals in the picture were also getting a lot of attention, and most of them seemed delighted. Vicente Morello strutted about like a king greeting his subjects, and Cecily was constantly surrounded by male admirers. He also noted that Tina appeared to be having a marvelous time, dancing, chatting, laughing, constantly pursued by good-looking young men. Twice he made attempts to speak with her, but getting through the crush was impossible.

Some time after midnight Arturo pulled him aside. "The maestro wants you to come upstairs. He wants you to meet somebody."

"Hey, later, man. I'm busy." Hendricks had been eyeing a statuesque redhead across the room.

"Listen, it's important."

Hendricks was about to ignore the producer's assistant and make his way over to where the girl was standing, but something in Arturo's tone told him that Morello considered the introduction a command performance. He shrugged. "Okay, let's go."

The private suite of rooms at one end of the third floor had once been Claretta Petacci's bedroom, sitting room, dressing room, and bath. The decor in the sitting room was still definitely feminine, with satin drapes at the windows and delicate furniture upholstered in pastel silks and velvets. When Hendricks walked in, he saw Morello standing talking with several men, most of whom he did not recognize. One of the men was Vito Zicci, the investor's representative who had been with the company in Spain. Hendricks had not seen Axface since they had returned to Italy. The young man was wearing a tight-fitting, midnight blue dinner jacket that accentuated his uncommonly broad shoulders and long arms. He nodded when he saw Hendricks, and the American inclined his head in reply, thinking that Zicci looked like a dressed-up ape.

Morello waved. "Ah, there you are. Come on over here and let me introduce you to a good friend of mine."

For some reason or other Morello seemed nervous, as if he were genuinely worried, a condition Hendricks had never seen him in before, even when they had run into all their difficulties on location. The producer took Hendricks's arm and presented him to a tall, powerful-looking man who was standing in the center of the group. "I would like you to meet Signor Mario Braciola."

The tall man's grip was strong, and he greeted Hendricks pleasantly, but his black eyes were coolly appraising above the acquiline nose. Hendricks sensed that this one was used to being in charge, to running things. He wondered if this man was the reason for Morello's nervousness. "Glad to know you."

Braciola's voice was deep and resonant. "You did an excellent job in the picture. I am very pleased."

You're pleased? Hendricks wondered what he meant by that, but he gave no sign. "Thanks."

Morello rubbed his hands unctuously. "Signor Braciola was a major investor in the picture."

Okay, that explained part of it anyway. "I hope you get your money back," Hendricks said.

Braciola smiled. "I think we will have a tremendous success." He waved a hand. "Let us sit down and have a drink. There are things we should discuss about plans for the future."

They took seats on the frail furniture, and two of the men, whom Braciola had not bothered to introduce, brought them drinks from a sideboard. Hendricks continued to wonder what was going on. He knew there had been outside money in the picture; that was why Zicci had been with them in Spain. But Braciola was hardly acting like some stiff who had merely put dough into Vicente Morello's venture. Instead his manner was that of a man who was calling the shots, or even more than that, the owner of the company. Who the hell was this guy, anyway?

Braciola raised his glass. "To *The Hired Gun*."

Hendricks saluted with his drink but only sipped the contents of the glass. He had had a lot to drink tonight, and he wanted to be alert for this discussion. He had a strong feeling that there was something pivotal about this meting; that Braciola somehow would turn out to be a lot more than the angel who had pulled Morello out of a hole.

The producer continued to look as if he were nervous and embarrassed at the same time. "Mario wanted to comment on how he feels we should follow up on this picture."

Braciola crossed his legs. He seemed perfectly at ease, displaying the air of a respected general meeting with his staff. "If this picture is half as much of a hit as we all expect it to be, then we should produce another just as quickly as possible. It should combine more or less the same elements as this one, and of course it should star our American friend here."

There were murmurs of assent about the room. Hendricks said nothing.

"It could even be a continuation of this story," Braciola went on. "For instance, the killer could go to another village, where he would run into a different situation, but naturally he would be the same kind of character."

Again there were expressions of admiration for Braciola's brilliant thinking. He looked at Morello. "What do you think, Vicente?"

"Oh, I like it, Mario. I like it a lot. And I think you are absolutely right that we should do it as quickly as possible."

The black eyes fixed on the American. "And you, Hendricks? What do you think?"

This time Hendricks caught just a hint of condescension in the man's tone. "I think it sucks."

There was a stir around the room, but Braciola's face showed no change of expression. "And why do you think that?"

"Because running out to make *The Hired Gun* all over again is the most obvious thing that could be done. I don't pretend to know a hell of a lot about this business, but from what little I do know, that's exactly what usually happens. Somebody hits with a World War Two movie or a horror movie and everybody breaks their ass to imitate it. And all that does is give the public something to yawn about. It's the original idea that gets them to come into the theaters."

Morello jumped in. "Not always. After all, how many great westerns did your Gary Cooper make? And every one of them was a hit."

"That may have been true a long time ago," Hendricks replied, "when going to the movies was a habit. But I think times have changed. You can't just keep on pumping out the same old shit."

Braciola continued to hold him in an unblinking gaze. "Very well, then. What do you think we should do?"

"I don't know," Hendricks said. He put his glass down on the table beside him and got to his feet. "I'll think about it. Right now I'm going back to the party."

"Sit down." It was Vito Zicci.

Hendricks looked at the narrow face, the mouth twisted

into something between contempt and anger, and then at the others in the room. "Look. I'm not sure what's going on here, but I think maybe I ought to let you know just where I stand. First of all, I'm not your tame bear who goes into his act when you snap your fingers. Maybe this picture really will turn out to be a big success. Okay, great. If it does, then I really fell into it. A fat piece of luck, and here I am. But what I do next, I don't really know. When I see some of the bullshit I'm expected to put up with, then I think maybe I was right in the first place. That where I really belong is on some tub where at least my life is my own. So what I need to do now is to get my head straightened out—to figure out what I want to do and where and how. Until then you guys can go right on playing genius. But don't count on me."

As Hendricks turned toward the door, Zicci started to move, but Mario Braciola silently raised his hand and the young man stopped. Hendricks walked out of the room and started down the stairs. What he had hoped would be the biggest night of his life was turning into something altogether different. He decided that he wanted a drink, and that he wanted very much to talk to Tina Rinaldi.

chapter 48

Scozza was enjoying himself. It was not often that he had an opportunity to attend a gala event under legitimate circumstances, and tonight he was not only carrying an engraved invitation, but also a press pass, compliments of *Il Mondo*. As he strolled through the palazzi, he glanced at his reflection in a gilded mirror, and that pleased him too. The paparazzo was wearing a tuxedo of silk gabardine so dark it appeared almost black, but which was actually, according to the tailor who had rented it to him, something called midnight brown. In Scozza's opinion, the suit made him look quite handsome, because it was cut and draped so that he seemed not as fat as he did massive. He also looked slightly mysterious, he decided with satisfaction, thanks to the huge, wrap-around dark glasses which obscured the upper half of his face.

A waiter passed, carrying a tray of champagne in hollow-stemmed glasses, and Scozza helped himself, sipping the cold, tingling liquid as he strolled over to one of the buffet tables. He did not care very much for the flavor of champagne, but what the wine represented, what it stood for as a high note of luxury, meant a great deal to him.

Waiters behind the tables were serving guests from silver salvers and platters. Scozza ignored them. He had his own way of dealing with buffets, especially one as elaborate as this. His eyes narrowed and his saliva ducts responded as his gaze swept the array of dishes. Holding his glass of champagne in one hand, he scooped up his choices, one at a time, with the other. Instead of filling a small plate, as other guests were doing, Scozza filled his mouth. First he ate a handful of Beluga caviar, sharply salty, the tiny, pearlescent black eggs bursting on his tongue. Then a chunk of lobster, of the fat, succulent variety from the North Sea, followed by a hot pastry shell filled with crab meat. Paper-thin slices of prosciutto, rolled into tubes, were next. Scozza dipped several of the cylinders of smoked ham into a piquant sauce and devoured them. A platter held tender spears of fresh asparagus vinaigrette. He emptied its entire contents, downing one delicate green shaft after the other. Steadily, methodically, the paparazzo walked back and forth along the table, not leaving it for a full twenty minutes as he gorged himself on the rich food, washing all of it down with glass after glass of champagne.

When he had eaten his fill, at least for the time being, he belched softly and drifted over to the bar, his purpose now to look over the guests and to see what might be a likely subject to photograph. He had already noticed a number of people who interested him, some from the world of show business, some with political backgrounds, some who were merely rich. Several photographers were busy in the villa, but Scozza held these in contempt. They had been hired by Vicente Morello's production company to cover this event, and they were merely the say-cheese type of idiot who wandered around popping away with a flash-mounted 35 mm camera, as if photographing a school dance.

In contrast Scozza covered a function of this kind, whether invited or not, without his subjects knowing he was shooting. It was for this purpose that he wore the dark glasses, which had been custom-built for him by Minox of Germany and which concealed an 8 mm camera in their heavy black frames. There was a double advantage afforded by their design; in addition to hiding the act of his taking photographs, the smoked lenses also made it impossible to tell what he was looking at.

He noticed a man standing at the bar talking earnestly with a young woman. Scozza decided that the man looked familiar. He was gray-haired, probably in his mid-fifties. The paparazzo searched his memory and identified him as a prominent businessman who had political aspirations. Scozza squeezed in next to the couple and asked the bartender for a brandy and soda. He lounged casually on the polished mahogany surface, all the while cocking an ear toward the conversation next to him. As he listened, it became clear that the young woman was the businessman's mistress and that he was trying to get rid of her. Scozza stood there for several minutes, leisurely sipping his drink. The businessman told the girl that he was becoming so busy with his burgeoning political activities that he would not be able to see her for a while, probably a long while, and suggested that she take a vacation. He would send her to a nice resort on the Adriatic coast. Or perhaps to France. The girl said she would throw herself off a bridge. The businessman explained that his wife was also becoming a problem. The girl said she did not give a shit. The businessman told the girl that he intended to give her a lovely present. It would be a sizable amount of money, he said. The girl replied that her heart was broken, but that such a present might help her to feel a little better. Not much, but a little. And it would depend on the size of the present.

While he stood at the bar, Scozza several times touched the tiny trigger which was concealed in the temple bar of the frames of his dark glasses. When he had thus exposed a suitable amount of film, and when he was satisfied that he had learned enough about the situation the businessman had gotten himself into, he finished his drink and went to the men's room, where in the privacy of a locked toilet stall he made notes in a small black book. He then reloaded the Minox, urinated, washed his hands, and strolled out to mingle once again among the gay, noisy crowd.

He went through more or less the same eavesdropping act with a number of other people, including a Greek motion picture actress, a homosexual director who was in the process of establishing a relationship with a supposedly straight and very upright banker, and the head of a shipping company. In addition he took random shots of anybody who was either recognizable or interesting or both. After a couple of hours of

272

this he was hungry again, so he approached another of the buffet tables and stuffed himself once more, this time paying greater attention to such hot meats as sliced beef and veal rollatini.

When he left the table, he climbed the stairs to the second floor. More people were dancing up there, some of the women with considerable abandon. Scozza leaned comfortably against a wall and studied the gyrating shapes. The writhing and jiggling stimulated him, and he began to think about engaging a whore when the party had ended.

A hand gripped his shoulder, and Scozza started.

"Caught in the act!"

The paparazzo turned to see Galupo grinning at him. "Christ, don't do that to me."

The editor laughed. "Why not? It should help to make you more alert."

"Don't worry about my being alert. There is very little I miss, let me assure you."

"That's wonderful, since you are working on my time. Come on over where we can have a drink and talk."

Galupo led the way to a small table. It was in the shadows and as far as possible from the bandstand, but the noise of the drums and the amplified guitars still reverberated like cannon fire.

When they had ordered drinks from a passing waiter, Galupo gestured toward the dance floor. "I must be getting old, but I find the new music hard to understand."

Scozza grunted. "You're not supposed to understand it. You just get up and move to it. Whatever it makes you feel, that's how you move."

"To me it is so much shit."

"Then you should squat down and grunt. The girls will think you are a sensational dancer."

"How is it going—are you having any luck?"

The paparazzo was intentionally vague. "Some. It's hard to tell. Even with very high-speed film, it's not easy to know what I'll get in this light."

"What about the people? You must be having a field day with this crowd."

Scozza shrugged. "A better than average mob, I'll grant you. I would even agree there's plenty going on here, but again, I have no way of knowing what I'll wind up with."

"We were delighted, you know, with the piece on Hendricks. Newsstand sales were way up, and the story generated a hell of a lot of talk. Our audience is more women than men, as you might guess, and they wet their drawers over this new combination of a pirate and a stud."

"Good. I'm glad it did well. I'm sure you'll want me to do another one on him. Maybe more than one."

The waiter returned with their drinks. Scozza was a little drunk, but he didn't care. Thus far he had had a marvelous time, and he was sure he had a lot of material in the tiny 8 mm magazines he had shot with the Minox and in the little black notebook in his jacket pocket. The thing was, he had to get it all sorted out in the next day or two, so that he would know exactly what he wanted to let *Il Mondo* have, and exactly what he would offer elsewhere. Some of it he might peddle to another publication, and some of it he was sure would provide absolutely first-rate material for blackmail. But one of the paparazzo's great skills was in knowing how to get the most out of stuff like this. He was confident that much of it would prove useful in giving him leads to follow up at a later point, especially the opportunities to sell information back to those who would be most embarrassed by what he had managed to ferret out about them.

Galupo was drinking whiskey over ice. He swallowed half the contents of his glass. "What did you think of the picture?"

Scozza curled his lips in disdain. "Absolute crap. But I think Morello has got himself a gold mine in this cowboy." At least, he thought to himself, I certainly hope so.

"Did you see the woman jump on him, outside this theater?"

"I heard about it. A cheap trick, no doubt the work of those half-assed publicity people Morello has running around."

"Or even the work of Morello himself."

"Yes, you may be right. It sounds like him."

"Don't be so quick to sneer. I have an idea we'll see that story in every newspaper in the city tomorrow morning."

"So? All that will prove is that editors are assholes. Present company excepted, of course."

"Of course. I would have had her do something much more dramatic. Like kill herself, for example."

"That would have been a nice touch, at that. No wonder your magazine is so successful."

"Exactly." Galupo drained his glass. "I'll leave you to your work. Be sure to come into the office, just as soon as you can. I may even have some new assignments I could put you into. Some of them quite interesting. And as I think you have seen, the money is very good."

Scozza lit a cigarette. "I would say fair. Certainly in the story on Hendricks you got a hell of a bargain."

The editor smiled and got to his feet. "Keep your shutter cocked."

"Ciao."

As Galupo moved away, Scozza returned his attention to the dancers on the crowded floor, studying the contortions of the women intently. He was particularly intrigued by a lush brunette who exhibited a marvelous talent for rotating her ass. He was about to get up from the table and move closer for a better look when a group of men coming down the broad stairway from the third floor caught his eye. Two of the men he recognized immediately. They were Vicente Morello and Mario Braciola, and they were talking together with some animation.

Scozza felt a small thrill of excitement. Braciola was as important in the photographer's eyes as any man in Rome, the embodiment of vast behind-the-scenes power. He was rarely seen in public and hardly ever at a big flashy party like this one. In fact he normally would have been almost impossible to photograph, even if Scozza had a market for the pictures. The trouble was, most publications would want nothing to do with printing anything on this man. Still Scozza prided himself on his keen nose, which was twitching now like that of a fox. What were those two doing together? Was it purely social—a matter of Braciola congratulating the producer on the picture, or was there something else? Could there be some deeper connection? The possibilities were fascinating to contemplate.

The paparazzo got up and strolled casually past the group, his hand touching the temple bar of his dark glasses. He tried to catch some of their conversation as the two men walked by, but he did not succeed. The group proceeded to go on down to the first floor, and Scozza decided not to follow them. As he had told himself, it could be nothing at all. But then again it could be something to think about.

He deftly lifted a glass of champagne from a waiter's tray and headed back toward the dance floor. Even as he studied the incredible gyrations of the brunette's ass, Scozza's brain continued to churn with thoughts of Braciola and Morello and what their being together could mean.

chapter 49

The Hired Gun was an instant, runaway success. The morning
after the premiere, the entertainment pages of Rome's newspapers were filled with stories on the picture. Mostly the
articles had to do with the glamour of the opening and of the
opulent party Vicente Morello had given to celebrate the
event, but there were also pieces about members of the cast,
and Morello himself, and Carlos Caserta, and most of all,
about Hendricks. Some of the material attempted to describe
his background, and depending on which newspaper you
read, he was a cowboy who had left the American cattle
country to go to sea, or a fugitive from the law, or simply a
soldier of fortune who had led a life of whoring, boozing, and
brawling until Morello had discovered him.

The gossip columns had a field day with the newly discovered
actor. He was generally described as a kind of insatiable satyr
who could not go for more than a few hours without a woman,
a rumor which had started in the pages of *Il Mondo*. One
writer had him in a desperate struggle with Morello over
Cecily Petain. Another wrote that Cecily had left the producer
and was living with Hendricks and Tina Rinaldi in a ménage à
trois. Still another let her readers in on the astonishing fact
that Hendricks's secret address was one of the biggest and
most expensive brothels in Rome.

Other articles honed in on the feud between Hendricks and
Carlos Caserta. There were pictures of the former soccer
player in his days as a famed athlete side by side with pictures
of him in the hospital in Spain. The latter were similar to the
one which had appeared in *Il Mondo* the week before the
premiere and showed Caserta looking ghastly, his black eyes
sunk deep into his cadaverously thin face. Galupo had a fit
when he saw these, but Scozza vehemently denied that he
had had anything to do with taking them, and least of all with
peddling them to other publications. That would not, the
paparazzo pointed out, have been ethical.

Critical comment on the picture generally agreed that it

276

was execrable. One reviewer said it proved that Roman taste had not changed one whit in two thousand years, and that the film should have been shown in the Colosseum, where it wou'd have been right at home. Instead of seeing gladiators cut each other to pieces, the citizens could have amused themselves by watching Hendricks kill half the population of a village and rape most of its women. Another proposed a different alternative. Rather than paying to see the picture, this one wrote, the same effect could be achieved by first visiting a cattle breeding pen and immediately afterward, an abatoir. You could watch the animals copulate, and then you could see them slaughtered, he suggested. The effect would be the same, and you would thereby save time and money.

Probably the most damning point of view was expressed in an editorial in one of the morning editions. The writer said that the picture was a compendium of everything that was rotten and base and vulgar in modern-day life and that it reduced the audience to the level of subhumans. Hendricks, it said, was the new high priest of filth, and that the only thing about him that was fitting was that he was an American. The fact that he was obviously irresistible to women only proved, it said, how far back into the primordial slime the female sex had crawled. The piece closed with the observation that such an abomination would never be shown in a communist country.

The church also condemned the picture, announcing that to view it would be the commission of a sin. It was time, the official release said, to join hands in a universal boycott of the entire motion picture industry, until it returned to the production of films fit for family viewing.

The result of all of this, of course, was to send people to see the movie in unprecedented numbers. The film was shown continuously from ten o'clock in the morning until midnight, and at no time of the day could you get in without waiting in line for at least an hour, and sometimes for as long as three. The lines wound all the way around the block, and when the auditorium filled up prior to a new showing, a roar of outrage would go up outside from those who had failed to gain entrance.

As a promotional idea, Morello had had an enormous cutout of Hendricks erected above the marquee of the theater. You could see it from blocks away, the huge figure of the blond cowboy with the blue eyes and the white teeth bared in a grimace, standing spraddle-legged with a smoking pistol in each hand. As one of the critics observed, there was nothing about this film, from its theme to its cast to its exploitation, that was not gross in its style as well as its appeals.

To Hendricks's surprise, he became an overnight celebrity, albeit a notorious one. The incident of the young woman who had attacked him while he had been on his way into the theater to attend the premiere proved greatly effective in stimulating further news stories. Numerous pictures of the assault were published in newspapers and magazines, along with articles conjecturing on his relationship with the woman. The consensus of these was that she had been the American's girl friend until he achieved success, whereupon he had thrown her out. Some others, however, took this idea farther, stating that she was actually his wife, and that she lived in a hovel with a brood of brats he had fathered before abandoning her. It was impossible to prove any of this, inasmuch as the young woman had mysteriously disappeared after the incident in the theater lobby, and no trace of her could be found. This, of course, led to further rumors, one of which was that Hendricks had murdered her and had dumped her body into the Tiber.

When he thought about it, the American realized that he had been naïve about what the publicity and the showing of the picture would do to his personal life. Everybody was talking about him, and about the movie, and their curiosity about him seemed impossible to satisfy. An additional problem for him was that, because of his height and coloring, especially his yellow hair, he was as easy to recognize as if he had worn an electric sign proclaiming his identity. As a result he was frequently stopped on the street and asked for his autograph, and sometimes when this happened, a crowd would gather, and often some jostling would take place as young girls tried to outshove each other to get close to him. On two occasions these events turned into small riots as one girl slugged another, and Hendricks escaped by climbing onto the Moto Guzzi and pushing off through the excited crowd. What was even worse, the fans sometimes decided to hunt souvenirs, snatching whatever they could from his clothing or his hair.

As a result Hendricks quickly learned to be extremely cautious when he went into the streets, and he disguised his appearance by wearing a knitted sailor's watch cap and the most ragged blue jeans he owned. The ruse did not always work, however, and when it failed, he would find himself surrounded by an imploring band of females who shrieked at him and thrust scraps of paper at him and tried to tear pieces out of his clothes or to snatch his cap off, all the while screaming that they loved him and offering him their bodies.

The boldness of the propositions from strange women he found the most bizarre aspect of all in his newly awakened recognition. Two days after the premiere he was having lunch in Ristorante Bobolo with Arturo when a good-looking, well-dressed young woman approached their table, sat down without waiting for an invitation, and told Hendricks she wanted to go to bed with him. She paid no attention whatever to Arturo, but locked her hand on Hendricks's forearm and demanded that he go with her to her apartment and spend the afternoon with her. Hendricks did his best to be polite, but the woman was adamant. She had seen the picture, she said, and Hendricks was the most desirable man she had ever laid eyes on. She didn't care what happened to her, she had to have him and that was all there was to it. People at nearby tables were watching this and grinning, and Hendricks could feel his face flaming.

"Look," he told her. "I can't. I'm busy. Some other time. Please leave me alone."

"I want you, Hendricks." Her voice was husky. "I will do anything to make love to you."

"And I said no. Now beat it, will you?"

"What's the matter—I'm not good enough for you?"

He sighed. "You're terrific. Really you are. But I can't. Now take off."

"You rotten, conceited American bastard."

"Holy Christ."

She swung at him, but Hendricks was ready. He blocked the blow and shoved her away. It took the manager and two waiters to get the woman out of the place.

Over the next few days Hendricks attended several meetings in Morello's office on the subject of what he would do next, and to the newly established actor's disgust, most of the ideas and proposals seemed to him to be as inane as what had been talked about in the palazzi on the night of the premiere. Morello had asked a couple of screenwriters to attend these meetings, but their suggestions didn't strike Hendricks as very intelligent either. They appeared to want to please Morello above all else, and whatever direction the producer's thoughts took, or whatever he threw out for discussion, they simply applauded. Hendricks also realized that when he expressed ideas of his own, no one paid more than minimal attention to what he had to say. It became clear to him that he wasn't expected to contribute, or even to be able to think. He was simply the performer, the attraction they would feature in whatever half-assed story idea they would eventually come up with. At first he was slightly mystified by their treating him as if he weren't there, and then he found himself becoming annoyed. What they were babbling about didn't seem to make all that much sense, and yet when he proposed a concept, or made an observation, they just looked blank and then either moved off in another direction or waited for Morello's next outpouring of brilliance. To Hendricks it was frustrating and galling, and when he left the meetings, he went straight to a cantina and took out his frustrations on a bottle of whiskey.

During those same days following the premiere, Morello's publicity people worked overtime pushing Hendricks into as many interviews as possible. The interviewers, he perceived immediately, held preconceived notions about him which were as unshakable as those of the screenwriters. He was seen by them as a half-civilized oaf who was incapable of thinking about much more than where his next woman or his next brawl would be coming from.

In one of these the interviewer was a female syndicated columnist whose material was carried in over seventy newspapers in Italy. They met over cocktails in the rooftop room at the Hassler. The interview had been arranged by Menotti, one of Morello's PR men, who sat at the table drinking brandy and looking bored.

The woman was middle-aged and fat, but she tried to dress much younger, striving for a chic, casual look that in reality came off as sloppy. Her blouse was unbuttoned halfway to her waist, revealing heavy breasts and rolls of flesh that jiggled when she moved, and there were ornate rings on most of her thick fingers. A small tape recorder lay on the table beside her drink, and she made notes in a spiral notebook as they talked. Her column was published under the name Vicki, and its contents were largely devoted to such matters as what star was sleeping with whom.

As the columnist threw questions at him, Hendricks had the distinct impression that it didn't matter what his answers might be, that the woman would find a way to bend them around to whatever she wanted to write about him anyway. In the few encounters he'd had with the press before this, he'd come to realize that the writers had their own ideas as to what their readers wanted to think about him, and that therefore they would simply jam him into the mold.

The columnist looked at his hair. "Is that natural?"

"Is what natural?"

"Your hair. Is the color natural, or do you touch it up?"

"God, of course not. Of course I don't touch it up. It's the same color it's always been, except maybe it was a little lighter when I was a kid."

"Do you think women like the fact that you're blond?"

"I don't know. I've never discussed it with any of them."

"Never?"

"Well, you know. I don't remember any big conversation on the subject."

"But they notice it, don't they?"

"Oh, yeah. I mean I guess so. Now that you mention it, I suppose some of them may have commented on it at one time or another."

"How about your own preferences. Do you like blonds better than brunettes or redheads?"

"Not necessarily. I like any kind of a girl if I like the girl herself. It doesn't matter."

"It's common knowledge that you like to treat women brutally. What's the reason for that?"

"Reason for what? Who says I like to treat women brutally?"

"Would you say it's a sexual thing—that you find sexual stimulus, or even gratification, in treating a woman roughly?"

"I wouldn't say any such thing. Knocking a woman around is not my idea of how to have a good time."

"And yet brutality has been such a basic part of your life."

Hendricks stared at the columnist. It was absolutely true. No matter what the hell he said, he knew that the story would come out that he was proud of being a dyed blond, he loved brutality, and he especially liked to beat up women for sexual reasons. Any kind of woman—blonds, brunettes, redheads—it was all the same to him. He glanced at Menotti, but the PR man simply returned his gaze with a blank expression and swallowed more brandy. He felt his anger come up, and then the whole thing suddenly struck him funny.

The woman leaned forward, exposing even more flesh. "Well, hasn't it? Haven't you dealt with most of your problems with violence?"

What the hell, Hendricks thought. Why not. "Yeah. That's

right. Anytime anybody gets in my way, I just knock them over."

She made notes on her pad. "Would you call the role you played in *The Hired Gun* a true portrayal of your character?"

"Absolutely. If anything it was a little tamer than the way I really am."

She made more notes. "Did your affair with Cecily Petain begin when you were together on location for the picture, or had you known each other before that?"

"We first met on a yacht in Portofino."

"Were you immediately attracted to her?"

"I thought she had great boobs." There, you want this kind of shit, I'll give it to you.

When the column appeared two days later, it was slanted exactly as Hendricks had expected it to be, and yet as far as he could see, there wasn't much different in the way this woman had written about him and what any of the others had printed. Just as Vicente Morello had predicted, he had become a personality—composed in part of the image he had projected in *The Hired Gun*, in part of the biographical nonsense that had been published about him, and in part of the public's own imagination. They saw Hendricks as a wild, two-fisting, hard-drinking womanizer, not only because that was what they had been led to believe about him, but also because that was what they *wanted* to believe.

Meantime *The Hired Gun* was setting box-office records.

chapter 50

The staccato bark of the Moto Guzzi grew in volume and intensity as Hendricks laid the machine into the uphill banked turn and opened the throttle. As the big bike climbed higher, the bark became a roar, and he felt as if he were riding a projectile, rocketing through the air with all the power in the world at the command of his right fist. He rotated the handle further when the motorcycle came out of the turn and onto the straightaway, and the response was electrifying. The bike leaped ahead, faster and faster, until the needle of the speedometer flickered at the 180 kph mark. Hendricks felt Tina's legs close on his and her arms tighten their grip around his waist. They shot along the autostrada, whipping past slower traffic as if the small Fiats and and Volkswagens were running backward, their shapes hurtling toward them and then disappearing in a blur as the Moto Guzzi howled by.

A few kilometers north of the city there were fewer vehicles on the broad highway. They pounded along steadily for over an hour, and several times Hendricks heard Tina shout something in his ear, but her words were lost in the beat of the engine and whipped away by the wind. He merely grinned and gunned the big bike on, delighted by the way it took the curves and flew over the road, exhilarated by the sense of freedom that riding a motorcycle at high speeds always gave him.

When they reached a point near Orvieto, some distance north of Rome, Hendricks swung off the autostrada and onto a narrow country road. This was even hairier than the main highway had been, with its tight turns and switchbacks through the hill country. Hendricks handled the bike expertly, negotiating the curves while deftly avoiding potholes and the occasional chicken or goat that wandered into their path. The sun was high, and the spring air was warm on their faces by the time he pulled the machine off the road and stopped at a small cantina.

The place was run by a smiling, rotund woman who greeted them jovially, obviously pleased at having two young people stop at her tiny roadside establishment. Hendricks had her pour glasses of Frascati, which they drank while she put up a lunch for them, and when it was ready they got back on the bike and rode on until he found an even less traveled road, this one little more than a pair of wheel ruts that ran through the forest. At the top of a ridge there was a grove of trees, and on the southeast side it opened onto a meadow where sheep were grazing. Hendricks turned off the road and stopped. He pushed the Moto Guzzi up onto its kickstand and pulled a blanket and their lunch out of the saddlebags and led Tina by the hand. He spread the blanket under a pair of tall pine trees, and they sat down on it and marveled at the view. There was a tiny lake far down the hillside, below the meadow, surrounded by evergreens and sparkling like a sapphire in the sunshine, and far off on the horizon, hazy in the distance, they could just make out the skyline of Rome.

Their lunch was fresh bread, warm and crusty, and cherry

tomatoes, and a big wedge of port salut, and garlicky slices of salami and pepperoni. There was also a bottle of Valpolicella, which Hendricks opened with the corkscrew in the knife he carried in his jeans.

Tina smiled at him as he filled paper cups with the wine. "Hungry?"

"Starved. God Almighty, I'm hungry most of the time anyway, and all you have to do is to get me out of doors someplace, especially when the weather's nice like this, and I could eat one of those sheep down there in a couple of bites."

"Don't do that. They're too pretty. And besides, we have plenty of good things to eat right here."

They touched their cups and drank, and Hendricks enjoyed the fruity taste of the wine, with its faint bite on his tongue that seemed to make him all the hungrier. They sliced thick pieces of warm bread from the loaf and cut chunks of the cheese, and Hendricks wolfed his food, popping the small juicy tomatoes into his mouth and chewing with gusto on the spicy meat.

He refilled their cups. "Hey, be sure you eat some of that salami. I don't want to be the only one with a killer breath."

She laughed. "Don't worry, I love it. And besides, garlic is good for you. Keeps you from catching cold and all kinds of other small ailments."

"I don't have any small ailments. Only big ones. The way I see it, if something is worth doing, it's worth doing all out."

Tina studied his face. "I guess you do see it that way, don't you? And what you've done is exactly that. You've gone all out, and you've made yourself everything you wanted to be."

He snorted. "Oh shit, Tina, I haven't done any such goddamned thing. Everybody keeps telling me that, but what's really happened? So I got shoved into the picture because Morello and Livorno were stuck and didn't know what the hell else to do with Caserta, and then with a lot of bullshit hype the movie stirred up attention in Rome. I keep telling people, that doesn't make me an actor, and it doesn't prove I have talent, and it doesn't mean I can do it again. Hell, I don't even know if I *want* to do it again."

Tina's mouth opened in astonishment. "You don't want to do it again? Do you know how many people in this world would trade places with you right this minute? Are you mad? And what happened to all the ambition you had in Spain? You were going to turn the world upside down—learn everything there was to learn about becoming an actor and then have a whole fantastic new career."

"Something like that."

"What do you mean, something like that? I was there. I heard you. I watched you. Now you've taken the first big step, you have it in your hands, and you're saying no, this isn't what you want? Hendricks, sometimes I think you really are crazy. Either that, or you have no idea what it is you actually do want. Maybe a combination of both those things."

"Maybe. But that's why I wanted to see you again, what I wanted to talk to you about."

She chewed thoughtfully on a crust of bread, her eyes gazing at him steadily. "I might have hoped it was just because you wanted to see me."

"Oh hell, that too. You know what I mean. I wanted to know what you thought. I wanted to, you know, discuss things."

"I was pretty upset when you moved out."

"I told you why, what that was all about. I mean, you were terrific to me, gave me a hell of a lot of help when I really needed it. But I didn't think it was fair of me to tie you down."

One corner of her mouth lifted in a sardonic smile. "You didn't think it was fair to tie me down? That's funny, Hendricks. What you didn't want tied down was you."

He exhaled slowly. "Okay. So maybe that was it too. But I'm trying to do this thing, you see? I'm trying to do this, and it's all new to me, and one minute I think I can really do it, that I can really turn it into something, and then the next minute I'm saying to myself, hey look, you dumb shit, where you belong is knocking around on ships. It's all you know and all you're good for, and the sooner you get back where you belong the better."

"How can you think that way? It doesn't make sense. The newspapers are full of stories about you, the picture is breaking records at the box office, and everybody says you're going to be a really big star. And here you are talking as if it was all a mistake, or as if it never happened. Or what's even crazier, as if it isn't what you had hoped would happen. I swear, sometimes I think it's just impossible to understand you."

He poured more wine for them. "Okay, so that may be, too. And if you think that's nuts, wait till you hear this." He handed Tina one of the paper cups and drank from his own.

"There's another thing that's bothering me, and I think it may be worse than any of the other things."

"Good God, what is that?"

"Well, here's another way to look at it. Let's say I am right. That I don't have any real talent, but that I do have some kind of appeal when you get me up on that screen and there's a lot of fucking and violence and all that shit that seems to turn people on. In that context they look at me and I seem to fit, and I get them excited. Or let's say it's a combination of me and that type of a story that gets them worked up. I think, if you boil it all down, that's what's really going on. Okay?"

Tina pursed her lips. "Okay. So what? That's exactly what we all wanted, you included. You may not have expressed it very elegantly, but yes, that's what goes on when the audiences see you in the picture."

"All right, so what's happened? So it looks as if the thing works. Whether I'm talented or not, whether I'm qualified or not, the thing works. And then what? Then Morello and his friends, the money guys, start looking at me like I'm some hunk of meat they can push around and do whatever they want to do. They're going to stick me in this kind of picture or that kind of picture, whatever *they* decide is going to be what they figure will make money. You see what I mean?"

She stared at him. "No. I don't."

He shook his head, struggling to express himself. "Well, you know what it makes me think of? One time I went to a prizefight in New Orleans. It was in a waterfront warehouse that had been cleared out and a ring and seats set up in the thing. The crowd was mostly guys off ships in the port. Everybody was drunk and yelling for blood, now the smoke was so thick it made your eyes sting, I remember that. Anyhow, there was this old guy, old for a fighter I mean, and you could see he'd been around plenty. His nose was flat, and there was a lot of white scar tissue over his eyes. They put him in against a young kid, a really beautiful young fighter, very classy and not a mark on him. Now you knew when you looked at what was going on that the old guy had no idea who he was going to fight, and that it didn't matter to him anyhow. He went in there in this cruddy old bathrobe and he looked at the floor while the referee talked to them and all the while the young guy is doing his little dance and looking all around to be sure everybody is watching him. Then the bell rings, and in the next few minutes what happened was exactly what everybody knew was going to happen. But you know what

286

else? It was exactly what everybody *wanted* to happen. The young guy cut him to pieces. He moved around with a lot of flashy steps and he showed everybody how nifty he was, and when he'd put on enough of a demonstration, he knocked the old guy out and the crowd went nuts and afterward everybody was talking about what a great future the kid had ahead of him."

Tina continued to watch him closely. "All right, so which one of them do you identify with, in your memory?"

He waved his hands. "That's just it, that's the point, don't you see it? I identify with both of them, because they were the same guy. At some time or another the old fighter had been just like the young one was that night. He was quick and strong and he figured nobody could lick him and he could go on forever. And someday the young guy would be going through the same thing. He would have caught some shots along the way, and he wouldn't be so pretty anymore, and not nearly as fast, and then along would come some other stud who'd flatten him."

She sipped her wine. "I understand what you're saying, and it's cruel and it's barbaric, but it's also the way life is. Not just for us, but for other creatures, as well. What you just described is also the way wolves live, and deer, and lots of other animals."

"Aha. Right. But with one big difference. What those guys were doing was not what nature made them do. It wasn't simply the way they had to live and struggle because that was the way it had always been and that's how the leaders of the pack or the herd established themselves. Those two fighters were being *taken*. They were in there because other people who were smarter than they were had held out a promise of money and glamour and a great life being a hero, and these guys had bought it; and by the time either of them, or any of them, figured out what the truth was, they'd had it. It would be too late, and they'd be stumblebums, and meantime the people who were running things, they would have found more young fighters they could live off."

Tina's eyes widened. "So that's it. You think that Morello and his backers are simply out to exploit you?"

"You're goddamned right I do. They're going to take me for as much as they can, as long as they can get something out of me, and then they're going to be on to something else. Hell, already I'm not really a person anymore. You saw the article in that fucking magazine and the other shit that's been printed

287

about me. And the broads. Now there's a whole bunch of women who want to screw me just because I'm in the picture."

She winced, but he didn't notice.

"Sure, that's every guy's dream, right? Well, now I know how fast that can wear off. But what's more important, all that does is tell you what's happening to me. I'm not me anymore. I'm this thing, this character created to pull people into theaters. King Kong on exhibition. Weaver was right. Morello has me on a piece of paper, and he's paying me what you'd pay a guy to wash your windows."

"Have you talked to him about that?"

"Oh sure, and what I hear back is a bunch of mumbo jumbo. He's got me by the balls, and he knows it. But what he doesn't know is that I just maybe won't play."

"Then what will you do—go back to sea?"

He looked down at the tiny lake far below them for a long time before he answered. "Hell, no. Like I said, I thought about it, and I wrestled with it, and I even got kind of serious about the idea. But that's self-generated bullshit. A way of kidding myself. Because you're right. I never had it so good, and a lot of the time I can't believe that all this is happening to me. But you know what? I'll be a son of a bitch if I'm going to let Morello and whoever the hell his friends are just take me and control me."

"What will you do?"

He turned to her. "I told you I had a crazy idea, didn't I? What I want to do is—I want to make my own pictures."

Tina's jaw dropped. She looked at his earnest face, and then she burst out laughing. "You want to make your own pictures? Hendricks, you are too much for me. One minute you are the complete amateur, hoping you might have some luck and maybe get somewhere. The next minute you have some success, more than you ever hoped for, and now here you are telling me you ought to be running things. Making your own pictures." She laughed again and shook her head in wonder.

"I told you you'd think I'd flipped out. But look at it this way. The people come into the theaters because they want to see me, right? Sure, they hear it's a wild picture, full of sex and gore and all those other good things. But more than anything else, they want to see what this new American cocksman is like. They want to see him rape the ladies and kill his enemies while they eat popcorn and get their rocks off. That's the truth, isn't it?"

She inclined her head as she thought about what he had said. "Maybe. Maybe you're right. I guess if I had to boil it down to one appeal above all others, I'd have to say that was the one."

He slapped his thigh. "Exactly. Now, I know all this sounds like I've developed the biggest ego in Europe, maybe the world. But I've thought about this until my head ached, and all I've tried to do was to be objective and to figure out where I should be going."

"And so you think you have?"

"Maybe. What I think is, if anybody is going to take me, then that somebody ought to be me."

They were quiet for a time after that, and then Hendricks put an arm around her and kissed her. He felt her stir as his mouth opened to him, and he pressed her down onto the blanket and opened the buttons of her blouse. It had been weeks since they had made love, and it was as if he were discovering her body for the first time, and perhaps better than that, because in fact he knew every inch of it. He kissed her nipples until her breath was coming in short, hot gasps, and then he opened her jeans and slid them down over the round, curving hips. He pulled off his own clothing hurriedly, and when he slid into her, she cried out and dug her nails into his back in the way she had done so many times. Their lovemaking was intense and demanding at first, and then later it was languid and unhurried, as they gently rocked together for hours, and when they were finally spent, the sun had disappeared below the hilltops and a cool wind was coming off the meadow.

They dressed and climbed back onto the Moto Guzzi, and it was dusk by the time Hendricks brought the bike back into the swirling traffic at the edge of the city. He dropped Tina at her apartment, and he kissed her lightly and said he would call her. But it was apparent to him that he had made a decision, a commitment, and that somehow the gulf that had appeared between them would grow wider.

chapter 51

Carlos Caserta opened his eyes and turned his head toward the window. The predawn light was only a shade above black, but he could make out a few ghostly shapes of trees and neighboring buildings in the gloom outside. He swung his legs over the side of the hospital bed and shivered a little. There was the expected twinge in his back, but it was not quite as pronounced as it had been. In the weeks since the cast was removed, he had been aware of slow but steady improvement. He stepped onto the cold tile floor and stretched carefully.

The bathroom was at the end of the hall. Caserta shuffled down to it, carrying his leather toilet kit. As he shaved, he studied his pale face in the mirror and decided that his appearance had also undergone a certain amount of recovery. He was not nearly so gaunt, and although his eyes still had the sunken look, the bluish patches under them had almost disappeared. In fact he decided that his color generally was much better.

Back in his room he lay down on the small cotton rug at the foot of his bed and did his exercises, a lengthy series designed to loosen his back muscles and to strengthen them. When he had first started doing them, the pain had made sweat pop out of his skin in beads, but now he was able to go through the entire routine with no great difficulty. Doing the exercises reminded him of his days as a soccer player, when getting into shape had always been easy for him, even after a long winter of carousing and consuming as much pasta as he desired. He thought about those times, his first taste of celebrity, when he was proud of his reputation as one of the dirtiest players in Italy, perhaps in all Europe. It was strange the way fate bent your life and sent you off in unexpected directions; if it had not been for soccer, Caserta probably would have gone to prison.

Near the end of his career he had established his character as a brute so firmly in the public mind that he began to pick up bit parts in movies in the off-season. He performed in thief and mobster roles with great authenticity, and by the time the owner of the soccer team told him he was washed up as a player, he was well on his way to building a new life as an actor. At first the money was small, compared to what he had earned in his halcyon days as a footballer, but as time went on, he got more important assignments and built a considerable following as a highly believable screen villain.

When he was chosen by Morello for the lead in *The Hired Gun*, Carlos Caserta believed he had achieved a new pinnacle in his career as a film star. He saw himself going on from that role to grander and grander parts, even imagining the day when he would become a romantic idol. All of this vanished like smoke in a high wind, of course, when Caserta tumbled from the roof of the church and crashed into the courtyard below. In the months following his fall, the big man's slow and painful recovery was spurred more than anything else by sheer willpower. He lived for the day he would take revenge on Hendricks. And when he read in newspapers sent him from Rome of the triumph the American was experiencing as the film became a hit, he was driven by a fury deeper than any emotion he had ever experienced.

This morning, therefore, he thought about the American with smoldering hatred, as he had every morning since his injury. When a nurse brought his breakfast on a tray, he ate slowly and deliberately, reflecting that he was one day closer to his return to Rome.

"Good morning, Carlos." It was Dr. Borales, wearing his usual idiot-pleasant expression and speaking with the standard phony cheerfulness he projected when making his morning rounds.

Caserta grunted.

"I have some nice news for you." Borales pulled a chair alongside Caserta's and sat down on it.

"What is that?"

The doctor smiled. "I don't see any reason why you shouldn't be getting out of here soon. Your recovery has really been quite remarkable."

"When?"

"Well, very soon. I would say within the next few days."

"If I am ready to leave why do I have to wait a few more days?"

"Oh, you know. We just want to be absolutely certain you'll be all right to travel. It is a long trip, back to Italy."

291

"Get my clothes."

"What?"

"I said I want my clothes. If I am well enough to leave your shitbox hospital in a few days, I am well enough to leave it now."

Borales sputtered a protest, but Carlos Caserta was not listening. He was thinking with cold savagery of the American with the blond hair and the blue eyes.

chapter 52

The funeral of Claude Lemont was stiffly formal. It was attended by distant relatives, by friends and former business associates, by a contingent from the vast chemical concern his father had founded, by his lawyers and his bankers and his investment brokers. Lemont's bereaved widow appeared upright and brave throughout the services, facing the world with dry eyes and looking smashing in a Dior suit of black wool trimmed in mink, which she had had made for the occasion. She accepted expressions of condolence with dignity and serenity, priding herself on how well she played the part. It was a beautiful day, warm and sunny, and at the cemetery she was grateful for the veil that covered her face. Without it, a broad smile would have been visible on her lovely mouth, because she was no longer able to contain her happiness. Estelle Lemont was now not only an immensely rich woman, but even better than that, she was totally free to enjoy the fortune her husband had left her.

The will would not be probated immediately, of course. That would take months. But Estelle's lawyers obtained a court order directly after Claude's death which made virtually unlimited funds accessible to her. Her life-style was not markedly altered, however; there was no reason for that to happen, for a while at least. She lived pretty much as she always had, dining with friends, shopping, experiencing Paris. The major difference was that the glorious change that had occurred in her life made it possible for her to plan to enjoy herself in a way that had never before been possible.

She thought about cruising during the coming summer on the *Chanteuse*. She would visit her favorite Mediterranean ports, Saint Tropez and Portofino and Monaco, and if that paled, she might fly to Maui, where she had friends, or to Brazil, where another of her intimates owned a sprawling cattle ranch. In the fall a number of people she knew were planning a world cruise on the *France*, and that might be amusing, she thought, and beyond that there would be the skiing and the parties during the winter season at Biarritz to look forward to. The important point was that she could decide to do any of these things, or she could decide to do none of them. She had the wherewithal to do exactly as she wished, with whomever and wherever she felt like it.

For a time she permitted herself a wider and more relaxed indulgence among the men she knew. It was no longer necessary for her to be as discreet as she had been while Claude was alive, and she could come and go as she pleased. But she became aware that the men in her life treated her differently from the way they had in the past. There was a kind of deference she could feel, a suggestion of respect or even awe for the money she possessed. It was a subtle thing, and at first it amused her, but then it became a source of annoyance. All her life Estelle Lemont had been appealing to men because she had a beautiful face, a ripe body, and a lusty appetite for sex which was direct, honest, and uninhibited. Now suddenly she found that men were also interested in her for another reason, and no matter how casual they appeared to be about her change of status, that undercurrent was always present. She was no longer only witty and sexy, she was also rich and eligible, and the men she knew, even the married ones, never seemed to forget it for a moment. As a result she became suspicious of their interest in her and put herself on guard with all of them. The more aware of this change in attitude she became, the more it took the edge off her pleasure.

Even her most trusted counselors showed a different side. The man who for years had overseen Claude Lemont's real-estate holdings in the wine country of Bordeaux had always been attractive to her, and one afternoon after he had presented a report on those properties, she offered him a drink. They were in the drawing room of her vast apartment on the avenue Foch, and after the second whiskey he made a grab for her. He was tall and good looking, with a craggy face and an unruly shock of brown hair, and the move he made was exactly what Estelle had been hoping for. He kissed her and put his hand under her skirt, and she returned his kiss and spread her legs, and then she unzipped his fly and took him into her mouth. He came that way, as she crouched over him on the Louis XV sofa, and then she grasped his hand and led him into her bedroom. They spent the next three hours making love in the same bed Claude Lemont had died in, and by the time Estelle felt as relaxed and surfeited as she wished to feel, it was growing dark outside.

The real-estate overseer, whose name was Jacques, lay on his back with Estelle curled up comfortably against his side. "That was lovely."

She snuggled closer. "Was it? Was I really good for you?"

"You were incredible. I thought about it, you know, many times, while I worked for your husband."

"I know. I could tell." She laughed. "And do you know how I could tell? Because I had exactly the same feelings myself. I would look at you and I would think, what an interesting man. He looks so powerful and so purposeful. I wonder what it would feel like to have all that energy inside me."

"And now you know."

"And now I know, and it was delightful."

"I don't suppose it ever occurred to you, Estelle, that I have been in love with you, during all those years."

Her senses sent up alarm signals at once. Love? Who said anything about love? A roll in the hay was one thing, but love? On the basis of what? She had never exchanged more than a few pleasant words with the man before this afternoon, and here he was telling her he had been in love with her for years. She thought back. Just as she had said, it was true that she had long felt a certain animal attraction to him, and that she thought she had sensed a response in him. And yet she had not even been sure that he would make an advance this afternoon and had planned to initiate such activity herself if that had proved necessary. And so far as his performance in bed was concerned, he had been acceptable but nothing special. As a matter of fact, she reflected, if anything he had been rather clumsy. And for a man of his proportions, his cock was certainly the most underdeveloped part of him.

Jacques tightened his embrace. "I was thinking."

"Yes?"

"Well, to tell you the truth, I have been planning for a long while to separate from my wife. We really have very little in common, and I have known for some time that our marriage could not last."

294

Oh Christ, Estelle thought. Here it comes.

"I was thinking about how wonderful it would be if perhaps we could spend some time together. Really together, and alone, you know? Perhaps a trip somewhere, just the two of us. What do you think?"

She exhaled slowly. "I think you had better get your clothes on. I just remembered that I have an engagement for dinner."

Another change in her personal relationships also manifested itself, and this one became just as galling to her. Her female friends, she discovered, were quietly but viciously jealous, although most of them all but stood on their heads to hide their true feelings. There had always been a certain envy of her radiant good looks, and of the fact that she had once been a fairly well established motion picture actress. She had long realized that her friends tended to reassure themselves by feeling superior to her because of her background, discounting it as cheap and theatrical. But now the notion that she was not only still reasonably young and unusually good looking but also very rich and unattached was more than they could cope with. At first she was too happy to be aware of this, but within a short time she became conscious of their feelings and developed counterresentments of her own.

At lunch one day in Chez Guerin she was listening idly to the latest gossip, recounted to her by Louise D'Arcel, a friend of some years whose husband was a stockbroker. Louise was a few years older than she and came from one of the better families of Brittany. She was slim and elegant, although Estelle had always thought that her jaw was too long and square and that it tended to make her look a bit horse-faced.

Louise toyed with her drink, a vermouth cassis. "They have been seeing each other for some time, and everyone seems to know it."

"Oh?"

"Everyone except Margot, that is. How she could be so ignorant of such a blatant carrying-on is hard to imagine."

"Perhaps she does know and doesn't care."

"Oh, she'd care all right. Not about Albert, that fool. But she would care very much about being laughed at. It would be one thing if Albert's little friend amounted to anything, but she's nothing but a model. You see her in things like perfume ads. I really can't imagine what he finds attractive."

Estelle smiled. "Men tend to look at such things somewhat differently."

"I'm aware of that. But after the first excitement of a

sexy young body, then what? And there is such a lack of breeding in these little trollops. Margot not only comes from money, but old money."

Estelle's manner was cool. "It doesn't seem to me that it matters whether money is old or new. It will buy just as much, either way."

Louise sipped her drink. "There are some things it can't buy."

"Maybe. But I haven't discovered what they might be." God, what a bore this woman was. To be young and sexy meant you were automatically stupid, and to be rich only counted if your family had been rich for a long time.

"Have you kept in touch with your friends in the motion picture business?"

"Not very closely. I hear from them from time to time."

"Vicente Morello is someone you know, isn't he?" Louise's tone made it clear that she considered Estelle to be still part of an inferior subculture.

"Yes, I know him."

"I read in *Paris Match* that he has a successful new picture that's just opened in Rome."

"Oh? I hadn't heard. That's nice."

"Yes, it's caused a lot of talk."

They chatted for another hour about nothing, over a lunch of quiche and a watercress salad, and Estelle was glad finally to get away. She promised Louise she would call her soon and privately resolved that she would do no such thing.

Estelle had all but forgotten their conversation when she arrived home in the late afternoon, but after she changed and a maid brought her coffee in her sitting room, she lit a cigarette and noticed a copy of *Paris Match* on the table. Remembering Louise's reference to Vicente Morello, Estelle picked up the magazine and leafed through it. When she arrived at the article on the producer and his newest triumph, the surprise she experienced was like an electric shock. There was a full-page color photograph of Hendricks, looking exactly as she remembered him—jaunty, devil-may-care, and strikingly handsome.

But what had he to do with Morello? She raced through the article to find out, and the more she read, the more dumbfounded she felt. The young man who had been mate for a time on the *Chanteuse*—*her* young man—was an actor? And not only that but he was the star of a new hit film? It was incomprehensible. She read through the piece again, slowly

296

this time. But when she finished, she felt that she still had no real understanding of how all this had come about. She thought back, recalling the night in Portofino when Hendricks had become embroiled in a fight with the captain of the yacht, and how in the midst of the altercation he had disappeared. Morello had been aboard that night, with Cecily Petain, and that at least explained how the American and the producer had met. The way the magazine told the story she recognized as patently a romanticized publicity hype, the kind of garbage Morello was a master at inventing. It was an absurd tale of the producer having discovered an American sea captain who had once been a cowboy.

As a matter of fact, Morello had said something to her that night about the film he was planning to do, a western, and she had scoffed at him. She looked at the photograph of Hendricks and realized that her fingers were trembling. For reasons she could not understand, she felt cheated somehow, that all this had gone on without her knowledge.

Estelle crushed out her cigarette and paced back and forth in her sitting room. She went to the sideboard and poured herself a stiff brandy, her mind working furiously. When she had downed the fiery liquor, an idea formed itself, and excitement spread through her. She could be in Rome, she realized, as early as the evening of the next day. She picked up the magazine and stared again at the picture of Hendricks.

chapter 53

Vicente Morello arose at seven o'clock and padded softly about the master bedroom of his apartment, taking care not to awaken Cecily. He went into his bath and shaved and showered, thinking as he did that he would have to hurry to make his flight. When he came out of the bath, Cecily was staring at him through sleep-heavy eyes.

She drew the covers up to her chin. "Where are you going?"

"Zurich."

"Zurich? What for?"

"I have an appointment with some banking connections there. I won't be gone long."

"How long?"

He opened a drawer of the dresser that extended across an entire wall of the bedroom and withdrew a pair of shorts. "I have meetings this afternoon, and dinner this evening. I expect to conclude my affairs then, and that should make it possible for me to be back in Rome by the middle of the day tomorrow."

"Mmm. Why aren't you taking me with you?"

He went on dressing, pulling on a gauze-thin batiste shirt of the palest blue color. "Because it is all business, and it would be awkward for you even to attend dinner this evening. I can't imagine you'd enjoy sitting around in a hotel suite waiting for me. The Swiss tend to be rather secretive, you know, and they frown on mixing business with pleasure."

Cecily pretended to pout. "Will you bring me a present?"

Morello put on his shoes, a new pair of black Buccellatis. "Of course I will."

"There are so many wonderful things to buy in Zurich. I love the jewelry stores, row on row of them. I could spend days there, shopping."

"I'm sure you could." He selected a single-breasted suit of lightweight gray worsted which had been finished by his Bond Street tailors and sent to him only the week before and put on the trousers. The tie he chose was a Charvet with small blue and white figures. He knotted it carefully.

"What will you bring me?"

"Something nice."

"Mmm." She rolled over and buried her head in the pillow.

Morello got a bag out of his closet, a slim Gucci of supple dark brown leather, and laid it open on the plum velvet bench at the foot of the bed. He put into the bag a suit similar to the gray in cut, but of medium blue with a narrow stripe. His toilet kit went in next, along with socks, shorts, shirt, and tie. He also packed slippers and a yellow silk robe.

He put on the jacket of his suit and studied his reflection in a full-length mirror with satisfaction. Cecily appeared to have gone back to sleep. Morello kissed her cheek lightly and left the room.

He was hungry, but there would be breakfast on the plane. He flagged a taxi on the street in front of his apartment house and told the driver to take him to Fiumicino. It was a mild, pleasant morning, and he would have enjoyed taking the hour-long drive to the airport in the Ferrari, but he made it a point never to leave the machine in such exposed places as airport parking lots. Car thievery was rampant in Rome these days, and the bright red coupe would have made a choice target. He was also intent on keeping a low profile for this trip.

Alitalia's flight number 347 was scheduled to land at one fifteen P.M. Morello was always fascinated by flying over the Alps, marveling at the spectacular views of majestic, snow-clad mountaintops thrusting skyward through the clouds. As the jet sailed over them at forty thousand feet, he stared down at the panorama below, his mind racing with his plans.

He was, he realized, taking an enormous chance. But he prided himself that one of his greatest strengths was having the courage to risk everything for a bold move when the stakes were high. So far his shrewdness, his uncanny ability to read the public taste and to know just what to give motion picture audiences, had served him very well. To be sure, he had had his share of failures. But in the instances when his films had been disasters, there had been circumstances affecting them that had been beyond his control. At least that was what he told himself. Far more important, he had never once lost self-confidence, never for an instant stopped believing deeply in himself and in his abilities.

The producer was also a great believer in his own destiny. If something went awry, it could only be part of a temporary reversal, a slight stumble as he went about climbing to the ultimate crowning successes he was convinced awaited him. It was this conviction, he knew, that provided the wellspring from which he drew, again and again, the indomitable will to win. Experience had taught him that unexpected twists and turns of fate were inevitable. When things were going smoothly, that was exactly the time to anticipate that they would suddenly go terribly wrong. And knowing that they would, and being ready, with his coolness, his strength, and his quick wit, was what enabled him so often to come out of even the worst messes far ahead. Some people, he knew, enviously ascribed such a knack to serendipity. The producer called it the Morello touch.

This was how, he reflected, he had managed to snatch *The Hired Gun* back from the edge of fiasco. Not many producers would have had the sheer balls, let alone the resourcefulness, to do what he had done when that idiot Caserta was injured. And even with Braciola and his loathsome henchman Vito

Zicci breathing down his neck, Morello had taken the picture on to what was already turning out to be his greatest triumph.

He thought of Mario Braciola and felt his anger mount. The idea of being controlled by this man—this overbearing hoodlum who thought that the use of his money gave him the right to take over everything Morello had spent years of his life struggling to achieve—was outrageous. All right, so the producer had been in desperate need at the time. But that did not mean that hereafter he would forever belong to Braciola and his organization, no matter what Braciola might think.

A stewardess brought him espresso and a snifter of cognac. He had eaten a huge breakfast of fresh fruit, an omelette, sausages, and a croissant, and now he felt relaxed and contented. Above all, he was sure his plan would work, however foolhardly Castarelli might consider it. He smiled at the girl, and she gushed over him. Morello loved being recognized, reveled in having people identify him as the famous motion picture producer. For a moment he toyed with the idea of making a date with her for a drink later on that night, but he quickly dropped the idea. This was one evening when he would not wish to have anything to think about other than the business at hand. Too much was riding on it.

The jet began letting down as soon as it crossed the highest of the mountain ranges, and from his seat on the left side of the aircraft, Morello could see Lake Geneva, and farther to the north the sparkling waters of Neuchâtel. Then Lake Zurich was directly ahead of them, the spires of the ancient city visible at the north end of the crescent-shaped body of water. A few minutes later the jet landed.

He went through customs in only a few minutes, and an official of the Bank of Zurich met him at the gate. A Mercedes limousine was waiting, and it drove him and the banker through the old city and across a bridge spanning the Limmat River into what was called the newer section, but which was still hundreds of years old, to the Four Seasons Hotel. The banker's name was Bouchard, and he was distantly polite. His conversation was carefully confined to small talk and to the topic of fluctuating currency values on the world money market, a subject of universal interest in Swiss banking circles. The air, Morello noted, was several degrees cooler than in Rome, and noticeably drier. He began to wish he had brought along a topcoat to wear in the evening.

The producer checked in at the hotel while his escort waited in the lobby of the venerable and quaint building. The

Four Seasons was the best in the city, but Morello much preferred the more modern places that were being built, mostly by American interests, all over Europe. They were lively, active affairs whose decor and style were much more to Morello's taste. This hotel, in contrast, was a holdover from previous centuries. The wood paneling in the lobby was a deep mahogany, burnished by time to a rich patina that made the wood look almost black. The staff wore cutaway morning coats and striped trousers and dark ties on stiff white shirtfronts. The only relief in the somber atmosphere was provided by huge vases of spring flowers, but this merely deepened Morello's impression that the hotel seemed more suitable as a place to hold a funeral than anything else. His suite was a little more cheerful than the lobby, at least, and it too was brightened by flowers. He unpacked, washed his face, and returned to his escort and the Mercedes.

The private meeting room in the bank was even more grave than the lobby of the hotel had been. Oil portraits of long-departed officials stared down from gilt frames on the walls, each of the subjects stolid, bearded men, their expressions cold and forbidding. The table had been set for a luncheon, and Morello's hosts offered him sherry. The producer did not much care for the wine as an aperitif, but to be polite he accepted a glass.

The men he had come here to see were René Uster, a senior officer of the bank, and Eric Weisshorn, a financier who controlled a motion picture distribution network which extended throughout Europe. Bouchard was little more important than a clerk.

Uster and Weisshorn were youngish, in their forties, Morello guessed. Both were conservatively dressed in the stiff, heavy suits typical of those worn by Swiss businessmen, and the manner of each man was direct and brisk. Morello always felt, when he was in the company of men like these two, that he had to be at his most alert at all times.

Weisshorn smiled pleasantly. "Well, Vicente. I congratulate you on *The Hired Gun*. From everything I can see, the picture is sure to be a fantastic hit."

This was disarming. Usually Morello was prepared to sell hard when he was dealing with the foreign rights to one of his pictures, but here Weisshorn seemed ready to concede that the property was a hot one. Did that mean the producer should agree, or would it be wiser to remain carefully neutral until he heard what the distributor would offer? He decided to project an air of total confidence. "This film is going to set records everywhere. There is absolutely no question in my mind that it will be the greatest attraction I have ever produced." There, by God. Let them know he expected plenty.

Uster raised his glass. "To success, gentlemen."

They drank, and Weisshorn remarked that he had studied the grosses the film had reported during the first couple of weeks of its run and had found them outstanding.

Morello nodded.

"You saw the print I sent you?"

Weisshorn's expression was one of pure admiration. "I screened it twice, and I want to tell you, I think the picture is absolutely remarkable. There is a frankness in it, a kind of raw authenticity which I found not only totally believable but compelling. I think I enjoyed it more the second time through than I did the first."

They finished their drinks, and maids brought in luncheon, vichyssoise followed by roast lamb. Normally Morello would not have eaten nearly so heavy a meal at midday, especially after what he had consumed on the plane, but the spirit of the conversation was so convivial and he was so flattered by the obviously genuine regard in which these men held his film that he relaxed and ate heartily. The wine, he noted, was a 1949 Lafite-Rothschild, a splendid year, and perhaps as great a claret as had ever been bottled. The more he ate and drank, the more expansive he felt.

Weisshorn wanted to know all about the talent in the film. He had never seen Hendricks before, of course, and was fascinated by the American. He also had good things to say about Cecily and about Tina Rinaldi, and he remarked that he thought Livorno's direction was extraordinary.

By the time they finished the meal and the maids had cleared away the dishes, Morello was confident that they would reach a highly favorable agreement. They spent the next several hours discussing grosses which could be expected in the seventeen countries in which Weisshorn's distribution chain would release the picture, and when they concluded the meeting, it was agreed that the distributor would make an initial deposit in Morello's account in the Bank of Zurich of three million Swiss francs against anticipated volume.

"The agreement will be forwarded to you by courier in the next few days," Weisshorn said. "I think this will be an excellent venture." He smiled broadly.

Morello was ecstatic. It was all he could do to maintain an air of cool confidence, as if to confirm that this was what he had expected all along. The fact was, he would have been delighted to settle for a million less. They sat around for a time over brandy and cigars and agreed to meet for dinner later in the evening.

The following morning Morello rose early and enjoyed a leisurely breakfast. Bouchard and the Mercedes picked him up at ten o'clock and drove him back to the airport. He left Zurich feeling he had accomplished everything he had hoped for, and by the time his flight touched down in Rome, he was more sure than ever that his plan was not only daring and brilliant but that it would go off without a hitch. He took a taxi from Fiumicino to his apartment, intending to drop off his bag and make a quick change before going to his office.

When Morello got out of the taxi, the doorman saluted and carried the producer's bag to the elevator. Morello's apartment was the only one on the fourth floor of the building. He let himself in, noticing as he did that the place seemed unusually quiet. He stood in the foyer for a moment, curious at the silence. There was no response when he called out, and he stepped into the living room still carrying his bag.

The apartment was empty. He walked through the rooms but found no one. Cecily was not there, and neither was the butler, nor the cook, nor either of the two maids. Puzzled, Morello put down his bag and went into the library. He sat down at his desk and picked up the telephone. Forcing himself to be calm, he dialed his office. His secretary answered, and in reply to his questions told him that she had heard nothing from Cecily nor had there been any calls from his home. Acting on a hunch, he asked to have his call transferred to Castarelli, but he was informed that the accountant had not come in. He told his secretary he would call back later and hung up.

Morello was puzzled. It was unlike Cecily not to leave word where she would be, and he knew of no reason for all the servants to be out of the apartment at the same time. One or two might be on a day off or out on an errand, but never all four.

And where the hell was Castarelli? He had been looking forward to telling the accountant how successful his trip had been and to putting phase two of his plan into action. He thought about calling Castarelli at home but hesitated.

The buzzer sounded in the foyer. Morello strode to the

instrument and answered the call. It was the doorman, telling him that a package addressed to him, marked urgent, had just been delivered. The doorman said he would bring it up.

chapter 54

The package was a Fabrikoid box fastened with straps, of the type commonly used to transport a can of film. Morello undid the straps and opened the box, noticing that although the label had his name on it, there was no indication of who had sent it, nor was there a return address. The shiny metal can contained a short piece of 35 mm film, apparently a few hundred feet at most, on a yellow plastic core. Morello wondered if the studio had sent it over, and if they had, why there was no accompanying note or explanation of some kind. He found it mildly exasperating.

But the producer had other things on his mind beside unmarked cans of film. He was about to put the reel aside when it occurred to him to look at a frame to see if he could make out what image it carried. He pulled a couple of feet of film away from the reel and held the strip of acetate up to the light. It was in color, and the picture seemed to be a close shot of a man. Curious now, Morello went back into his apartment and entered the small screening room off the library. He threaded the film into the projector and sat down, flipping off the lights in the room as he started the machine.

The man in the picture was Castarelli. The shot was a tight close-up, harshly lighted, and the accountant was staring into the camera. His features were beaded with sweat, and there was a cut in his lower lip from which a drop of blood oozed. In the bright light the drop was a brilliant scarlet against the puffy, bluish flesh of the accountant's mouth. His eyes were wide, and a pinpoint of light danced in each pupil. Morello had never seen a more abject expression of terror on a man's face.

Near the bottom of the picture there seemed to be a rope or binding of some kind across Castarelli's chest. There was a rasping sound, and Morello realized that it was coming from

304

the sound track on the film, and that what he was hearing was Castarelli's hoarse breathing.

In the picture a shadow appeared behind the accountant, and then a wire loop dropped over his head. To Morello the length of wire was as fascinating as a snake. For several seconds it lay motionless on Castarelli's chest, the metal gleaming dully in the hot light. Then the wire began to move, so slowly that its progress was almost imperceptible.

Morello felt as if he were in a nightmare, struggling to wake up. But he was awake, and this was happening, and he was powerless to stop it. The small screening room was eerily quiet except for the hum of the projector and the sound of Castarelli's ragged breathing. Almost a minute elapsed while the thin length of metal slowly crawled up the accountant's chest and gradually closed around his neck. When the wire tightened on the flesh of his throat, Castarelli gasped, but the garrote bit relentlessly deeper.

Morello saw that the wire stretched across the accountant's neck at a point just over the Adam's apple. The strain on the metal strand increased, and suddenly Castarelli's mouth flew open. A scream, like the howl of a trapped animal, poured from within his throat. The loop drew still tighter, and the scream trailed off to a stutter and ended in a gurgling cough. His head moved from side to side in short, spasmodic jerks.

The wire was now no longer visible. There was only a reddish furrow across Castarelli's neck. His eyes bulged as if they were about to burst from their sockets. The sound of breathing stopped abruptly, and the color of his flesh slowly turned to a mottled purple. The accountant struggled once, convulsively. Then almost gently, the bloated features relaxed, and a dull film spread over the eyes. His lips curled, and from between them the tip of his tongue protruded obscenely.

The tail of the film ran through the projector's gate with a clatter and the screen went blank. Mechanically Morello reached over and turned off the machine. He snapped on the lights and got to his feet. There was a lavatory off the screening room. He went into it and vomited into the toilet.

chapter 55

The Grand Hotel was the oldest and most splendid in Rome. Originally built as a palace by the Medici family, its walls were nearly four feet thick, and although it was on the Piazza del Republica, in the heart of the city, none of the horrendous street noise could penetrate its bastions. Therefore the first thing about the place that Hendricks noticed when he entered the lobby was the quiet. He approached the desk and asked the clerk for Estelle Lemont.

"Signora Lemont?" The man was tall and slim, his ascetic features registering obvious distaste as he looked at the visitor. "Is she expecting you?"

Hendricks suddenly realized what an impression he was undoubtedly making. He was wearing the clothes he donned regularly now when he didn't want to be recognized, which was most of the time, the old knitted watch cap pulled down on his head, his body encased in a ragged denim shirt and frayed and patched blue jeans. "Yeah, she's expecting me. Name is Hendricks."

The clerk frowned. It was unlikely, his expression said, that Signora Lemont, or for that matter any guest of the Grand, would have a reason to see this bum. Nevertheless he lifted a telephone and dialed. "This is Signor Attazzi at the front desk. There is a, ah, Signor Hendricks here, who says Signora Lemont is expecting him." He waited a moment, said thank you, and put the phone down. He stared again at Hendricks. "You may go up. Signora Lemont's suite is seven forty-one."

Hendricks saluted with a forefinger. "Thanks, pal. Hell of a nice hotel you got here."

The clerk cleared his throat and gazed at the ceiling as Hendricks strode to the elevator.

A maid answered the bell and led Hendricks through the foyer to a drawing room. She was young, he noted, French and cute. "Will you sit down, please? Madame will be with you in a moment."

Hendricks remained standing. He grinned at the girl, and

306

she blushed, curtsied, and left the room. The watch cap, he realized, was still jammed in place. He pulled it off and tossed it onto a chair. The room was as elaborate as any he had ever been in. The furniture seemed to be all antique, beige and lemon-colored woods trimmed in gold leaf and upholstered in heavy satins and brocades. The chests and tables all had marble tops, and the walls were decorated in hand-painted murals. The scenes appeared to be of Rome perhaps a hundred years earlier. A number of vases held bouquets of gladioli in vivid colors. And just as the lobby had been, the drawing room was virtually silent, with no hint of the raucous traffic that swirled in the street below.

Hendricks dropped into an armchair and cocked a sneaker-shod foot on a nearby coffee table. Estelle was, he supposed, waiting to make a suitably dramatic entrance. He thought back to the last time he had seen her, in his cabin on the *Chanteuse*. Jesus, that was a million years ago.

Double doors at the far end of the room opened and Estelle Lemont swept in. She was wearing a gown of some thin material in a soft orange hue. Her smile was radiant, and the gown set off her dark coloring handsomely. "Hendricks, darling. How marvelous to see you."

"Hi." He got to his feet slowly and she clung to him, kissing his mouth and his neck and holding her body tight against his. Despite his studied casualness, Hendricks felt himself respond.

Estelle broke away and looked him over from head to toe, as if she were trying to swallow him with her eyes. "I can't believe it. I can't believe it's really you. And you look so, so, you know, *basic*."

"Basic? What the fuck is basic?"

"Darling, you know what I mean. So unaffected. So natural. People everywhere are wearing jeans now. They're really very in."

"Uh-huh."

"Please sit down. Let me get you a drink." She pressed him down onto a sofa. "What would you like?"

"Oh, maybe a beer, if you've got it."

"Of course." She swung open the doors of a commode whose interior contained a liquor cabinet and a small refrigerator. "Is Dortmunder all right?"

"Yeah, sure."

She opened a dark brown bottle, poured a glassful of amber liquid, and handed it to him. "There you are, love."

"Thanks." He watched as she poured herself a vermouth over ice.

"Cheers, darling. Wonderful to see you."

Hendricks swallowed half the contents of the glass and belched.

Estelle sat down close beside him on the sofa. He was aware of her perfume, and that she was lightly brushing his arm with her breasts as she talked.

"As I told you on the telephone, I just can't get over all the fantastic things that have happened."

"Yeah. Sorry about your husband."

"Poor Claude. It was terribly sad. He had so much to live for, it really makes you stop and think."

"It was a heart attack, you said?"

"Yes. He, um, strained himself. Overdid it, and was gone like that."

Hendricks thought of Lemont as he had looked on board the *Chanteuse*, strolling imperiously about the big yacht's decks. He couldn't imagine the fat prick overdoing anything.

Estelle's expression clouded, and then she seemed to shake herself out of it, and her mouth curved again in a broad smile. "But life is for the living, darling. That's what we have to think about, what we have to remember."

"Sure." He drank more of his beer."

"So tell me. How is Vicente?"

"Morello? Okay, I guess. Hustling, as usual."

"I think the picture is marvelous. The first thing I did when I got to Rome was to go to see it."

"You liked it?"

"I loved it. Rough and crude, but above everything else, it was *real*."

"Critics ripped the shit out of it."

"Bah. Critics. What do they know? They panned everything I ever did, except for one arty little horror that didn't even earn back its negative cost."

"Uh-huh. That's right, I'd forgotten you were in this business at one time, weren't you?"

"For several of the happiest years I ever spent." She laughed. "It was hectic and crazy, and I loved it, even when I was starving."

"So why'd you get out?"

"Because I had a chance to marry Claude, and I took it. I thought that what I really wanted was enough money so at I'd never have to think about it again."

"And now that's what you've got."

Her eyes narrowed. "More or less. It's what we all want, isn't it?"

"I don't know. It's not what I want. At least, I don't want it the way you got it."

"That's cruel."

"Maybe. I mean, I want money, sure. I want as much as I can get. But I don't want to make the kind of trade you did. When you talk about being happy, you talk about when you were struggling. But you weren't happy all those years you were married to Lemont." He studied her face. "You hated the son of a bitch, didn't you?"

She looked away.

"So when I make it, if I ever do, I want to do it on my own."

"If you do? Darling, I would say you were well on your way."

"That's what you think. When Morello picked me up, I was on the beach with nothing. He gave me a chance, and I signed a contract. It pays shit."

She laughed. "How typical. Vicente always did believe in slavery."

"Maybe he does, but I sure as hell don't."

"You mustn't worry about it. Contracts can be broken. And besides, we shouldn't waste all our precious time talking business." Her voice became throaty. "You can't imagine how I've missed you, how much I've thought about you."

"Yeah? That's nice. I thought about you, too."

"Liar."

He grinned. "Sure I did. I thought about what a great piece of ass you were."

Her mouth opened slightly, and he knew she wasn't used to being talked to this way, wasn't used to having a man treat her as if she were of no importance. Her fingers brushed over his fly.

"That gives me a hard-on."

Her hand closed on him and moved rhythmically. "That's what I wanted it to do. I remember how good it was, on the yacht last summer."

"Uh-huh. When I was your seagoing bellboy. You wanted to get laid, you just pushed a button, and there I was."

"Don't be nasty."

He shrugged. "It's the truth, isn't it? The way I saw it, screwing you was part of the job. Maybe a pretty good

309

part, but I was still just another one of your servants."

"You were much more to me than that, Hendricks. Believe me you were." She zipped down his fly and freed his penis. He was fully erect now, and she held the engorged shaft in her hand, staring at it. "God, what a fantastic thing." She bent down and encircled the glans with her lips.

Hendricks first gripped a thick mass of hair at the back of her neck. "That's another one of your talents. You're a first-class cocksucker."

She looked up at him. Her voice was small and almost pleading. "Please let's go into the other room. I want you to. Now. Right away."

He got to his feet and followed her into the bedroom.

Estelle closed the door behind them and slipped out of her gown, which fell away in a soft, shimmering orange cloud. Her body, he noted, was as trim and taut as he remembered it, the breasts full but erect, tipped with broad, dusky nipples tapering to points.

He began to unbutton his shirt, but she grasped his hands. "No. Let me."

Hendricks stood still, watching quietly as she moved about him, first gently pulling off his shirt, then unfastening his belt and sliding his blue jeans down over his slim hips. She undid his shoelaces, and he kicked off the sneakers and stepped out of the jeans. Estelle's hands fluttered over his body, touching him, stroking and exploring. She knelt before him, finally, and took him as far into her mouth as she could. She held him, her tongue working, and then her head slowly bobbed, and he felt her sucking him, her movement urging him to come.

But he didn't. Hendricks pushed her away roughly, and she got to her feet. She was wide-eyed, and he noted with satisfaction that she was unsure of herself.

"Please. I want you to make love to me." She looked away from him and lay down on the bed, her legs apart. He saw that she was wet and glistening.

Hendricks approached the bed. "Turn over."

"What?"

He grasped one of her legs and rolled her onto her belly. "I said turn over." He slid an arm under her and pulled her up into a crouching position.

Estelle made a small whimpering sound as Hendricks grabbed her buttocks and forced her legs apart. He plunged into her and the whimper became a sharp cry. "Now, you bitch." The

310

muscles of his buttocks contracted as he took her, ramming in and out of her until she threw her head back and he felt her tremble as the orgasm swept over her. Then Hendricks was coming too, and he held her in a tight grip until he was totally spent.

Estelle's body grew limp in his hands, her breath coming in shallow gasps. Hendricks pushed her down onto the bed. "From now on, anything that happens between us is on my terms."

chapter 56

Vicente Morello walked into the studio and headed for his office, his face ashen under his tan, his stomach a cold, contracted lump in his gut. His secretary intercepted him. "Signor Morello, before you go in, Signor Zicci is inside. I tried to stop him, but he pushed past me. I explained—"

Morello nodded wearily. He had not slept in thirty-six hours, and his eyes were sandy and red-rimmed. He raised his hand to silence her. "It's all right." He stepped inside and closed the door behind him.

Vito Zicci was sitting at the producer's desk, lounging in Morello's deep leather swivel chair. A small, cold smile raised one corner of his slitlike mouth. He nodded toward one of the visitor's chairs drawn up before the desk. "Sit down, Vicente. I've been waiting for you."

Morello sank into the chair.

"Cigarette?" Zicci extended a pack.

"No."

Zicci shook out a cigarette and took his time igniting it with a gold lighter. He exhaled a cloud of blue smoke and regarded the producer. "We're making a few changes in this operation."

"Yes?" Exhaustion was an enormous weight, pressing down on Morello's shoulders.

"Yes. From now on I'll be taking what we'll call a more active role in the day-to-day running of the business here."

"As you wish."

"Uh-huh. Braciola and I feel it will be more efficient this way. We won't lose time communicating to you what we want done. Under the new arrangement, I'll be right here. You understand?"

Morello nodded. He wondered vaguely at Zicci's less respectful reference to Mario Braciola, and at the slim young man's implication that the change he was announcing had come from himself and Braciola jointly, but he made no comment.

Zicci drew on his cigarette. "The first thing that needs to get done is to put another western picture into production."

"We don't have a story."

"So get one. Go to whoever wrote this last piece of shit and tell him to turn out another one."

"It's not as easy as all that."

"It's not, eh? Well, I say it is."

"We need a concept. A production is not only a story line."

Zicci grimaced. "I know that, for Christ's sake. And I have one. It is a sequel to *The Hired Gun.*"

"Braciola is pushing that again?"

"I'm pushing it. I want the same cast, the same people, but above all, the same kind of action. Let the killer go on to another village. He can screw and kill as well in one as in another."

Morello sighed. "I don't even know if I could get those people together again."

Zicci punched out his cigarette in an ashtray. "I think you will. As a matter of fact there are a lot of things you'll be doing from now on that will surprise you."

"Oh?"

"That's right, a lot of things. So now you get a writer and pull together that cast. You'll be pleased to know I've even started the work for you."

"How's that?"

"The casting. I've lined up one of your stars for you. He wasn't in *The Hired Gun,* but he should have been." He picked up the telephone and spoke into it. When he returned the instrument to its cradle, he looked at Morello and the cold smile again twisted his mouth. "An old friend of yours. I'm sure you'll be delighted to see him."

The door opened and Carlos Caserta walked into the room. Morello stared at the tall dark actor. Caserta was thin and his eyes were sunken, but he looked nothing like the scarecrow whose photograph had appeared in the article in *Il Mondo*. Morello stood up and extended his hand. "Carlos."

Caserta's grip was firm. "Hello, Vicente. Surprised to see me, eh? You thought that after the fall I was finished, didn't you?"

"Not at all. I was confident that you would recover and resume your career. It's good you are back."

Caserta sank into a chair, and Morello resumed his seat.

"Carlos is delighted he will soon be working again," Zicci said.

Morello nodded. "Good. I'm sure he is."

Caserta looked at the producer. "What did you do with that thieving bastard of an agent of mine—buy him off?"

"I haven't had any contact with him since you were hurt," Morello said. "As you know, the studio paid all of your medical expenses."

Caserta sneered. "How generous. But I may still sue the shit out of you."

"There was a hazards clause in your contract," Morello said. "You'd have no grounds to sue."

"Which explains why I haven't heard from my goddamned agent. He agreed to that crap."

Zicci gestured impatiently. "Accidents happen. Now let's get on with this new project. Our producer is developing a sequel to *The Hired Gun* that will be even better than the original, aren't you, Vicente?"

Morello felt numb and totally defeated. "Yes. That's what I'm doing."

Zicci turned to Caserta. "After all the stories, all the publicity, think of how excited the audiences will be at the prospect of seeing you and Hendricks together."

Caserta nodded. "I think about how excited I am myself at that prospect. I have dreamed about having such an opportunity for months, ever since I was injured."

"You seem to be recovering rapidly," Morello said.

The dark actor's expression was cynical. "It is a matter of conditioning, as much as anything else. I learned how to strengthen my body during my soccer days, and that experience is serving me very well now."

"Yes. How soon do you think you would be ready to work?" Morello asked.

Caserta shrugged. "Another couple of weeks, at the most. I am only a little stiff now, and even that will be gone soon.

What I need most is to put on weight. I lost more than fifty pounds, and I have recovered only half of that."

"Rome is the best city in the world to be in if you want to gain weight," Zicci said. "You stuff yourself here and you will have those pounds back in no time." He slapped the desk. "Plenty of pasta and bread and good red wine."

Caserta looked at Morello. "What will be the relationship between me and the American, in the new picture?"

"I don't know yet," the producer replied. "That is, we're only beginning to plan the project. But it will be one of conflict, as had been the original plan in *The Hired Gun*. You will be rivals of some kind, or perhaps enemies. I don't know yet."

"Good, good," Zicci said. "That is what the audiences will want to see, as well. And we should make as much of the off-screen rivalry as possible. The more the public believes they hate each other, the better. Even though it's not true, of course."

"Of course," Caserta said. "I was extremely disappointed to be out of *The Hired Gun*, I admit. But all that garbage that appeared in print was simply a lot of lies. I have no ill will toward the American. His success in the picture will only help the new one."

"You're right," Morello said. "It will help a great deal. I admire your calm, Carlos, and your strength. Your attitude is a good one. It would not help you if you were only bitter about your misfortune."

The actor scowled. "I am not bitter. I am only anxious to get back to work, to begin rebuilding my career." He got to his feet. "And now, if there is nothing more to talk about, I want to leave. Too much of this tires me."

Zicci and Morello wished Caserta well, saying they would be in touch with him as soon as they were ready to discuss the new picture in greater detail.

When he had gone, Zicci threw his head back and laughed. "Fantastic, isn't it, how things sometimes turn out? The great Carlos Caserta has an accident, and that tragedy only provides an even better opportunity than what we had before. Hendricks makes a big success, and we are in far better shape than we would have been if that stone-headed ball player had not fallen off the church. And, of course, if I had not seen what a brilliant stroke it would be to put the American into the lead."

So now Zicci was taking credit for that, too? It was not

314

surprising, but Morello was beyond caring about such things. It seemed trivial, now.

Zicci's narrow face hardened. "I think, Vicente, you have learned some lessons. Our organization is not one you may try to deceive or to play cheap little tricks with. We are very serious about our plans for you and this studio, and you will do well to cooperate to the maximum hereafter. What Braciola told you we expect is exactly what you will deliver, and I am here to see that you do." He sat back in the deep leather swivel chair and lit another cigarette. "Incidentally, we are putting some of our people into key positions here." His eyes fastened on Morello's face. "The head of the accounting department, for example, will be one of our men. I believe the position is open."

Morello stared in fascination at the cold, narrow face, as if he were watching a cobra.

"And then there is the matter of your girl friend."

"Cecily? What have you done with her?"

"Don't talk like an asshole, Vicente. We have done nothing with her, except to have a little chat. We suggested it might be well for her to take a vacation for a few days. You know, get away and think about her career and her life. You'll be hearing from her soon, I'm sure of it. The important thing is that you understand your position here exactly, you see, and that you understand your relationship to the organization. It's not a thing for you to take lightly, Vicente. Do you follow me?"

The producer took a deep breath. His exhaustion was weighing ever more heavily on him now, and he had developed a piercing headache that threatened to crack his skull. "Yes, I follow you."

"I think Braciola explained to you a long time ago that when you enter into partnership with us, it is a bond that lasts forever. He did explain that, didn't he?"

Morello's voice was dull, toneless. "Yes, he explained that."

Zicci stood up. "All right, Vicente. I'll let you go now. I know you have work to do. Be sure you get together with me tomorrow, and we can discuss your progress on the new venture. Have a good day."

Morello got to his feet, and the pounding in his head increased its intensity. He was being dismissed from his own office. He opened the door and walked out into the hallway, closing the door behind him softly.

chapter 57

Il Ristorante La Stanzo exemplified the new Rome. It was the fashionable, hip place to be seen, the most modern dining facility in the city. The walls of its rooms were clad in mirrors and stainless-steel panels, and the atmosphere reminded Hendricks vaguely of the interior of a spaceship. But he appreciated the fact that gentlemen were not required to wear coats and ties, so that he could be comfortable in an open-necked sport shirt. Estelle clung to him as they walked in, looking chic in a silk blouse and tight pants. They made a striking couple, and the maître d' showed them to the best table he had.

A captain hovered over them. "May I get you something from the bar?"

Hendricks ordered a bottle of Verdicchio, and the men hurried off.

Estelle glanced about. Other diners were noticing them, and that was another thing she loved. "Is it time for me to make my proposition?"

Hendricks frowned. "Your what?"

"My proposition. I have a wonderful suggestion to make, and it concerns a way for both of us to be very happy."

"What is it?"

"Well, I have that huge suite in the Grand, with nobody to share it with but my maid. So I was thinking that—"

"Forget it."

Her face fell. "Forget it? But I was only going to say that it could be nice for us to be together."

"Yeah. And I told you I'm not one of your servants. You don't mean anything more to me than a better than average screw. Somewhat better, that is."

She swallowed. "Hendricks, you really don't have to be quite so cruel to me."

"I'm not. I'm just being straight. I don't want your money, or any other fucking thing. When I want your company, I'll ask for it, and not because I'm living with you. And I want it only so long as you don't turn into a pain in the ass."

"But, darling, I understand that. Honestly I do. I'm not trying to buy you. I'm only saying that it could be fun for us to be together. No strings, just to enjoy each other. And I promise not to be a pain in the ass."

A waiter arrived with an ice bucket and their wine. He opened the bottle ceremoniously, and Hendricks tasted it and nodded. The waiter poured for them.

Estelle touched her glass to Hendricks's and they drank. "Don't you see?"

He rolled the Verdicchio around on his tongue. It was cold from the ice, and its big, fruity flavor was round and delicious. "No, I don't. The last broad I shacked up with started to think she owned me."

She moved closer to him. "I give you my solemn word I won't do anything like that. You'd be free to come and go as you please, believe me. And besides, I think I can help you."

"Help me what?"

"Well, I think I could advise you, you know, on what you want to do. After all, I was in that business for a long time. I really think I could be helpful."

"I doubt it."

"If only to bounce ideas off? Think about it."

Hendricks studied her face. He was, he knew, taking a certain perverse pleasure in turning the tables on her, in treating her as if she were dirt. Maybe all the shit they'd been writing about him was true after all. But at the same time, to his surprise, he was discovering that he actually found Estelle likable, in her own way. It was hard to figure.

"And then too," she went on, "you say you don't like being in that situation with Morello and his backers."

"So?"

"So, if you really want to produce a picture, why not let me finance it? I have plenty of money, and as I said, I know quite a lot about the business."

"Jesus, you're full of all kinds of great ideas, aren't you?"

"Well, I think it's a real possibility, a way for you to get what you want."

"And I told you, I don't want your money."

"I heard you, and I understand. This would be strictly a business proposition."

He was silent for a moment. "All right, look. You're really a lot more okay than I gave you credit for. Or at least, more than what I thought you were when I was your pet stud on

317

your old man's yacht. That's a generous offer, and I appreciate it. But I'm telling you that right now Morello and his friends have got me by the balls. I can't just walk out. If I want to play, I've got to play with them. On the other hand, I know I've turned into their hot property. They're scrambling like hell to jam me into another picture while *The Hired Gun* is doing so well."

"Of course they are. They know what's making the picture go. It's all you."

"Yeah, I'm a big part of it. But you know, Morello did have a hell of a concept when it came down to it. He figured that what the fans really want is the same thing they wanted when the Colosseum was going full blast. So he gave it to them, and it worked. Sure, I fitted in just fine. But the basic idea was every bit as important, probably more so. The thing is, I think it could be done even better."

"How?"

"Well, I know that if you feed an audience big doses of sex and violence, you're giving them what they're eager for, what they'll respond to. That's what *The Hired Gun* does. They identify because they're seeing their fantasies played out in the picture. But what I think could be even more effective would be to take those fantasies one step further. Instead of just showing them somebody getting beat up or killed, let the somebodies be people they hate. Do that, and they'll really get their rocks off."

Estelle drank some of her wine. "All right, but that's not a new idea, is it? You show the villain getting his in the end, and they all applaud."

"Sure. But what I'm saying is, let that idea be the theme of the entire picture. Do you see?"

"I'm not sure that I do."

"So look. What Morello and the rest of them want me to do is just *The Hired Gun* all over again. That's out—I won't do it. On the other hand, I think that if I played a modern character who had the same style and the same characteristics as the killer, then I say that could be effective as hell."

"Ah, I think I understand."

He poured more wine for them. "Hey, we should order something to eat. You are hungry, aren't you?"

"Starved."

"Okay." He snapped his fingers, and a waiter scurried to their table and handed them menus. They studied the oversized cards for a few minutes and agreed on l'orata and a salad.

Hendricks gave the waiter their orders and returned to his idea for a film.

"For instance, let's say the central figure is a cop. But not an ordinary copy. He's a guy who doesn't just try to arrest a thief or a murderer. Instead he kills them. He's like a one-man vigilante outfit. Then those scum, like a kidnapper, or a murderer, or what the hell ever, they get exactly what the audience feels is coming to them. No trial, no judge, no jury, no jail. Just zap. A bullet in the head, or maybe the cop beats their brains out. You know what the crowd would do? They'd go crazy, that's what."

"They might, at that."

"You bet your ass they would. And the sex. A lot of it ought to be involved with the crimes. A murderer is not only a miserable bastard the audience wants to see dead, he's also a rapist who has weird sex habits."

"What does he do?"

"Hell, I don't know. Maybe he's a compulsive pussy eater."

"He sounds wonderful. I love him."

Hendricks laughed. "Okay, you know what I mean."

"Yes, and you're probably right. Now who do you get to write the screenplay?"

"I don't know that either. But it shouldn't be too hard. What I'm describing isn't exactly the highest form of drama ever invented."

"No, but don't kid yourself. A good script could mean the difference between getting what you want and turning out the same idea so that it didn't come off at all."

He thought about it. "Yeah, I suppose that's possible."

"I know very well it is. If you want it to work, then you've got to have a solid foundation to build it on. And that means a script that lays it out the way you want it, at least on paper."

"All right, I'll buy that."

"So now, who are you going to get to write it?"

"Christ, I haven't the vaguest idea."

"Who did *The Hired Gun?*"

"Some hack Morello dug up. Or no, now that I think about it, it was two guys. But it didn't matter, that thing was so far from the original script by the time it was shot, the writers never would have recognized it. Morello fucked around with it, and so did Livorno, and even the script girl had a hand in making changes."

"Were the writers with you on location?"

"No, I never even met them."

"So then Vicente simply paid them to write it, and then after that he and whoever else was involved made whatever changes they pleased?"

"Yeah, that's more or less the way it was, I guess."

"All right, darling. Rule one. If you're serious about the creative end of this business, start with a good script. It's absolutely true that motion pictures are a director's medium, but it's just as true that a good director works with good material."

"That makes sense."

"It certainly does."

The waiter returned with their food. After he served them, he poured the last of the Verdicchio into their glasses. Hendricks ordered another bottle.

Estelle sighed.

"I warned you I get parched. And besides, this is a pretty good conversation. I actually think a couple of the things you're saying could even be called helpful."

"I told you I could give you some worthwhile advice, if you'd let me."

"All right, so what I need first is a script."

"What you need first is a writer. And a good one."

"And where do I get one? Morello is nobody to go to for anything that's remotely like quality. Quality costs money, and he is the cheapest son of a bitch alive."

Estelle thoughtfully chewed a mouthful of red snapper. "I read in a newspaper that Betty Barker is here in Rome."

"Who's Betty Barker?"

"An American playwright. She wrote a couple of Broadway plays, and then the movies grabbed her. She was up for an Academy Award last year for *Dark of Night*. Did you see it?"

Hendricks shook his head.

"Wonderful picture. About a hooker living in New York who gets involved in a murder. Barker didn't get the award, but she should have. She's somebody you ought to talk to."

He stared at her. "A woman? You are actually telling me to think about getting a female writer to turn out a script on the kind of story I described to you?"

"It was just a suggestion. But the thing is, she's no hack. If you buy the idea of starting with worthwhile material, you need a capable writer. And it doesn't seem to me that it matters whether that writer is male or female. What you're looking for is ability."

Hendricks ate rapidly, as he always did. The l'orata was

320

delicious, spicy with tomatoes and red peppers, the tender fish sweet and fresh and juicy. "Okay, I'll think about it. Meantime I've got a meeting with Morello and the others this afternoon. I think it's about time they found out where I'm coming from."

She put her hand on his arm. "Hendricks, will you think about what I said?"

"About what?"

"You know, about sharing my suite with me, for a while, at least?"

He looked at her and grinned. "Yeah. I'll think about it. It might not be such a bad idea at that. So long as you understand you have no hold on me."

She returned his smile. "In other words, provided I'm not a pain in the ass?"

"Exactly. On the plus side, it could be convenient."

Her smile widened, and she reached under the table and stroked him.

chapter 58

The conference room in the studio was a small bare cubicle. Morello was sitting there, and Vito Zicci, and Antonio when Hendricks walked in. The American nodded and sat down at the table.

Antonio spoke first. "You have been having a nice vacation? Feels good, doesn't it, to know you're in a smash hit. Like money in the bank."

Hendricks did not answer.

Zicci leaned forward. His ax-blade face was intent, his eyes cold and hard. "The thing is, we have to get going on a new production. You've been asked a couple of times to come in here for a talk, and you didn't show up. Now it's time to get down to business."

Hendricks looked at Morello. The producer seemed different, somehow. He was wearing one of his raw silk suits, and his strong face and his bald head were tanned from the sun, as usual, but something about him seemed to have changed.

Hendricks had first noticed it the night of the premiere, when Morello had been so eager to please Mario Braciola, and now the producer was even less of the aggressive man in charge he had always been. He looked listless, indifferent.

"We have a new property being worked on right now," Zicci went on. "Another western. Really a powerful idea. It's a follow-up to *The Hired Gun*. Script's being written."

Hendricks took a deep breath. "I told you, no."

Zicci stared. "What?"

"No," Hendricks said. "I won't do it."

Axface's eyes narrowed. "What is this, you won't do it? You have a contract."

Hendricks sat back in his chair. "I don't give a fuck what I've got. I'm not doing another western, and that's final."

Zicci and Antonio both appeared stunned, and for the first time, a change of expression flickered across Morello's face. He looked slightly amused, Hendricks thought.

Antonio was conciliatory. "Maybe you want a little more time off before you start work again, is that it?"

"No," Hendricks said. "That's not it. What I'm saying is, things have changed. It doesn't matter what you guys want. If we make another picture with me in it, and notice I said *if* we do, then we make it the way I want it. Otherwise you can forget it."

Zicci thrust out his jaw. "And what do you think happens to you, if you refuse to work in this picture? Do you think you can just go elsewhere? Do you think that because you are a big thing now, because everybody in Rome is talking about you, that you can just go to another studio somewhere and they will welcome you with open arms? Do you really think that is how it can be?"

Hendricks studied him. Jesus, the young Italian was one ugly bastard. "No, I don't. And who said anything about going to another studio?"

Zicci exhaled sharply. "Don't talk nonsense. What else would you do?" His slit mouth turned down in contempt. "Go back to your ships?"

"Yeah," Hendricks said. "That's exactly what I'd do. That way, I'd at least be my own man." He looked around the table. "And what the hell is so wonderful about what I've got here? So I'm in a picture, and the press writes about me like I'm some kind of a baboon, and that contract you're jabbering about pays me shit in small dribbles. What am I supposed to do, get down on my knees and thank you for all the great things you've done for me? What things, for Christ's sake? As far as you making decisions about what to do with me next is concerned, I'm telling you, you can forget it."

Zicci opened his mouth and closed it again. His eyes darted a look at Morello.

The producer cleared his throat. "Hendricks, you're talking about wanting to do something your way. What is it, exactly, that you want to do?"

The American laid his big hands on the table, palms down. "What I want is three things." He raised a finger. "One, if we do another picture, it's going to be based on a concept I have. No western, but a modern cop story that takes place here in Rome. Yeah, I agree with your ideas, Vicente, on what an audience wants to see. And so my character in this one would be even rougher than what it was in *The Hired Gun*. I'd play the cop, of course, a cop who's more or less outside the law. I'd hand out my own justice, with a gun."

Morello nodded. "Interesting idea. A possibility, certainly. What else?"

Hendricks lifted a second finger. "Two, we tear up that silly fucking contract and pay me what I'm worth." He noticed that Morello shot a glance at Zicci before answering.

The producer again nodded. "I think something could be worked out there. After all, a lot has happened since we drew up that agreement. In fairness, Hendricks, let me remind you that at the time you had done nothing but a screen test. I was the one who was taking the chance, not you."

"Okay," Hendricks said. "I'll grant you that. But the way it's turned out, I ought to be making real money, and that's what I expect to get."

"That's not unreasonable," Morello went on. "As I said, I think something can be worked out."

"Okay." Hendricks raised a third finger. "The third thing is, in this picture, I direct."

There was a tense silence in the small room. Zicci broke it. "You do what? You direct the picture?"

Hendricks's gaze was steady. "That's right. I direct it."

Axface was incredulous. "How could you do that? You have no experience. You have done one picture as a beginning actor, more of an amateur than anything else, and now you're talking about being a director?"

"Three conditions," Hendricks said. "Not one, or two, or two and a half. I know what I want this picture to be, and I know I can direct it. Working with the right cameraman, It wouldn't be any big deal."

Zicci leaned back, his dark eyes fixed on the American, and lit a cigarette.

Hendricks kept his expression impassive, but he wondered what was going through their minds. Christ, he thought, even to me it sounds wild. A few months ago I didn't know my ass from my elbow in this business, and maybe I still don't. But I know enough not to let these crapheads push me around. No matter how they cut it, the key to this whole damn project is me. So fuck 'em. It's my way, or no way.

Axface exhaled a stream of smoke. "A friend of yours was in here the other day."

Hendricks looked at him. "Yeah? Who was that?"

"Carlos Caserta," Zicci said. "We are planning to use him in this next picture."

"Caserta is back?" Hendricks had supposed the hulking actor would return to Rome sooner or later. But he hadn't thought much about it, or cared. As far as he was concerned, Caserta could have stayed in the clinic in Spain forever.

"He looked pretty good," Antonio said. "A little thin, but he's coming along very well. Really amazing."

"Quite an idea, don't you think?" Zicci asked. "Bringing the two of you back together. After all the publicity, the public would be very excited about seeing you in the same picture. It would be irresistible to them."

Hendricks thought about this. The former soccer player was a murderous pig—a brutal, self-aggrandizing monster who demonstrated a willingness to destroy anybody who got in his way. And now they were talking about having him work with Caserta again? He looked over at Morello.

The producer inclined his head. "It's really not such a bad idea, when you consider it. Zicci is right. The public would be very excited to see you together. And the publicity opportunities would be unlimited. But best of all, the natural conflict in the film, the believability of you two cast as enemies, would be terrific."

Zicci dragged on his cigarette. "How do you think Caserta would fit into this idea of yours, this concept you have for a film?"

Holy Jesus, Hendricks thought, they're buying it. They're actually going to let me do it. So long as I play my hand right, that is. "I don't know. It might work, might not. I'll have to think about it."

Zicci continued to hold him in an unblinking gaze. "Do you have any idea, Hendricks, how much it costs to produce a motion picture?"

Hendricks shrugged. "I don't know—a few million lira, I guess, depending on locations and so on. Why?"

"The point I am making," Zicci said, "is that you are asking me to commit an enormous amount of money to an idea you have, without any real property in hand. It's just an idea at this point, and nothing more. And to do it, we would be abandoning a formula that has a proven record of success. That hardly seems like a reasonable decision for us to make. Even if your concept were a good one, and even with the power of having you and Caserta appear together."

Now is the time, Hendricks thought, to squeeze. "Look. I've told you what the deal is. I'll work, provided you meet the conditions I've laid out. It's my picture, I get paid what I'm worth, and I direct. As far as working with Caserta goes, yeah. That's an interesting idea. I'm not saying okay to it, not yet at least, and certainly not until I'm sure we have an agreement. All I'm saying now is that it's possible that it might work."

Zicci turned to Morello. "How long would it take to get something written on this idea of his?"

The producer pursed his lips. "A treatment? Not long. I could have a story conference with a writer in the next few days, and we would have something to look at perhaps a week later."

"You can forget that, too," Hendricks said. "I told you what I have in mind, but I'm not going to sit still while one of your tame monkeys turns out some shit script. If we do it, it's my picture, and that means we start with my script."

Zicci ground out his cigarette in an ashtray. "Your script? Who writes it?"

"I have a writer in mind," Hendricks said.

Axface was insistent. "Who? You have a writer, tell me who you are talking about. You don't actually expect us to agree to this thing when we don't even know who you have in mind?"

"It's an American," Hendricks said. "An American screenwriter, and a damned good one, who happens to be available right now. So what the hell am I asking you to commit to? A lousy few thousand lira to get the concept on paper. Is that so much to a bunch of high rollers like you guys? Or do you have to run off and get Braciola's permission?"

At the mention of the name Zicci flinched. "I don't have to get anybody's permission to make a decision."

"So make it," Hendricks said. "The picture gets produced, on my terms, and I'll be responsible for coming up with a script."

A crafty look came over Zicci's narrow features. "And you agree to work with Caserta?"

Hendricks returned his stare. "Yeah. I agree to work with Caserta."

Zicci sat back in his chair and lit another cigarette. "Very well. Your conditions will be met. You have a deal."

"All right," Hendricks said. "What about my contract?"

"Your contract will be revised," Morello said. "Have your agent call me."

Hendricks nodded. "I will." As soon as I get an agent. Jesus, I must get the biggest rube in the history of pictures.

"We should be together again as soon as possible," Zicci said. "Another meeting, as soon as you can get something written. Perhaps by the end of next week?"

Hendricks stood up. "Agreed. I'll see you then." He left the room and walked out to the street. A group of ragged children watched as he unlocked the chain binding the Moto Guzzi to a tree.

For a moment, as he swung a leg over the machine, he felt exultant. Goddamn it, he thought, I've done it. But hey— done what? So far, I'm running about eighty percent on bluff. Who was that American screenwriter Estelle was talking about? I don't even remember her name.

He kicked hard, and the Moto Guzzi fired. The kids cheered, and Hendricks gunned the engine as the big motorcycle moved into the traffic.

chapter 59

The girl was small and pale, with lank blond hair and bruises on her legs that stood out darkly against her white skin. There was also a scattering of red sores on the insides of her forearms. Scozza looked at her in disgust and pushed her away.

She thrust out her chin belligerently. "You owe me ten thousand lire."

The paparazzo shrugged. Naked, the girl appeared virtually defenseless. "So I owe it to you. Now get out of here."

"No, damn you. I want what is coming to me."

Scozza sighed. He was sitting on the bed in the cluttered room he called his studio. Lights were suspended from a rack on the ceiling, and others were mounted on floor stands. An old four-by-five Graflex stood on a tripod in the center of the room. There was a bottle of cognac on the table beside the bed, three quarters empty. Scozza poured a couple of ounces from the bottle into a glass and tossed down the fiery liquid. He shuddered and scratched among the hairs on his distended belly.

"Give me my money," the girl persisted.

The paparazzo stood up. He was wearing only a pair of shorts, and the fat on his body hung from him in rolls. "I don't have it right now. And besides, you're exaggerating. It shouldn't be nearly that much."

The girl's eyes blazed. "It should be more. For the screw, and then that sick thing of yours on the floor, and the pictures. For the pictures alone I should get ten thousand."

Scozza grinned. There was an innate cruelty in the man that gave him perverse pleasure in a situation like this one. The girl was powerless, and now that his lust had been satisfied, she was of no interest to him. If anything, she was repellent. "For the pictures, you should go to jail."

"What do you mean?"

"Suppose they were to end up in the hands of the police, with your name clearly printed on them. Now get your clothes on and get out of here."

But the paparazzo underestimated her. The girl drew back her lips in a snarl and moved toward the chair on which her clothes were piled. When she reached the chair, she opened her handbag and groped in it, her eyes fixed on him. A click sounded, and a slim steel blade extended from the girl's fist.

"Shit." Scozza snatched a blanket from the bed. As the girl sprang at him, he held the blanket taut and then tangled it around her flailing knife hand. She cursed and tried to bite him, but Scozza gripped her wrist through the blanket and twisted until she cried out in pain and fell to the floor. He pulled the blanket and the knife away and bending over punched her nose, crushing it.

Scozza stood looking down at her, panting from his exertion.

He closed the knife and put it into a drawer in the bedside table. The girl lay on her side, sobbing, her hands clutching her face. Blood seeped between her fingers and ran in tiny rivulets to the floor. The sight of the crimson streaks on her white skin was exciting to him, and he felt himself stir. He thought briefly about pulling her back onto the bed but dismissed the idea. He had had enough of her. He reached down and grasping her arms hauled her to her feet.

The girl was past struggling now. She continued to press her hands to her face, blood trickling down the backs of her hands and onto her wrists. Scozza scooped up her belongings from the chair and pulled her to the door. He opened it and pushed her into the hallway, tossing her clothing after her. He slammed the door and locked it.

For a few moments he could hear her muffled crying from the hall, as he returned to the bed and poured himself another drink. But by the time he downed it and lit a cigarette, the sounds had abated. He exhaled smoke and took stock.

Scozza was nearly broke. He had sold almost all of the photographs he had taken in the villa palazzi the night of the party celebrating the premiere of *The Hired Gun*. Some had gone to *Il Mondo*, and some he had surreptitiously sold to other publications in France and Germany, as well as in Italy. Others he had sold, along with the negatives, to people who had appeared in them. But the proceeds had gone quickly, as they always did when Scozza was flush. He had spent much of the money on his usual pleasures, cocaine and rich food and whores, and the remainder he had gambled away. So now he was reduced to trafficking with creatures like the little blond.

There was one group of photographs from the night at the palazzi he retained, however. These were the shots of Vicente Morello and Mario Braciola. Scozza was positive now that there was an important link between the two men. Twice he had followed the producer to the white marble building on the Via del Babuino, and he had observed that one of Braciola's men had assumed a position of great authority in Morello's production company. The trouble was that information like this was not only dangerous to try to sell, it was dangerous even to possess. Nevertheless Scozza had spent hours trying to figure out a way to use it. The recurrent dream that haunted the paparazzo was that at some point he would stumble across an opportunity not merely to make a sizable amount of money, but a vast amount. He would uncover a way to make a golden strike, to become a truly rich man.

Scozza poured himself the last of the cognac and permitted himself to enjoy this dream as he drank.

He dozed for a time, and when he awoke, he was cold and hungry. What he needed now was a worthwhile subject to shoot. There had to be a good opportunity somewhere. He hated to go into the streets and hang around the doorways of clubs and restaurants mindlessly, the way so many paparazzi did, lurking like jackals in the hope of spotting a prey. Scozza considered himself far above these rabble, a much more skilled and sophisticated practitioner of his art. His mind shuffled various possibilities, and when he thought of Hendricks, a question which had teased him recently returned to his thoughts.

Several times over the past few weeks he had seen the American actor in the company of a remarkably beautiful woman. The trouble was, Hendricks had become highly adept in avoiding paparazzi, even one as clever as Scozza, and the photographer had not be able to get close enough for a good shot. Now Scozza again began to think about the woman. Who was she? Because it was part of his trade, he took pride in his ability to identify celebrities of all kinds, and especially those from the world of show business. Pictures of these people usually brought the highest prices, and Scozza had the nose of a ferret when it came to sniffing them out. The woman he had seen with Hendricks looked familiar, somehow, but he could not place her.

Scozza had a suspicious way of looking at nearly everything. Suppose, for example, that this woman was someone who would not wish to be identified. Suppose she were someone's wife, who would not welcome having her relationship with Hendricks become public. There had to be something valuable there, beside the obvious attraction of photographs of the new American star. Scozza had seen them go into the Hotel Grand together. Was the woman a guest of the hotel? That would mean she was not from Rome, unless they were simply using the Grand for a liason, which was unlikely. It was too prominent, and besides, they had marched in as if they didn't care who saw them. That tended to contradict his theory that she was married and simply having an affair with Hendricks, but you never knew.

He looked at his watch. A little past four. On a hunch he got dressed, slipped a 16 mm Minolta into his jacket pocket, and went to Giovanni's, a sidewalk café across from the Grand. He ordered a vermouth and settled down to wait.

An hour went by, and Scozza sipped his drink and relaxed and watched the strollers on the sidewalk along the Corso Vittorio Emanuele. In the late afternoon the heat of the day eased, and the air became soft and mild and very pleasant. People sat at the tiny tables in the outdoor café and drank coffee and Cinzano and ate spumoni from little paper cups. Scozza admired the girls, fantasizing over some of them, all the while keeping one eye on the massive front of the old hotel across the street.

He was about to order another drink when a taxi pulled up in front of the hotel and Hendricks got out, the mysterious dark-haired woman with him. Hendricks was easy to identify, with his height and his blond hair, and as soon as he saw the American actor, Scozza got up from his chair and, dodging between the cars, quickly crossed the street and scurried up the broad front steps leading to the lobby of the Guard.

Scozza caught up to Hendricks and the woman just as they were entering the doors. He stayed close as the couple walked through the lobby, making no effort to withdraw the Minolta from his jacket pocket. It was there, if an opportunity should present itself, but what he had in mind now was something quite different. The front desk was busy with guests of the hotel requesting keys, information, and mail, and the paparazzo pretended to be one of them, ostensibly paying no attention to Hendricks and the woman.

As Scozza watched, a clerk looked up and smiled broadly. "Ah, Signora Lemont, good afternoon." The clerk collected a key, telephone-message slips, and some envelopes from one of the boxes, and handed them to the woman. She and Hendricks headed for the elevators, and Scozza turned in the opposite direction and walked into the bar. He walked through it and into the passageway leading to the men's room. There was a pay telephone on the wall. Scozza dropped a coin into it and dialed the number of a friend who was an assistant entertainment editor of a newspaper.

For several minutes Scozza talked to the editor about various people he might be able to supply photographs of. Some of them were nobodies, and some of them, like De Sica and Loren and Lollabrigida, were choice subjects. But all of it was nonsense, a smoke screen. When he had gone on for a time, he asked casually whether a woman named Lemont meant anything.

There was a pause, as the editor thought about it. "Yes. Sure. Estelle Lemont. Former actress living in Paris. Her husband died not long ago and left her a hell of a lot of money."

Scozza's pulse quickened. "A lot of money? Really a great deal?"

"More than you or I could ever count, my friend. Her husband was a playboy who inherited the Lemont Chemical fortune. Why—what about her?"

"Nothing. We must be talking about two different people. The one I mean is an old lady who lives in Bardonecchia."

"No, never heard of her. Listen, Scozza. It has been some time since we have seen anything from you. I know you shot all that stuff on the new Morello picture that appeared in *Il Mondo.*"

"So?"

"So why aren't you coming to us with material like that?"

"Because your rates are so niggardly, of course. Give me what I am worth, and I will see to it that you get first crack at my best work."

"Can I count on that?"

Scozza was indignant. "You know you can trust me."

The editor sounded mollified. "Okay, if you run across anything good, come and see me, will you?"

"Of course. But be prepared to pay me." Scozza hung up and walked back into the bar. He eased his bulk onto a leather barstool and ordered cognac, the liquor he liked to drink while thinking. The bartender set a snifter in front of him and Scozza sipped its contents.

He swallowed the brandy very slowly, feeling it burn its way across the back of his tongue and down into his throat. The editor's words kept returning to his mind, and Scozza rolled them over in his brain even more lovingly than he had the cognac in his mouth. *More money that you or I could ever count.*

He recalled a picture of Estelle Lemont to his mind's eye. Of course. A former French actress. No wonder she looked familiar. He must have seen one of her films at some point or other. She was remarkably beautiful, which would give Hendricks two reasons to be fascinated by her.

More money than you or I could ever count. Scozza sipped his cognac and wondered if, at long last, he had come upon his golden strike.

chapter 60

Hendricks read through Betty Barker's treatment slowly and carefully. He was in a small office in the Giandelli Studios, his feet propped up on a battered desk. There was only one tiny window high up on the wall, and the room was stifling. He was wearing his usual uniform of jeans, denim work shirt, and ragged sneakers, and the clothes were sodden with his sweat. Nevertheless he was drinking coffee from a heavy white mug on the theory that the strong hot liquid would help him to be, at his most alert.

The treatment was very good. Several times he felt the hair rise at the back of his neck as he read, and he was pleased to note that the concept of the film seemed to have a compactness, a way of neatly fitting together, that gave him a feeling of confidence. The damn thing would work. It would actually work. Until this moment, he knew, he had been going on bravado and bluff as much as anything, but what the screenwriter had done with the premise was put it into a form that would make the story manageable and well paced. She had followed most of Hendricks's original ideas but had changed some others and added many of her own. The result was a taut, cohesive piece of writing that he was convinced would enable him to bring the idea of the picture to life on film. He liked her title, too: *The Dead of the Night.*

He tossed the sheaf of papers onto the desk, stood up, and stretched. The door of the office opened and there stood Matthew Weaver. Hendricks let out whoop, and the two men wrapped their arms around each other in crushing bear hugs.

When they pulled apart, Hendricks looked at the cameraman and laughed. "For somebody coming off a three-day drunk, you don't look half bad."

Weaver grinned. "What do you mean, three day? It was more like three weeks."

The fact was, Hendricks decided, Weaver was a little thinner, and there were signs of fatigue under his eyes, but except for those telltale indications the man seemed fit enough. His beard was neatly trimmed, and his jeans and checkered shirt were clean and crisp. Hendricks rested a hand on the cameraman's shoulder. "I had a hell of a time tracking you down."

The grin stayed on Weaver's hairy face. "Yeah, well. When we wound up the shoot, I figured London was as good a place to cool out as any. And besides, a lot of the crew were from there. We had a ball."

"I'll bet."

"Yeah. But hey, I'm glad you found me. I think what you're doing is the greatest thing I ever heard of. I read all about how *The Hired Gun* hit, just like I told you it would. And just like I told *you* would. Now for you to be making this next one, hell—that's fantastic."

Hendricks squinted. "You think I'm crazy?"

"Of course I do. You'd have to be. But I think the concept is a good one. After you told me about it on the phone, I thought about it a lot, and the way I see it, we'd have a real chance for a winner."

"You want some coffee?"

"No, but I could stand a drink."

They went to a small cantina a block away from the studio, and Hendricks filled Weaver in further on his plans for the new picture, including his hiring of Betty Barker. The cameraman knew Barker's reputation and was impressed that Hendricks had gotten her to agree to do the script.

Over a Scotch Weaver asked about Vicente Morello. "The thing I can't figure is that he'd go along with you. If there ever was an egomaniac, he's it. So no matter how much good you did him the last time around, I can't see him agreeing to let you run this show."

Hendricks shook his head. "Something's going on here that could make it clear. You remember Vito Zicci from the shoot in Spain?"

Weaver grimaced. "Axface? Christ. How could I forget?"

"Okay. Well, he's the guy who's actually in charge of the company these days. When he snaps his fingers, Morello jumps. It seems that Zicci works for an outfit headed by a guy named Mario Braciola. Ever hear of him?"

Weaver whistled softly. "And how I've heard of him. An octopus. They say he's involved in everything going in this city—loan-sharking, whores, gambling, and every kind of legitimate business he can get his hooks into. Man, that explains a lot of things, including what went on in Spain."

"And it also explains why Morello has been pushed into a back seat."

"Sure. Zicci doesn't know shit about making pictures, so they can't throw Morello out altogether. Instead they use him while they skim his business."

"If that's how it works."

"Believe me, that's how it works. So then it was Zicci who agreed to let you do this?"

"Right."

"What about Braciola?"

"I don't know. I guess he goes along, gives Zicci a free hand. I only met him once, and he had a lot of silly ideas about pictures."

"Yeah. But don't kid yourself, there's nothing dumb about that guy. And I would bet anything you'll be hearing a hell of a lot more from him as this project goes ahead."

"Probably."

"Bet on it. Now what about the rest of the cast?"

"I'm pulling them together. The principals, at least. And wait till you hear this. Caserta's back."

Weaver's jaw dropped. "And don't tell me he's going to be working with us?"

"Sure, why not?"

"Because I remember what the son of a bitch tried to do to you in Spain, even if nobody else does."

Hendricks's voice was flat. "I made a deal, Matt. To get this picture made, with me calling the shots."

"Jesus—some deal."

"All right, but think of it from the standpoint of box office. Publicity could be terrific."

The cameraman remained doubtful. "Yeah, maybe. But you know how far I'd trust him."

"Yeah. About as far as I would."

"Right." Weaver swallowed the remains of his drink. "Hey, do you know how much work there is to do?"

Hendricks smiled. "I have a rough idea."

"Well, let me tell you. It's more than even you can imagine. What kind of help can you expect from Antonio?"

"Plenty. Morello may be shell-shocked, but Antonio has already done a lot for me."

"Okay. Now listen. I guess you knew I would be, but I want to tell you. I'll be up to my ass in this with you, all the way."

"I was counting on it."

Weaver climbed off his stool and dropped a bill onto the bar. "So let's get going."

For the following several weeks both men worked an average of eighteen hours a day. The size and the scope of the project was nearly overwhelming to Hendricks, even though he had thought he had some idea of what to expect. There were script conferences, and location scouting, and the problems of who would play which part, and questions of set design, and wardrobe okays, and the planning of a shooting sequence, and a thousand other details.

At every turn, Vito Zicci was a hindrance. He haggled over everything Hendricks tried to do, arguing that it would cause budget problems, and he intruded himself into every subject area, including the ones he obviously knew nothing about. His ideas of how the story should develop were absurd, but he insisted on being included in the story conferences and was petulant when the others disagreed with him.

"If I were you," Weaver said to Hendricks after a meeting in which Zicci had been particularly troublesome, "I would go to Braciola and tell him to get that clown off your back."

"Yeah. I just might do that."

Meantime Vicente Morello merely went through the motions, while Antonio did most of the actual organization of the work. The producer was nothing like the man who had hammered *The Hired Gun* into a successful film, and if anything, he didn't appear to give a damn about what happened to the new venture.

For a long time it seemed to Hendricks that no progress was being made and that they had nothing but confusion to show for their efforts. And then one night he and Antonio and Weaver looked at each other and realized that they actually had an agreed-upon shooting schedule.

The cameraman lit a cigarette. "Goddamn. Would you believe it?"

"No," Antonio said. "I would not. It's a small miracle. God, but I'm tired."

Hendricks smiled. "Hell, we all are. Let's get out of here. I could use a drink and some sleep."

Weaver got to his feet and yawned. "I hear you, man. Let's go."

Antonio said he had a couple of more things to clean up, and the two Americans left together, Weaver accepting a ride on the back of the Moto Guzzi.

They were about five blocks from the studio, heading north,

when a gray Lancia sedan pulled up alongside the motorcycle. They were only inches separating the bike from the Lancia on one side and the row of parked cars on the other. Hendricks was about to gun the machine to pull ahead when he saw the Lancia begin to close the gap, gradually veering into the motorcycle. Instead of accelerating, Hendricks rolled the throttle shut and hit the foot and hand brakes at the same time.

"Hang on!" he shouted to Weaver as tires screeched and the big bike skidded from side to side, Hendricks fighting to keep it under control. Just ahead of them the Lancia sideswiped a parked car with a shriek of metal, bounced off, and then hit the next vehicle in line.

For an instant Hendricks thought they had made it, but then the Moto Guzzi slammed into a parked Volkswagen, and both men went flying. Hendricks felt himself go completely over the car, landing in a heap on the sidewalk. He lay there, stunned, for several minutes.

Weaver's voice was a croak. "Hey, you okay?"

Hendricks moved his arms and legs tentatively. He ached here and there, and his head was ringing, but there seemed to be no real damage. He pulled himself slowly to his feet. "Yeah, I'm all right. How about you?"

"I'll make it, I think." Weaver was crouched on one knee, examining a bloody knee through a hole in his jeans. "That son of a bitch must have been drunk."

Hendricks looked up. "He wasn't drunk. In fact, I think he knew exactly what he was doing."

chapter 61

The bedroom was starkly decorated, containing no furniture other than the huge bed and a scattering of upholstered benches. There was a bank of windows, but they were obscurred by heavy draperies, and the only light in the room came from clusters of spots in the ceiling. Some of those shone on the Impressionist paintings that hung on the walls, and some of them illuminated the large, heavily muscled man who lay naked in the center of the bed. A few feet away from him a television camera stood on its platform, its lens staring at him like the eye of some futuristic animal. Alongside the camera was a TV receiver with a wide screen, and a video-tape recorder.

A door opened, and a girl walked into the room. Her nude body was slim and graceful, with long, beautifully turned legs and high, pointed breasts. Her deep auburn hair tumbled in thick, lustrous waves about her shoulders. She looked at the man and smiled, arching her back a little so that her breasts would be more prominent, and raising herself on her toes. The man returned her smile and, without taking his eyes from her body, reached behind his head and flipped switches on a panel in the headboard of the bed. Soft strains of Debussy sounded in the room, and a red light atop the television camera went on.

The girl began to dance, moving her body in slow, gentle pirouettes around the bed, each movement bringing her closer to the man. After a time she knelt beside him and brushed the ends of her hair against various parts of his body. The auburn strands gleamed in the columns of light from the ceiling as they made contact with the man's skin. He lay quiet, motionless except for the pulsing of his penis, and she moved about him.

Finally he reached up and pulled her down to him, his hands stroking her, his mouth moving over her. The girl emitted small sounds of delight as they explored each other's bodies. They twisted and turned on the bed, and then the man gripped her in his strong hands and entered her. She cried out as they pressed against each other and parted, moving from one position to another in an unending ritual of love. The man thrust into her from above, and then from behind her. Later he lay on his back as she mounted him, their bodies intertwining in an almost infinite variety of attitudes. At last the man groaned and they trembled together and then he relaxed and they were still.

He rolled over on his back. "Was it good?"

"It was wonderful."

He laughed softly, a rumble deep in his throat. "Then let us see whether it was or not. Let us make sure." He reached back to the panel of switches. The music continued to fill the room with lilting rhythms, and now the television receiver glowed with light. As they watched, a picture loomed into view, and the machine played back the action it had recorded on video tape.

The man studied the flickering images, an amused smile on his hawklike face. From time to time his eyes narrowed, but beyond that he did not move. The girl lay beside him, stroking him, her eyes fixed on the television screen.

He laughed again. "Not bad, Cecily, at that. I believe this may be one of your better performances."

She smiled. "They say an actress is only as good as her costar, Mario. I think it is true."

"And you also think you're ready for more important roles, don't you?"

"I know I am. I don't see why I should have to be in another stupid film with the American. I'm ready to play the lead in pictures created just for me."

"You'll do that soon enough. But first you'll play what I tell you to."

The girl sighed. "I don't know that I can be patient forever."

"Who said anything about forever? After you finish this next film, I'll think about something different for you."

"All right, but you can understand my impatience, can't you?"

"Of course I can. But you'll get what you want, in time."

"I hope so."

"What has been happening with Vicente of late?"

She shrugged. "Nothing. He acts like a whipped dog. I don't know what has changed him so."

"Perhaps he is just getting old."

"No. It's something more than that. He sits in the library alone at night for hours."

"Keep an eye on what he does. If anything unusual happens, or if he talks about anything that concerns his business or his plans, I want to know about it."

"Yes, Mario. I've been very careful to keep you informed. His trip to Zurich, for example."

"That's exactly what I mean. I want to know everything he does."

"Whatever you say."

He patted her flank. "Very good."

She was quiet for a few moments. "When do you think I might have a film that's really my own?"

"I told you, Cecily. Soon enough. Or more precisely when I truly believe you are ready. In the meantime you will do as

338

I say, and be grateful that your career is in such capable hands. Is that clear?"

"Yes, it's clear." She continued to stroke him.

The taped sequence on the monitor came to an end and the screen went blank. The man's fingers sought the switches behind him. "That was fascinating. Would you like to see it again?"

The girl hesitated for a fraction of a second. "Of course, Mario, if you would."

"Yes. You often see things you missed the first time through."

chapter 62

When they were ready to begin shooting, Hendricks called the cast and crew together and told them what he expected and how he intended to work. They were on one of the big sound stages, and his voice seemed small to him as the group gathered in the cavernous space. Weaver was there, and Antonio and Zicci, as well as Cecily, Tina, and Caserta, along with the actors who would be playing lesser roles.

As he spoke, Hendricks felt his confidence grow, and he was buoyed by a sense of excitement for the project. "The first thing you're going to see is, I'll make mistakes. Okay, fine. I fully expect to. But Matt and Antonio will keep me headed in the right direction, and you will too. If you think what I'm trying to do in a given scene is wrong, or that the way I want you to deliver a line doesn't work, or whatever, I want to hear about it. I'll be fair, and I'll listen, because above everything else, I want this picture to succeed, and so do you. If that's going to happen, we've all got to help each other and be as cooperative as we possibly can be."

He looked at their faces. Most of them appeared to be taking his words well, and to be in agreement with the spirit of what he was saying. He thought he saw something like thinly disguised hostility in Caserta's dark features and what might have been a cynical smile at the corners of Cecily's mouth, but generally they seemed willing enough to go along with him. "One thing I'm going to be a stickler on is punctuality. I want you here on time every day you're working in a scene, with no excuses. And I want you to come in prepared. Know your lines and be ready to work. Remember, this film belongs to all of us. How well it turns out is going to depend very much on how well we all pull together. Now let's give it everything we've got to make a picture we'll all be proud of."

Antonio followed, giving the cast and crew shooting schedules, and as the associate producer talked, Hendricks felt a little foolish, wondering if he had come off like a coach addressing a schoolboy athletic team. He decided that if he had, it was just too damned bad. One way or another he was going to get the job done.

As shooting got under way, Hendricks tried, with Weaver's help, to maintain a brisk, no-nonsense pace. But from the first setup, they ran into nothing but trouble. There were equipment breakdowns, and at one point a three-hour power failure in the studio, and endless hangups with niggling details of lighting and wardrobe and set construction. But none of these things approached the problems Hendricks experienced with the cast. Except for Tina, who was as warmly supportive toward him as she had always been, the actors and actresses were dull, almost sullen, as they stumbled through their work.

At the end of the first couple of days Hendricks asked Weaver about it. They were sitting in a prop room drinking cans of beer, and both men were feeling the aftereffects of a long, frustrating day.

The cameraman rubbed the back of his neck. "I don't know. Some of the stuff that's happened you can almost count on. You know, this busts, or that set isn't ready, or what the hell ever. But what I don't get is the cast. Christ, they act like they're half asleep."

Hendricks swallowed some beer. "I can't figure it either. It's almost as if they didn't give a damn about how this thing turns out. I know that sounds crazy, but that's how it feels to me. And what's worse is, I don't know what to do about it."

"Okay, so the first thing is to figure out where the problem's coming from. You don't find a cast or a crew stumbling around like this by accident. Something's going on here that has these people pissed off, or at least unhappy about the way we're doing things, or something."

"Yeah. Say, Matt?"

"Uh-huh?"

"You suppose it's me?"

"Oh, hey. I don't—"

"No, I mean it. You know, it could be the way they see it, I don't know a hell of a lot about what I'm doing, and they resent the fact that they've got a new boy as a director. So they're dragging their feet. Possible, isn't it?"

"Yeah, it's possible. But hell, I don't believe it. The last time out, let's face it, you really saved everybody's ass. We were really out of it until Morello shoved you into the lead, and if you want to boil it down, that's what saved that picture and turned it into a success. So what's to resent about you? And besides, I think you're doing a damned good job."

"Thanks, Matt. I really appreciate the help you're giving me. Fact is, I couldn't be doing this without you, and I know it."

"Forget it. What we've got to concentrate on is getting some life into this outfit."

The first setup the following morning was a scene which called for Caserta to enter a room where he encountered Tina. They were to exchange a few words, Tina was to shout at him to get out, and he was to strike her, knocking her to the floor.

Hendricks had wanted to get the action shot and out of the way as quickly as possible. They had several other scenes to do that day, and remembering the foul-ups on *The Hired Gun*, he wanted to avoid falling behind in his schedule. He had planned the scene for eight o'clock, and when Caserta still wasn't out of makeup by eight thirty, Hendricks was fuming. He looked around and saw that the crew was being nonchalant about it, some of them clowning around, others exchanging gossip as they smoked and drank coffee.

Hendricks turned to Antonio. "Get Caserta the hell out here."

The assistant was apologetic. "He's still in makeup. I think he was a little late getting in this morning."

Hendricks felt a surge of anger. "Tell him he's got sixty seconds, no matter what the makeup looks like."

A few moments later Caserta shuffled onto the set, wearing an expression that was somewhere between a smile and a sneer. Hendricks forced himself to remain calm, although it irritated him to see the big actor exchange knowing looks with some of the crew members. A few snickers sounded, but Hendricks pretended not to hear them.

The action required Tina to look up in shocked surprise as

Caserta entered the room. Hendricks walked through the shot with them, and when he was satisfied, he asked for a take. There was another delay while Weaver checked his reading, and then at last they were ready to go. Antonio shouted for quiet on the set, and Weaver announced that he had camera speed. Just as Hendricks opened his mouth to call for action, Caserta went into a coughing fit. He roared and hacked and doubled over, clutching his throat, while the technicians' grins grew wider.

There were two more false starts before they got a complete take, and Hendricks knew it was lousy. Caserta did everything but yawn as he moved through the shot.

"Cut." Hendricks looked at the script girl. "We won't print that." He walked over to Caserta. "Look, Carlos. Let's make another one, but this time put some anger into it, will you?"

Caserta looked blank. "Anger? You want anger?"

Hendricks felt his ears get hot. "Yeah, that's right. I want to see some passion, some savagery. This scene is supposed to be violent, do you understand?"

"Of course." Caserta went back to his marks. "Anger. What you want is anger."

They rolled film, and this time the hulking Italian was much more emotional in his expression and his movements. But when he approached Tina, he barged into a small table and set it crashing to the floor.

"Cut." Hendricks's tone was relaxed and pleasant. "Okay, everybody. We still need to settle down for this one. Let's take a little break."

Antonio yelled for the electricians to kill the lights, and a babble of conversation arose from the members of the crew. Weaver looked over and shrugged, and Caserta headed for the coffee table. Hendricks stepped over to it also, and when he got there he moved close to Caserta. "Say, Carlos, you got a minute?"

The actor scowled. "What is it?"

"Come on over here. I want to show you something." Hendricks turned and walked to Caserta's dressing room, the Italian following. When both men were inside, Hendricks closed the door. He spun around and grabbed Caserta's shirtfront in his fists. Hendricks's voice was a low hiss. "Listen, you son of a bitch. If you don't want to work in this fucking picture, then all you have to do is say so, understand? I'll replace you, and I don't give a shit whether Zicci likes

342

it or not. But if you are going to work, then goddamnit, you're going to *work*. Do you hear me?"

Caserta bared his teeth in a snarl. "Let go of me."

But Hendricks held on. "Your choice, Caserta. What's it going to be?"

For a moment the actor tensed, but then he relaxed, and his voice reverted to its usual sullen tone. "I said let go of me. I'm here to work."

Hendricks released his grip and stepped back. "From this point on, I don't want any more crap out of you. Now let's go."

The tenor of the shooting improved after that, and Caserta seemed more cooperative, but Hendricks was nowhere near satisfied. It still took longer to get acceptable takes on film than the tyro director believed it should have, and there was still an undercurrent among many members of the cast that suggested that they were going along only grudgingly with Hendricks's instructions.

At the end of the week an incident occurred that left them all shaken. Hendricks and Weaver were inspecting a set that represented the interior of a crumbling tenement. As they looked it over, Antonio joined them, and the three men talked about how the action was to be blocked. Carpenters went on with their work as the impromptu conference continued. A brick wall about three meters high had been erected at one end of the set, and Hendricks stepped over to it to illustrate how he thought a bit of business should take place.

Weaver rested one foot on the arm of a chair. "Where do you see him making the turn?"

Hendricks pointed. "Right about there. He knows I'm behind him, he spins around, and he realizes he can't get away from me. So he pulls the gun from his back pocket, goes down on one knee, and gets off a shot. Like this." Hendricks whirled and crouched, pantomiming the action he wanted. The move probably saved his life.

Weaver saw it first. "Look out—the wall!"

The brick wall beside Hendricks toppled forward and disintegrated in a violent crash on the floor of the set. If he had been standing, it almost surely would have struck him with full force. As it was, when Weaver shouted a warning, Hendricks instinctively threw himself toward the base of the wall. Some of the falling bricks struck his head and shoulders, but the damage he sustained was slight, and nothing like what it could have been. Hendricks lay in the rubble for a moment shaking his head, choking on the clouds of cement dust, and then Antonio and Weaver were pulling him to his feet.

The carpenters crowded around them, and other technicians and crew members came running from all directions.

Weaver held Hendricks's shoulder. "Hey, man—you all right?"

The director had a cut on his forehead, but he managed a small grin. "Yeah, I'm okay, I guess." He looked around at the men who had been working on the set. "You guys are going to have to try harder than that."

It got a laugh, and then everybody was talking at once. In the first-aid room they stuck a plaster on Hendricks's forehead, and Antonio handed him a shot of whiskey. The liquor produced a raw burning in his belly, but an instant after he downed it, he felt better.

Zicci burst into the room. "What is going on? What happened? Damn it, I have told everyone I expect them to be cautious and to observe good safety practices."

Hendricks glanced at Weaver, and the cameraman tugged at his beard and rolled his eyes upward.

"I guess," Hendricks said, "not everybody was listening."

Zicci fumbled about for a few minutes, making a couple of more inane remarks, and left the room.

Weaver glanced at the door. "Pulls at your heartstrings, doesn't it, having him worry about you like that?"

"Yeah." Hendricks touched his fingers gently against a bruise on his scalp. "Although, if I had to judge how he sounded, I'd say it was disappointed."

chapter 63

In her lifetime Estelle Lemont had never experienced anything quite like Hendricks. For a time while they lived together in her suite in the Grand, she wondered if it were simply that she could not own him that bothered her. She had always had any man she wanted, and now that she was rich and independent, she felt particularly frustrated. The way

344

Estelle saw it, she had the wherewithal to buy anything she desired. But the one thing she wanted most, she could not have, at least not on the permanent basis she wished.

Then she conjectured that perhaps it was merely Hendricks's independence that was so maddening. Here she had offered to finance a film, if that was so important to him, and he had brushed off her approaches on that subject as if they were nothing. But of course, backing a picture was simply another way of buying him, or trying to, she forced herself to admit. And yet, damn it, the business of making motion pictures was one she knew quite a bit about, certainly in so far as being able to give him some good advice was concerned. And most of the time he wouldn't even listen to that.

But the fundamental reason for her frustration, she was convinced, was that Hendricks was the most attractive man she had ever met, and certainly the one who was better able to satisfy her then anyone else ever had. And what she wanted was not Hendricks for a few days or a few weeks while to him she was as much a convenience as anything else, but Hendricks as her man—even her husband. And when Estelle Lemont wanted something, she got it. To her the only question was how she would go about bringing him around, how she would be able to gain the upper hand. She thought about it for hours at a time while he was at the studio, developing plan after plan, testing each in her mind before rejecting it.

Finally she decided on a scheme that was as bold and brazen as she could devise. If making films had become such an obsession with Hendricks, then the way to control Hendricks was to control his film making.

When Estelle entered Porfirio's, Morello was already waiting for her. The maître d' led her to his table, and when he rose to greet her, she was shocked by what she saw, even though the stray remarks she had picked up from Hendricks had prepared her. Instead of the athletic, purposeful male she had known for so long, the man who took her hand now seemed limp and lacking in resolve. Even this color looked different to her. He was gray, somehow, under his tan.

"Vicente, darling, you look marvelous, as always."

"So do you, Estelle. I had no idea you were in Rome. Why didn't you let me know you were coming?"

She offered her cheek for his kiss and sat down. "It all happened in such a rush, I hardly knew I was coming myself. I certainly had no time to think about it. After Claude's death

I was terribly distraught, of course, and I simply turned in on myself and grieved for a long time."

He nodded sympathetically. "Quite understandable, to say the least. It must have been a dreadful trauma for you."

"It was ghastly. Poor Claude."

"You said on the telephone he had been ill for some time?"

"Yes. For months, in fact. After his funeral I simply woke up one day and realized I must get away from Paris. I needed a change, you see, and when I read about your great success with your western, I wanted to see you. And Vicente, I have a confession to make. I also wanted to see Hendricks."

His face went blank for a moment, and then he understood. He threw his head back and laughed, and for the first time he seemed to her to be a little like his old self. "Of course. You and he were friends, eh, in the days when he worked on your yacht? And now that you are no longer, ah, encumbered, you wanted to renew your relationship."

Estelle smiled. "For the most part, that is correct."

A waiter appeared, and Morello ordered drinks for them, vermouth over ice.

Morello studied her. "And now there is something you want, isn't there? Something you believe I can help you with."

"Exactly. You understand me very well, don't you, Vicente?"

"Of course, my love. I always have."

"And so I won't waste time fencing. I want—"

He raised a hand. "Wait. Let me guess. You want a part in this new picture."

"No. That's not it at all. What I want is to invest in it."

His surprise was genuine. "To invest in it? You want to put money into this thing? My God, what irony."

"Irony? How?"

"I was thinking about the times I desperately needed financial backing, and how often I was turned down. Even by you, on one occasion."

"That was different. These circumstances are not at all the same."

The waiter returned with their drinks, and they wished each other health and drank.

Morello shook his head. "Now I have the opposite problem. Too many people want to put money into this venture."

"Because of the success of your western?"

"That, too. But I can't even discuss it with them."

She was puzzled. "In heaven's name, why not?"

His shoulders sagged. "I'll tell you, Estelle, because we have been friends for a very long time. But I would advise you to forget what I am about to relate to you, for both our sakes."

When she agreed, Morello told her about Braciola, and about the producer's relationship to the organization. She already knew much of it from what Hendricks had told her, but the fear in Morello perplexed her. "Vicente, he can't force you, really? You are too important. I mean, those people are always around the fringes of the business. In France as well as here. But a major producer? I simply can't—"

"Estelle, believe me. There is more, a lot more that I can't tell you about. The man who was my—" He caught himself. "Take my word for it, my situation is a very precarious one."

She was silent for a moment. "I want to see him."

"Who?"

"This man. This Braciola."

He was incredulous. "You want to meet him? Good God, what for? Ah, you wish to see if you might not negotiate with him directly, eh? Estelle, that would be a very unwise thing to do."

She covered his hand with hers. "As you point out, we have been friends a long time. Do this for me. Arrange a meeting. And don't bother to worry. I can take care of myself."

There was sadness in his eyes as he raised his glass and drank. "I hope you are right."

The building on the Via del Babuino reminded Estelle of some of the newly erected ones along the Champs-Elysées. With its clean lines of cool white marble it had a look of self-assuredness, of the new directions in which money and power were going. When she was shown into Mario Braciola's suite, she was mildly surprised by its tastefulness and the quality of its furnishings. But Braciola himself, from what she had heard about him from Morello, and what she had learned through her own sources, was about what she had expected. He exuded strength and self-confidence, and yet secretly she held him in contempt as inferior to her. She was sure she could handle him without difficulty.

The expression on Braciola's hawklike features was clearly one of admiration. "You look lovely, Signora Lemont. It is an honor for me to meet you and to have you visit me. I remember you so well from your films, of course. To me, you haven't changed in the slightest."

Estelle was pleased and flattered in spite of her warnings to herself to be cautious. She smiled radiantly. "It's sweet of you to say so, but it's been many years since I made a picture. I wasn't much more than a child at the time."

He led her to a sofa. "Please sit down, won't you? May I offer you something to drink?"

"Thank you, no." Estelle sank to the seat with a practiced grace. She was wearing one of her newest Diors, a peach-colored silk that set off her dark coloring with striking effect.

Braciola sat opposite her and inclined his head respectfully. "I was terribly sorry to learn of the passing of your husband."

She composed her face. "It was a terrible shock. So totally unexpected. We were very happy, you know. Only a marriage so full of joy could have enticed me away from the motion picture business."

"I'm sure that's true. I understand very well how you must feel, and I offer my deepest and most sincere condolences."

"Thank you." She smiled again, gently this time. "May I call you Mario?"

"Of course. And may I call you Estelle?"

"Certainly. I think it's always better to do business on a first-name basis. It makes everything move along much more quickly."

His eyebrow arched. "Business?"

She crossed her silk-encased legs and was gratified to see his glance flick over them. "Yes, business. You see, now that poor Claude is gone, I have reawakened my interest in the motion picture industry. I really feel it would be a terrible waste of my talents and my energies if I were to be more or less inactive, concerning myself only with my favorite charities. I could be so much more productive and self-fulfilling if I were to become involved once more in a field I know and love so well."

"You wish to return to acting?"

She laughed. "Oh no, nothing like that. At least, not right away. Perhaps later on, but not now. For the present I'm only interested in the possibility of investment."

His eyes narrowed almost imperceptibly. "You want to invest in motion pictures?"

"That is correct. You see, the inheritance of Claude's estate has left me quite comfortable and in control of a rather wide range of holdings. But to me, things like stocks and bonds and real estate are so dry and lifeless. They lack the emotional appeal that such a venture as film making holds."

He frowned. "Then Morello told you of the relationship between him and me?"

"Only in the briefest terms. I was pressuring him to give me a position in the new film his company is working on now."

"Yes." He was quiet for a time, and behind the dark, heavy-lidded eyes, Estelle knew his brain was working at high speed. "Morello has been approached by many others, as you would expect, with similar propositions. After his remarkable success with the western, that was only to be expected."

"Of course."

"To be perfectly frank, I find it hard to see what reasons I would have to give you the opportunity you are asking for. Capital is not a problem for us; we have ample resources. Aside from the fact that you know something about the business, why should I agree to let you in on what anyone could expect would be a highly profitable venture?"

Estelle took a deep breath. "The answer I can give you will surprise you, Mario. But I sense that a man of your breadth of experience will understand."

He waited, expectantly, for her to continue.

"I would say that the success of this next film depends, more than anything else, on one factor."

"And that is?"

"That is the amazing new talent who is its star and its director: Hendricks."

His eyes were those of the consummate diplomat or the professional gambler. Their expression was impossible to read. "Very well. I would agree that what you say is true. Now what about it?"

"Just this. Hendricks and I have been close friends for a long time. In fact, we are deeply in love and are living together."

"Ah, I see."

"Yes. It is extremely important to me that I play a role in his work as well as in every other aspect of his life. And that is something that he wants very much as well. The returns to you would be more than the investment capital you say you don't need. It would also be your assurance that he would be happy and eager to do his best work."

For the first time she noticed a change in his expression. He looked, she thought, just the least bit apprehensive. It was amazing, really, that she could manipulate men so easily.

Braciola sat back in his chair. "And what is the scope of the position you hope to achieve? What is the percentage you want?"

"A major one, Mario. At least fifty-one percent."

He nodded. "This is a matter I will have to give considerable thought."

"Naturally."

"But I must warn you, the answer may be no."

"That would be unfortunate, for both of us. But if you were to ask my opinion, I would think it would pose more of a problem for you, in the long term. There are other places in the world, you know, where one can produce motion pictures. Provided, of course, one has the money."

"I understand. And I promise you, I will give all of this my most careful consideration."

"I'm sure you will."

They chatted for a few more minutes, and then Estelle left. She was confident that she had made a brilliant move, and that everything would turn out exactly as she intended.

Mario Braciola kissed his visitor's hand and wished her a good day as he escorted her to the foyer and showed her out. When he returned to his suite, he touched a button on the telephone and Vito Zicci entered the room.

"You heard?"

Axface smiled. "After what Morello told us, it was about what you would expect."

"Yes. She has an inflated estimate of her abilities. Did the report come in from Paris?"

"I have it right here." Zicci placed a manila folder on the table in front of Braciola.

The older man opened the folder and studied its contents for several minutes before he spoke. "Even better than I thought. It's like having a dove beg to join the hunting party."

The slit mouth opened, and Zicci emitted a toneless laugh.

Braciola closed the folder. "I believe it will come as quite a surprise to Signora Lemont when she eventually learns just who owns what."

"I'm sure it will."

"You know what to do. The sooner the better, and no slip-ups."

"Consider it done."

chapter 64

Hendricks looked up as Tina walked onto the set. She was wearing a simple light dress that clung to her body in a way that revealed every curve and hollow, and it was more erotic to him than a brief costume would have been. "Good afternoon."

She turned to him. "Notice that I am on time. I know my lines, and I am ready to work."

He smiled, aware that she was teasing him. "Okay, so that's what you're supposed to be. Matter of fact, you're even a couple of minutes early, and we're not quite ready for you. So how about some coffee?"

They walked over to where the huge old nickel-plated urn stood on a table, and Hendricks poured them each a cup.

Tina sipped the steaming black liquid. "For a mean, hard-driving taskmaster, this is an unexpected act of kindness."

"Hey, I'm not really that bad, am I?"

She returned his smile. "No, not really. To tell you the truth, I am amazed at how patient you are, and how you are getting this done."

"It's still driving me crazy, the way things keep going wrong."

"Part of the job, isn't it? And anyway, who ever heard of a production going smoothly all the time?"

"Who said anything about all the time? I'd settle for any of the time."

"How is your head—are you all right now?"

"Yeah, I'm okay. You can't hurt me with a few bricks."

"No aftereffects at all?"

It was interesting, the way she could go to the heart of something that bothered him. "Well, maybe a little headache, now and then. But it's nothing to worry about."

She put her hand on his arm, and in the large dark eyes he could see genuine concern. "I hope you'll be careful. You know I really care a great deal about you."

"Yes, I know you do." On the other side of the set he could

351

see Cecily Petain watching them. He felt awkward, standing here like this, feeling a sudden surge of tenderness for Tina, aware that other members of the cast and crew were probably taking in this little scene as well. And yet he had to admit that when he thought about the women who had been part of his life over the past year, there was only one who seemed to have no hidden motives, no guile in her dealings with him. Tina was all straight ahead, all out front. She didn't lie or maneuver or manipulate. She was just Tina, warm and supportive and more real than any of the others.

Antonio called that they were ready, and the moment was gone. They took a few more hurried sips of coffee and walked quickly to the setup.

The scene called for him to protect Tina from an attack by a sniper in an alleyway. Hendricks had to push her to the ground and then shield her with his body while he attempted to return the sniper's fire. They ran through the action, and as soon as Hendricks and Weaver were both satisfied, they went for a take.

When the set was quite and the camera running, Hendricks shoved Tina down and threw himself on top of her, pulling a gun from his pocket. The lights were hot, and about twenty people were watching, but Hendricks found that he was responding to her in a way that didn't require acting at all. As the scene developed, Hendricks was supposed to stay with her until it was evident that the sniper had gone and they were safe, and as he continued to lie on top of her, they were to react to each other. It was crazy, but even with everybody looking on, he could feel himself growing hard. He was aware of her breasts and her legs under his body, and of her warm breath on his face as she looked up at him.

There were a few lines of dialogue, and under the circumstances, they suddenly seemed silly. Tina began to giggle, and Hendricks called for a cut. She moved her hips just a little, so that none of the others could see it, and whispered, "Why don't we tell them to go away for a few minutes?"

Hendricks grinned. "I'm the director here. And I'll decide what's going to happen."

"Yes, sir."

They reset the action and got an acceptable take, and when they had finished, Hendricks found himself wishing he could spend some time with Tina in her dressing room. They had planned to do one more scene that day, and he was a little surprised that the contact with her had so aroused him. He

352

decided that after the work was done, he just might pay her a visit, at that. He and Weaver were looking at the camera angle that would open the next scene when Antonio approached.

The assistant pulled at Hendricks's sleeve. "Say, excuse me, but I've got to talk to you."

Hendricks brushed him off. "Not now, man. I'm busy."

Antonio seemed agitated. "Listen, this is important."

"All right, so what's on your mind?"

"They want to have a screening of some of the selected takes we've shot so far."

Hendricks stared at him. "Screening of selected takes? Who does?"

"Well, uh, frankly, this is coming from Zicci."

The American snorted. "Tell him I'm busy. Some other time." He turned back to Weaver.

Antonio leaned closer to Hendricks and lowered his voice. "Hendricks, I got the impression this is a command performance. Mario Braciola wants to see how the work is coming along."

That was different, and Hendricks knew it. "Braciola is coming down here? Now?"

"Right."

"Okay, so let's show him. Tell the editor I want a reel put together of takes from the first half-dozen scenes. They're all out of sequence, of course, but so what? At least he'll get an idea of what we've been up to."

The assistant nodded. "I've already done it. Just as soon as you finish this next scene, we're to meet in the screening room."

Antonio hurried off, and Weaver watched him go, an amused smile on the cameraman's bearded face. "So the big man wants to know how the slaves are carrying out his wishes."

Hendricks scratched his jaw. "What the hell, you can't blame him for that. He's paying the freight, and so far I haven't heard too many bitches about overages, or the fact that we're behind schedule, or anything else."

"Yeah, but neither has he seen any of the footage."

The director smiled. "What's the matter—you nervous?"

"Who me? Yeah, a little."

The attitude of the people in the screening room was one of studied casualness, but Hendricks could feel the tension when he walked in. Antonio was there, along with Weaver and several cast members, among them Tina, Cecily, and Caserta. Hendricks exchanged remarks with some of them about the work they had done that day, chatting idly about this take or that one, and he glanced up to see Vicente Morello enter the room.

God, Hendricks thought, the man looks shell-shocked. Morello had lost weight, and for the first time since Hendricks had met him back in Portofino the previous year, the producer seemed not to be suntanned. Instead his skin was an oddly sallow color, and there were deep circles under his eyes. There were also lines at the corners of his mouth, and his cheeks were gaunt. Morello sat down in one of the folding theater seats, not speaking to any of the group.

Hendricks dropped into a seat alongside the producer. "How's it going, Vicente?"

Morello shrugged. "I should ask you."

It was awkward, but Hendricks refused to be ruffled. "We're doing okay, I guess." He smiled. "Or maybe I should say we'll know when Braciola gets here."

"Yes. Then you'll know the state of the world."

The door opened, and Mario Braciola stepped into the screening room. He was rather formally dressed, in a gray sharkskin suit and a black tie, and it occurred to Hendricks that the heavyset man looked more like a banker than anything else, which in the circumstances did not seem inappropriate. There were two other men with him whom Hendricks did not know, and Vito Zicci, unctuous as usual in Braciola's presence.

Braciola sat down beside Hendricks, and the others took seats in the rear of the room.

They exchanged perfunctory greetings, Braciola cool and distant, and Antonio stood up in front of the small audience and explained in nervous tones what they were about to see. "The takes are not cut. That is, they're not trimmed to length," the assistant fumbled, "and the scenes aren't even in order. I mean, some of what you'll see actually takes place at the very end of the picture, instead of up at the beginning as you'll see them here. But it should give you an idea of the quality of the work. I, ah——"

Braciola raised his hand. "Excuse me, but I did not come here expecting to see a finished film. All I wish to do is to get a feeling for what you are doing."

"Sure," Hendricks said. "Antonio, let's roll the footage."

The lights went down, and in the first few seconds the American became so involved in what he was seeing that he forgot about Braciola's presence. The scenes were awkward, some of them, even stiff. But there was a harsh, semidoc-umentary quality about them that gave them great authentici-ty. As in *The Hired Gun*, the action seemed absolutely real, as if the camera had somehow intruded itself into life and was revealing what went on when a mugger assaulted his terrified victim, or in another sequence, when a homicidal rapist attacked and murdered a defenseless girl. To his surprise and satisfaction, Hendricks saw that his own performance in the scenes where he appeared was much smoother than he had been. He moved easily and naturally, with a poise that conveyed a sense of confidence that came off not as the personality of a cocky wise guy but as that of a self-assured cop facing a tough, dangerous job.

When the lights went up, the room was quiet for a mo-ment, and Hendricks knew they were all waiting breathlessly for Braciola's verdict. For an instant the whole situation struck him as ludicrous. Here they were, on the edge of their seats, hoping for approval from a man who didn't know his ass from a zoom lens. He turned to Braciola, and in calm tones asked, "Well, Mario—what do you think?"

The hooded eyes were momentarily expressionless, and then Braciola nodded. "I think it is excellent. It was exciting, even in this form. It seems to me that what you have here is the beginning of a very good film."

"Thank you, Mario." It was Zicci. "And I would like to pass along my own congratulations to everyone here for the hard work and the dedication that shows so clearly in what we have just seen."

Hendricks glanced back at Axface. Was the son of a bitch actually trying to take credit for this? Of course he was. Hendricks also noted a black scowl on Carlos Caserta's swarthy features.

Braciola turned to face the American. "It becomes evident that you have as much natural talent for directing a film as you do for acting in one. It is very interesting to see your hand in this. I believe your abilities will grow to be extremely valuable."

Hendricks had not expected praise, even if Braciola liked what he saw. He was surprised and flattered.

"What is the title of the film?"

"We're calling it *The Dead of the Night*, but that's just a working title. We may or may not use it."

Braciola stood up. "Thank you, everyone. It is good to

see such progress. I look forward to another visit soon."

The tension broke, and everyone began talking at once. Braciola left the room, the others following, and as Hendricks walked out, it occurred to him that Braciola had not spoken one word to Vicente Morello. It was as if the producer had ceased to exist.

Weaver caught Hendricks's eye and mugged approval. Hendricks winked.

For a long time Morello sat alone in the screening room. It seemed strange to him that, in marked contrast to what he had felt in recent weeks, he now experienced no sense of anxiety, no hint of the terror and the deep depression that had gripped him relentlessly. At this moment he was calm and relaxed. Even the crushing weight of fatigue, caused by a seemingly endless string of sleepless nights, had lifted from his shoulders.

For the first time since this nightmare had been brought home to him, he could look at his situation more or less dispassionately. He had gambled, and he had lost. And in the losing, he had been stripped of everything. He had lost his studio, he had lost his future and with it his hope, and worst of all, he had lost his dignity. He had been degraded in front of his world.

He had even, he reflected with irony, lost Cecily. Not that the little trollop had ever really meant anything to him. But she had betrayed him, he was certain, and that added to his debasement.

It was as if Braciola had made an incision in Morello's body and had drawn off all that made him a man, leaving in its place a dried husk. But none of that mattered now. It was over, and the knowledge soothed him. He thought about his life for a few moments, about some of the good times, about some of his triumphs, but he found no pleasure in them. All that was meaningless.

Morello reached into his inside jacket pocket and withdrew a Baretta automatic pistol. It was a 7.65 mm caliber, small and flat, and its blued metal and checkered grip felt faintly oily in his hand. The pistol was warm from the heat of his body. He drew back the breech and released it, thereby inserting a cartridge into the chamber and cocking the hammer. It was odd, but he felt no emotion at all.

He placed the barrel of the gun in his mouth, its muzzle pressing against his palate. His finger exerted pressure on the trigger, and in the millisecond before the pistol fired, he heard a distant scream, and he realized with surprise that the sound was coming from his own throat. There was a brilliant flash of light, and a thunderous explosion, and bits of Vicente Morello's brain erupted through the top of his skull in a crimson and gray geyser, and he ceased to exist.

chapter 65

The newspapers had a field day with the death of Vicente Morello. They ran stories on his career, or his romances with various actresses, and on his successes as well as his failures. Much space was devoted to his relationship with Cecily Petain and to his discovery of Hendricks. The articles also speculated, sometimes wildly, as to why he had committed suicide. One stated that he had become addicted to drugs, another that he had been crushed by gambling debts, another that he was suffering from a mysterious, incurable disease. Still another implied that he was the victim of a diabolical plot.

The funeral was small and private, attended mostly by members of Morello's film company. Hendricks noted that Mario Braciola was not there. Most of the cast and crew were in a state of shock, but Hendricks was preoccupied with what all this was doing to his production schedule, and how the company would be run, and by whom.

He did not have long to wait. The following day Vito Zicci called a meeting at the studio and announced that he was now fully in charge and that any question regarding the running of the company should be addressed to him. Hendricks noticed a sullenness about the people in the room, most of whom had originally been hired by Morello, but no one challenged Zicci. Jobs weren't that easy to come by this season, and anyway, what difference did it make in the long run if Zicci was now the head man? As far as they were concerned, they had simply traded one variety of martinet for another. The thing to do was to stay alive and look out for yourself.

When the meeting ended, Hendricks hung back.

Zicci's narrow face wore an insolent expression. "Yes?"

"There are things I've asked for that I'm not getting, at least, not when I need them."

"Such as?"

"Such as finding that ship I want to use for a location—the tanker. And what about the set for the interior of the police station? We are scheduled to shoot two scenes there at the beginning of the week, and it's still nowhere near ready."

Zicci shrugged. "It is a matter of expense. Only by putting an extra team of carpenters on that job could we have had it ready. I told that to Antonio."

Hendricks was puzzled. "For Christ's sake, man. It costs more to tie up the crew and fall behind schedule than it does to knock some lousy flats together. And what about the extras for the scene on the bridge? I didn't have anywhere near the people I wanted. The shot looks thin, phony."

"I cannot work magic. We are operating on a tight budget."

The American felt a flush of anger. "Tight budget, my ass. I'm trying to turn out a picture that'll make this company a hell of a lot of money. And here you are crying poor mouth over a few lousy lire."

Zicci extended his hands, palms up. "There is nothing I can do. Absolutely nothing. I have only so much to work with, and no more."

Hendricks's instinctive reaction was to knock the sneer off Zicci's face, but he held himself in check. He turned and strode from the room, slamming the door behind him.

The offices of *Il Mondo* were wildly disorganized, as usual, with members of the editorial staff scurrying in all directions, even though it was after ten o'clock in the evening. Scozza made his way through the clutter to Galupo's office, and the editor rose to greet him.

When Scozza had been seated and a paper cup of brandy thrust into his hand, Galupo squinted shrewdly at his visitor. "I'm going to come directly to the point, Scozza. I have another assignment for you, a big one this time."

The paparazzo swallowed some of his brandy. "Good. I need the money."

"Uh-huh. But there are some considerations."

"Such as?"

"Such as, you are going to have to be a great deal more discreet about this job."

Scozza blinked. "More discreet. Me? I am the most careful and closemouthed man in the world about my work. And when I am on a special assignment, I am like the Sphinx."

Galupo's smile was cynical. "Perhaps. But I'm telling you for your own good, this is something unusual. It comes directly from close friends of the owners of this publication, so you had better handle it with great care."

"What an honor."

"Don't be sarcastic. You will do very well to heed my words, believe me."

"All right, then, get on with it. What is this vastly important mission, and how much are you going to pay me? As I have told you, I think each time I have worked for this rag of yours in the past, I have been screwed."

The editor looked pained. "That is ridiculous, and you know it. We pay top rates, more than you could possibly get anywhere else."

Scozza finished his brandy and extended his cup for a refill. "I did not come here to debate your generosity. As you have heard, I have my own opinion on that subject. What is it you want me to do?"

Galupo poured cognac into the photographer's cup, then into his own. "There is a woman here in Rome, a French woman who is visiting from Paris. She is staying at the Grand Hotel."

Scozza's jaw dropped.

"What is it? You seem surprised."

"No, nothing. I am merely trying to concentrate on what you are telling me."

"All right. The woman's name is Lemont. Estelle Lemont."

The paparazzo could not believe what he was hearing. He became aware that his heart had begun to beat rapidly. Was it possible that for once a stroke of luck was coming his way? God knew it was about time. But, would it be good or bad?

"What we want," Galupo said, "are pictures, of course. But these pictures are not for publication."

The device in the back of Scozza's head, the one that unfailingly alerted his suspicious mind, began to whir. "Not for publication? Then what do you want them for?"

"That is our business, frankly. And I would advise you not to strain yourself thinking about that aspect of our little project."

Scozza sipped his cognac, slowly this time. "And what should the nature of these photographs be?"

The editor leaned forward in his chair. "They should tell us as much as possible about the lady's sex habits. And the more bizarre those habits might turn out to be, the better."

359

"Ah, I see." And of course, he did see. Whoever was behind this wanted Estelle Lemont to be in such a position that she would either pay large sums of money or else do something she would not otherwise do in order to suppress those pictures. The trouble was, a ploy of this kind was one which in various forms Scozza had engineered himself many times over. He wondered for a moment who wanted this done, and who the actual owners of *Il Mondo* were. That, he knew, would be difficult to learn. There would be corporations overlapping corporations. But whoever they were, the net result was that they would be taking Scozza's pigeon away from him. He would be hired to do for them what he could very well be doing for himself. It was outrageous. But he kept himself carefully under control.

Galupo's voice became soft, almost dulcet. "The good part of this is that your fee will be enormous."

Scozza stared at the editor. "Do you realize what you are asking me to do?"

"Of course I do."

The photographer drew himself up in his chair. "Then you must understand that this is totally out of the question. I am not an extortionist. My profession is taking pictures, and I am extremely skilled at it. The notion that I would be a party to what you are proposing is shocking to me."

The cynical smile returned to Galupo's face. "Is it?"

"Absolutely. So I thank you for the brandy, but I must go." He tossed down the remainder of his cognac.

Galupo's expression did not change. "Scozza, you have heard only a part of the proposition."

"I have heard enough."

"No, you haven't. Here, let me give you just another touch of brandy. You see, there are two sides to our offer. A pleasant side, and an unpleasant side. Let us begin with the former. Your fee, Scozza, will be fifteen million lire."

In spite of himself the photographer inhaled sharply. One could buy quite a number of women, to say nothing of vast amounts of cocaine and other pleasures with a sum of that magnitude. It was more, he reflected, than he had ever made from any one single job in his life. But, on the other hand, it was probably nothing compared to what he could get if he were to undertake this project for himself. Goddamn it.

Galupo poured himself more cognac. "But as I have said, there is also an unpleasant side to this." He drank from his paper cup and wiped his mouth. "Our friends are determined

360

people. When they say they want this to be done, they expect that it *will* be done. If it is not, you could expect that they would be very disappointed. And that could be most unlucky for you."

Scozza made a number of swift connections in his mind, as sweat trickled down his sides. He could well imagine just how unlucky he could become.

The editor belched. "I have always considered you a prudent man, Scozza. Surely you see that it would be more fortunate to have fifteen million lira than to have an accident."

"Yes, I can see that."

"Good man."

Scozza also saw that as long as he was trapped, he should make the best of it.

"But you are asking me to assume considerable risks. I think my fee should be five million higher."

Galupo nodded. "Very well. I'm sure our friends will agree that your efforts will be well worth that."

The photographer drank off the cup of brandy. Mother of God, that was a lot of money. But it continued to rankle him that hypothetically, acting alone, he might have made much more. "When do you want this work done?"

"Just as soon as possible. Our friends are not noted for their patience."

An idea suddenly struck Scozza, and again he grew suspicious. The man he knew Estelle Lemont was seeing was Hendricks. Could it be that they expected shots of her with the American? Pictures of that kind would be worth a fortune. He decided to try a cautious probe. "The French woman. Does she have a lover, or a number of them?"

Galupo's eyes narrowed. "That is another interesting aspect of this assignment. We would like her to be photographed with someone new—someone she might not choose herself to have a, ah, relationship with."

Scozza stared at the editor. "Have you lost your mind? You want pictures that under any circumstances would be difficult enough to get. But now you want them to show her with somebody she does not even know?"

Galupo laughed. "Not only that, but someone she probably would not want to know. In fact the unlikelier he is, the better."

The paparazzo sighed. What they were asking him to do was merely to perform miracles. Yet, oddly enough, ideas were already forming in his mind, and the challenge was exciting to him. What was more, he was confident that he would find ways to exploit this to his own advantage.

"More cognac?"

Scozza shook his head. He was already a little drunk, and he needed to think clearly. "I will require a large advance. There will be considerable expenses."

"Of course." The editor reached into a drawer of his desk and withdrew a stack of bills. He counted off lira notes and scribbled out a receipt which he had Scozza sign.

The paparazzo stuffed the money into his pocket and got to his feet, a little unsteadily. "You'll be hearing from me soon."

"Good. And Scozza, for your own sake, don't mess this up."

In her dressing room at the studio Tina Rinaldi took a long, hot shower, letting the water pound her back and shoulders, easing the tension and the fatigue she felt from the day's work. When she stepped out, she rubbed herself dry with a thick, terry-cloth towel and put on a light cotton robe. She sat down at her makeup table and examined her face in the mirror closely. Not a line, not a blemish. It was amazing. She would not have been surprised if she had looked old and haggard as a result of the strain she sometimes felt.

Working with Hendricks was a joy, and yet much of the time she was terribly frustrated. It was disturbing to her to be near him, sometimes playing romantic or sexy scenes with him, and then simply to walk away at the end of the day. And then there was the pressure of working with people who barely disguised their hostilities, each of them secretly maneuvering to achieve their own selfish ends. Cecily was fiercely jealous of Tina and was constantly trying to elevate her own role in the film, much as she had done in Spain. And Tina trusted Caserta even less than she had in the past, if that were possible.

A knock sounded at her door. "Who is there?"

"It's me, Vito Zicci."

This was a surprise. Tina made it a point to stay as far away from this cold young man as possible. "Yes? What is it?"

"May I come in? I want to speak with you."

Reluctantly she opened the door. Zicci stepped inside, a crooked smile at one corner of his mouth. He straddled a straight-backed chair and studied her breasts under the cotton robe.

"Yes? What is it?"

His gaze moved upward to her face. "I wanted to tell you

that I have been watching you and that I think your work is excellent."

Tina pulled her robe close about her. "Thank you. That's very kind of you."

"I mean it. In fact, I am so impressed I've decided your role should be made more important. Much more."

"You have decided?"

"Yes. I have decided. I am now the head of the company, you know, and ultimately all decisions are my responsibility."

"I think you should discuss such things with Hendricks and not with me."

"I'll let him know what I want, soon enough. But first I am letting you know what I want." He tilted the chair back a little, his gaze continuing to roam over her. "This could be very fortunate for you, you know."

"What could?"

"Oh come on, Tina. You know very well what I mean. I want us to be friends. Close friends. With me looking out for you, a lot of good things can happen to your career."

Tina felt a surge of anger, but at the same time she was fascinated. "Such as?"

"Such as, a starring role in a film created for you. That's what you want, isn't it?" His tone mocked her. "Your highest ambition?"

"Perhaps it is. But I don't intend to achieve it by exchanging favors with you. Now if you'll excuse me, I want to get dressed." Tina stood up and moved past him to open the door. As she came near, Zicci gripped her wrist. She struggled to break free. "What are you doing? Let go of me!"

He tightened his grip and twisted, and with his free hand he tore open the front of her robe. He stroked her breast. "Beautiful."

"Damn you!" Tina bent her head and sank her teeth into his hand.

He roared in surprise and pain as he pulled back from her. Then he doubled his fist and drove it into her belly.

Tina fell to her knees, shock and nausea rolling over her in waves.

"Stupid little bitch!" He stepped to the door. "Remember this, Tina. If I can help you, I can also hurt you." He opened the door and left the room.

Tina stayed on her hands and knees for several minutes, until she was able to control an urge to vomit. Her stomach

363

hurt like hell. She got to her feet, finally, and slumped into a chair. She knew that this would be only the beginning of her troubles with Vito Zicci.

chapter 66

Estelle Lemont was stunned by the news of Morello's suicide. She was aware that he had been in desperate trouble, but the idea that he would be so overwhelmed by his misfortune that he would take his life had never occurred to her. She felt a sense of loss, and of sorrow. They had known each other for a very long time.

But the feeling did not last. Estelle had other matters to think about, other problems to cope with. She was more determined than ever that her scheme to gain control of Hendricks would work, and that eventually she would have him. Whether or not she would still want him at that point was a question she could not even ask herself. All she knew was that she wanted him now to the point that it had become an obsession with her.

After Morello's funeral Estelle asked Hendricks how the studio would be run. They were at dinner in Da Giggetto.

"Braciola's got all the marbles now. It's his show. And he has Zicci in there playing executive."

"I take it you don't think much of his abilities."

"Zicci? A weasel. Knows nothing. From what I can see, he'd probably make it very big in this industry in the States."

She laughed. "What do you know about Hollywood?"

"Not a hell of a lot. Just what I've heard from people who've worked there. Weaver, for instance. Sounds to me like the same crap as here, but on a much bigger scale."

"Have you thought about that? Going there yourself, I mean."

He put his fork down. "Sure. Of course I have. If I'm ever going to make it in this business—really make it and not just screw around with spaghetti westerns and cop movies, then that's where I've got to go. It's where the money is, and the big market."

She nodded. "Then you really have a lot riding, don't you, on this *The Dead of the Night?*"

"You're damn right I do."

And that made it all the more important that her plans must be implemented, and the sooner the better.

Carlos Caserta sat sprawled in a deep chair of chocolate-brown leather, surveying the room. It was modern, with a lot of chrome and glass, and one wall was a bank of windows through which he could see a panoramic view of the northeast section of Rome, a vast pattern of lights that seemed to stretch to infinity. Music from huge floor speakers pulsed steadily with the beat of one of the new American rock records. He was drinking Scotch from an oversized glass, and the whiskey and the music were making him feel expansive. He waved a hand. "Not bad."

"It will do." Zicci was sitting opposite the hulking actor, his crossed feet resting on a glass table. "At least for the time being."

Caserta swallowed some of his whiskey. "For the time being, eh? It sounds to me as if you may have ambitions for yourself."

Zicci's eyes were cold and steady. "I have my goals."

Caserta laughed. "And what are they? You are going to ask Braciola's permission to do art films?"

"I don't have to ask for anything. What I have in mind is that the company will make pictures with some of the biggest stars in Italy, maybe in the world. At the same time I know that I can make deals with distributors that will insure that my films get preferential treatment."

"What do you mean, 'your' films? You are merely an employee. And as far as making pictures is concerned, it becomes more and more apparent that the key man in your company is Hendricks. He is the one who will really be running things, in time."

Axface sneered. "That's ridiculous. He is merely fumbling about, making clumsy attempts to direct."

"Yes? *The Hired Gun* was a big success, and I think *The Dead of the Night* will do just as well. In fact, it should do better, now that Hendricks is established. And what do you think will happen then? Braciola will give him anything he wants, and believe me, Zicci, he will want more and more. Then we'll see whose films your company produces."

"You think so, do you?"

"I'm sure of it. And when that happens, what will become of all your fancy promises to me? You will have no power to keep them."

Zicci thrust himself forward in his seat, the muscles working in his narrow jaw. "I will do exactly as I have told you I will do. And if you really want those things to come about, then you must help me."

Caserta grimaced. "You know how I feel about that American bastard."

"Exactly. And that is why we must work together. It is in our mutual interest, do you see?"

"What are you saying is that your previous efforts have not worked, is that it?"

"What do you mean?"

Caserta drank more whiskey. "Don't fence with me, Zicci. I am no fool. It is obvious to me where many of these problems have come from in the production of this new picture. And despite your efforts, Hendricks is turning out a good film. Not only do the rest of the cast and crew know that, but so does Braciola."

Zicci's voice was hard and flat. "And that is why you must help. I know exactly what must be done."

"Then count on me. If you have a good plan, it would be well for us to carry it out."

"I have a good plan, Carlos, as you will see. Have another whiskey, and I will tell you about it."

Mario Braciola opened the folder on his desk and leafed through the papers it contained. The receipts on *The Hired Gun* were gratifying. The picture had already earned back three times its negative costs, and foreign exhibition had not yet even begun. And from what he had seen of the new picture, it could do even better. He opened a second folder and glanced at the sheaf of notes his accounting department had prepared. There were several columns of figures. One of these represented cash surpluses it would be impossible to justify if government tax officials were to examine them. Despite the large sums he regularly paid to many of these same men, it would be extremely troublesome if information on those unaccountable surpluses were to fall into the wrong hands. He closed the folder and thought about the problem.

It was time, Braciola decided, to make the film company much more active. Instead of producing one or two pictures at a time, he would step up activities to the point that as many as a dozen film projects would be in development simultaneously. Under those layers of activity, a great deal of money could be moved around. What a fool Morello had been to blow his brains out, and what an inopportune moment he had chosen to do it. Just when he had been needed most.

Braciola got up from his desk and walked to the window, where he could see the cool foliage of the Villa Borghese. If there was one human weakness he despised above all others, it was a lack of courage. Morello was dead because, when it came right down to it, he was a coward. So be it. All that meant, simply, was that he could not have been depended upon in any event.

What Braciola needed now was a strong man. He stared out at the view of the gardens as his mind turned over his options. As he considered his choices, he concluded that one course of action made more sense than any of the others. He returned to his desk and opened the second folder once again.

chapter 67

The helicopter rose straight up over the rooftops and hovered for a few moments at an altitude of three hundred feet. The pilot inclined the nose, and the craft moved out to the southwest, its main rotor thrashing the air with a steady staccato beat. Hendricks sat in the right-hand outboard seat, Weaver in the middle between him and the pilot.

Weaver shouted above the nose. "Sure better than screwing around with that traffic."

Hendricks nodded. It was his first ride in one of these machines, and he was fascinated by it. The chopper's airspeed indicator read eighty knots, and the sensation of wafting over the typical midday snarl of cars and trucks in the streets below them was exhilarating. It was also interesting to see Rome from this perspective, to be able to pick out familiar landmarks so easily, and to see how the features of the city related. He spotted St. Peters and the sprawl of the Vatican City, the column of Marcus Aurelius rising above the Piazza Colonna near the vast Palazzo Chigi, and farther on the Piazza Venezia, which marked the center of modern Rome.

A few minutes later they flashed over the outskirts of the city, and then the topography below them became grids of verdant fields interspersed with stands of olive and fruit trees. There were farmhouses and country villas and small towns and villages, and shortly after that they reached the coast. The Mediterranean was a deep blue, almost cobalt in the bright sunshine, a paler aqua in the shallows close to shore. They swung south along the beach, and the pilot pointed. A vessel lay out there, and Hendricks raised a hand in acknowledgment. The helicopter turned and slowed as it approached the ship.

It was an empty tanker riding at anchor, her bow high, her stern down in the water with the weight of her engine. Even from here Hendricks could see rusty patches on her decks and superstructure, and reddish stains along the sides of her hull. He signaled, and the pilot gently lowered the chopper down onto the tanker's flying bridge. When the machine settled onto the steel deck plates, the pilot killed the engine and the whirling blades of the rotor gradually came to a halt. Hendricks climbed out, Weaver following. The pilot remained the the machine. "Just stand by," Hendricks called to him. "We won't be long."

Weaver indicated with a tilt of his head. "Here comes the welcoming committee."

Hendricks turned to see a man dressed in a ragged khaki uniform and carrying a rifle climb the steps from the lower wing of the bridge up to where they stood. "It's the guard. He's been told to expect us." He waved, and when the man approached, Hendricks explained that they were there to inspect the vessel for use as a film location.

The man nodded. "Help yourself. Take as much time as you like. I don't get that many visitors."

"Okay. We'll just wander around." Hendricks led the way down the outside ladder down to the bridge deck and from there down the boat deck, Weaver behind him.

The cameraman squinted at the scaling gray paint. "Looks like this one has been to the wars and back."

"She has. This is a type T-two, built during World War Two."

"So how come it's just sitting out here rusting?"

Hendricks walked under the midships lifeboats, looking up at the davits. "Not much demand for ships like this today. Everybody's building much bigger ones. This old tub only goes about eighteen thousand tons, and the new ones are anywhere from a hundred thousand up."

Weaver whistled. "A hundred thousand tons?"

"Right. And some of them are a hell of a lot more than that. There's a race on to build them bigger and bigger, with the Japanese leading the way. They figured out that a tanker is nothing but a string of containers, with a bow on one end and an engine on the other. So theoretically there's no limit to how big they can go. And the more cargo you can carry in one, the more cost-efficient it becomes."

"So what happens to the old ones like this—they just rot?"

Hendricks swung down the steps to the forward well deck. "The owners try to pick up whatever short-haul jobs they can, and if they can't keep them going, they send them to the boneyard and break them up for scrap."

"End of ship."

"Right." He waved an arm. "But it makes a damned good location, don't you think? There are more nooks and crannies and hidden passageways on one of these things than you could ever count."

The cameraman's gaze swept over the midships house and up to the forepeak. "I believe it. And yeah, I think we can get a lot of good stuff here. It's different, and it's kind of spooky. Make a great place for the bit where the dope smuggler tries to kill you."

"That's what I figured. Matter of fact, we might even want to stage another sequence here. Let's think about it."

"Sure."

They poke around for a half hour or so, and then started back up to the flying bridge. As they passed one of the tank tops that studded the deck, Hendricks heard muffled sounds. He stopped. "What the hell was that?"

Weaver turned to him. "What was what?"

Hendricks held up a hand. "Listen. Do you hear it? Sounds like somebody yelling."

The cameraman froze, his head cocked to one side. He held the position for a few seconds and shook his head. "No, I don't."

The sound repeated, louder this time. Hendricks stepped quickly to the tank top. It was a mushroom-shaped projection rising about three feet up from the deck. The cap of the mushroom was a door, held in place by steel dogs. He grabbed one of the dogs and began spinning it open. "Christ, there's a man in this tank. Give me a hand, will you?"

The steel door was a little more than four feet across. When they had freed each of the dogs, it took all the strength both men could muster to heave the door open. They looked down into the cavernous tank, its dark recesses still stinking faintly of crude oil. The sounds were clearer now, echoing hollowly from the bottom of the tank, alternating between groans and what sounded like cries for help.

Hendricks leaned over the edge of the opening and peered into the gloom. He shook his head. "I can't see much. It's blacker than hell down there."

The noises from the tank became varied. A sound of thrashing against metal was interspersed with the human cries. Hendricks swung a leg over the side of the tank top and stepped onto the narrow steel ladder attached to the side of the tank and leading down into it. He pointed to the bridge. "Matt, go up and get that guard. Get him to bring a light down here, and fast."

Weaver turned and sprinted across the deck toward the midships house.

Hendricks hesitated. The fumes in the tank could be poisonous. Its interior apparently had been cleaned by the method called butterworthing, in which a rotating nozzle was lowered into the tank and a mixture of hot water and detergent was blasted against the steel walls under great pressure, but there still seemed to be enough residue to be hazardous. The unmistakable sulfur odor of the crude oil was there, and it produced a stinging sensation in his eyes and the membranes inside his nose.

The cries were louder now. They sounded as if whoever was down there was in considerable pain. Hendricks glanced over his shoulder, but Weaver and the guard had not appeared. He took as deep a breath as he could suck into his lungs and let himself down the ladder, one rung at a time. The atmosphere was close and heavy, and he could feel a clamminess that seeped through his shirt. There was an oily film on the rungs of the ladder, and it made slippery going for his hands and feet. He continued to peer into the darkness below him, hoping his eyes would adjust to it and that he'd be able to see, but except for the narrow shaft of light from the opening above him, there was only a black void. When he had gone about a half-dozen steps down the ladder, the steel door of the tank top crashed shut. Now he was in total darkness.

When the telephone rang, Estelle Lemont was alone in her suite. She had sent her maid out on an errand, and she was about to take a bath. She lifted the instrument, hoping the call would be from Hendricks. "Yes?"

"Signora Lemont?"

"Who is calling?"

"My name is Tomaso. Signor Hendricks asked me to call."

"This is Signora Lemont. What is it?"

"I am a free-lance journalist. I am doing a piece on Signor Hendricks and his new film, and I was scheduled to see him for an interview. He was detained at the last minute and suggested that I speak with you."

Estelle was delighted. "Did you wish to come here?"

"Signor Hendricks suggested we meet at a cantina which is not far from the studio. He said you and I could talk until he arrived."

"Very well. It will take me a few minutes to get ready."

"Please, don't rush. Our appointment was not until five, so we have time. And anyway, I am grateful that you will do this for me. It's kind of you to take the trouble."

Estelle glanced at her watch. "No trouble at all." She got an address from him and hung up. The bath would take too long. She decided on a shower instead and was in and out quickly. She thought carefully about how she would dress, deciding finally on a simple top and a linen skirt. She wanted to look a bit more businesslike than chic, and the outfit she chose would help to convey that impression.

She also thought about how she might handle herself in the interview. The most important thing, she decided, would be to give the reporter the kind of information that would please Hendricks. This was the first time he had provided any kind of opportunity for her to share in what he was doing, and she intended to make the most of it. And the way to do that would be to give him as many reasons as possible to see that he could trust her and depend on her. Later on it would be just that much easier when she let him know of her financial involvement with Braciola and the film. That could be a tricky problem, she knew, but she was confident that she could handle it, just as she was confident that ultimately she could handle Hendricks. The thing was, you had to ease a head-strong man into the realization that he needed you. She selected a pair of sunglasses and a shoulder bag of pale soft leather. Her reflection in the mirror was exactly the impression she wanted to make. Estelle smiled and left the suite.

There was a crowd at the front entrance waiting for taxis, and several minutes went by before she could get a cab. The traffic was atrocious, as usual, and it took twenty minutes longer than she had planned to get to the address the reporter had given her. She thought further about what she would say to him and concluded that she would be wise to avoid revealing anything about herself on her own career. It was highly unlikely he would know anything about that anyway.

Estelle was mildly surprised when the taxi deposited her in front of the cantina. It was a seedy little place, much like the kind of cheap café that dotted the Rive Gauche in Paris and not at all where she would expect a writer to conduct an interview with a screen personality and his friend. Nevertheless it was true that it wasn't far from the studio, and that no doubt explained why he had suggested it. There were a few small tables on the sidewalk, and the patrons sitting at them looked as dingy to her as the cantina itself. She walked past them and through the door.

The interior was rather dark, and she took off her sunglasses and tried to adjust her eyes. After the brilliant sunshine outside, it was difficult to make out much of anything for a moment, but her impression of the inside of the cantina matched what she had seen on the way in. There was a bar with a handful of customers standing at it and more small tables. It smelled heavily of stale cooking.

"Signora Lemont?"

"Yes?"

"Hello, welcome. I'm Tomaso. Here, please sit down."

She seated herself opposite him at one of the little tables. "Sorry I'm late. I thought I'd seen heavy traffic, but this afternoon was unbelievable."

"I assure you, it is no problem at all. We have plenty of time; Signor Hendricks did not know just when he could get away. What would you like to drink?"

"Oh, I guess a Campari and soda."

The reporter snapped his fingers, and a waiter shuffled over through the gloom. He ordered her drink, and when the waiter had gone, he smiled at her. "This is a great honor for me. Not merely one famous person, but two."

It was another surprise, but not an unpleasant one. As long as Estelle had been away from the business, she nevertheless always found herself pleased and flattered when she was recognized. She feigned indifference. "Thank you, but that was a long time ago."

"Not so long. I remember many of your pictures. I was delighted to know that I would be meeting you. In fact I wondered if I might be learning that you perhaps have plans to resume your career."

Estelle returned his smile. "You're not the first person to wonder about that, but I can tell you positively that I have no such intentions."

"What a shame. I'm sure your fans would be delighted if you were to change your mind."

As the writer spoke, Estelle's eyes became accustomed to the semidarkness, and she decided that he was a remarkably ugly man. He was fat, with oily, pockmarked skin, and as he spoke, his thick lips became flecked with spittle. His clothing was ill fitting and unkempt and contributed to the overall impression he made of sloppiness. She also found herself no longer responding favorably to his fawning remarks.

The waiter returned with her drink, and the writer raised his own glass. "Salut." He appeared to be drinking brandy. She raised her glass and tasted the Campari. Its bitterness made her shudder a little, and she looked at the journalist with growing distaste. She would be glad when Hendricks arrived.

The writer downed his drink and extended a package of cigarettes. She shook her head, and he lit one for himself. He exhaled, smoke curling from his thick-lipped mouth. "So tell me, how is your friend's new film coming along?"

"It seems to be working well. From what I am told, the cast is very pleased with his direction. He has a great deal of natural talent, you know, an instinct for getting the most an actor has to offer."

"Is it true that the concept for this new picture was also suggested by him?"

"Absolutely. The entire idea was his, and he hired an excellent screenwriter, an American named Betty Barker, to do the script. You've heard of her?"

"Of course. One of her films made a big splash at the Cannes festival, last year. How did he come to choose her? I mean, wasn't it a little unusual, that he wanted a woman to do this work?"

"Not at all." Estelle drank more of her Campari. She wanted to avoid letting him know that the choice of screenwriter had been the result of her suggestion. That was the kind of thing Hendricks would want to see in print. "He knew her reputation, and he wanted to be sure he would start this project with a first-rate script."

"Yes." He smiled and dragged on his cigarette. "That's important, isn't it?"

It occurred to her that there was something insolent, now,

in the man's tone. She finished her drink and glanced impatiently at her watch. It was too dark for her to read its face. Or was it? She held her wrist closer and squinted, but the hands and numerals were a blur. She looked up at the reporter and saw that his smile had become a broad grin. She started to ask what he thought was so funny, but she found that although her lips formed the words, she was unable to issue the sounds from her mouth. A strange numbness was spreading through her body. She shook her head to clear it, but it would only move in slow motion, wobbling on her neck. The image of the writer was not so distinct as it had been, and she was annoyed that he had begun to laugh softly. Again she tried to speak, but she could not.

Everything had slowed to an incredibly languorous pace. Moreover it suddenly was not so disturbing to her as it had been only a few minutes ago. Somehow it seemed natural that she was in this state, her body turning to rubber, her mind taking this all in as if from a great distance. There was a roaring in her ears, and that seemed strangely comforting. She listened to the sound wonderingly. As she watched, the reporter took some bills from his pocket and put them on the table. He stepped over to her and pulled her to her feet.

Estelle felt that perhaps she should resist him, but she could not. In fact it really wasn't that important. She could barely stand up, let alone walk, and it was so much easier simply to go along, to let him half carry her out of the cantina. He held her up with one arm around her body under her armpits, and the door he took her through was not the one through which she had entered. It led into an alley where a small car was parked. The sunlight was blinding to her, lancing her eyeballs with pain, and then she was slumped in the car, and the man was driving it out of the alley.

chapter 68

The interior of the tank was silent, and then Hendricks heard the rush of water. It took a moment for the meaning of the sound to register on his brain, but when it did, he grasped that somewhere in the impenetrable darkness below him, seawater was being let into the tank. A vessel of this type depended upon its liquid cargo to maintain a stable, seaworthy attitude when it was under way. When it ran without cargo, the tanks were filled with seawater to provide ballast. Now someone had opened the intake valve which would admit water into the space in which he was trapped. The water roared through the pipe and slopped and sloshed on the welded steel plates. It was coming in fast, and he could smell it, a briny top note above the stink of the foul air. He opened his mouth and shouted as loudly as he could, but he could not even hear his voice over the roar of the inrushing water.

Each tank on one of these ships had a capacity of something around twenty-five thousand barrels, he knew. And the intake system was designed to load ballast rapidly, inasmuch as a light tanker was dangerously unseaworthy. He wondered how long it would take for the tank to fill up. An hour, probably. Perhaps less. Where the hell were Weaver and that guard?

Hendricks climbed up the greasy ladder until he reached the underside of the door over the tank top. Bracing himself, he placed his shoulder against the door and heaved with all his strength. The door did not budge. He slumped over, his feet on the topmost rungs of the ladder, and fought for breath. The bad air was getting to him now, cutting his lungs with its sulfurous edge. He hauled himself back up to the door and strained against it until his muscles trembled and the pain was fiery in his back and his shoulders and his legs, but he could not move it a fraction of an inch. He stepped down again and hung on the ladder, again struggling to breathe. Below him the sound of the pounding water told him it was continuing to rise, reaching up toward him.

The room was small and dirty, and its single window had been painted over. In her strange dreamlike state Estelle saw what looked like lights on tripods and a large, old-fashioned still camera. She realized she was in a studio of some kind, and she wondered why. There was a bed in the center of the room, a low, rumpled affair with a brass headboard, and the reporter pushed her down onto it. She found that she was unable to rise or to move her head more than the slightest bit, and yet she could see, although her vision was blurred.

She heard a voice, and she realized that there was another man in the room besides the reporter. Her eyes sought him out, and when they found him, she saw that he was oddly shaped. His torso was long and massive, but his arms and legs were truncated, hardly more than flippers. His head was hideous. It was huge, bulbous, even more disproportionate to his body in its oversize than his limbs in their brevity.

The two men spoke to each other, and the smaller one laughed. They approached the bed and began roughly pulling Estelle's clothes off. When she lay nude on the tangled bedding, the small man disrobed, continuing to grin at her as he threw his clothing into a pile on top of hers. He is a dwarf, she told herself. How strange. I have never seen a dwarf up close.

For so short a man, the dwarf's penis was enormous. It stood up like a thick red club, its purplish head twitching. For an instant the oddly disproportionate combination of trunk, head, arms, legs, and penis struck Estelle as funny, and she might have laughed if she had been able to. But then it was suddenly grotesque, and she became frightened.

The seawater swirled around Hendricks's body as he jammed himself into the small pocket of air contained in the tank top. His lungs burned from each breath of the acrid atmosphere, and he tried to take it in short gasps. From time to time he pounded a fist against the steel door over his head, but the effort seemed puny, and the sound faint. After awhile he stopped, conserving his energy as he tried to think of some way to escape from the trap.

A ship of this type would have ten tanks like this one, he knew. He wondered if all of them were being flooded simultaneously. If they were, the ship would be settling in level trim as she took on the ballast, but it was impossible for him to tell, crouching here in the darkness, caught like a rat in the hold of a sinking vessel. The water was up to his chest now, splashing against his face. Some of it got into his mouth and he had to fight to keep from gagging on the mixture of oil and salt. He wondered how much time he had left.

The dream sequence in the small studio had become a nightmare. The grinning dwarf crawled over Estelle's body like a jackal feeding on a piece of carrion, while the fat man who had called himself a reporter crouched behind his camera, illuminating the room at intervals with brilliant flashes from strobe lights. The dwarf shoved his bulbous head between her legs and sucked at her noisily, muttering to himself.

Estelle tried to push him away, but her efforts produced little more than a feeble pawing.

As the fat man continued to photograph them, the dwarf raised himself and climbed up onto her, thrusting his huge penis into her. His mutterings became a cackle, and as Estelle looked up at him, she saw stumps of rotting teeth in a wide red mouth, and she was nauseated by waves of fetid breath. She turned her head a little, and the bursts of light from the strobes were blinding. They seemed to fill her head with explosions, coming one after another. She managed to shut her eyes, but she could feel the dwarf continuing to work on her, moving from one position to another as the lights erupted over and over again.

Hendricks knew he had reached the point at which death was minutes away. His face was pushed up against the steel door of the tank top, and the water swirled inexorably higher. He opened his mouth and pulled the pungent air deep into his lungs, wincing as it stabbed his chest. He climbed a few steps down the ladder and plunged ahead in the black water, hoping his sense of direction was correct, and that he was swimming toward the bow of the ship.

His chances were slim, but if he had stayed where he was, he was certain to die. This way, he would at least be trying. Each tank on these ships had, as he remembered, a hatch which led into the next tank, so that the liquid contents could be balanced between them. When the ship was trimmed, the valves controlling those hatches would be closed. But with the ship light and riding at anchor, there was a possibility that they would be open, especially when the tanks had been cleaned. He swam through the cold seawater until his hands touched the steel bulkhead, and then he began to feel his way along it, searching for the hatch.

It was no good. He was exhausted, and his tortured lungs threatened to burst in their desperate craving for oxygen. Tiny points of light danced in his head, and he felt the last vestiges of strength slip away. He had heard that drowning was not a painful way to die, but he was in agony. As his muscles convulsed, his hand touched the hatch. It was open and water was spilling through it into the next tank.

With the last scrap of energy he could summon, Hendricks pulled himself through the narrow hatch. There was air on the other side, and he gulped it greedily, sobbing with the effort. The water in this tank, he judged from the sound, was some distance below him. He hung by his hands from the edge of the hatch for a moment, and then let go. The sensation of falling through the darkness was eerie. He hit the water hard, plunging down into it until his feet struck the bottom of the tank. He bobbed to the surface and groped for the ladder that would lead to the top. When he found it, he crawled upward, forcing his spent body from one rung to the next. When he reached the inside of the tank top, he offered a silent prayer that this one would not be dogged shut. He put his shoulder against it and heaved. The door gave. He was able to move it only the slightest bit, but he could move it. He clung to the ladder for a moment, nauseated now from the seawater he had swallowed and from the bad air, and then he set himself to heave against the door once again.

After a time the fat man waved the dwarf away. He left his camera and climbed onto the bed with Estelle. She was no more able to resist him than she had the dwarf, who stood watching them, the wide grin twisting his hideous features. At least she could not feel what the fat man was doing to her. When he finished with her, he and the dwarf pulled her off the bed and dressed her, and the dwarf put his own clothing back on. She was still unable to walk without support, although some mobility had returned to her arms and legs. The two half carried her down to the street and threw her into the front seat of the small car. The dwarf disappeared, and the fat man got into the vehicle and started it.

The drive through Rome seemed to go on forever, and the car was cramped and uncomfortable and jounced terribly. Estelle felt herself alternately nodding off and coming awake in some pain as more feeling returned to her limbs. Her muscles were twitching, and she felt tiny needles jabbing at them as her circulation quickened.

When they arrived at her hotel, the fat man reached across her and opened the door. He shoved Estelle out of the car, and she staggered onto the sidewalk. It required great effort for her to walk, and she felt as if her legs did not really belong to her. She put one foot in front of the other, lurching forward, and when she got to the entrance, she grasped the brass railing, but she could not ascend the steps.

There was the usual crowd waiting for taxis. A number of people glanced at her, and Estelle knew from the expressions on their faces that they thought she was drunk. Some of them seemed disgusted and others amused. She wanted to crawl away and hide, or better still to disappear. Never in her life had she experienced anything like the degradation she felt now.

The doorman glanced over at her, and his features registered recognition and then shock. He called a pair of bellmen from the lobby, and together the two men got her into the lobby and from there to the elevator and finally to her suite.

It took a long time to heave the heavy steel door open far enough to permit the passage of Hendricks's body. When at last he had cracked it about eighteen inches, he crawled over the side of the tank top and fell heavily to the deck. He lay there on his back, deeply breathing the sweet, clean air.

chapter 69

Scozza parked the tiny Fiat in the lot behind the hotel and slammed the door contemptuously. After today he would be driving a vehicle more in keeping with his status. With what he had recorded on film, he was convinced that he would become a rich man. It was as if his entire life had pointed him toward this one great opportunity, preparing him for it. And Scozza would make the most of it. He hummed to himself as he entered the back entrance of the hotel and climbed the stairs. The effort caused him to breathe hard, as it always did, and he could feel his heart pounding. This dump, too, would soon be a thing of his past. When he got to his door, he fumbled for his keys, a smile on his thick lips.

Inside, he closed the door behind him and dropped the chain into place. He snapped on the lights, thinking as he did that he had earned himself a good big slug of brandy.

"Hello, Scozza."

The paparazzo blinked. Two men were standing in his studio. One of the men held an automatic pistol, its muzzle pointed at Scozza's chest. The other man was a stranger, but he looked vaguely familiar. His body was slim, with wide shoulders and unusually long arms. But the most distinctive

379

thing about him was his face. It was strangely narrow, like the blade of an ax. Scozza had seen this man before, he was sure of it. But he could not remember where.

"Sit down, Scozza." The man with the narrow face indicated a chair, and Scozza slumped onto it. He looked about his studio and was shocked by what he saw.

The big Graflex had been smashed into an unrecognizable mass of twisted metal and shattered glass. It lay in a heap in the center of the floor. All the drawers in his chests where he kept his equipment had been pulled out, their contents dumped and strewn everywhere. His Nikons had also been wrecked. The rolls of film he had shot of Estelle lay where he had left them, on top of one of the chests.

The narrow-faced man gestured, and the one with the pistol stepped quickly to Scozza, pulling a loop of wire from his pocket. He put the pistol away and lashed the paparazzo's hands behind his back.

The first man gestured toward the rolls of film. "This all of it—everything you shot of Estelle Lemont?"

Scozza was baffled. How did this intruder know what he had photographed? What did he know of Estelle Lemont?

The one who had bound him brought the back of his fist against the photographer's face, hard. The unexpected blow made Scozza's head spin.

"I asked you a question. This all of it?"

Scozza nodded. "That's everything."

The slim young man scooped up the rolls of exposed film and stuffed them into his pockets. He nodded to his companion. Scozza winced as the man behind him grabbed his hair and jerked his head back. He saw a glint of light on the blade of a straight razor, and then he felt excruciating pain in his throat. There was a tugging sensation mingled with the pain, and he saw a crimson fountain burst from beneath his jaw and arc out into the room. The man with the narrow face grinned at him, and then Scozza remembered. He had seen him the night of Vicente Morello's party, when the man had been with Mario Braciola.

Scozza opened his mouth to scream, "I know you," but the only sound he could make was a ragged gurgle. There was a distant wail echoing in his head, and the light faded. As it did, the pulsing from his throat grew weaker and weaker, until he no longer felt any sensation at all.

Hendricks had no idea how long he lay on the deck of the

tanker. It was hard for him to deal with any thought beyond the realization that he was alive, and that his body was sore and bruised and the inside of his chest was raw from breathing the foul air he had encountered inside the ship's tanks. After a time he pulled himself to a sitting position, his back propped against the tank top through which he had escaped. The sun had gone, and it was growing dark. The wind came up, blowing in off the sea, and he suddenly felt very cold.

What the hell had happened to Weaver? Why hadn't he and the guard come searching for him? He got to his feet, feeling light-headed and unsteady and looked up at the flying bridge, but he could see no activity up there. Hendricks walked gingerly to the base of the midships house and slowly ascended the steps. His body ached, and he could feel himself trembling from the cold and from the battering he had taken.

When he got to the flying bridge, his gaze swept the area, and he saw that the guard and the chopper were both gone. The ship appeared to be deserted. He was about to go back down when a dark mass on the deck near the steering station caught his eye. It was hard to tell what the shape was, even when he got close to it, but as he knelt down, he saw that it was Weaver.

The cameraman was alive, but not by much. The top of his head had been split open, and his hair and his face were encrusted with dried blood. The stuff had run down his jaw and stuck in his beard. Hendricks had to make several attempts before he could feel a pulse, and when he did, it was weak and fluttery. Instinctively he knew that if he didn't get Weaver warmth and shelter to counteract the shock, he would die.

Hendricks pulled the cameraman up off the deck as gently as he could and slung the inert body over his shoulder. Weaver was heavy, and Hendricks staggered under the burden as he carried him down to the boat deck. He put him down and tried to get into one of the cabins facing onto the deck, but the doors were all locked. These were the officers' quarters, and Hendricks speculated that there might still be blankets on the bunks. He looked around until he found a fire ax in its holder on a bulkhead, and with the ax he chopped and smashed his way into one of the cabins.

He was right, there was still bedding on the bunk. Hendricks carried Weaver inside and laid him down and covered him with a blanket. The cut on his head was bleeding again, and his breathing was shallow. He muttered a few words, but Hendricks was unable to understand them.

It had become totally dark. Hendricks went out onto the deck and climbed up one of the davits. He freed the lashings on the canvas cover of the lifeboat hanging from the davit and climbed into the craft. The boat's gear was intact, and he found a lantern and a first-aid kit. Back in the cabin he lighted the lantern, and in its light he cleaned Weaver's wound and bandaged it. There was a small bottle of brandy in the first-aid kit, and Hendricks managed to get Weaver to drink a little of it.

The night was long and cold, and by the time dawn broke, Hendricks was feeling stiff and miserable. He checked Weaver and was relieved to find that the cameraman was conscious.

Weaver groaned. "Goddamn, my head hurts."

Hendricks bent close to him. "What happened?"

"I don't know. I ran up to the bridge, looking for the guard, and when I got up there, the roof fell in."

"You feel good enough to get off this tub?"

"Yeah. At least, I'll try. But how do we get ashore?"

"I don't know, but I'll figure out something."

Hendricks went back out onto the deck. He could see fishing boats putting out on the roiling early morning sea, bobbing in the swells. The problem was how to attract attention from one of them. He climbed back up into the lifeboat and rummaged around until he found a signal pistol. Back on deck he waited until one of the boats came fairly close to the tanker, and then he fired the pistol directly at the fishing vessel. The flare arched out over the water, a fiery red ball. It missed the cabin of the boat by inches, and the vessel hove to. Hendricks leaped up and down and waved his arms, and the boat turned and made for the ship.

A light chop had come up, and getting Weaver off the ship and onto the boat was tricky. Hendricks and the fishermen finally managed it by rigging a bosun's chair and easing the injured man from the well deck of the tanker down onto the pitching craft. They put him on a bunk in the forepeak, and Hendricks told the crew of the boat that Weaver had been injured in a fall. Nobody questioned him too closely, and a half hour later the boat put into a small fishing village.

There was a clinic in the village, and the doctor there examined Weaver and put him to bed, telling Hendricks he would take X rays and keep him there for a day or two. When Hendricks was satisfied that Weaver would be all right, he left the clinic and found a taxi that would take him to Rome.

chapter 70

Tina hesitated before the office door. Something was wrong, and she didn't know what it was. She had come to the studio for a ten o'clock call, but Antonio had told her that shooting had been suspended for the day. Hendricks was not in the studio, and no one seemed to know where he was. Now she had been summoned by Zicci. She knocked on the door, and a voice from within the office told her to enter.

Zicci was slouched in Vicente Morello's old chair, one foot on the edge of the massive desk. His mouth formed the insolent smile she found so irritating, and he waved her to one of the visitor's chairs facing the desk. "Hello, Tina. Looks like you have a day off."

She sat down, feeling tense and wary. "Where is Hendricks, and why are we not working?"

The slim man got up from his chair and walked around the desk to where she sat. "I have no idea what happened to him. He makes all this noise about maintaining schedules, and then he doesn't bother to show up." He leaned against the desk. "Maybe he and his cameraman friend went on a drunk. Weaver didn't come in today either."

Tina felt her sense of anxiety deepen. It would be totally out of character for Hendricks to go on a binge and ignore his responsibility to the production. More than that, it would be an impossible thing for him to do, she was sure of it. He was too deeply committed, too much involved with giving everything he had to making *The Dead of the Night* a success to simply turn his back on it. In fact no matter how exhausted he sometimes became through his backbreaking efforts and long hours, no matter how much she knew he sometimes drank at night to relax, he was always on the set in the morning, ready to go.

Zicci's gaze swept over her body. "Have you thought about what I said to you the other day—about our becoming good friends?"

Tina looked at the oddly narrow face and into the cold eyes. "Yes, I've thought about it."

"Good. Then maybe you've finally come around to being sensible. It really would be a great waste, you know, if you were not to take advantage of this opportunity."

"I said I'd thought about it."

"And?"

"And I think you are repulsive. I'd sooner kill myself than have anything to do with you."

Zicci threw his head back and laughed. "That's what I like. A woman with spirit. One with some fire in her. No wonder I feel something when I look at you."

Tina got to her feet. "I don't care what you feel. I'm leaving. If you want to talk to me again, do it through Hendricks or Antonio."

Zicci's angular features twisted into a scowl. He pushed the heel of his hand against Tina's face and shoved her back down into the chair. "Goddamnit, you will do as I say, when I say! Do you understand me? I am in charge here. Not Hendricks, not anyone else. This studio is mine, and I will decide what is to happen."

Tina was furious, but as she looked at Zicci's suddenly wild face, her emotion turned to fear. There was something terrible, something twisted, just under the surface of this man. Now that she had touched it, a savage rage had swept over him. As she stared at him, she saw a further change take place in his expression. She realized with a jolt that he was aware of her fear, and that it was stimulating him. She gathered herself, to make another effort to leave the room, to bolt from it this time, but Zicci anticipated her attempt. He gripped a handful of her hair and wrenched it, forcing her down onto the carpet.

Tina opened her mouth to scream, but Zicci struck her face hard with the back of one hand and then the other. The blows were numbing, and she felt her mouth filling with blood, the faintly salt taste running over her tongue. Her cry was little more than a choking cough as she gagged and fought for breath. He straddled her and ripped open the front of her dress. She was wearing only a pair of pants beneath it. She struggled under him and clawed his face, and his response was to strike her harder, this time with his closed fist.

As his punch hit her, a blinding light burst in front of Tina's eyes. Her senses reeled, and for a minute or two she lost consciousness. When she came to, she realized that Zicci had torn her dress and her pants completely away from her, and that he was holding her arms in a viselike grip. He twisted them so that they were bent backwards at an odd angle, and the pain in her elbows and her shoulders was unbearable. He bent over her and bit her breasts, sinking his teeth into her flesh again and again.

Hendricks paid the taxi driver and got out of the cab. He stepped quickly over the sidewalk and unlocked a door that led onto one of the huge sound stages. Inside he saw that the area was dark, and he felt a flash of anger. This was where he had planned to shoot a scene today, and possibly two. Instead it was a miracle that he was here at all. On an adjoining stage he could see a group of technicians at work, but with that exception, the studio seemed deserted. He moved through the shadows toward the front of the building, where the administrative offices were, taking care to stay out of sight.

When he got to the hallway that led away from the sound stage, Hendricks crouched low. He knew that his appearance here today would be a stunning surprise to some people, and he wanted to keep that advantage. He looked around the corner cautiously, waiting to be sure no one was between him and the offices at the end of the corridor. Satisfied, he crept silently into the hall.

Hearing the steps behind him was more a matter of instinct than the actual detection of a sound. Hendricks spun around, and there was Carlos Caserta. The big actor's face was constricted into a grimace, nostrils flaring, teeth bared, like that of a rabid dog. In his right hand was a rigger's knife, the kind the prop men carried, long and slim with a curving blade. Caserta let out an enraged howl and sprang at Hendricks, swinging the knife in a flashing arc.

Turning as he did saved Hendricks's life. He twisted sideways, and the blade missed his throat by an inch, ripping through his shirt and slicing a bloody furrow in his pectoral muscle. The force of Caserta's attack carried him into Hendricks, and the two crashed to the floor. Caserta was on top, and his reaction was instantaneous. He again slashed at Hendricks, this time aiming at the American's face.

Hendricks had faced a knife in a brawl more than once. He caught Caserta's wrist and bent it in an attempt to force the big man to drop the weapon. At the same time Caserta scrambled to regain his feet, and when Hendricks twisted the actor's wrist, Caserta fell forward onto the blade. The knife entered his belly cleanly, slicing upward under his rib cage and puncturing his heart. Caserta's mouth opened wide, and he gasped a series of small guttural noises as his life ran out through the gaping hole in his gut. His eyes stared at Hendricks in disbelief, then slowly glazed over as his big body flopped convulsively and finally became still.

Hendricks pushed Caserta aside and stood up. His clothing was drenched with blood, some of it his own, but most of it from Caserta. He stepped quickly down the hallway to the office that had been Vicente Morello's, and which had been appropriated by Zicci. Outside the door Hendricks could hear sounds of a struggle inside the office. A woman was crying and protesting, and the voice was unmistakably Tina's. He slammed his shoulder against the door and burst into the room.

Tina was lying on her back in the center of the floor, Zicci on top of her. There were cuts and welts on her body, and her face was contorted with pain and fear. Hendricks reached them in one leap, gripping Zicci by the back of his neck and hauling him to his feet. He drove his fist into Zicci's mouth, knocking him over a chair and leaving him in a heap on the floor.

Hendricks turned and bent over Tina, who sobbed uncontrollably, her shoulders shaking, her hands gripping his arms as she clung to him desperately. "Don't let me go, don't let me go."

Hendricks pressed her head against his chest. "It's okay. I'm not going to leave you. Are you all right?"

She nodded, and as she looked up at him, her eyes again widened in terror. Seeing her expression, Hendricks instinctively rolled aside, and the heavy lamp base in Zicci's hand smashed down onto his shoulder. The shock was tremendous, but Hendricks got to his feet fast, his right arm hanging devoid of feeling and useless at his side, and rammed his head into Zicci's belly. Axface was driven backward into a bookcase, its glass doors shattering in a cascade of glass. Hendricks followed, aiming his left fist for Zicci's jaw, but before he could throw the punch, Zicci's foot lashed upward, catching the American's kneecap.

Hendricks fell heavily onto all fours, and Zicci's next kick caught him flush on the jaw. He collapsed, and Axface was on him like a panther tearing at its prey, raining blows to the back of Hendricks's neck.

As terrified as she was, Tina felt something stronger than fear when she saw Zicci beating Hendricks into unconsciousness. She pulled herself upright, searching desperately for a weapon. There was a brass letter opener on the desk. She snatched it up and plunged the blade into the back of Zicci's neck. The shaft passed completely through the column of vertebrae, sinew, muscle and flesh, its pointed tip emerging from the front of his throat. Zicci's head rolled back, his eyes wide with horror, and a strangled cry issued from his mouth. His hands jerked upward, and then he fell silently to the floor.

Hendricks climbed slowly to his feet, shaking his head to clear it. There didn't seem to be an inch of him that was free of pain. He looked at Tina and she again began to cry, but he grasped her shoulder with his one good hand. "Don't. You can't break down now. Come on. Can you cover yourself with something?"

She nodded, and still trembling, put on her pants and the torn ruin of her dress, holding it together in front of her. "What are we going to do? Somebody will be here any minute."

He shook his head. "There's hardly anybody here. They must have let them all go when they knew we wouldn't be shooting. Come on."

Hendricks lifted Zicci by the dead man's belt. He dragged the body to the door, which he opened and peered through into the hall. Signaling Tina to follow, he pulled the corpse down the hallway to where Carlos Caserta lay in a drying pool of blood. Hendricks dropped Zicci's body on top of that of the actor, and taking Tina's hand stepped cautiously to the same doorway by which he had entered the studio. He unlocked the door, and they slipped through it into the street.

chapter 71

The rooms in the tall white marble building seemed to Hendricks to be more like an elegant apartment than a suite of offices. He looked at the deep, comfortable furniture and the flowers and the paintings, and it occurred to him how incongruous the setting seemed in some ways, and how appropriate in others. It was, in that respect, much like Braciola himself.

The tall, hawk-faced man indicated a chair, then sat opposite the American. "Will you have a drink?"

Hendricks shook his head. "No. Nothing, thanks."

A faint smile passed over Braciola's features. "Most unfortunate, all these terrible things happening. Zicci and Caserta must have really hated each other, to have had such a battle."

Hendricks stared at the other man, saying nothing. It had been several days since the fight, and he continued to feel sore and stiff.

"On the other hand," Braciola went on, "it is quite possible that the police were wrong, and that the two of them did not actually kill each other in a fight."

Hendricks waited patiently for Braciola to reveal just how much he actually knew about what had happened that day in the studio, and what he intended to do with whatever knowledge he might possess.

Braciola studied the tips of his fingers. "Nevertheless, that is as good an explanation as any. Both of them had a history of violence, and there were records of their difficulties with the law." He looked up at Hendricks and gazed thoughtfully at the American's face before continuing. "So in one sense, the official view is the most satisfying one, and also the one least likely to lead to further investigation, or further trouble." His deep voice became quieter. "Which is one reason that I encouraged the authorities to come to that conclusion."

Hendricks understood, then, what was being communicated to him. He decided to open up a little. "Both of them tried to kill me. Not once, but a couple of times."

Braciola showed no surprise at this. "How, and when?"

Hendricks told him about what had happened when he and Weaver had attempted to scout the tanker as a location.

When he had heard the story through, Braciola nodded. "But you have no proof that Zicci was behind that."

"No, but I didn't need any. Only he and Antonio knew where we were going that day. For whatever reasons, Zicci didn't want me to get off that ship alive."

"I know the reason."

Hendricks arched his eyebrows. "What is it?"

Braciola sat back in his chair. "Vito Zicci suffered from a disease that sometimes infects hot-blooded young men. He became carried away with ambition, and greed, and with a sense of his own importance."

"So?"

"So you were a rival to him. He wanted to control that

studio absolutely, with no competition from you, and no inter-
ference from me. His design was to get rid of you, because
after that fool Morello killed himself, you were clearly the one
threat to Zicci's authority. As long as you were content to be
simply a stupid actor, appearing in whatever role you were
told to play, you were no problem. But as soon as you insisted
on directing this new picture, Zicci was consumed by jealousy. Not only were you getting all the attention from the
public and the press, but you had the creative talent as well."

Hendricks thought about this, his curiosity rising. "So you
knew about it, but you did nothing to check him."

The small smile returned to Braciola's harsh features. "You
can be sure that I would have, when the proper time arrived.
You merely saved me a lot of trouble."

"And so, what happens now?"

"What happens now is that you get your wish."

Hendricks didn't like speaking in riddles. "What wish?
What are you talking about?"

A door behind Braciola's chair opened, and Cecily Petain
walked into the room. She was wearing a long filmy white
gown that revealed her full breasts, the nipples pressing out
against the thin material, her auburn hair tumbling around
her shoulders. Seeing her here was startling to Hendricks.

Cecily smiled. "Hello, Signor Director."

"Hello, Cecily."

The girl stood behind Braciola, her hand gently caressing
the back of his neck. As he watched them together, Hendricks
realized that this explained a number of things, as well. he
returned his attention to Braciola. "You were saying I would
get my wish."

The heavy-lidded eyes fixed the younger man in a steady
gaze. "That is correct. You wanted to make pictures? Very
well, you shall make them. I needed a strong man to run the
studio, and now I have one."

The full import of what he was hearing struck Hendricks
hard. "You mean you're going to put me in charge of the
operation?"

"That is precisely what I mean."

Hendricks leaned forward. "And what if I say no? What if I
say the hell with it, I'll work somewhere else?"

Braciola sighed. "You won't, for a number of reasons. One
of them is that you'd never get a chance like this one again. I
think you realize that." His voice softened, but his gaze
remained cold and direct. "Another is that once you work

with me, you are always with me. There is no part of the world you could go to where I do not have connections, where I do not have influence."

"And if I agree, does that mean I would have a completely free hand?"

Braciola's lips curled in amusement. "Of course not. But you would be able to make the kind of pictures you want to make."

"I see."

"Yes. I think you do." He reached up and put his hand over Cecily's, stroking it. "And by the way, your friend, Signora Lemont, regrets that she had to rush back to Paris without saying good-bye."

Again Hendricks experienced a jolt of surprise. "Estelle? What do you know about—"

"There are many things I know, Hendricks. Signora Lemont and I have some business dealings together. She is an investor in this film company. But I think that from here out she will be content to participate from a distance, and purely as a financial contributor."

So Estelle had tried to go around him, after all. Hendricks thought about her, as ruthlessly ambitious a woman as any he had ever known. He glanced at Cecily. But perhaps not as clever, or as lucky, as some. He got to his feet. "All right, Mario. We have a deal. I guess there's nothing in this life that doesn't have some kind of strings on it, someplace."

Braciola stood up, his face solemn. He shook Hendricks's hand. "I think you have made a very wise decision. From this point forward, your career will truly have no limits."

"Yeah. I'm sure of it." Hendricks nodded to Cecily and left the suite.

Back out on the street, he looked at the flood of cars and trucks along the Via Babuino, the vehicles shimmering in the August heat. The Moto Guzzi was chained to a nearby lamp-post. Hendricks unlocked it and fired the engine. There was only one thing he wanted now, and that was to be with Tina. Through it all she was the one bedrock truth, the one dependable thing in the crazy whirl of events his life had become.

He pushed off into the traffic, the bark of the motorcycle's engine blending with the roar in the street.

THE GIRL WITH THE GOLDEN HAIR

Leslie Deane

They were the talk of Hollywood. The small-time model whose sensual beauty and thrusting ambition brought her superstardom. The husband, whose liking for young starlets threatens to destroy all around him. The lover whose pitiless methods can make or break careers, reputations and lives.

Together they turn their glittering kingdom into a nightmare world of jealousy, lust and revenge.

The Girl with the Golden Hair is a story of success beyond all dreams, of public acclaim and private tragedy, of love betrayed by ambition and greed.

£1·25

STARRS

Warren Leslie

People who have never been to Starrs know its reputation: it is the most opulent, fashionable and expensive store in the world. Built by Arnold Starr, his wife and three sons, it draws its clientele from the wealthy of three continents. It has made the Starr family the shining merchant princes of the world.

But from behind Starrs' glittering jewels and sleek furs, secrets begin to emerge . . . secrets of ruthless ambition, family hatred and misplaced love that threaten to topple the legend, the family and the whole Starr empire.

£1.85

BALLERINA

Edward Stewart

Stephanie Lang and Chris Avery share dreams, loves, hopes and fears. Together they suffer the rigours of dancing school, the cruel but brilliant tutorship of Vollmar, leader of the National Ballet, the attention of Bunin, relentless sexual conqueror from the Kirov. But only one can reach the top – and at a tragic cost of heartbreak and rivalry. Searingly authentic, *Ballerina* is an unforgettable novel of love, ambition and friendship.

£1·25

TO CATCH A KING

Harry Patterson

His previous bestsellers include *The Eagle has Landed*, *The Valhalla Exchange* and *Storm Warning*. Now Harry Patterson (alias Jack Higgins) has transformed the facts of history into his most compelling thriller to date.

July 1940. While the world awaits the invasion of England, a plot unfolds in Lisbon that could change the course of the war. Its instigator: Adolf Hitler. Its target: the Duke of Windsor. Its aim: to catch a king. Only one man could have conceived of so daring, so deadly a plot. Only the maddest moments of history could have made it possible.

£1·10

BESTSELLERS FROM ARROW

All these books are available from your bookshop or news-agent or you can order them direct. Just tick the titles you want and complete the form below.

☐	BRUACH BLEND Lillian Beckwith	95p
☐	THE HISTORY MAN Malcolm Bradbury	£1·25
☐	ENTERTAINING Robert Carrier	£4·95
☐	A LITTLE ZIT ON THE SIDE Jasper Carrott	90p
☐	AUCTION Richard Cox	£1·25
☐	FALLING ANGEL William Hjortsberg	95p
☐	AT ONE WITH THE SEA Naomi James	£1·25
☐	IN GALLANT COMPANY Alexander Kent	85p
☐	METROPOLITAN LIFE Fran Lebowitz	95p
☐	AFTER THE WIND Eileen Lottman	£1·95
☐	THE BETTER ANGELS Charles McCarry	£1·50
☐	SPORTING FEVER Michael Parkinson	£1·25
☐	THE MASQUERS Natasha Peters	£1·95
☐	STRUMPET CITY James Plunkett	£1·95
☐	A SHIP MUST DIE Douglas Reeman	£1·10
☐	A JUDGEMENT IN STONE Ruth Rendell	95p
☐	TO THE MANOR BORN (Book 2) Peter Spence	£1·00
☐	THE FOURTH MAN Douglas Sutherland	£1·25
☐	THE YEAR OF THE QUIET SUN Wilson Tucker	80p

Postage _____

Total _____

ARROW BOOKS, BOOKSERVICE BY POST, PO BOX 29, DOUGLAS, ISLE OF MAN, BRITISH ISLES
Please enclose a cheque or postal order made out to Arrow Books Limited for the amount due including 35p per book for postage and packing for orders within the UK and 45p for overseas orders.

Please print clearly

NAME ....

ADDRESS ....

....

Whilst every effort is made to keep prices down and to keep popular books in print, Arrow Books cannot guarantee that prices will be the same as those advertised here or that the books will be available.